ALSO BY GILES FODEN

The Last King of Scotland

Ladysmith

Ladysmith

GILES
FODEN

Alfred A. Knopf
New York
2000

THIS IS A BORZOI BOOK
PUBLISHED BY ALFRED A. KNOPF

Copyright © 1999 by Giles Foden

All rights reserved under International and Pan-American Copyright Conventions.
Published in the United States by Alfred A. Knopf, a division of Random House, Inc.,
New York.
Distributed by Random House, Inc., New York.

www.aaknopf.com

Originally published in Great Britain by Faber and Faber Ltd., London, in 1999.

Knopf, Borzoi Books, and the colophon are registered trademarks of Random House, Inc.

Library of Congress Cataloging-in-Publication Data
Foden, Giles, [date]
    Ladysmith / Giles Foden. — 1st American ed.
        p.   cm.
    ISBN 0-375-40920-3. (alk. paper)
    1. Ladysmith (South Africa)—History—Siege, 1899–1900 Fiction.   I. Title.
PR6056.027L33   2000
823'.914—dc21   99-40731
                                                             CIP

Manufactured in the United States of America
First American Edition

In memory of J. C. A. Foden

Think of the days of yore;
consider the years; generation
upon generation past.
Ask your father; let him
narrate it; let the old one
recount it for you.

DEUTERONOMY 32:7

Ladysmith

Prologue

If you hold the bottle up against the light as you pour it into the glass, you will see what colour Guinness really is. Just where the cheerful liquid flows over the lip of the bottle, you will see a beautiful deep colour glittering like a jewel. It is a moment in time, and it is called the ruby point. The landlord told me that.

Oh boys, how it all comes back. Before her death, I worked at the Guinness brewery in Dublin, shovelling steaming hops into the fermentation bins. The place was full of heat, like it was somehow alive. We had to strip off our shirts, and the smell of the malt went into the very pores of our skin. When I got home, she would say that she could taste it on me. And now I am tasting the bitter brew myself, sitting in the Cock and Anchor at Liverpool docks, waiting for a ship. Little Bella and Jane are fast asleep in a room upstairs. They keep asking about their mother, and I do not know how to tell them that her story is over.

How did it begin? It began with a battering ram, which the landlord's men—another landlord, as different from this friendly Liverpudlian as could be imagined—brought and erected outside my family's cottage in Tarbert. It was a huge trunk of timber, over twenty-five feet long, which they hung from a tripod and swung at the door, behind which I had barricaded myself with my brother Michael. The pair of us had carried in ledges of limestone. We could hear the shooting outside, and then the battering started. It didn't last long, the door splitting in straightaway and the ledges falling over. Then the ram came right inside, sending pots and kettles flying above the hearth, and smashing my drinking cup. Its chips fell onto the floor, along with the grindings of the limestone, which was like yellow flour. Then one of the constables fired in a bullet, which took my brother full in the chest, killing him on the instant.

They beat me afterwards, and left me for dead also, on the edge of a peat bog. When I woke up, there was blood in my mouth, and my body was bruised and raw. Everywhere around me were the blocks and pyramids of the peat stacks. I dragged myself up a boreen to the house of a member of the Brotherhood, Joe Ward, and he gave me a bath, some new clothes, and a fry. Also some money, with which to go to Dublin. There was nothing left for me in North Kerry now: my parents dead, my brother killed. Even if I had been able to get another smallholding, the land had been squeezed dry of nourishment, and there would be no respite from the rents. I don't know, anyway, that I would have been able to make it work. Since the death of our mother and father, Michael and I had done our best to keep that pocket of ground going, setting potatoes wherever we could, even along the cliff tops. But every day, the lack of food scrabbled at our stomachs, and I think we both knew that things could not last.

The roads to Dublin were heavy with travellers. Everybody was on the move. Most were starving, most thought they would get to America, most would die. On the way, I fell in with a sweet girl called Cathleen. She and I would go foraging for food together. It was on one of these trips, looking for mushrooms in some dark corner of forest, that we had our first flourish, her pulling up her petticoats on a bed of leaf mould. I think, maybe, that it was there that Bella was conceived.

On arrival in Dublin, I made contact with the Republican Brotherhood again. It was through them that I secured the job at Arthur Guinness and also lodgings in Kevin Street. My first work for the Brotherhood was to go on a parade in Phoenix Park, where Cathleen and I, on seeing the son of Randolph Churchill, secretary to the Lord Lieutenant, frightened his donkey and made him fall off. He was out for a ride with his nurse, who I believe was called Mrs. Everest.

That was our first action. In later years, Cathleen and I got caught up with a mightier crowd, a grouping within the Brotherhood that was responsible for many of the great patriotic feats of the time. Led by John MacBride, it included James Devine, Christopher Fallon and Finbar Sheehy in its ranks. Devine was the commander of our cell, which had arranged to meet at a pub in Middle Abbey Street at ten o'clock. The reason given for the meeting was to plan the bombing of a police station—but I knew that MacBride, or Foxy Jack as we used to call him, suspected Sheehy of being an informer and wished Devine to interrogate him.

Dublin was misty that night, and where the gold of the gas lamps hung suspended, each one had a little muffler of grey. Cathleen remained outside in an alleyway underneath one of these, keeping watch, while I went into the pub with Fallon and Devine. Waiting for Sheehy, we sat in the pews in a fug of stout, Sweet Afton and Gold Plug. A man in a cap was playing an old air on the piano. Half an hour passed. There was still no sign of Sheehy. Devine decided to abandon the meeting in case the authorities had been put on the alert. We came out of the pub, and it was then that I heard Cathleen's warning whistle. I turned and saw that there was a party of men shadowing us. Sheehy had betrayed us.

They were detectives, carrying revolvers and sticks. One of them shouted "Arrest that man!" and they ran up towards us, attempting to lay hands on Fallon, who was hindmost and had taken his gun out. He turned and fired two shots, killing one of the detectives and hitting the hat of another. Fallon was then hit himself, and his limbs became wrapped up with those of the policeman who had tried to lay hold of him. Devine had meanwhile grabbed one of the others by the arms and was wrestling with him, at the same time trying to draw his own revolver from a hiding place in his trousers. There was great confusion and noise of discharging guns, but among it all I heard Cathleen's signal whistle again. Fearing for our lives, I ran off in her direction, the opposite way the police would expect. As I did so, another detective fired after me. It was that bullet which did it, for on reaching Cathleen in the dark alley, I found her knocked down, with a hole in her throat.

I could hear the running steps of the detectives in the cobbled street behind me, and did not know what to do. I picked her up. There was blood all down her front, and in the gaslight her face looked as pale as an angel's. I could see at once that she was dead. The running steps were getting closer. I let her body go. It slid down the wall, and her head fell to one side, making the awful, blood-filled hole gape wider. I cannot get the picture out of my head. When I ran from the scene, it was as if I was running into that hole. There were lots of people around by now also, and their open mouths were like that hole, too.

I have been running ever since. Taking the children sleepy-eyed from their beds, I took the first packet from Dun Laoghaire the next morning, and arrived here. It is not safe, as I see from the newspaper that I am being sought, and we must flee again. Once more, the Brotherhood has helped me, paying for passage to South Africa, where many of our brethren have gone—in part because there is work to be done there, fighting the empire in whose name liberty is being suppressed, as it has been in Ireland this last hundred years or more; in other part because there are opportunities for enrichment in the gold and diamond fields. MacBride is also thinking of coming out, if things get too hot for him.

Myself and the children leave in the morning . . . My God, is this to be her memory? The account in this newspaper styles my wife a common prostitute. Up in the room with the girls is something that tells a different story—a photograph taken by an Englishman who came to Dublin to make pictures of "the Irish poor," as he put it. He gave me it as a gift, and when he did I never knew it would become so precious. As for the other gifts the English have given me and my country, I swear it, if I do anything else in my life, I will make them pay.

Crossways

1

These items for sale also, the notice in the window said. To wit: three mother-of-pearl looking-glasses, four scissors, three large and two small combs, ten vials of perfume and an equal number of bottles of hair oil, all laid out in a neat, symmetrical pattern. The young woman in the straw hat regarded the scissors charily, as if they might put her hair in danger; then, seeming to make up her mind, opened the door and went in.

High above Bella Kiernan, as she stepped into the barber's shop, four horsemen were coming down the road from Helpmakaar, cantering between the heavy shadow of Bulwan and the smaller shade of Umbrella Hill. As Bella greeted the barber, they reined in their horses, and came to a halt.

"Here will do well enough," said Steevens to the others.

For all concerned, it was a matter of perspective: in front of Bella was a row of well-cushioned leather chairs, each set before a mirror; below the horsemen lay the town of Ladysmith, as seen from a particular point of view and distance. She sat down; they surveyed the town, sitting in its dusty amphitheatre of ridges and kopjes—surveyed it, and said to each other, yes, we can easily make a stand here. One produced his brass spyglass and took a closer look.

"Solid as the Bank of England," MacDonald muttered. The others agreed, and the spyglass was closed up with a snap.

The horsemen were wrong: sure as the crowned eagle stooping above them would catch its prey that day, they were wrong to a man. A proper soldier would have deemed it a tight place to defend, the rocky spurs and flat-topped hillocks being so disconnected and irregular, so mutually overlooking, that each vantage point was disadvantaged by another.

They kicked their mounts on, splashed through a spruit, and cantered on down towards the town. A little nearer, aching after their long tour, they paused on Pound Plateau. A spyglass again, Nevinson's this time; out of the quiver-like brown leather case it came, to be extended and trained upon Ladysmith, in the late afternoon.

It always amazed Nevinson what a panorama the glass's sovereign-sized portion of light could reveal—the serried roofs of the tin town, the garrison the English called the Aldershot of Africa, the tented camp on the barren plain two miles out of town, the racecourse in an oxbow of the Klip River, the V where the zigzag narrow-gauge line from Natal divided (one line to the Transvaal, one to the Free State), the convent, the desultory scattering of thorn trees beyond the cricket pitch and golf links, the rows of wooden-fronted houses with little squares of orchard or vegetables, and the wide main street with its stores, hotel and all-round saloon-bar feel.

Five miles to the north was the haystack-shaped Pepworth Hill, and high above that, above all of it—the whole shooting match, as it were, or would be—towered the precipitous Drakensberg, along which ran the barbed-wire fence dividing British Natal from the two Boer republics. Maybe, Boers or no Boers, the horsemen would have been better up there among those cool blue peaks, needful of a still further uplifted vision of Ladysmith: such a parched, ordinary place it was, after all; one unaccustomed to the kind of attention they were giving it.

They rode on down and came, in their turn, under scrutiny. Their observer, Antonio Torres, had a rich yet opportunistic imagination, seeing, in one moment, the Apocalypse in those riders and, in the other, four more heads to cut. He watched them ride slowly past the window, and tried to remember how it was in the legend. Pestilence, famine, war and death, was that it? Death seemed a little superfluous in that company, he reckoned, though in fact these four seemed altogether well enough in themselves, as their horses plodded up Ladysmith's main street, passing, Torres noted, Mrs. Frinton on her bicycle. One—whom he recognized, having cut his hair earlier in the day—was in civilian clothes. The others were in military uniform and would easily have passed for soldiers.

"Many correspondents about now," he said, lifting up a dark fringe between his fingers to get a line on it and then, with a deft movement, snipping it shorter. The fine hair fell on the bridge of Bella's nose and he moved to brush it off. But . . . she had already begun to sneeze, and he stood back a second, watching her head come back, and then forward, onto her dress.

"Excuse me," exclaimed the young woman, looking up at the man her father called "Don" Antonio, and seeing him touch his long, tanned face. It was, she thought, not unhandsome; rather mysterious, with eyes that sparkled in such a way as to suggest that there was more about him than his mild manner allowed. He had a devil's-fork beard, too, which served to increase his air of intrigue.

It was true that nobody in Ladysmith knew much about Mr. Torres, who had come from Portuguese East Africa and set up his shop only recently. Bella had decided she rather liked him: with his elegant dark suits and soft white shirts he had a sense of style about his person which few men in Ladysmith could match. But he wasn't suitable for her, of course: too old (ten, perhaps fifteen years her senior), not to mention his Portuguese blood. What would Mrs. Frinton think of that?

Thinking she might laugh, she in fact sneezed again, and apologized to the barber once more, looking up into his black eyes as they regarded her in the mirror.

"Do not be foolish, Miss Kiernan. It is my fault for certain. Or the dust. Yes, this terrible dust. Ever since I came here, I have not grown accustomed to this dust. And so much more now, since the number of soldiers grew larger. Let us pray there will not be war. I do not think there will be much hair cutting if everybody is fighting."

"Father says it might come to a siege," said Bella.

"Well, let us hope that it does not," Torres replied. "But you saw the natives on their way, and when they are on the move it's a sure sign that something is happening."

Bella had seen them, on the train as it passed through from Newcastle to Maritzburg: black faces behind the bars of the cargo vans, crying out for bread and meat—the Xhosa boy clicking in his strange language, clicking like Mr. Torres's scissors on her head, the Zulu in his animal-skin kaross, face downcast with loss of pride. Not that there weren't white faces, too, on that train: smart men in hats, rough-looking miners and boilermen from Cornwall and Lancashire, whole families with tin trunks and servants, all packed in coal trucks or cattle trucks, travelling three days and nights under African skies down to Cape Town. These were the Uitlanders: uit meant "out" in the Taal, and the Boers were, in effect, kicking them out of the republics.

"Like the Great Trek in reverse," said Bella, repeating a remark of her father's.

"Only this time it is the British and the blacks," said the barber. "Well, at least the Boers are in a majority in their country now. It is what they have always desired."

It was in part this, the fact that the booming, mainly British population in the mining towns of the Boer republics didn't have the vote, that had set the machinery of aggression in motion.

"I think it must indeed be our fault then," Bella said. "To some degree, anyway. All the Boers I have spoken to—well, I haven't actually spoken to that many—say they are afraid that Britain will take their land away, as they did with Cape Colony. That's what caused the original Great Trek up to their republics, isn't it, Mr. Torres?"

He moved her head with the fingertips of both hands, straightening her up.

"Yes, and if the British hadn't threatened the Boers, brought so many soldiers here, all this talk of war might not be around. And all these refugees. If only they wanted haircuts as well as food."

Bella laughed at the thought of so many people stopping off at Ladysmith to get their hair cut. Then she sat up straighter still in Torres's chair. It wasn't a laughing matter, the food crisis. The demand for bread at the station had forced the price up generally; it was now a shilling a loaf and, as her father had said, "Old Star is coining it." Mr. and Mrs. Star, Ladysmith's bakers—Bella could see their shop across the road from where she sat in the comfortable leather chair—were generally thought greedy by the populace. As she told Torres what her father thought of the Stars' behaviour—"criminal" had been one of the words he used—a slight frown passed across the barber's face. Bella wondered if she had been a little too confiding.

Torres looked back at her in the glass, at her face, at her neck, at the cream-coloured, light cotton frock below. With its brown eyes, thin lips and slightly angled cheekbones, it was quite a pale, austere face that regarded him from above the jars of hair oil and the india-rubber bulbs of the perfume sprays. And becoming all the more so as, inch by inch, layer by layer, he cut off more hair, for with every lock that fell the young woman's face seemed graver and more serious in its contours.

Perhaps it was just that it saddened him, this particular haircut. The truth was, the dark tresses of Bella Kiernan reminded him of those of another Bella, or more properly Isabella, whom he had left behind him in Lourenço Marques. She had married another, the family choice, and he had left the city of his birth, left his parents' rich estates, left everything, rather than have to see her every day on the arm of another man—left with sadness in his heart, and wandered, and ended up here, among the British. He had learned to cut hair on the way, from a Lithuanian Jew at Komati Poort.

Antonio, you are dreaming again, he said to himself, remembering the time he had nipped Mrs. Frinton's ear with the scissors . . . and forced himself to concentrate on the overwhelming question of Bella Kiernan's haircut.

Because they are questions—he pruned off another tress—haircuts are questions, their outcome indeterminable and weighty. Definitely weighty, in the instance of Bella Kiernan; but it was what she had wanted, however he had tried to counsel her otherwise. How strange it was, he thought, the way that women will suddenly take drastic measures with their hair; as if, by some new coiffure, they might achieve a particular object or, in a mysterious scheme that went beyond the bounds of earth itself, change their soul utterly. He looked in the mirror again.

Bella realized that Mr. Torres hadn't said anything for a while. She wondered what he had been thinking about. He wasn't the gossiping type usually associated with his trade, but she liked to hear what he did have to say. His Latin dignity and style, combined with occasional flights of fancy, marked him out from the brash, pioneering bravado of most of the Ladysmith men.

"I don't think the Stars are the only ones growing rich from the misfortunes of others," she announced. "I think the gold people and the diamond people in the Cape want to get their hands on the Boer fields. Father says that Sir Alfred Milner, the Cape Governor, is in cahoots with them, to get money for the Empire, and that's why he's so keen on war."

"Maybe so."

"What do you think will happen?"

"I don't know. There are certainly lots of rumours about. The town is full of wild fantasies. Mr. Greenacre's son was in here yesterday and he said he saw nearly a thousand Boers watering their horses."

There was silence—except for the clicking scissors—as the two of them thought about this; although, as Bella remarked to herself, Bobby Greenacre was a notorious fibber.

As she sat there, a strange sound began to fill the silence. At first she thought it was just the scissors, but then she realized it came from outside. It slowly grew louder, the clip of horses' hooves and the jingle of harness, and then the low murmur of a large body of men in the distance. A bugle sounded, then fife and drum, and soon the main street was filled from end to end with tramping feet. Torres stopped cutting and both turned to watch as more troops came in from the railway station, after disembarking from the armoured train with horses and supplies. He and Bella had seen it several times before that week, the arrival of rank upon rank of these seasoned men in khaki, the best the British Army could muster, but each time it was a sight to behold. The sun had begun to go down and the cavalry lances cast long shadows on the ground. Behind them came scraggy mules and long-horned oxen pulling wagons in teams of ten, driven by African boys who handled their long, leather-tongued stock-whips with astonishing skill. Then came the infantry, rifles on their shoulders, puttees round their calves, expressions both grim and grinning on their faces.

"They look very strong, don't they?" said Bella. "Father says they have come from India and are very skilled from fighting the difficult tribes there."

"Pomp and circumstance, that is what you British say, isn't it?" Torres replied, with a chuckle. And then, correcting his levity: "But I hope they send many more, anyway. It is very frightening, all of this. My great-grandfather died in the Napoleon war, you know, that is why my father had to come to Africa. But I will tell you my story on your next haircut, Miss Kiernan, because"—he touched her on the shoulder—"this one is finished."

"It looks wonderful, Mr. Torres," said Bella, turning her head to inspect. "In fact, I'm so pleased I think I will buy one of those looking-glasses you have in the window, if I may."

"Of course," said the barber, smiling at her. "I will fetch you a new one from the store. I have some still in their box."

Once she had paid for the haircut and the new looking-glass, Bella said goodbye to Mr. Torres and left the salon. At the door, she paused, deciding whether or not to put her straw hat back on. In the end, she did, betraying a slight uncertainty as to her ability to carry off the new style. This nervousness was in no small part due to the large numbers of soldiers that filled the street outside. As she walked past the shop fronts, with her mirror box under her arm, she felt the military gaze falling upon her, and kept her own eyes demurely down. All the same, in several places she had to lift up her petticoats to keep them from the dust, and this manoeuvre brought a certain amount of exhilaration to both Bella and her observers.

Jane, her younger sister—heavier-set, less nervous, and blonde—was already behind the bar when Bella walked into the Royal Hotel. Proprietor: Leo Kiernan, their father, who had had them working as barmaids since their early teens. Now, at twenty and eighteen, they were expert at mixing all manner of drinks and their slim white wrists had grown strong pulling the tall beer levers that lined the bar like—well, she and Jane had a secret about that.

It was certainly true that there were a lot of men in the bar of the Royal Hotel that evening, so many that the noise of their talking drowned the sound of the musical box playing in the corner. As decorously as possible, Bella made her way through: past men in uniform from the Green Horse, the Natal Carbineers, the Naval Brigade and other regiments, past men in homburg hats from the town, past farmers in corduroy suits from the outlying districts, and—at one table, as Bella noticed—the four men who had ridden by Mr. Torres's window not long earlier.

Her father was down at one end of the bar, Jane at the other, dextrously squirting soda into a line of whisky glasses while chatting to a pleasant-looking young naval gunner. Bella lifted the hinged flap in the bar counter and went through. Looking up from the line of tumblers, with one ear still open to the blandishments of the sailor, Jane mouthed, "You're late!"

Bella pulled a face and took off her straw hat. She reached down below the bar for a cloth to wipe up the spillage which, even though it was still very early in the evening, had accumulated on the varnished wood. Rising, she came face to face with her father. It was one of the curiosities of the Kiernan family that although Bella (as her mother had been) was dark and Jane blonde, their father was the deepest red. This being a time when genetics was a science in its infancy, and also a time when other so-called sciences (involving transmigrating souls, Ancient Egyptians and the shape of the skull) were very much abroad, it would not have been improper to assume that Leo Kiernan was not their father at all. Because he was, quite simply, very red-headed indeed. In terms of its texture, too, his hair was curious: closely, tightly curled.

As it happened, it was hair that concerned Mr. Kiernan as Bella came up from beneath the bar, not on his own account, but on his daughter's.

"What," he exclaimed, "have you done to yourself? You look like a convict! Who did this? Torres?"

"Yes," replied Bella, boldly. "But I asked him to, and it is nothing to do with him. Or you, Father. A lady must wear her hair as she pleases."

"A lady? So you're a lady now, are you?" He seemed, if anything, to be getting redder.

"I think it's rather fetching," said a voice from the bar. Bella—and her father—looked up to see a stocky young trooper, clutching a shilling in his hand. He had green eyes, a biggish nose, and his fingernails were dirty.

"What you think is not the point," said Mr. Kiernan, glowering. "Come on, what do you want?"

"I'll have a gin, if I may." He smiled at Bella. "Tom Barnes, Green Horse."

Like your eyes, Bella said to herself.

"I'll deal with you later," her father said to her, as if he knew her train of thought, "and I'll please you, sir, not to exchange pleasantries with my staff." Mr. Kiernan pushed the gin across the bar to the soldier, and turned to his daughter, pointing at the floor. "Take that crate of empties down to the cellar. And bring up a full one while you're about it."

"Don't be hard on her, sir," Bella heard the soldier say as she went out. He seemed a decent fellow, she thought, as she struggled down the cellar steps with the crate. Though really it would have been better if he had kept quiet.

The fellow in question returned to his table. Tom Barnes was sitting with four war correspondents. They were quenching their thirst after a tour, having ridden down the Helpmakaar road and stopped for a breather on Pound Plateau. The journalists hadn't had permission for the scouting expedition and now he had been assigned by the censor's office to keep an eye on them. This was a lucky chance since it meant he got a night out. Having ignored him at first, they were now—the quartet comprising George Steevens of the *Mail,* Henry Nevinson of the *Daily Chronicle,* Donald MacDonald of the Melbourne *Argus* and William Maud, the *Graphic's* "special artist"—quizzing him about the army's readiness for the impending war. In particular, Nevinson—a bearded, elegant character—was worried that the British had pushed up too far from the Cape.

"Look," he said, cupping his glass with his hand, "I was up in Pretoria earlier this month. I saw it. The Boers may be ragged and disorganized but they've quite simply got more men than us—nearly twice as many. Twenty thousand to our ten. And we don't know the land so well. They do, and they are full of passion, too. I saw their General Joubert when I was up there, and do you know what the first thing he said to me was?"

"What?" queried Maud, on behalf of all.

"He said: The heart of my soul is bloody with sorrow."

"Typical Boer rhetoric," sniffed MacDonald, lighting his pipe.

"No, it's good," countered Maud. "I can see it as a caption."

"Just for effect," said MacDonald. "You shouldn't have been taken in."

"On the contrary," exclaimed Nevinson. "He meant it. Joubert was one of the ones who desperately wanted peace. He feels about this in a way that we don't, and that passion, conveyed to his troops if it comes to war, could prove dangerous."

"Passion doesn't always win a war," said Steevens. "Guns and food, that's what you need."

"Oh come on. Passion is necessary too," said Nevinson. "Absolutely."

"Not if you're an Englishman. There is a simple argument to it. If we win, it will be through brute force and logistics. If they win, it will, as you would say, be through passion. For although I've only made a sketchy study of the Boer character, I have learned one thing about that race."

"What's that, then?" said MacDonald.

"That they are a people hard to arouse, but harder to subdue."

Tom Barnes took a drink and looked at the men around him. They all seemed a little foolish. None had yet quite got to grips with the realities of "the coming scrap," as it was now known. From the tiny ration of water from the pumps, the dysentery and enteric, the hot sun beating down on your head or, if you were off duty, the breathless haze of your tent, to the white ants and flies on every-thing—your food, your tobacco, your writing paper, even your underclothes—it was no picnic. Not to mention the dust in your mouth and in the workings of your fob-watch, or the likelihood of getting shot at by an army of men who never showed themselves and who saw warfare in the same light that they saw hunting antelope. Stalking was the Boer way, the old hands from Majuba said, which was why all the training the British cavalry were doing—charges with lances, for God's sake—seemed pretty pointless; and all the training the infantry had been doing—marching forward in close order, easy to pick off—totally so. He had tried to describe all this from India in a letter to Perry, his younger brother, once he'd heard that he, too, had signed up and was headed for the Cape: the sheer drudgery of a lot of soldiering—young lieutenants shouting at you or having you flogged, blisters on your feet, boils on your thighs, food not fit for dogs . . .

He had the idea that Perry—two years his junior—believed that soldiering was a bit like the ferreting expeditions they had gone in for on the farm when they were younger: an adventure, a lark with a prize, a bloody one to be held up by its hind legs and presented to Ma for skinning when you got home. The fact is, you were more like rab-bit on the battlefield than ferret or ferreter. That was what he had said to Lizzie, their sister, in another letter—written on board the *Lindula*, en route from Princes Dock, Bombay, to Durban—in a last-ditch attempt to get her to persuade Perry to think again. He couldn't forgive himself the possibility of his younger brother being killed because Perry wanted to imitate him, as he had done all his life.

Thought of these letters reminded him that he hadn't written home recently, something he had done religiously in India. There was the voyage to cover, for instance, and the medical and veterinary inspections beforehand. How there had been a case of anthrax at Deolali, and B and C Squadrons had had to be left behind. How he himself had had to apply for two replacement horses on the way, one cast from the ship, lame in two feet, the other injured in the train from Durban to Ladysmith, having slipped on the iron floor of the truck after heavy rain.

He looked about him at the members of the press. They were still talking about passion. It seemed to him—mindful as he was that they were scholars and he was only the son of a farmer—an inappropriate word to describe fighting. He had seen quite a bit (they'd been at Sialkot, in the Punjab), even if it was only against the curly-slippered armies of bedizened maharajas. The Indians didn't have Mausers, as Brother Boer was known to have, just scimitars and muzzle-loading muskets. Still, he had seen them make some hot wounds in men he had liked to call friends. But passion, no: that word made him think of women. In particular it made him think of the slender, crop-haired girl at the bar. He looked down at his gin. It was half full. That could be quickly remedied.

Bella saw the young man drain his glass, standing up in the same movement, and moved herself into a position along the bar where he'd necessarily come towards her rather than Jane or, Lord preserve us, their father. She needn't have bothered. The trooper, his green eyes twinkling, was making a beeline for her. So, unfortunately, was Jane. Her own admirer, Gunner Foster of the Naval Brigade, had returned to his table, slightly worse for the wear of too many whisky-sodas—bought, Bella had said, on account of love rather than necessity.

"I meant what I said about your hair," said Tom to Bella, putting both his elbows on the bar. "It's very bold."

"You'd better keep quiet. Our father will hear you," said Jane, bustling up beside her.

"Same again?" Bella asked breezily, flashing her a hard look.

Tom looked at Jane. "You're sisters then?" He held up his hands in a gesture of surrender. "Ah well, it's nothing but the truth. You've both got bold hair!"

"What'll you have?" said Bella, her tone a little less friendly. "Another gin?"

"I think I'll switch to beer," he said, nodding his head in mock seriousness. "I've got a bit of a dry throat. A Castle, if you please, miss."

2

The Biographer sat on the deck of the *Dunottar Castle,* watching them put it in. Whenever the hoists rose there was a din of ironwork gears, overlying the harsher, continual scrape of steel on stone. He was wearing a pair of black boots, and between his toecaps—his crossed feet were resting on the glossy lower bar of the balcony railings—he could see the stokers. They were black, too, stripped to the waist and sweating as they shovelled away, under the sunshine of Madeira. For the island was an Admiralty coaling station in those days.

He reached into the pocket of his white canvas jacket and removed a square brass lighter. The smoke danced in front of his sunburned face. In spite of the grime that covered them, he could recognize some of the men working on the dock. That was Perry Barnes there, the young Warwickshire farrier, clipping horses on the quayside next to the marine office. A long line of animals were waiting for his attentions, having come down from hill pasture, to which they had been taken from the ship for grazing. He and the farrier had talked on the train to Southampton, finding common cause in their Midlands background. The Biographer watched as another horse was brought forward, and the curly-haired, good-looking Barnes took it in hand.

Lucky boy, to have escaped coaling duty. Officers as well as men had been drafted in to help the regular stokers, such was the urgency of the *Dunottar*'s journey. Ships of the Castle Line ate coal like monsters on a normal run to the Cape, but this time it was different. Speed was of the essence. The Army Corps (of which this was only the advance guard) had to get to South Africa as soon as possible. The ultimatum of President Kruger—demanding, among other things, withdrawal of British troops from the Transvaal borders—had expired, and a state of war existed between the Empire and the Transvaal Republic. For months the two sides had been negotiating, but that time was now over. As Kruger had reportedly said to Milner, the High Commissioner, before walking out to his carriage, "What you really want is my country." It was true. Milner's despatches were warlike and—although he was far more prudent—the Secretary of State for the Colonies, Joe Chamberlain's, use of words like "suzerainty" in Parliament had enraged Kruger and his parliament, the Raad.

The Biographer wondered where it was all leading, now that negotiations had come to nothing. It was true that an air of great responsibility hung over some of the officers and men on board. Others, sadly, were prone to giving out loud cries for vengeance for the battle of Majuba, where the British had suffered a heavy defeat and four hundred casualties at the hands of the Boers, eighteen years before. There was a naked ferocity about these cries, one that turned to empty words the boasted progress and civilization that were said to be the spirit of the age.

The Biographer had watched this kind of thing during his dinners on board in the junior officers' mess: some of them behaved like oafs when they were drunk. He never said anything—it wouldn't do to seem a fish out of water among military men . . . Did they think him effeminate, he wondered? There was a story about a correspondent being debagged by soldiers while covering the war in the Sudan, just because he wore his hair fashionably long. Some of the other correspondents, like Churchill and Atkins, had managed to get themselves a place at the Captain's table with Buller's staff, but the Biographer had not been admitted to this inner circle. He suspected it was because his type of journalism was not taken seriously. Some said it was unnatural to fix life's transitory moments in the way that he did.

Well, time would tell whose record of Buller's expedition was the most lasting. Already the Biographer had caught him—General Sir Redvers Buller, VC—on still plates, caught the heavy moustache, the Crombie with a buttonhole of violets, the felt hat, the stolid figure and big, kindly face. He had also made a number of moving Biographs of Buller and his staff, and of various other scenes concerning the Advance Guard's entrainment for Southampton and embarkation for South Africa. He was particularly proud of a description of the crowds on the platform at Waterloo, civilians and soldiers in a mêlée of uniforms, suits and dresses, all singing and shouting and leaning out of the train windows waving hats, and then, finally—as they'd pulled out with a hoot and a jolt and a puff of steam—what John Atkins had remarked upon, "the long frieze of faces drawn past one's carriage." Atkins was the *Manchester Guardian* correspondent, who was allowed upstairs with the others. A good man.

To the Biographer's eye, if not his lens, there had been among those faces many suddenly saddened by an intimation of the greater loss that war might bring. But the grief-stricken ones and the glad, the womenfolk wise and foolish, and the double-chinned Cockney porters leaning on their trolleys—all of them had merged into one as the train picked up speed. The Biographer had been worried that his machine would produce nothing but a blur in trying to record this final part of the scene; but all its mysteries had not yet been revealed, and the answer would not be known until his packet of plates and film reached London and his colleagues at the Biograph Company. Sometimes, in any case, he thought the image came out better when shrouded in gauziness.

One way or another, he hoped that in that packet would be pictures of the train journey—attempts to catch, as they skimmed past, gleaming pastures and hedgerows full of birds which, like the locomotive's human cargo, would be in Africa that winter. Pictures, too, of the ordinary soldiers, sat among kitbags and clouds of tobacco. If only he had been able to portray their chat as well, their lively humour and fatalistic cracks. As if to compensate, he had used more film than he need have done, spun it out, just as the train had spun across its ringing web of steel through the downland and forest of Surrey and Hampshire—to Southampton.

At Southampton Water the *Castle* had awaited them, a towering vessel, almost too big for his lens. There was a medieval quality to the scene, one most appropriate to the ship's white-painted name (over that too his lens had panned). The mass of people and the little boats nosing about under the quay walls had been like traders or importunate beggars on the banks of a moat, the busy gangplank serving as a drawbridge. For a while there had been a stable little world there on the quayside: a large crowd of cheering patriots standing, or perched on roofs and dockside machinery, singing "Rule Britannia" and "For He's a Jolly Good Fellow." Then the tin trunks and weapons and officers' valises had gone up, followed by Buller's stallions, Ironmonger and Biffin, and all the other horses. Finally, the moment for departure had come and, in the month of October at the end of a century, the foghorn had blooped and the great prow had ranged forward.

He twisted in his canvas chair to look at one of the paddle-boxes, a great fairground wheel of a thing criss-crossed by struts. Then he glanced back down at the stokers. The pile of coal on the dock had gone down somewhat, but they would not be done till dusk. Only then, when the sun came down over the island, would the furnace be red again, its beastly maw secure of its black food for two thousand tons' worth of nautical miles.

"Hullo," shouted a smart voice from above him. "You—down there."

The Biographer raised himself from the canvas chair and looked up. Sticking out from under the white rail of the deck above was a pair of brown calfskin boots. Tucked into these were faded khaki trousers and above them a tunic of the same fabric, the collars of which framed the eager, button-nosed face of Mr. Winston Spencer Churchill, correspondent of the *Morning Post.*

"You're the Biograph fellow, yes?"

"That's right."

"Well, Atkins spoke to me about your plight. I've arranged for you to join us at Captain Rigby's table tonight. No more slumming."

"That's very kind of you."

"Six o'clock sharp."

The brown boots were suddenly gone, and the Biographer found himself looking into the sky. He felt a rush of gratitude towards Atkins and Churchill. Perhaps he might be taken seriously after all. Then he twigged that Churchill probably just wanted to get himself on film; he was said to have a genius for self-publicity. He had lately been a parliamentary candidate for Oldham, and apparently wanted to follow his father, Lord Randolph, into politics. What lives these people led; a different world from the Birmingham tenement in which the Biographer had grown up. Still, it was his early apprenticeship in the watchmaking quarter of that city that had taken him, by roundabout routes, into the photography business, a trade in which he found great satisfaction. The nobs could keep their glamorous careers; they were already outmoded.

The sound of a whinny caught the Biographer's attention. He

turned to see Perry Barnes taking up the hind leg of a horse, the last of the line, between his own legs. It struck him that it would make a good picture, and he went off to his cabin to fetch his tripod and camera.

On the dock below the Biographer's empty canvas chair, Perry Barnes watched as another sliver of browny-blue hoof fell to the ground in front of him. He liked clipping horses; it reminded him of home. The farm at Radford. Lizzie, his sister—she had a passion for horses. Anything was better than coaling, anyway. But that was the last one. He put the heavy clippers into the pocket of his tunic and went over to pick up the big shoe pincer, which was leaning like a layabout against the clapboard wall of the marine office. He pushed a hand through his hair and looked at the wall, its white paint smeared with coal-dust. Layabout: Tom had called him that once when they were pitching hay and he'd sat down under the yellow stook for a swig of lemonade. His brother was already out in the Cape, having been in India. A garrison town called Ladysmith. He had followed in Tom's footsteps—too many brothers for thirty acres, with Arthur the eldest as well—but hadn't managed to get into the same regiment. Bloody army.

"You couldn't just clip another horse for me?"

Perry looked up to see the photographer fellow he had talked to on the train, struggling with a bundle of outlandish equipment.

"They're all done, I'm afraid."

"Can't you just go through the motions?"

Perry squinted up at him. "I can't really. We've got to get moving. Anyway, what would be the point?"

"Never mind," said the Biographer.

Once the coaling was over, the decks were swabbed to rid them of dust, and the coalers queued up for showers. Perry joined them. The water coming down over his creamy, adolescent flesh smelt of the tank, and the young blacksmith suddenly missed the butt of fresh rainwater under the downpipe on the farm. They used it for making tea, and for washing their hair once a week. Three brothers washing their hair before going to the Red Lion on a Friday. The image made him feel homesick. Still, snap time soon, he thought; half a pint of beer and some corned beef hash on a tin plate would do very nicely . . .

The Biographer took the opportunity of having brought out his equipment to take a covert shot of the showering men, and another of General Buller, climbing up onto a skylight to escape the deluge of the deck-swabbing.

"You can catch me if you can, but I won't pose for you," the General called down to the cameraman, as he balanced on the sloping glass. "Not up here, at any rate."

Afterwards, a common sailor asked him to come down, so that he could wash the skylight too.

"Now you wouldn't wash me off, would you?" Buller chuckled, and then jumped down onto the slippery deck. For an oldish man, he kept his footing very well.

A little later, a gong called the inner circle to the Captain's dining saloon. There was more music inside, where a band played popular airs as the diners took their seats. The conversation, the Biographer discovered on his own uncomfortable entrance, was at first exclusively political. He soon became aware that the members of the General's inner circle were far more blasé about the outcome of the war than the ordinary soldier. The General's staff, presenting themselves as a band of stout-hearted experts, seemed to think the war would be over very swiftly.

Of the correspondents, only Atkins would countenance any sense of the justification of the Boer cause. "It is, after all, their land," he said, as the waiters brought in a great silver tureen of mulligatawny. John the Baptist, the Biographer thought, as they lifted off the round lid—as large as Buller's head—and started ladling it. "Well, there are the natives . . . ," he ventured nervously.

Silence fell over the table, and the Biographer's long, pointed nose descended towards his soup plate. There was an awful moment in which the clank of cutlery was all that could be heard. Idiot, the Biographer thought.

"Oh my goodness," called out an aide-de-camp, eventually. "Someone's invited a kaffir-lover to the Captain's table. If we'd known you were of that stamp, we wouldn't have asked you."

"He'll learn, I guess," said Churchill. "He's the new photographic chappie, everyone. So keep on your toes and mind your tongues, lest he creep up on you with his camera and show you in an unfavourable light."

The Biographer's nose descended further, like that of a dog which has been firmly admonished, and he felt cravenly thankful for Churchill's remark, condescending as it was. At least it let him off having to explain himself.

But the incident was soon forgotten, as the conversation moved on. "They are both inferior races, anyhow," someone else said. "Boers and natives. What was it Milner said? The ultimate end is a self-governing white community."

"Supported by well-treated and justly governed black labour from Cape Town to the Zambesi," picked up another. "But that means Boers, too."

Milner: there was a justice of the peace called that in Birmingham, the Biographer remembered. But this one, the Cape Governor, was a real jingo, responsible for pushing the Boers over the brink.

"Milner told Asquith you just have to screw Kruger, sacrifice the nigger completely and the game is easy," shouted one of the swells.

The Biographer wished he was elsewhere. These people, these colonels and aides-de-camp, these Major Pole-Carews and Lord Gerards, these civil servants and silver-tongued correspondents, even genial old Rigby, the *Dunottar Castle's* captain—they were like another breed. Even the way they held their bodies was different. Look at Churchill now, for instance, listening as another one of them blathered on. Even when he wasn't the centre of attention, he had a patronizing air, a way of holding his head that said, "I'm cock of the walk." The Biographer never felt like that. He wished he had his big camera by him; with its armour in front of him—its huge elm-wood box, glass plate and hood—he felt protected, in control, unassailable.

He looked across the table again at Churchill, who had begun to hold forth about Boer armaments. He had the slightest wisp of ginger moustache and, also slight, a lisp which distorted his pronunciation of the letter "s." Yet in spite of this impediment, and of his aristocrat's arrogance, he had something about him. His remarks displayed the kind of interest and depth that was absent from the other talk round the table.

On the way in to supper, for instance, he had whispered conspiratorially to the Biographer—"Isn't it odious, a voyage? The sea's heavy silence all around; you keep expecting something to leap up out of the water. But it never does."

There was nothing to it, really. It was just an odd, slightly elaborate fragment of conversation; but still, fools didn't make observations like that. The Pole-Carews and Gerards simply didn't talk in that way. Atkins, perhaps, but not the officers. Buller, though, he was something else: full of the wisdom and caution born of years of campaigning. But an air of worry hung about him tonight as they tucked in to crown of lamb. The jollity he had shown on deck had quite disappeared, and he kept looking up crossly whenever one of the gathering made an inflammatory remark.

"Listen here," he finally growled. "I don't like dinner becoming a political discussion. We are on our way to do a difficult job. It is important for us to resist the prejudices and antipathies of religion and race if we are to have a clear view of the military task."

One consequence of Buller's statement was that a substantial portion of the rest of the dinner was spent discussing Scintillant's recent by-a-neck victory over Ercildoune in the Cesarewitch at Newmarket. This, oddly enough, had taken place at almost exactly the time Kruger's ultimatum had expired. Many of the diners seemed to have been at the course, and one had landed a hefty wager. The Biographer smiled to himself. He had watched a different kind of sport that week—Villa tackling Spurs, in the first round of the Cup. Now he lifted to his lips another cup, a porcelain one full of coffee, and glanced across the table into the penetrating eyes of Winston Spencer Churchill. No, these weren't his people. They even drank coffee differently, holding up the saucer daintily as they sipped.

3

The coffee bushes were in blossom with little white flowers. Muhle Maseku noticed these, and thereupon chided himself. For this was not the time for beauty. He heard the crack of the long whip behind him, driving one of the bullock carts upon which the ill and infirm were piled, and all around the murmuring tramp of seven thousand men and their families. Seven thousand! They had been mineworkers on the Rand, most of them, out of Natal, and with rumours of war they had lost their jobs. At the back was the white man, Marwick, tending the sick, at the front the concertinas, mouth organs and drums of the mine band.

The tunes were painfully jaunty, for such a miserable time. Otherwise, all was solemn calm. Muhle himself was worried about his wife, Nandi, and their young son, Wellington. They were marching alongside Marwick's bullock carts at the back, with the other women and children. Muhle was worried that his own family or he himself would become sick soon. His feet were a mess of blisters from the walking, and what little food they had been able to bring with them was exhausted. He turned against the flow—thirty abreast, in some places—and went back to the women's group. Looking through the crowd, where the heads of babies peeked out from between the shoulder-blades of their mothers, riding in knapsacks made of folded cloth, he could see neither Nandi nor Wellington. He became anxious. Then he spotted them stumbling along, both clutching bundles of precious possessions. A tin mug, a mirror, a bag of maize meal: all that was left of their life on the Rand.

"I salute you," said Nandi, "but your son is tired now, and we must rest and find food." She touched the beads at her plum-coloured throat, and Muhle felt tears prick his eyes at the sight of it.

"I am not tired," countered Wellington from beside her. "I can march as well as Father, as well as any. My heart is full, my muscles are strong."

He lifted up a bony arm, as if to show that strength, and Muhle looked down at it, following the contours of the flesh up the dusty forearm to where a biceps swelled, then over the shoulder where the skin was smoother and cleaner, flowing into the neck and face: that face which reminded him of his own father's, with broad cheeks and stubborn forehead, eyes the colour of honey from the acacia blossom of Natal and small ears set back flat against the skull.

"What are we going to do?" demanded Nandi.

Maseku could see the strain in her face, but did not answer. There was no appropriate reply to make. Instead he put an arm round her, reaching down at the same time to take Wellington's hand. The boy— he was only twelve, but looked older—smiled at him. So handsome, Muhle thought, just one year younger than he had been when he married Nandi, but still just a sapling. A furrow creased his brow then. Already on this long march some other boys had tried to bully Wellington. He had beaten them fiercely off his son. Only Nandi's urgent cry had stopped him from chasing after them.

Now, as they walked towards a ridge of hills, the cry was coming from Muhle's belly. Every time they passed a store by the side of the road the shopkeeper would turn them away. They were frightened, these Boer traders, Muhle could see that; frightened of the crowds of his people and their pain.

They marched on, passing other groups of refugees: Hindus in bright saris, wearing bangles and gold nose-rings, a company of whites—Scots and Irish—on horseback, a Boer family in an ox wagon, going in the opposite direction, the mother with a baby clutched in her arms. At one point they came upon an accordion, dropped in the middle of the road: the column just opened up and passed round it, paying little heed. They knew what it meant, though. For all, like Muhle himself, had left behind households, possessions, livelihoods. And now they themselves, no less than their belongings, were flotsam scattered on the veld, by the wave of impending war.

Late in the day, a long murmur came down the column, and it slowly eased to a halt. Muhle saw Marwick—the kindly Englishman from the Natal Native Affairs Department—go up to the front, where there was some commotion.

"Stay in this spot," he said to his wife. "I will go to see what happens. Maybe there is some food." He followed Marwick past the ranks of black men—Zulu and Xhosa, Sotho, Swazi and other tribes from Natal and the Cape, and not a few from the north also, strangers from Nyasa and Bulawayo.

This curiosity—no, it wasn't that, it was responsibility—was the undoing of Muhle Maseku. For they had just crossed the border into Natal and on the British side were some Boers, on horseback, with their rifles in their hands and their trademark slouch hats upon their heads. The Boers were engaged in strenuous argument with Marwick, every now and then interjecting their broken English with the *nee* and *ja* of their own strange tongue. Marwick looked ill and afraid, Muhle thought. As he watched, many more Boers appeared and began sectioning off a part of the crowd of marchers, herding them with their rifles. Muhle panicked, trying to move back away from the vanguard. But then one young Boer with pale blue eyes prodded him back, and he began to be carried along by the flow of the rest. Terrified of being separated from his family, Muhle shouted out to one he recognized on the other side of the cordon, a comrade from the mines.

"Mbejane! They are taking me. You must tell Nandi that if I do not see them soon they must foot it to my kraal. I will see them in the old place."

But Muhle never knew whether Mbejane had heard him, as the rifle of the young Boer with pale blue eyes was behind him, and he and the stolen four hundred were first walking up the hill, then running in the slow jog that is the custom in those parts. Muhle, swept along with them, looked desperately back for his wife and son, but all he could see was a mass of faces, each as frightened as his own.

All that afternoon, the Boers made them drag heavy siege guns up to the summit of the next hill, taking the whip to those who did not comply fast enough. It soon began to rain, which made the task more difficult and the Boers bad-tempered. They did not spare the sjambok then, its tongue stinging all the more where it sizzled on wet skin. But Muhle was tough, he had worked in the hardest mines—the Ferreira, the Robinson Deep—so he did not slack from weakness. As he pulled on the chains attached to the gun carriages, he thought only of staying alive and getting back to Nandi and Wellington as soon as possible. The dark spectre crossed his mind that he would not get back, that these Boers would keep him here to fight in this white man's war for ever—but he dismissed it, and then swore as his feet slipped in the mud.

The scene at General Joubert's artillery laager, to where they were pulling the guns, was a strange mixture of busy-ness and ghostliness. In the wake of the rain had come mist, its eerie tendrils draping the aloes and acacia trees. Through it, and all around the emplacements, moved the bullock carts and horses of the Boer burghers. At one point, Muhle caught sight of the General himself, his long beard ruffling in the breeze which, that evening, came to sweep the mist from the hills. Sitting on his horse, surveying his dispositions in the half light, he looked coolly competent: blue frock coat, brown slouch hat with a crepe band, and shrewd, piercing eyes. Muhle shivered, and saw how his own breath, like that of the General, and of the General's horse and the stamping lines of bullocks, was making shapes in the cold air.

They worked late into the night. The Boers brought out torches, lengths of wood soaked in pitch, and the oily yellow flame of these combined with the light of the moon to make the laager a still stranger place. As he toiled, Muhle thought of his wife and child. He was not the only one with such thoughts, for amid the sweat and groans of the four hundred men taken by the Boers came the murmurs of others concerned about their families. When, at last, the final gun was in place and the order came for the men to disband, it was as if the lid had been taken off a boiling pot. All four hundred ran pell-mell down the hill, sliding like children in the rich brown mud.

Someone was bound to get hurt and, as the gods disposed it, it was bound to be Muhle Maseku. In the rush down to that dark valley whose small firelights signalled the place where Marwick's column of refugees had camped for the night, he tripped and fell. No, more than that, his foot found its way into the hole made by an aardvark in the edge of an anthill and he broke his ankle. As he fell, Muhle realized that he had heard the sound many times before. It was the sound acacia branches made when you snapped them off for firewood. Then the pain tore through him and—before he could begin to cry out for help, for at least someone to fetch Nandi to him—Muhle Maseku fainted in the hills outside Ladysmith.

4

Stood on a blazing kopje, Henry Nevinson of the *Daily Chronicle* lifted his spyglass to his eye and surveyed the yellow-brown plain in the pan. Three or four miles wide, and like the town itself surrounded by hills, it was almost circular in shape. It reminded the correspondent of a shield. Not an African one, made of dried cowhide and wattles and good for rapping your assegai on to frighten the enemy, but a Greek or Trojan one. For it had come into Nevinson's head that he was some classical character—King Priam's trusted herald Idaeus, perhaps—and the plain of Ladysmith that of Ilium.

Actually, the classical speculation had first been that of Steevens. The *Mail* man, who was well read in Greek, had accompanied Nevinson on an earlier visit to the plain. Today, unable to maintain his colleague's analogy, Nevinson put the idea out of his head. He lowered his glass, musing on how, in these days of ratiocination, analogy was no longer the intellectual power it once had been. The kings of the old time are dead, as a poet friend of his once put it. Now all was facts and evidence. And moving photography. Other members of the press corps in Ladysmith had heard how a representative of the Biograph Company was headed for the Cape with General Buller, and sneered accordingly; but Nevinson had kept his counsel. He could see it had potential, this new art. Or was it a science?

He secreted his spyglass in the shade of a bare rock, and picked up his notebook. Balancing it on his knee, he began to write. Already, since the invasion and the declaration of martial law, he had filled two booklets with his tidy hand. For the time being, the wire was intact, and from these scribblings he would assemble the atoms of the telegraphs he would send back to his office—via Durban and the cable, passing deep under the sea, up to Zanzibar, Aden, and finally through to London, centre of the known world. But what if the wire was cut? Preparations had been made with carrier pigeons, and a squad of native runners, yet the former could be shot by keen-eyed Boer marksmen and the latter intercepted by sentries and their messages turned open.

The answer to the problem lay nearby, on Signal Hill, where lately the heliograph and flagmen had been working, trying to blink and flap messages in Morse and semaphore to troops at other stations. But so far, in the anteroom of crisis, they had not got through, and weren't likely to do so until loyal forces were able to fix another heliograph station at Weenen on the Kolombo mountain, thirty-five miles away. In that, as in everything, Nevinson thought, we await General Buller's grace. It struck him that it was possibly interesting to his readers, this question of how what they were reading was borne unto them, out of a moment of emergency—but it wasn't the sort of item Major Mott, the military censor, would let him put in a telegraph.

Nor, though he had done the calculations, would he be able to put in the figures which would no doubt determine the outcome of the whole affair. There were now 13,500 soldiers in the town, about 5,500 civilians and—he made this distinction without hesitation—2,500 native Africans and Indian immigrants. There would have been a lot more of those to feed, had General White not ordered all non-essential servants to be dismissed. Even so, with a total ration demand of around 21,500 mouths, the town could last only about two months. Ignoring, that is, the problem of 12,500 livestock—horses, mules and oxen—for which they had only a month's forage in store.

None of this could go in his despatch. But there was plenty of other material to write about. Armoured trains crammed with military stores had been steaming into Ladysmith station all week, filled with compressed beef, compressed forage, jam, oil, sardines, ammunition and more—all the necessities of army supply. Last Wednesday, General White himself had arrived with his entourage. Nevinson had noted how decrepit the man charged with the defence of Natal had seemed: his old riding accident was plaguing him in the heat, making him limp. It didn't augur well, that gammy leg.

Neither did the news of the Boer advance, led by the other general, Joubert. "Slim"—cunning—Piet, as he was known. And cunning he was proving to be. Creeping down mountain passes from the two republics, the Boers' three columns now controlled most of northern

Natal. Joubert himself had come by Laing's Nek. Although both Charlestown and Newcastle had been captured, there had been little serious action, as the British residents had mainly already left. What had taken place was mostly bloodless—some police and a passenger train captured. The worrying thing was how well supplied the Boers appeared to be, especially with Krupp artillery, which was reported to come with skilled German gunners supplied by the factory. More worrying still was the speed of the advance: at this rate Brother Boer would be in Durban within the month.

So far as the inhabitants of Ladysmith were concerned, the point was that a large number of Boers, perhaps twenty-five thousand organized into commandos, had massed within fifteen miles of the town. The outposts of both the Carbineers and the 5th Lancers had been engaged on successive nights, and heavy firing was beginning to be heard in the distance. People were saying that the first real shots of the war had been fired at nearby Dundee, to where a column had been rashly thrown forward. This was under Penn Symons, the impetuous man in charge of forces in Natal until the arrival of Generals White and—if he ever would arrive—Buller, with his Army Corps.

Other noises than those first shots at Dundee had maintained an air of normality in Ladysmith itself, albeit normality of a rather infernal character: the other day the band of the Leicesters had played scales all morning. Slow time, Nevinson had observed. That was the awful thing: the whole place was just waiting for the Boers to come on. Not surprisingly, this feeling of dreadful anticipation had given rise to suspicion. The few Dutch left in the town had been arrested, and now the military police were rounding up suspicious characters. This seemed pointless to Nevinson: most of them were simply refugees displaced by the war, mine-hands and uitlander servants down from Johannesburg.

He rubbed his face—the sun had brought out a rash—and made a note to himself to get a hat with a wider brim. Below him, the dipping slope which the kopje crowned was swaying its tall grasses with a hypnotic motion, and for a second it seemed that the emptiness he saw, still further below on the plain itself, was nothing but a mirage.

It had all changed so quickly, testament to fear as much as to military necessity. Before, the lines of white bell tents had been busy with activity. Pickets with fixed bayonets had kept guard, and mounted patrols skirted the perimeter. Men had played cards, cleaned their kit, smoked their pipes. Yesterday they had dismantled the camp, it being deemed impossible to defend, and moved into town. Wagons had stirred up great clouds of dust, and kit had lain revealed on the ground, ready to be packed up. Now it was nearly all gone, and the tents were being repitched beside the river.

He looked out over the sun-scorched, stone-freckled plain again. It wasn't vast enough to be a desert, but the bare expanse he could see created that impression: freedom, space, a kind of totality that was also crushing. It absorbed one ineluctably, drawing the eye towards the infinite. As Steevens had said, of coming up on the train, "You arrive and arrive, and once more you arrive—and once more you see the same vast nothing you are coming from." Here all was gaunt and wild, as the Cape, with its Dutch gardens, had been cultivated and picturesque; how far away those dark greens and purples seemed today, as if situated in an altogether different realm. For now, without the soldiers, the plain was truly desolate. There was only dust, litter, a few goats browsing, and—he noted in his glass—the occasional African poking about in the debris.

It was with this pitiful sight in mind that Nevinson packed up his belongings, remounted, and made his way back to town. At least he had a good pony. The horse which had brought him down the Helpmakaar Road, after his initial tour with Steevens and the other correspondents, had gone lame. He had had to get another. This would have cost him a sovereign, but he had brought several boxes of cigarettes with him and an officer of the Hussars had been willing to exchange his polo pony for one.

After the scene on the plain, the outskirts of Ladysmith itself seemed idyllic—cottages with rose gardens and honeysuckle about their shady verandas. One was the house commandeered by White, the commander-in-chief. Nearby, with many a merry shout, a detachment of the Green Horse was pursuing a football. He saw Tom Barnes among them, and waved from his horse. Barnes, bare-chested, waved back, and then scrambled into a tackle. Like the gardens—some had trees bearing that buttery fruit, avocado, that he had tasted here for the first time—the football pitch was a calming sight, for all the world such as one might encounter in a village of Herefordshire or Worcestershire on a Sunday afternoon in the middle of summer.

The impression didn't last long. Entering the main street was to throw yourself into a chaos of steaming horses, pannier-laden mules and bellowing oxen, of stacked firewood, Lee Metford rifles, lances and cavalry sabres, bales of forage, soldiers in uniform, volunteers in riding boots and shirtsleeves, and African drivers cracking their whips. Nevinson had to dismount and tether his pony. There was a general mood of fear and anticipation and want of confidence, a feeling that things would very soon change. Of all the evidence of people preparing for the worst, the most affecting was the sight of a large number of lady cyclists with their wicker baskets piled high with provisions bought in panic. One of these, a thin, ascetic-looking woman, with an abundance of grey hair and a long black gown, nearly ran into him as he watched, and in doing so, almost fell off her bicycle. Steadying her, he grabbed hold of the handlebars. Some of her goods fell to the ground.

"Careful, young man," she snapped, dismounting. "You should watch where you are walking."

"I'm sorry, madam," said Nevinson, going down on his knees to pick up the provisions. "I was taking in the scene."

"Were you indeed?" She stood over him with one hand on the bicycle, the other on her hip—the very image of indomitable womanhood.

He straightened, putting the paper bags and cartons back into the basket. "I am afraid one of these eggs seems to be broken." He cupped the goo of the broken egg in his palm and flicked it onto the ground.

"And so we shall all be cast down," said the woman.

"I'm sorry?" queried Nevinson, wiping his palm with a handkerchief.

"This unspeakable war. It is a curse from the Lord, a judgement on the pride of the politicians and generals. On both sides! If they were nearer the light, this state of affairs would never have arisen."

"I am sure you are right," said Nevinson. "To whom do I have the pleasure of speaking?"

"My name is Mrs. Frinton. Now if you will excuse me, I must get to Star's bakery before the bread runs out."

She remounted her bicycle and rode off. Nevinson watched her thread her way through the crowd, wobbling dangerously, and reflected that perhaps her premonition of disaster was right. Women had a sixth sense about such things, he believed. The laying in of essentials and home comforts by the ladies of Ladysmith seemed to him a certain sign that the greater comfort, the way in which the town had hitherto complacently risen and settled into itself each day, sun-up to sundown, could not persist. He retrieved his pony and led it back to the cottage he had taken with Steevens and MacDonald, wondering where it was all going to end. For if Ladysmith fell, why not Natal, the Cape, indeed why not, as subject peoples everywhere saw that it was possible, the Empire itself?

It was a question that came back to him later that evening, when he was exploring the new cottage. The landlord had a surprisingly extensive library, which included a set of Gibbon: the 1872 edition, annotated by Doctor Smith. Steevens, who was a Gibbonian, had been delighted when his attention had been drawn to it. For want of anything else to read, Nevinson carried the first volume up to bed with him that night. He wouldn't have time to get through much of it, of course, but just a few words from the great man would be a dose of good for his own prose.

But he found it as heavy to read as it was to carry, and after half an hour went downstairs again in his pyjamas to find something a bit more congenial. It wasn't that he couldn't stomach true learning. He was as well read as Steevens and had already published two books on German letters—one on Herder, one on Schiller—in addition to *Neighbours of Ours,* his Cockney fantasia about ordinary life in the East End. It was just that he wanted a good read to take his mind off things. He scanned the shelves: *Kloof Yarns, The Phantom Future, Women Adventurers, In the Heart of the Storm* . . .

Ah, here was just the thing. *Illusion: A Romance of Modern Egypt.* On taking it up to bed and settling down with it, he found that although the author wrote with great assurance, she took little pains with her style and employed an often clumsy extravagance of diction. Her figures, too—the officers of a dragoon regiment quartered in Cairo—had not quite the air of being true to the life of the historical period that they portrayed, of some forty or fifty years ago.

But as he got deeper into the sensational story, Nevinson began to entertain a very much higher opinion of the author's talent. For, notwithstanding all her literary deficiencies, she was very effective. The plot seemed impossible, but it was dramatic; the figures seemed unreal, but were well grouped; and the hero, a captain, was thrown into due prominence: a rather commonplace, highly respectable man with many virtues and but one redeeming enthusiasm—his profession.

The story, which Nevinson finished that very night, went some way along these lines: one night, the captain is discovered hopelessly drunk, but he is popular with his regiment and the affair is concealed. Yet it happens again, and when he disgraces the uniform a third time he is court-martialled and dismissed from the service. He sets off south and is captured by the dervishes and made a slave. Here the honest, puzzled man rises to a great occasion, and after showing the courage of a martyr for the faith that he has, somewhat conventionally, held, he escapes, to find eventually that his disgrace was an "illusion," and that he had been drugged by the enemy.

The novel was more striking than this bare analysis of its plot would indicate. It was written with an admirable sincerity and, thought Nevinson on going to sleep, was altogether uncommon.

In the morning, when he awoke, he thought it was rubbish.

5

The Biographer, sick from the effects of typhoid inoculation, could hardly focus upon the chalked words. BOERS DEFEATED—THREE BATTLES—PENN SYMONS KILLED. When he and the other passengers of the *Dunottar Castle* saw the blackboard hung on the side of the other ship—the *Australasian,* on its way from the Cape—at first not a word was spoken. Then, slowly, some people began expressing their desire for vengeance at Penn Symons's death; others, including Churchill, were simply anxious that the fighting would not be over before they reached South Africa.

The remainder of the voyage was passed in heavy anticipation. The deck games of cricket and tug-of-war lost their gaiety, and people began packing, and sharpening their rusted swords. A special machine—somewhat like a bicycle, with a grindstone for a wheel— was brought out on deck for this purpose. As farrier, Perry Barnes was called upon to do the work, and by the time he had put an edge on six hundred swords, he was heartily sick of the sight of steel.

The Biographer filmed him during his labour, and also got a good sequence of General Buller walking up some steps and looking directly into the lens.

"That'll do," the General said afterwards. "If you take any more, I'll have you thrown overboard."

The last days of the voyage passed. When the rocky shores of Robben Island came into view, Churchill, standing next to the Biographer at the rail, muttered that it was "a barren spot," and retired to his cabin, complaining of the terrible slowness with which they were approaching the anchorage. But finally they arrived, and he came out and with the Biographer gathered round those bringing on despatches from Cape Town. Thereby they learned of the three battles in more detail—and of a shameful retreat to Ladysmith and the imminent besieging of the town. Buller landed in state the following morning, to the cheers of an enormous crowd, and the Biographer caught a good image of the early-morning sun shining upon his face. In a battered hansom cab Churchill, together with Atkins of the *Manchester Guardian,* went up to the Mount Nelson Hotel to plan their campaign and to conduct interviews with the military staff staying in that grand residence, before leaving for East London by rail, therefrom to catch the mail packet to Natal. They hoped in this way to gain a few days on everyone else in the race to Ladysmith.

"For that," said Churchill to the Biographer on bidding him goodbye, "is where the bulk of the Boer army is massed, and where the outcome of this struggle will be determined. Though I cannot foresee any serious reverse for our troops."

The Biographer was more circumspect, taking his time to explore Cape Town, while waiting for official acceptance of his formal petition to be allowed to follow the army. He found the town and its Table Mountain a very picturesque location; it was no surprise that the Boers loved this land and were willing to fight for it. The rich and varied grandeur of the place, with its gardens and vines and well-matured oaks, was worthy of a Claude or a Poussin. But the landscape did not awe him to such an extent that he did not film it: with a lens, if not a brush or a pen, the world was at his disposal.

He filmed the arrival of the New South Wales Lancers during this period, in the process of doing so discovering the considerable fascination that his equipment had for the natives, crowds of whom kept reaching out and touching his apparatus. He also took steps to procure a draft harness and a cart in which to carry his materials, hoping to add mules or horses to them at the next stopping place.

Finally the petition was granted, and the Biographer, together with his cart, rejoined the *Dunottar Castle,* which was to proceed to Natal with Buller and his staff. This it did, through five days of rough seas, arriving at Durban on November 10, to be greeted by a crowd of fifty or more rickshaw-runners. Yelling and capering about, they were dressed in outlandish costumes of horn and feather to attract custom. The Biographer took great pleasure in picking out from these magnificent specimens of manhood a figure he considered a veritable Umslopagaas, worthy of Rider Haggard. A horse could not have gone faster, and as he rode high in the seat the Biographer watched the droplets of sweat running down the Zulu's muscular bare back.

Having installed himself in a rather grubby hotel (the town was full of refugees from the war, and rooms were difficult to secure), he made preparations, over the next few days, for his great trek north. The cart and harness were brought off the ship and united with a pair of horses. A tent was bought to cover the cart, and cooking utensils and tinned food purchased. The Biograph itself was strapped to the back of the cart in such a way that it could be raised and lowered at a moment's notice, and also swivelled from right to left. It had rather the appearance of a gun, a passing soldier remarked, and got "shot" for his cheek. Some of the other pictures the Biographer took during this period were less heartening. One in particular remained in his head as well as on the film he sent back in his last London box before the column departed: that of a refugee black woman, weary and downcast, feeding her child. She looked up at him with a cold eye as he secured the image. He wondered if she knew what he was doing.

Of the other things the Biographer did, in the long waiting time before the column set off (for an army with a mission, it had an extraordinary supineness about it), one was to visit a Hindu temple. There were many such temples in Durban, he discovered, to service that city's large Indian population, brought over, fifty or so years before, to work as indentured labourers on farms and railways. Lately, many of them had turned to trade, and their success had drawn others to come from India and settle in South Africa as merchants.

He was called on to remove his boots before going into the temple. The inside of the place was filled with burning incense lamps and the frightening statues of various gods. It was also, as the Biographer discovered on entering an antechamber, the scene of a political meeting. He had heard from men in the Durban garrison that the Indian community had for several years been militating loudly against pass laws and restrictive taxes, and clamouring for representation. He supposed this was the purpose of the meeting. There was a large banner on the wall, reading NATAL INDIAN CONGRESS, and the main speaker was a small, slight young man with sharp black eyes that darted here and there from behind round spectacles. He seemed to have the audience in his spell, and once the meeting was over the Biographer quizzed him as to what he had been saying.

"Are you trying to throw down the government? Is that what all this is about?"

The man smiled, and looked down at the ground as they walked towards the Biographer's rickshaw. The Zulu was seated in the dust with his back against the wheel, smoking a clay pipe with a prodigiously long stem.

"Oh no, not today. We are engaged upon a discussion about the war. I feel it is our duty, if we demand rights as British citizens, to help in the defence of the British Empire. To that end, myself and my colleagues are collecting together to have our services accepted as an ambulance corps."

"But I thought you people wanted emancipation from the British?"

"We do, sir, we do. In fact, my own sympathies are entirely with the Boers. But it is my honest belief that we Indians, here and in our homeland—and, for that matter, these Zulus and other oppressed races—will only achieve our complete freedom within and through the British Empire. Not by shooting bullets at you fellows, but by persuading you of the error of your ways."

"What error?"

"Well, for instance, thinking that we Indians are cowards and only ever do things in our own self-interest. That is one reason why this ambulance corps is being formed—although above all it is a humanitarian impulse that is behind its formation."

They had reached the rickshaw, and the Zulu sprang up with alacrity. The Indian held out his hand to him in greeting, at which the African looked askance. He gave the Biographer a look of great discomfort, and went to fasten himself between the shafts of his vehicle. The Indian appeared pained at the Zulu's reaction, and then, to the Biographer's astonishment, started undoing his shirt buttons, exposing the flesh of his chest.

"Let me tell you something, sir," he said.

"Very well," replied the Biographer, mystified.

"This brown skin is my birthright, and it does me honour, but in my heart I consider myself a black man. When I am treated as such, as so often by people of your own colour, I feel pride, not self-disgust."

The Biographer nodded contemplatively.

"You nod, sir, but in truth you have no idea of what it is to be considered a 'coolie' or, worse still, a 'kaffir.' All of our parts and graces are circumscribed by these labels—my friends are thought of as 'coolie merchants,' while I am nothing but a 'coolie barrister.' Our bodies, even when we eschew meat and liquor as I do, are considered unclean. I once went to a white barber in Pretoria, and he refused to cut my hair—so I cut it myself with a pair of clippers, and was happy to do so, in spite of my friends laughing at the mess I made of it. What they did not appreciate is that we Indians make similar distinctions in our own culture, refusing to allow our barbers to cut the hair of untouchables. Every time we suffer prejudice in South Africa we reap the reward of our own sinfulness in this regard."

Although he had difficulty following the man's logic, the Biographer was impressed with his passion, and it struck him that the Indian would make a good photographic subject.

"Do you mind if I take your picture?" he asked. "I'm a cameraman, you see, the representative of the Mutoscope and Biograph Company. I have my pocket machine here with me."

"I would happily oblige you," said the Indian gentleman, doing up his shirt buttons. "But in most instances I believe photography to be the handmaiden of pride, and an enemy of humility."

The Biographer was put out by this refusal. "You'll be facing fiercer enemies than the camera if you join Buller's army," he said.

"A bullet, sir, is not the worst fate a man can suffer. Nor is a beating. I myself have been badly boxed and beaten by whites enraged against my political activities—kicked and pelted with stones by a great crowd. But I bore my bruises with humility and did not prosecute my assailants, in spite of Mr. Chamberlain cabling the Natal authorities and asking them to do so."

"Really?" queried the Biographer, disbelieving that the Secretary of State for the Colonies would take an interest in the activities of an Indian advocate in far-flung Natal. "Is that true?"

"Why should I lie to you?"

"No, of course, you wouldn't. Anyway, I suppose I must climb into my vehicle."

His companion looked at the Zulu, crouched between the traces of the rickshaw, and sniffed. "I do not like those things."

"A man's got to get about. Well, I'll look out for you at the front. What's your name, by the way?"

The Indian had taken off his glasses and was cleaning the lenses with a cotton handkerchief.

"Gandhi," he said. "Mohandas K. Gandhi."

6

"This place where I am now at has been christened Green Horse Valley," wrote Tom Barnes from Ladysmith, in his first letter home since arriving. And then he stopped. He never knew what to say to Lizzie, his younger sister. Anyway, it was uncomfortable writing on the ground, and his calves were itching where dust had found its way between the folds of his puttees. He had borrowed Bob's drum, propping it between his legs and using the skin to lean on. As he sat there, his pencil poised, he could hear Bob himself—seated nearby on a biscuit box in the opening of the bell tent—sucking on the briar that was poking out through his whiskers. The company drummer and Tom's best friend, Bob Ashmead was engrossed in a magazine.

"What you reading?" asked Tom, pushing a finger down between the khaki bands to scratch his leg.

Bob grunted in reply, let out a puff of smoke, and then held the magazine up to show its title: *Band of Hope, incorporating Sunday Scholar's Friend.* Two shields on either side of the curly-leafed, Arcadian legend, the one saying "Get wisdom, get understanding," the other "For wisdom is better than rubies."

"Didn't have you down as a Bible basher."

"My mother sends them," Bob explained gruffly. "Haven't got anything else. It's pious rot most of it, but there's news too . . ."

With mock solemnity, he read out an item. "Last month, a London publican, residing in the highly favoured parish of Islington, was charged at Marylebone Police Court with nearly killing his own daughter of nineteen years of age. The man (although a kind father when sober) had got tipsy on ale at his own public house . . ."

"Ale . . . ," murmured Tom, dreamily.

"Me too. I'm as thirsty as a Derby winner. Let's go to the hotel next time we're off duty."

Tom thought about the girl there, the one with the unusual short hair. "I'm on. If they'll let us. Bloody beer will have run out if this lasts much longer. You'll have to sub me even so; if I get that bastard who took my belt I swear I'll shoot him. God, I hope we get out of here soon!"

"Use the Mauser, then it'll be like a Boer did it."

They both looked at it where it lay in the opening of the tent—the pistol they'd taken off a Boer corpse.

"How long do you think we'll be here?" asked Tom.

"It'll be over in a tick, believe me. They're just a bunch of farmers."

"So am I, if you'll excuse me. Anyway, they can shoot better than us. You saw how sharp that sniper was the other day?"

"Mmm," said Bob, and then they stopped talking. Neither wanted to remember the sight of Private Mouncer falling from his horse, hit by a bullet in the throat. Tom shivered. He had seen Mouncer in hospital. The nurses said the poor fellow would never be able to speak again. What a thing. Tom thought he would rather be dead.

Lord, it was hot. Above the two of them, the sun was beating down, enforcing quietness on the camp as effectively as a sergeant-major: all that could be heard was the occasional neigh of horses and sounds of men chatting in muted tones in front of their tents. The heat merely added to the nervous torpor that had settled over Green Horse Valley since the last action. It was all waiting, waiting, waiting. But the net was closing in. The telegraph wires had been cut, and the bombardment proper was expected to begin tomorrow. In some ways he wished it would: given the deadlock of force on either side, at least it would represent some kind of progress. But he knew that wasn't true really: he had been under shellfire in India, and it wasn't pleasant. And the Maharaja had not had such powerful and accurate guns as these Boers were understood to have.

He heard a splash and looked over to where Lieutenant Norris was sitting in a tin bath, scrubbing his neck. His hat, wide-brimmed in the Boer style—probably pinched off a dead one, thought Barnes—was still on his head and the skin of his back was white as the milk that Lizzie used to carry in each morning at home, in the big tin pail. Better do that letter, he thought. For he was on picket duty that evening, and wanted to get some kip beforehand. He set his pencil to the paper.

> We have had serious reverses at Dundee and Nicholson's Nek, and three battles said to be victories for British arms—Talana Hill, Elandslaagte and Rietfontein—but I am not so sure. At Nicholson's Nek, nearly a thousand of "our boys" were taken prisoner and are now going under escort to Pretoria, the Boer capital. All British forces in the area have made a desperate, mud-covered retreat to Ladysmith, where I am now shut up with General White. The Boers have about twenty thousand within striking distance, so it is not a happy business, although very exciting. They say that General Buller has eighty thousand men on their way to save us from Cape Town. The town is all talk of when he will arrive—and of when we might come under Boer shell. But don't worry, I will keep my head in one piece, and if I get a knock, put it all back together again!
>
> The command of D Squadron has gone to Captain Mappin, who is reasonable, and Major St. John Gore has assumed command of the regiment as a whole—Colonel Baden-Powell being in command at Mafeking, which the Boers are also thought to be investing. We are very crowded here in camp.
>
> Before our confinement, I went out on a few patrols, joining in a chase after some cattle and sheep and a Boer laager. We captured some hundreds of sheep on one and drove them into town, your humble having to walk as I fell off my horse—necessit. a third remount on return—and having some new boots on I blistered my feet very badly on the way back and had to go into hospital which prevented me joining in some of the later actions. I lost myself on the veld for a while and only rejoined my unit after a trying time in which I got on the wrong side of a bog in the company of some lads from the Leicesters.
>
> It turned out that Johnny Boer was waiting for us to get bogged, so that he could have us at his mercy. The bullets came much too close to be comfortable. So we lay down in the reeds and returned the salute, and by covering one another's retreat, we got clear of the bog.

Thank God.

In the emergency hospital (the Town Hall) I discovered a relative of ours. Mrs. Frinton, she was a Miss Parker, the same family as our cousins, and her father once kept the White Lion at Southam. She knew Mrs. Oram and her brothers well. She herself is a widow, her husband having died of a snake-bite some years ago. I have also seen an Irish girl at the Royal Hotel whom I rather like the look of. I hope to meet with her soon. I have made a new chum as well, a gunner from the Naval Brigade called Foster. A seaman in the veld, I hear you ask? The reason is that they rushed up a detachment of naval guns from Durban (I think they came off HMS *Terrible,* or *Powerful,* or *Tartar,* or something like that) at the start of the war, on account of our lack of artillery here in Ladysmith. Anyway, this Foster, a bearded bluejacket, has his eye on the sister of my girl.

On another patrol we came upon an abandoned Boer farmhouse and burnt the whole lot to the ground. We had a jolly time in it before it was burned, there was a splendid piano and a pile of music mostly in Dutch. The whole lot was burnt of course. It was very hot that day and we were deceived in our water supply. The stream where we should have halted had run dry.

My first real action was at Elandslaagte (a Boer name said as, Elands-lockty), where our infantry and artillery triumphed and we mopped up after together with the 5th Lancers. The pig-stickers, as we call them. Some shells fell among us beforehand, but we took it well. On the way in a funny thing happened, a pointer bitch, prob. a Boer gun dog, attaching herself to us and taking a great deal of interest in the shell-holes as they came. She didn't like the vapours much as they came out of the hole, drawing her nose away sharply, but still looked in every one. She even followed us back into town, but I don't know where she is gone now. I was surprised how these shell-bursts do not kill everything near around, often just going directly into the ground with a thud. Once the explosion has died down, the melinite vapours start to emerge from the hole—as if from the bowl of a pipe, only smelling much worse!

To get through at Johnny Boer we had to cut the wire on

either side of the railway line, which Captain Mapping did. The ground was bad, but Boer ponies are no match for our horses at close quarters (though the enemy are often better riders and their mounts have much more stamina) and we overhauled those trying to escape and gave them the points of our swords or speared them with lances, as the case may be. It is quite hard charging over a mile in near darkness, flashes of guns and rifles going off all the while. That night we bivvied at the railway station, making fires with coal from the mines and eating tinned meat and biscuits.

The following morning, we found ourselves next to a farmhouse in which a Boer woman was hiding. When we got to her, she was crouched in a shed with her arms round a goose. Seeing us approach, she buried her head in its feathers and started crying. As we surrounded her, she kept repeating something in Dutch. An African scout who spoke the language said what she was saying was: "Leave me my man-goose! Do not take my man-goose! Do not hurt my man-goose!" We had to take her in of course, but we let her keep the goose. As she was a farmer, I felt sorry for her, but they have plenty of our fellows in Pretoria, so there. Although they have released some injured and let them come to the hospital.

After we had taken the Boer woman and her goose into captivity, in a shower of rain we went over the ground we had charged, searching for wounded; but the ambulances had done a good job, as we found only disembowelled ponies, wagons, and dead oxen, one with its head blown clean off. There were also, still alive, riderless ponies and some Africans wandering about sadly. We took them all back to town and also the breech-blocks of two guns we had captured. We got a bit of personal loot as well, my friend Bob and I, including a Mauser and bandolier, some ostrich feathers and a jackal-skin rug, the last two of which I intend to send to you, assuming you have no need of a pistol!

And that is more or less it, as I must lay down my weary head before night sentry duty. I had a letter from Arthur and a parcel, but no sign of the note money you sent me, worst luck. I had my belt stolen with £8 in it the day I came back from hospital, with three others also losing theirs with more or less in it.

Tell Ma and Pa and brother Arthur I am all right, except for the fact of being shut up here. It's not so bad, until it rains, which oddly brings on my toothache. Otherwise, I am in good health and feel honoured to have seen—before the siege began—something of a grand country. It is the blooming season here (diff. to home of course) and the blossoms on the trees look splendid. The flowers growing on the veld also put most of our garden flowers in the shade. The corn here has just got well into ear and until the siege began we were cutting it all off.

I suppose you are prepared for Winter at home now. I wonder how the ferreting will prosper. I suppose Arthur will lessen the rabbits as usual. Is he as ardent a sportsman as ever? I myself should like a bit of shooting out here of the animal, rather than human, kind. There is, or was until we became townbound, lots of game of all descriptions. On the way up here we saw thousands of deer and springbuck running along in front of us and in the distance they looked like a lot of mounted men, which gave us a scare. I haven't seen any rabbits like English ones. They are like a cross between a rabbit and a hare. Everything here is different like that: it makes you feel that the world is a much bigger place than Radford Semele, I can tell you.

I hope Aunt is keeping well and yourself and all the rest at Radford. Shall write again soon, if I have time. It is uncomfortable writing while sitting on the ground. You try it.

Your loving brother,

Tom

p.s. My remount is a handsome colt, whom I have named Bashful in honour of Perry. Did he get himself a girl before coming away? No news of him, sadly, but expect he will be here to rescue me soon.

7

Muhle Maseku had no illusions about being rescued. Ilanga, the sun, had risen seven times since he had been brought into the Boer camp with his injured leg. He was a big man, and it had taken three of the Boers' servants to carry him. They were Xhosa, and at night in the black quarters as he lay there on his pallet, he had listened to horses' hooves, the noise of sticks being broken: their click-click language. Now it was morning, and they had gone out to work, and still he lay there, immobile, powerless.

Outside, beyond the makeshift straw huts in which he and the other Africans stayed, were the guns and wagons of General Joubert's camp. Through the opening in the hut, Muhle could see Dr. Sterkx, the man who had helped him. When the Boer guards had found him lying on the ground the morning after the accident, they had been ready to shoot him, convinced he was a spy. Eventually, he had per-suaded them that in fact he was there because he had been pulling the guns, and they had turned to go off—leaving him lying there on the slope of Bulwan, half naked (he had lost his kaross and his cooking pot), nursing his injured leg. Only the intervention of this doctor, who had ordered that he be brought into camp, had saved him. In the days that followed, Sterkx had come into the hut from time to time to rebind his ankle and to give him some food. Muhle had gathered from the doctor that the splints would have to stay on for at least a month.

This morning was the same. Sterkx—a small, stooping man with gold-rimmed glasses and thinning hair—came in and bent over him in the semi-darkness, readjusting the pieces of wood and wrapping the bindings ever more tightly.

Muhle gasped at the pain. "Why are you helping me?"

Sterkx pulled at the fabric again. "The week before we found you, the British burned my farm—the wagons, the house, the furniture, everything gone . . . They even burned my piano and music . . ."

The doctor stood up, and looked out through the oval gap that served as the hut door. His voice was strained with feeling. "But that was nothing, for they also took my wife into Ladysmith as a prisoner. I fear for her safety there, and thought of her when I saw you lying there on Bulwan."

Muhle didn't understand. "But I am a black man. You don't usually give us charity."

Sterkx turned towards the pallet, and looked down at him. "You are God's creature. Since my Frannie was taken from me, I have been full of anger and bitterness. And then a calm came, and I prayed to the Lord, and I realized that I must offer kindness to others, in the hope that the same will be offered to Frannie in the town there."

"My family . . . ," said Muhle, and then paused.

"What?"

"My family are missing also."

"Then you know what I am feeling, in spite of being a kaffir. Here, have some biltong."

Sterkx reached into his pocket, and pulling out a long strip of the dried meat, handed it to him. "This war is a terrible thing. Even though we are on the side of right, even though the Germans and the French and the Americans are on our side also against the English oppressor, I regret it, for whatever happens it will come to no good . . ."

Muhle sat up and chewed on the tough meat. He felt its goodness seep into him as the Dutchman talked on, and he reflected that never before had one of this race talked to him man to man—that is, as if he too were a man—and then, as Sterkx continued, he slowly understood that this Dutchman was really talking to himself, wrestling with his own pain even as Muhle's ankle throbbed on the bed beneath him. And yet he was also kind, saying that he would have one of the Xhosas bring him a pot of water . . .

"And once the bone has set, I suppose we can get some crutches fixed up for you too."

"Thank you, nkosi," said Muhle.

The Dutchman turned to go.

"Wait," Muhle said. "When I am able to walk, they will let me look for my family, yes?"

Sterkx stopped by the doorway. "I am sorry. I do not think we can let you go now—in case you fell into the hands of the British, you see."

"But you understand—about my wife and my son. I must find them!"

"I am sorry," said Sterkx. "They would not let me." And then he left.

Muhle stared at the oval of light in the doorway. The ragged edges of it, where the straw stuck out, represented to him the pain and anger he felt—pain in his ankle, anger at being forced to stay here, a prisoner of his body and the hateful Boers. For even the good doctor had become hateful now, as did everything he saw through that hole, from the horsemen, as they came and went, to the guns looming behind them.

In the days that followed, the commando in which he was held fought a number of battles with the British. The rattle of Maxims, the crackle of Mausers and other small arms could be heard in the hills around the camp, underlaid by the deeper echo of field artillery. Going out, the Boer horsemen were an impressive sight: the men cool in the saddle, bandoliers of ammunition across their chests (the beards of the older ones flowing down over the belts of shining cartridges), Mausers in rifle buckets on their saddles or slung over their backs, boots of soft hide pushed into their stirrups, and assorted kit—bedding rolls, tin pots for cooking—strapped to their saddles. Their clothes were mostly grey or brown, home-made, except for those of the officers, who favoured more formal black suits: coats with claw-hammer tails, and half top hats.

Coming back in after an engagement, officers and men alike looked sorry creatures: slumping in the saddle, soaked with rain and blood and mud, the wounded piled up in ox carts behind. In other carts came the dead, their staring eyeballs fixing on Muhle through the ragged gap. He saw in those eyes images of Nandi and Wellington, and knew more deeply than ever that as soon as he was able, he would flee this place and find them.

In the meantime, the oval of light played on: from where he lay,

Muhle could see the big gun he had helped pull up the hill. Its spoked wheels were huge, glittering with steel plate and rivets; in between, the dark grey of the barrel stretched up high against the sky. In front of the gun, Boer and African diggers had built up a great mountain of earth, to protect it from British fire. Soon, Sterkx had said, they would start the bombardment of Ladysmith.

"And then," the doctor had said, "God preserve my Frannie and any other innocent shut up in that town."

Around the emplacement scurried the gunners of the *Staats Artillerie,* their blue uniforms and gold epaulettes sharply different from the country clothes of the ordinary horsemen. Now and then, Muhle would also see striding around the tall, broad-shouldered figure of General Joubert, his iron-grey hair and white beard making him a natural man of authority. His headquarters was a large marquee in the middle of the camp, over which fluttered the *vierkleur* of the Transvaal. As the Zulu gazed silently upon the flag, wagons crossed to and fro, obscuring his field of vision. From these, as the oxen snorted and moved about in the shafts, men unloaded sacks of sugar and coffee and corn, all brought in from the surrounding farms. The sight of the food made Muhle feel hunger again: the biltong Sterkx had given him had taken the edge off it, but he craved some maize porridge, something to fill him up. Thought of maize made him wish he was at home, back at his kraal, watching the fields of bright green ears swaying in the wind, or watching Nandi drying the kernels on a mat, or Wellington shooting at a chicken with his sling, to frighten it away from the glossy white pile on Nandi's mat.

But these were all lies. These were images of his own childhood. Since Wellington had been a young boy, Muhle had worked down in the mines in Johannesburg, sweating and cursing with the others in the galleries, swinging pick against rock, sparks flying up, or pulling gouts of red clay out of the wall with the big hoes. Then every night back to the dreadful shanty with its stinking water and thousands of inhabitants from all over southern Africa. Every day, in the mines, he had longed to be back in Natal; every evening, in the shanty, Nandi had said to him how she hated their life, and he had promised to bring her back as soon as they had saved enough money. Now, by force of circumstance, they were in Natal, but apart, and far from home.

Later on in the week, once Sterkx had brought him his crutches—home-made, they were little more than two branches of thorn tree—Muhle was able to get up and move around the camp. It was important, he knew, that he get himself fit enough to slip past the sentries one night. He was often challenged about why he was wandering round the camp, but usually his explanation—that he was an injured labourer—was sufficient to allay any suspicion. He was wise to be wary, however, since the Boers were shooting any African who had worked for the British: already he had seen some twenty killed by firing squad after having been captured at the battle of Elandslaagte, had watched the Xhosas go to bury them where they lay in a heap afterwards. From their appearance, it was clear that many of the dead were also Xhosa, and one man from the hut let out a terrible wail when he saw that a relative was among the corpses. It was a sound that cut Muhle to the core, as he thought about his own family, and where they might be.

Once during his wanderings, on the morning of a great battle, Muhle encountered his saviour.

"I have to go and wait for the wounded by the ambulance," Sterkx said. "Why don't you come with me? You ought to keep that leg moving."

But there were few wounded—few Boer wounded—in that battle, and for most of it the ambulance wagon stood idle. Together they watched, black man and white, from the high hill. On the plain below, men moved like ants, sweeping hither and thither in waves, great clouds of dust and flame spurting up as shells dropped among them. Sterkx let Muhle use his spyglass to watch for a while, and on the ridge beyond the plain (its English name was Nicholson's Nek) the Zulu saw the Boer sharpshooters creeping on their bellies, and the British soldiers lifting their heads cautiously above their fortifications. Nearly always, a Boer bullet found them. Dead soldiers lay behind every earthwork or pile of rock.

Sterkx took back his glass and Muhle lay next to him, his crutches at his side. He listened to the Boer's exclamations—*Geluk hoor! Los jou ruiters!*—and prayed that wherever they were, Nandi and Wellington weren't in the middle of it.

"The English are bringing up their guns," said Sterkx.

Muhle looked again, and sure enough, the British gunners had limbered up and were riding in a column down towards the main site of battle.

"Surely they can't come any closer?" Sterkx said, this time as much to himself as to the Zulu. "They will be cut to pieces."

Even without the spyglass, Muhle could see that the column was too close to the hidden lines of Boer riflemen, who lay everywhere in the grass, some with their horses lying quietly next to them, as they had clearly been trained to do. The sixteen-gun column came on. Its horses, by comparison, were nervous and jumped in their traces as the crack of the Mauser bullets grew ever closer. Still they came on, and then the horses began to fall in their own tracks and the column became a jumble as guns and limbers jackknifed; even from up here, the noise of the bullets striking the gun barrels was audible. It sounded as if a crazed blacksmith were at work down there on the plain. The horses and men around the column—there was no noise as the bullets found these targets—fell into a mess of harness and trace, wheel-spoke and steel. In the face of the onslaught, the column jerked and writhed like a wounded animal, and then, soon enough, lay lifeless.

"Almagtig," breathed Sterkx. "Almighty God."

The Boer riflemen moved forward, swarming over the wrecked gun teams, then moving up the ridge.

"Now we have got them."

Horrified, Muhle watched as the Boers gained ground. Soon, the sound of a bugle was heard and a white flag went up on the other side of the ridge.

"Come on," said Sterkx. "We'd better move down. It seems I will be searching for Boer bullets in Englishmen today."

An hour or two later, at the bottom of the hill, Muhle watched the British prisoners march in with dragging steps and downcast faces.

"They were mostly Irish," Sterkx told him later, "and will be sent to gaol in Pretoria."

8

The capture of more than a thousand prisoners, mostly Dublin Fusiliers, at nearby Nicholson's Nek, the falling of heavy shells on a number of farms near the town, and the army's shameful retreat were each in themselves cause for consternation. Together, they made a disastrous impression on the morale of Ladysmith. These events also had the effect of speeding up the "evacuation," as the military were calling the rush from the town. That it was a shameful business was confirmed to Nevinson on a sticky, thunderous Natal evening, when he went down to the railway station. A strange and disturbing sight greeted him there.

In a yellow light, three trains were waiting, amid great confusion and congestion. Panic-stricken whites mixed with a vast crowd of Indians and Africans. The cause of the alarm was the Boers' imminent closing of the railway line. Out of the windows of the carriages poked the excited faces of white children, and the anxious ones of their mothers; in the open trucks, the other races were thickly packed. The general idea among all seemed to be "save your skin"—plus the cloth-wrapped bundle of goods upon your head, if that was your unfortunate lot—and, whatever its colour, every one of those skins dripped with sweat in the oven-like heat.

Nevinson looked about, and was shocked by what he saw. The native police were hitting both Africans and Indians with knobkerries, or prodding them as if they were livestock. It was cruel and pointless, not least since the more they were beaten and prodded, the more they shouted, pushed and pulled. Thinking there might be some copy in the scene, Nevinson took out his notebook and shoved his way through the crush. As he was scribbling down some notes, he heard an Australian voice in his ear.

"Well, at least we're clearing the town of its human refuse."

He recognized the voice as that of MacDonald, his fellow correspondent, and a bit of a jingo. He carried a swagger stick and affected the more ostentatious kind of uniform. Many of the press corps wore khaki and other officers' equipment—sword belt, sun helmet—in some combination, but MacDonald's outfit, together with his wide-brimmed Australian hat, was so carefully calculated as to suggest considerable vanity.

"I think it's rather sad," Nevinson replied, levelly.

"Do you really? Myself, I have no doubt that the mass of Hindus and kaffirs will one day furnish Natal with its greatest social and political problem."

"Perhaps so. But I don't think, just now, we're in a position to make any prophecies."

"Well, at least we're staying here. Only thing a solid bloke could do. See those white bleeders. Look at them! In my opinion, Nevinson, manhood is besmirched by flight in such company."

"Some have been ordered out, you know."

"Is that so? I know Burleigh has gone."

"For good?" Nevinson was surprised that the *Telegraph* correspondent hadn't decided to stick it out.

"Yes, fled the coop. Say, do you fancy a drink at the Royal later?"

"I won't, MacDonald, if you don't mind. Feeling a bit weary."

He pocketed his notebook and walked off, suddenly wanting to get as far away as possible from this Babel, and from MacDonald. It made him flinch, the way the race hostility rankled so deep in the Australian. He regretted having billeted with him. Steevens, who shared the cottage with them, was extremely pleasant. A refined and thoughtful scholar who could also cut it with Fleet Street's yellowest, he put the point upon honour but softened its edge with an easy wit. MacDonald's coarseness, on the other hand, made their little cottage rather tiresome at times.

The sun was almost down when he got back there, having strolled round the town picking up colour in the interim. At one point he stopped and watched a group of native women dancing at a street corner. Dressed in brightly printed wraps, they were moving with somnolent ease to the combined music of a mouth organ and a thumb piano. Nevinson stood entranced by the simple rhythm. He watched the feet move in the dust, and then slowly lifted his eyes. The women looked back at him unblinking, with something halfway between interest and resentment in their eyes. Nevinson met their gaze momentarily, then looked down and continued his journey.

"The last train has gone," he told Steevens, on entering.

The hero of the *Mail*—balding and bespectacled, though scarcely thirty—was sitting writing at the kitchen table.

"So we're stuck here then," he said, removing his glasses. Small, brown-eyed, white-faced, he didn't seem the war correspondent type, but his confidence under fire—and in print—was already legendary.

"Looks like it."

"Beleaguered."

"Well, let's see how it goes," said Nevinson. "Place for the story, though. Although Burleigh seems to think otherwise—he's gone, MacDonald tells me."

"Has he? The bugger. When I send my next despatch I'll put him down as missing in action. That'll ginger up the boys in the *Telegraph* offices."

Steevens got up, walked over to the window and looked out—into darkness, for in the few seconds since Nevinson had entered the room, night had fallen in its quick, tropical way, like a heavy curtain at the theatre. Steevens's torso was marked out against the blackness of the pane.

"Beyond is the world," he declaimed, ". . . under the wide and starry sky."

He turned round, and leaned against the windowsill, his stiff white collars contrasting brightly with the black glass. "I used to watch the sky in the Sudan, of a night. Glorious, the open desert."

"Rather refreshing, I should think," said Nevinson, taking a seat at the table.

"Yes. It didn't attack the nerves, being on campaign, like this place does. Well, until Omdurman, when the death toll was too much for one to entertain any thought but that of the grave. The bombardment, it did the job, but by Christ . . . Heads without faces, faces without anything below, and black skins grilled to crackling."

Nevinson paused, thinking about what Steevens had said. Eventually, he spoke. "Will it come to that here, do you think? If they bring Kitchener over to help Buller? There's rumours of it."

"Let's hope they don't need to. Anyway, this is different. A white man's war. I wonder how long it will last, though."

"They say Buller will be here in a week or two. But I'm not so certain."

"Nor I," said Steevens. He hit the window sill with the side of his hand. "What irks me about all this is how unnecessary it all is. The swaggering figure of Universal Trade is the man with his finger on the trigger, and yet no one is saying it."

"I take it you mean the gold-bugs," said Nevinson, who was already aware of Steevens's Radical sympathies—despite his working for a Tory halfpenny paper, where such political inclinations, not to mention literary ones, were held in contempt.

"Indeed. Milner, Rhodes, even Chamberlain is culpable to some degree. They are all after the gold and diamond fields really, and to my mind that makes the whole thing stink. Blood shouldn't be spilt for such things."

Steevens certainly had passion, thought Nevinson, even if he didn't think it crucial to a victorious military campaign. Maybe it was that which had brought him recognition at such a young age. Exciting books about India and the Sudan campaign, incisive reports from America and the ranks of the Turks at Thessaly . . . What was the title of that one, *With the Conquering Turk*? . . . Nevinson had been on that campaign too, on the other side, but he hadn't heard Steevens's name in those days. He ought to have done. Head boy at his school, fellow of his college, Steevens had left both behind and swept Fleet Street before him. Nevinson felt a twinge of jealousy; he had worked in journalism for a decade longer. But there was, it was true, a brilliant austerity about Steevens's writing: by picking out the right details, he gave you a very powerful picture of a scene, making you feel as if you were there.

"What's this then?" Nevinson said, looking down at the pages of manuscript in front of him on the deal table, and catching a glimpse of a Greek name.

The prodigy came over from the window and picked up the pad. "Oh, you don't want to look at that."

"Come on, George, what is it?"

Steevens held the papers to his chest, like a modest virgin, and then sat down in the chair, looking a bit embarrassed. "Oh, nothing. Well . . . you know I published a book before I came out, *The Monologues of the Dead.*"

"Of course," said Nevinson, who acted as literary editor of the tiny-staffed *Chronicle* when he wasn't on campaign. He remembered getting the review in: classical figures, historical and invented, tell their story in modern speech—Troilus, Themistocles, the Mother of the Gracchi, Constantine the Great. "The Lucan imitation," he added.

"That's right," said Steevens. "Well, I thought I'd try to write something in the same manner. About this place."

"Voices of a siege, you mean?"

"If it comes to that." Then the young man grinned. "Though I'm not sure that's the title for me. Might have to be *Monologues of the Dead,* Part Two, if those Boer guns do let rip."

The sound of a heavy tread on the porch steps interrupted them, followed by the noise of the front door opening.

"That'll be MacDonald," said Nevinson. "I ran into him down at the station. Cursing the kaffirs as usual."

"I know what you mean. No gentleman he."

Nevinson stood up from the table. "I'll turn in, I think. Lest we face a monologue—on the virtues of Australian butter."

"Or mutton," replied Steevens, before giving a harsh guffaw. MacDonald's paeans to Australian produce, and its superiority over the South African equivalents, had already become a regular feature of the journalists' evenings in the cottage.

As MacDonald opened one door, Nevinson closed the other. "Have I missed a joke then?" he heard the Australian say. "Hope I'm not the butt."

9

Nevinson watched a man sink to the ground—shot as he lifted the butt of his own rifle to his shoulder—and saw the stretcher-bearers run towards him. The correspondent crouched down further in the sangar, and listened to the tearing, roaring sound of shells passing overhead and the rattle of Mauser bullets chipping the fortification's rock wall. The town was now utterly surrounded, and they had been under fire for two days. It was on a Thursday, November 2, that the first of the Boer shells came crashing into town, from their big gun— "Long Tom" as it had been christened. A woman was wounded by a shell splinter, but Nevinson had still not got her name, such was the confusion. On the Friday, the bluejackets, the naval gunners who had been rushed up from the coast, fired their own first cannonades back at the Boers. The sailors' battery had some reasonably sized guns, but they were small fry compared with the Boers' great piece. It seemed, as he thought, a desperate case. In all earnestness now, the straitened state, the siege, had begun.

The effect on all was considerable. Donald MacDonald had come into the cottage visibly shaken, after seeing what he described as "a mass of splintered shell come hurtling over the camp and take off the leg of an unfortunate kaffir." On the first day, the shells had pitched mainly among military positions—the outer camp lines (where Nevinson now was), and the military stores near the railway line— but on the second, streets and houses had begun receiving attention. The heart of the town was blasted by no fewer than three big guns. The townsfolk stood transfixed in their doorways listening to the roar, and then rushing back inside if it sounded as though the deadly charge were coming their way.

Some of the naval men had been badly hit, one losing his legs—carried off on a stretcher, he died in the hospital—another mortally wounded in the groin. Through his glass, Nevinson could watch the Boers come out from behind their guns, stand with hands on hips to watch the fall of shot and then, when the response came from the British guns, dash back behind their shelters. Already many people in Ladysmith were complaining that Sir George White had left too many superior positions to the enemy. They overlooked the town from almost every point of the compass.

Confidence, on that first day, was not high among the British. Everywhere people were ducking and dodging for shelter whenever they heard the report. Some civilians were taking more careful steps, beginning to dig themselves caves and holes in the south area of the town, where the Klip River ran close and softened the earth. Others stayed in their homes, or—if they had a conscience, and many did—went to help in the hospital that had been set up in the Town Hall.

The casualties were slowly beginning to mount, adding to those injured in the earlier battles outside the town. A cavalryman on patrol had taken a bullet in the back of his head: MacDonald, who seemed to be a magnet for wounds, had seen this too, had watched helpless as the poor man lay there on the open veld, bleeding to death, his horse grazing next to him. In addition, two of the Natal Volunteers had fallen, another two had been shot through the upper arm, and three troopers of the Imperial Light Horse had been first mown down by Maxim fire and then, as if to seal their fate, rained upon by a hail of shell splinter. Another volunteer had been shot through both cheeks: an awful injury, but at least he lived and his jaw remained unshattered, such was the exactitude of the Mauser bullets with which the Kaiser had supplied the enemy.

From noon till night, this hell had persisted. A cottage had been exploded, and the Royal Hotel had suffered—if that was the word—a near miss. Cavalry and artillery flying behind teams of horses had been sent out, but were almost immediately driven back. The Ladysmith war balloons, sent up for observation, had proved consistent targets for the gunners of the *Staats Artillerie,* although so far they had escaped unscathed—and even now one hovered in the darkening sky above the crouching correspondent; a symbol, as he saw it, of misplaced British faith in technical capability.

Nevinson carefully put his head above the parapet, and then ducked down again immediately as a Mauser bullet sang past him. He lay down again, and waited for the firing to slacken. When it did, he slowly crept back to the opening of the sangar behind him. Bidding farewell to the men inside—they were too fraught to reply, even though it appeared that this day's assault might be over—he left the line of rocky circles that marked this outer perimeter of defence, and walked nervously towards the main part of the town.

Night began to fall in earnest. His way took him down a gradually inclining slope, so that below him he could see the dim flickering lights of camps and houses, lit in expectation of darkness. So far the Boers had not fired at night, so a lantern, candle or bonfire was not conceived of as a dangerous attraction. But how long before they did? Then those lights would die, and in dying give the lie to the swagger that had persisted in the Empire before the war had begun. He felt it was his duty to support the British, but all the experience of his early youth, from Ruskin and the Christian Socialists at Oxford to his time with the reformers at Toynbee Hall, teaching the poor in the East End, went against it. His youthful abhorrence of the State and all its enormities—he had known Peter Kropotkin and the other London anarchists in those days—seemed out of place here in Ladysmith. But what was the suppression of the Boer republics if not a liberal cause?

It was pitchy black by the time he reached the cottage, and he might have had trouble finding it if it had not been for the clucking of some fowls they had been keeping in a pen in the garden; it was MacDonald's idea, a way of supplementing their food supplies. On going inside, he expressed some of his thoughts about the siege to Steevens, who was sitting with his feet up on the kitchen table, smoking a pipe. He was inclined to enthusiasm about the present fight, and about the Empire too.

"I used to be against it all, like you. But then I went to India. Have you seen Bombay?"

"I haven't," Nevinson said.

"Well, you must go there. Any Englishman would feel himself greater for a sight of that city. I came back a changed man. It was no more long hair and crush hat for me after Bombay, I can tell you."

"I've heard it's an appalling place."

"Not at all. All human life is there, and therein lies the glory."

"Do you really believe in that stuff anymore, after what we've been through these last few days? Is Empire really worth it, George, after all? I saw a man horribly shot today, and I really began to doubt it."

"I'm with Thucydides, I'm afraid. On the Athenian Empire. It may seem wickedness to have won it—" A shell went off, but he continued speaking, without hesitation or change of tone. "—but it is certainly folly to let it go."

"But the purpose falters, George," said Nevinson. "With every despatch you or I or MacDonald gets out, detailing another defeat or setback, the world laughs at us. They are calling Buller 'Sir Reverse' rather than Sir Redvers now, you know. It is the farce that comes when you strip away the illusion, the theatre."

"Cheek, I call it. Product of socialists and cigarette-smoking new women. Well, actually, I have to concede that the Bull is being rather slow at the business end."

His colleague's mishmash of attitudes puzzled Nevinson. Steevens's Radical antipathy to the moneyed classes didn't seem to sit well with his support for Empire.

"I don't see how this squares with what you were saying last week," he ventured.

Steevens looked back at him. "It's the vital ideal of Empire one must hang on to—however tawdry the reality, however full of outrageous postures and cheap tricks. We've got to keep aiming at something beyond the truth. I suppose, at base, it is all to do with spreading light."

"Or what we think of as light. I don't understand you, George. I hope you don't mind me saying it frankly."

"How do you mean?" Steevens seemed almost pleased that his character should be seen to give rise to such confusion; if Nevinson had been a malicious man, he might have styled the expression his colleague wore as one of arrogance.

"I mean . . . You've been about, seen a bit of life, and yet you still have these high-flown notions. The *Mail* will have you writing leaders soon if you carry on in this vein."

"Already do, sir, already do."

"I might have known."

Suddenly brisk, Steevens brought his feet down off the table. "Sleep calls me to her bower. MacDonald's already gone up. I think all this shelling has knocked the stuffing out of him."

He stopped at the door. "By the way, you know there's this meeting tomorrow. I'm going to go along."

"So am I," said Nevinson as the door closed. He went over to the water jug to pour himself a glass to take upstairs, and found it empty. He held the iron jug in his hand and lifted it, weighing its emptiness, and once more said to himself, so am I.

10

"So I am meant to run away, Mr. Kiernan? Personally, I should have thought that a very un-British action."

"And your view is that we should just sit here, letting our families be blown to pieces?"

Mr. Grimble—a bearded, beak-nosed gentleman—and the red-headed Leo Kiernan stood on either side of the podium. The other civic dignitaries were still seated at the long table behind. The audience was seated on wooden chairs, or crowded at the back. As someone had remarked, it was the first meeting of the town council ever to have been attended by large numbers of the public. Bella, the correspondents—Nevinson, Steevens, MacDonald—and Torres the barber were among the audience.

"Come, come," said Farquhar, the mayor. "We've got enough to worry about without falling out amongst ourselves."

"That's right," said the military censor, Major Mott, who was representing the army. "We've all got to work together. It's the only way."

The occasion of the meeting had come out of an earlier request by the council to General White—namely, that he communicate to Joubert a message asking that all wounded and non-combatant civilians in the town be allowed to evacuate southward. This the General had done—reluctantly, since it smelt of cowardice.

Major Mott now had the paper sent back by Joubert in his hand. He read it out to the assembled company: "Respecting your request that the townspeople may be allowed to leave for the South, this I cannot possibly agree to. The wounded, with their attendants and doctors, may, as requested by you, be taken to a chosen place, and I shall agree that the people of the town shall also be removed there.

The numbers of the civilians must be communicated to me and the removals of the wounded and civilians must be effected within twenty-four hours of the receipt of this, and the locality must be distinctly marked. I must further make it a condition that under the name of civilian there must not be sent out any who have taken up arms against the Republic."

People were shouting by the time Mott had finished. "How dare he make such demands?" said one. "We shall not be dictated to in this way," said another.

And then the Major continued: "General White has agreed to these terms, and suggested the establishment of a neutral camp at Intombi Spruit. He advises the town to accept the proposal."

Again there were cries of indignation. One man flamboyantly pulled out his white handkerchief and said, "This is not my banner. I am a patriot and shall not be known by the name of coward. It is right that we should put our lives in danger for the Queen." Then, with theatrical defiance, he flung the kerchief on the floor.

Others, in particular those who had suffered injury to family or property from the bombardment, were all for leaving the soldiers to it and getting out from under the shadow of shell.

Leo Kiernan was one of those who spoke in favour of accepting the offer.

"It would be criminal not to allow non-combatants to take advantage of this arrangement," Bella heard him saying. But her father was again roundly shouted down by Grimble. He was one of the local farmers (mostly fruit, with a bit of arable thrown in), and a leading light in the Carbineers, the settlers' volunteer force.

"We humble ourselves too much to ask for the forbearance of such scoundrels," he now said. "I suppose we shall be knocked about a good deal, but, well, I am getting old, and care little about danger these days. I will not leave my property."

"Sir, there are other lives at stake than your own," said Bella's father. "They must be considered."

Archdeacon Barker—who, tall and dog-collared, had the benefit of divine authority—eventually carried the day. "Our women and children shall not go out under a white flag. They shall stay with the men under the Union Flag, and those who would do them harm may come to them at their peril."

There were loud cheers—though not from Bella's father, who looked cross. The decision having been made, the townsfolk filed out of the hall, the low chunter of their discussions filling the interior air until, as they passed out into daylight, it was swallowed up by the noise of horse and soldier and the distant boom of shell. It was too far away to be the Boers . . . could it, wondered Bella and a hundred others, be Buller?

As she walked back to the hotel behind her father, Bella reflected that he was a respected curiosity in Ladysmith. Various women had set their cap at the widower, but he had rebuffed them all; the only intimacy he kept was his own, and the only things he cared about in the world, she believed, were his daughters and his hotel. Now all three were in jeopardy.

He turned round. "You go on back. I'm going to the Commissariat to see what I can squeeze out of them. Perhaps you might clean up the stoep this morning. I notice it has become very dusty."

It was a strange way of referring to the near miss that had thrown a shower of debris onto the porch of the Royal on the first day of shelling. Bella had already swept most of it away, but there was still a fine coating of red dust all across the wooden boards.

"Very well," she said.

She watched him try to cross the road, waiting for a gap to appear in the khaki and brown thicket of horse and man that filled the street.

Back at the hotel, Bella took out a mop and bucket and set to work, dragging the little tails of the mop across the wood and then curling them up in the bucket drainer. Lifted out, the mop head would hold its moulded shape for a second, and then collapse again into a hundred dull grey strings.

"The mountains look pretty, don't they, Miss Kiernan?"

She had been so absorbed that she didn't think the voice was addressing her.

"Don't you think?"

She looked up, surprised, to see Tom Barnes on his horse.

"I was saying," he called down, "that you have a nice view from here." He gestured out above the town, towards Bulwan and the other hills, stretching green and blue into the bright, mid-morning sky.

"Why, yes . . ." She stopped mopping and leant against the mop handle. The soldier's horse stamped and moved to one side, uneasy at having to wait while the rest of the squadron passed by.

"Shame them Boer guns are up there, or I'd take the liberty of asking you for a hill walk one afternoon."

Bella blushed and pulled the mop handle into her chest. "I suppose it is a shame," she said, trying to compose herself in view of the massed eyes of the body of men, as they moved behind the soldier.

"I would say so," he said, and smiled. "Perhaps I might come by some time, and my friend Foster too, to see you and your sister."

"Perhaps you might," she replied, a little bolder.

His mates were laughing at him now, and when he raised his helmet in farewell, several others did the same in mockery. Bella blushed again, lifted four fingers from the mop handle to offer a modest wave, and then stood back to watch the rest of the column pass by. As she watched, her eyes slowly focused on something else beyond them: the stout figure of her father approaching from the other side of the street. He came up the steps and stared at her hard as he went through into the bar.

The afternoon brought shelling—already it had become a matter of course—and, once the bar had closed, the night found Bella sitting in the parlour mending a blouse. She could hear the clatter of bottles and crates from next door as her father cleared up.

Later he came in, and sat down next to her.

"It frightening you, Bel, this shelling?"

She looked up, surprised. He rarely addressed her with this pet name, which was one mainly used by Jane.

"Not so much, Father."

"Don't let the soldiers talk coarsely to you."

"I won't, Father."

"Good girl."

He got up and made his way to the door. Reaching it, he paused with his hand upon the knob. Her eyes took in his thickset body and clothes—his laced-up heavy boots, his legs in brown corduroy, the auburn hairs on his strong forearms (his shirtsleeves were rolled up), and the way his head, with its close-cropped red hair, sat low, like a ball of lichen-covered stone, upon his broad shoulders.

"Sleep tight," he said, without turning round.

Her father passed through the doorway then, and she heard his feet upon the stairs, and was happy. For there was a bond between them, after all. The thought ran through her head that she should run after him and throw her arms around him on the landing, but she felt as if she had been pinioned to the chair, and sat there for some minutes afterwards immobile, the light from the lamp throwing strange, mesmeric shadows all around her.

Brushing her hair in their bedroom that night—using her new looking-glass, she was sitting in her nightgown on the window seat— Bella related to Jane what the soldier had said, how he and the naval gunner wanted to come and see them.

"Herbert is a silly name," said Jane, sitting up in her bed. "But his manner is pleasing. What do you think of yours?"

"I don't know. He's not overbearing, and I like that, and he seems as though he might be reliable as well as charming; those are the qualities I would want in a man, sis."

Jane made a noise, a kind of disparaging sigh which expressed both impatience and amusement. In the looking-glass, Bella saw her raise her eyebrows.

"Who cares about that, right now? We're in the middle of a siege, Bella, in case you hadn't noticed. The point is, do you like the look of him?"

"I'm serious, Janey. I want to leave here. I want to see more of the world, and I want the kind of husband who will let me run my own household. I can't see that happening with anyone in Ladysmith."

"So you reckon this soldier's your best chance?"

"Perhaps."

"You couldn't leave me here with Father. It's not fair. Anyway, your Tom could be killed any day."

Bella put down her looking-glass and brush and made her way over to her bed, getting in without saying anything.

"Honestly, Bel, you're too moony for words. You haven't even done anything with him yet. You never think things through."

"It's not him, really," said Bella, looking at the lamp flickering on the wall. "I'm just feeling a bit wretched about—about everything."

"What?" said Jane, slightly impatiently.

"You know . . . what I said before. Father, working here . . . not to mention the siege."

"It's just how things are. We can't change it."

"It would be better to be a man."

"Is that why you cut your hair off?"

"I don't know. I never thought of that."

"Well, it looks all right all the same. Maybe it will catch on. Anyway, night-night."

She blew out the lamp.

"Night-night," said Bella, into the darkness.

11

If you drew a line, crossways, from Bella to the starlit mountains of the Berg, it would pass through Torres's shop on Keate Road. There, sat in his leather chair, his feet upon the counter, the barber was drinking a glass of sherry. Its golden liquid was illuminated by the glow of a candle which, burning with absolute steadiness, also shined up still further his well-polished boots. His thoughts turned on manes extravagant: in particular, the triple coil of his lost love, dark-haired Isabella Teixeira de Mattos. Where was she now, he wondered, that other Bella? Caressing her husband? Undressing herself before going through to him? His spirit soured at the thought.

Yet in truth it was not bitterness he felt, but a strange wistfulness. It seemed odd, more than anything, that they would never again walk arm in arm through the lovely streets of the city, as they had used to do. One day in particular had retained its place in his memory, a Sunday at the end of the long rains when they had visited the municipal rose gardens after Mass. It was a time of year when the dark earth swelled with life; chameleons turned an unnatural green to keep in with the new shoots of grass, and the tight pink buds of the roses appeared to open every instant.

With Mass over and the clouds of morning gone, they had strolled together between the flower beds, small white pebbles from the Mozambique Channel crunching beneath their feet and the great sky of hope above. Isabella was wearing a delicately embroidered green mantilla, he recalled, which rustled slightly as she walked. In those days, it had never occurred to him that he would not marry her; but even at its height, that very day, their love was intent with its own loss—just as, had they inspected them, the new petals would have revealed blackspot and mildew.

He remembered her removing her arm from his own with gentle awkwardness, and then turning towards him. As she did so, the green covering that shaded her eyes fell back, revealing her pale, aristocratic face. He thought she was about to allow him to kiss her, but instead she spoke.

"You must know."

"Must know what?" he replied.

"It is Luís who is the choice."

Her eyes quickened with grief, and then she pulled her mantilla about her and ran away from him. Once more, from far away in Ladysmith, he beheld her figure as it fled through the flower beds in the direction of the glimmering square where, sitting on a bench outside the cathedral, her chaperone awaited her. Bewildered, he had sat down under a bit of broken tree. He must, he recalled, have sat there for hours, staring at the white pebbles, for by the time he went home it was evening and the moon above the city was a hard pebble itself and the streets had become unlovely.

Torres heaved a sigh. He should have rescued her from that hidebound world, not run away from it himself . . .

The vista of the years resolved itself in his barber's mirror, where he found he was reflected. The flame of the candle, disturbed by some parvenu draught, was flickering now, playing about his and its own image. Standing up, he shook himself and, picking up his glass, went out onto the porch to finish his sherry. As he stood there, looking out into the infinite country of the night, he heard—over the whisper of the oil lamp hung by the door—the faintest *pad-pad-pad*.

Across the street, a shape emerged, silvered by moonlit rays. Suddenly, there at his feet, was a flap-eared, long-tailed dog. He recognized it as a pointer. His father had had one for hunting, its keen tail signalling anything from duiker to partridge; even trout once, wading into a stream near Beira. Crouching down, he put his glass on the boards and patted the animal on the head, and then went upstairs to his lodgings to find it something to eat. But there was nothing in the meat safe, and when he came back down the dog was gone. He went to bed wondering if it had been a ghost.

12

Intombi Camp was about four miles southeast of the town, down the railway line. The first train during the twenty-four-hour ceasefire had left about five o'clock the day after the meeting—a great long snake of a thing filled up with wounded lying in their green "doolies," as the litters were called, and with tearful women and children, and not a few of Ladysmith's menfolk. The moans of agony coming from beneath the green covers, as the doolies lay in the station yard waiting to be loaded, had been terrible to hear.

This, as everything, had to be recorded. Every day, Nevinson would take his report to the censor, Major Mott—a man who, according to MacDonald, "combined the directness of the soldier with the literary sagacity of the sub-editor." Since the telegraph had been cut, it was increasingly difficult to get messages in or out by any means: the proposed heliograph link had not yet been established, and some correspondents were making use of the homing pigeons.

It was a method Nevinson had found to be unreliable. The only other options, so far, were the official military messengers or amateur kaffir boys. All put their lives in danger. Sometimes the enemy took the runners in for questioning; sometimes they shot them on sight, like the pigeons. As a consequence of the danger, the boys (it was a cant term, since many of them were fully grown men, and others could only be described as old) were charging £20 or more either way. This was a preposterous figure, as it was far, far more than they might earn in a year; but considering the trip might cost them their lives, he supposed it was a bargain. And it could indeed be a journey that would cost them dear, since the Boers had laid bell wires everywhere to alert them to any movement.

If an official runner was used (and under the martial law that now governed Ladysmith, it was strictly illegal to use any other), the message had to go through Major Mott. In the early days, when the British still had the telegraph wire, he had been harsh; in these present times he was merciless. The slightest suggestion in a correspondent's copy of Imperial weakness would be struck out in red ink—even the notion that the town needed the relief column to arrive at all. As the Boers knew this was not the case, and the British knew this was not the case, and the Africans and Indians caught in the middle knew it also, the process was clearly a nonsense.

"You mean to give the impression that we're cowering behind kopjes?" demanded Mott, on the day after the ceasefire had expired. "That the British Empire is on its knees behind an anthill?"

"Well, we are overstretched . . . ," came Nevinson's rejoinder.

"Certainly not! It's a question of tactics."

"But Major, the report will be in cipher."

"Ciphers can be broken."

"Oh well, cut it if you must."

That afternoon, irritated by the Major's intransigence, Nevinson determined that he would get himself his own African runner, independent of Mott's man. He let it be known to the loafers who hung around outside the Royal that he would interview candidates at the cottage the following day.

When morning came, he went out before breakfast to find a line of some twenty Africans waiting for him. Wearing crumpled hats or wrapped in blankets (Ladysmith mornings could be misty, in spite of the heat to come), most seemed to him too old to make the run, or had a look about them which made him suspect that they would dump the letters.

He had almost got to the end of the line when a bony young kaffir with a melancholy face presented himself.

"What's your name?" Nevinson asked him.

"Wellington Maseku."

"Wellington? Well, I hope you're as brave as the general because this is a dangerous business. You realize what it entails?"

"Yes, nkosi."

"That if you are caught the Boers might shoot you?"

"I understand."

"Good. I would like you to leave tonight. Your destination is Maritzburg—or, failing that, the nearest British outpost you can find. They will, in all likelihood, give you a packet of letters to return to me. Do you follow?"

"Yes, nkosi."

"Right. Come back tonight at seven o'clock and I will give you some food for your journey, and the first part of your payment."

Having watched the boy go off, Nevinson retired inside the cottage. He felt weary and a little bilious, a condition that did not improve the breakfast of coffee, dry bread and an old rind of Dutch cheese that was all the larder could offer him. There were also a tin of corned beef and a box of biscuits, but he decided that he ought to save those for the boy, as they would travel better than bread and cheese.

Making the rounds of his informants later that day, he found weariness everywhere. Expectation of early relief had fallen off, and sorties—the only real excitement, unless shell-dodging could be called excitement—were an increasing rarity. Townsfolk and soldiers both were so oppressed by the vagaries of bombardment that even life-saving work had become a tedious chore.

Nevinson visited Green Horse Valley in the course of his tour, and watched Tom Barnes and his chum digging shelter trenches, throwing all their frustration and boredom into every strike of spade and pick-axe. But they had evidently had a more eventful breakfast than he, if the large shell crater in the middle of the work area was anything to go by. Tom and Bob Ashmead told Nevinson the tale over a cup of tea— "Fancy a brew, sir? We ain't got no milk, but we've got the leaves, the means of the boiling, and the cups to go with it."

. . . They told it to him, and he wrote it up: how Tom went off to find his mess-tin, and Bob leaned on the safety rail the carpenters had erected around a newly dug trench, thinking, as he had put it, "I would have myself a smoke." As he was searching his pockets for tobacco, a shell hummed over. Before he could dive into the trench, the railing—hit further along—gave way and he fell into the hole. Tom was no less lucky. Once the bombardment had ceased, he came to their tent, to find it rent and tumbled over, raked by shrapnel. The mess-tin he had been on his way to find had been squashed flat. The occasion was only lightened by the sight of Lieutenant Norris who, in the midst of taking his customary morning bath, had suffered an

upset. A shell had struck a tree, bounced off a rock without explod-
ing and, rolling into the camp, turned over the bathtub with him
inside it.

Said Bob: "You should have seen 'im there, standing by his tent
naked as the day he was born, holding the metal bathtub in his two
hands and staring at the dent in it."

The dent in it... wrote Nevinson in his journal that evening. It
had begun to rain, and the tin roof above him was pitter-pattering
with the noise of it. How strange it was, the way these stories possessed him . . . no, not just him, but all of them in Ladysmith, as if in
each individual death or hairsbreadth escape, everyone was given a
foretaste of their own demise, or of some extravagant piece of personal history on which they would be able to look back and say, "I
was there, this happened." But which of us—Nevinson wrote the
words down, and felt a black tremor in his soul—will be here at the
end? It was a drama with all the makings of a Greek tragedy, yet it was
already dragging on too long for the modern stage.

His train of thought was interrupted by a knock at the door. He
went to answer it, and was almost surprised to see standing there the
young African boy he had commissioned that morning. He hadn't
really forgotten that he had told him to come back but—between
shell and the story of shell, shell and the image of shell—it had half
slipped his mind.

"I am here, nkosi."

"Good, good. Hang on there a moment." Nevinson looked at
him in the doorway, dripping with rain. "Actually, you had better
come in."

The boy took a step forward, and stood there mutely in the hall.

"I'll just go and get the packet," Nevinson said. "I suppose I had
better wrap it in view of the weather. In fact, it might be better if you
go early in the morning, once things have dried out; otherwise the wet
might show your tracks. Or you'll trip on the wires. You know about
the wires?"

"Yes, nkosi."

"Up to you."

"The morning is when I will go. Before sunrise."

"Right. Come through."

The boy followed him into the kitchen. Moving his journal aside,

Nevinson took out his pocket knife and cut a piece out of the oilskin cloth that covered the table. Then he fetched the cardboard package of reports and letters (he had collected several on his rounds that afternoon, including one from Tom Barnes) and tied the oilskin around it. This he then gave to the boy, who stood there immobile for a moment, as if puzzled, and then tucked the oilskin packet between his black chest and his rag of shirt.

"I've got you some food, as I promised," Nevinson said, and retrieved the tin of bully beef and the packet of biscuits from the depleted larder. The boy stuffed them into his trouser pockets.

"And here's the money." He handed him £20 in Bank of England notes. "You'll get the rest when you come back. All right then? You're not going to run off? I'll catch up with you if you do, believe me."

"Don't worry. You can trust me very well. You will see my face again."

Nevinson led him through to the front door. "Well, good luck then."

"Thank you, nkosi," the boy said.

On a sudden impulse, Nevinson held out his hand. Wellington took it and they shook, then the boy turned round and trudged off into the clouded moonlight, his feet slushing through the mud that the evening rain had brought. As the thin figure disappeared, Nevinson realized how cold the boy's hand had been: it was as if it had left an icy imprint upon his own palm.

It didn't surprise him, as he was turning to come back inside, to hear a shell burst: they were generally now given a few at bedtime, to make sure no one slept too soundly. He stopped and waited for it to fall—somewhere near the Town Hall, he reckoned, or maybe the Royal Hotel.

On going up to bed later that night, he looked in on Steevens, who had been rather out of sorts the last few days. But the *Mail* man was asleep. Nevinson stood by the open door for a second, listening to his colleague's regular breathing.

The morrow saw a fuller bombardment, during which all sat down to be shelled. Running for shelter, Nevinson saw a shell burst and a great splash of red suddenly appear on the window of Major Mott's office. With the bombs still falling all around, he rushed inside, expecting to find struck down the man who had struck him out so often. Then—as he looked from side to side—he felt ashamed that such a thought, at such a time, could have passed through his mind. But as it turned out, it didn't matter. The ruined office was empty, and the "blood" was only a pot of red copying ink that had been thrown off the upturned table and dashed against the window.

So that day the censor escaped the unconscious wish of the correspondents—although as he had been on the lavatory at the time, it didn't really count as a hairsbreadth escape. Some did escape by such a measure. That night, a shell entered the room in which Bobby Greenacre, the town scamp, was sleeping. His father rushed through smoke and masonry dust into the room, to find the boy absolutely unhurt.

It seemed, however, that the Boers were intent on a sequel. Bella Kiernan went round in the morning to congratulate the parents on this lucky escape, only to see Bobby's pet rabbit cut in half by a shell splinter as she left. It was a sign of the deteriorating food supplies that even this mess of fur and flesh was taken to his tent by a soldier for stew—and had Bella known that the soldier was Trooper Barnes, it might have given her pause in her precipitous imaginings of some kind of life with him.

Or perhaps not. Hunger, until now an uncommon experience in Ladysmith (among whites at any rate), created a certain moral latitude. Walking past Star's bakery that afternoon, and seeing Mrs. Star kneading dough in the window, gave Bella an intense desire for freshly baked bread. She stood watching Mrs. Star's hands working the dough in the wide tray, folding the white paste over and over, stood smelling the scent of baking bread coming out of the vent above the door—and could not resist going inside.

"Can I help you?" said Mrs. Star, rubbing her hands over the tray, so that the pieces of dough fell back inside.

"I was hoping to buy a loaf."

"You and the rest of town. Have you got a coupon?" The woman's face, dry and red below her linen cap, could not be described as a generous one.

"I haven't. I was just hoping . . ."

"Miss Kiernan—you know very well that I can't sell anything nowadays without receiving a coupon. Not a crumb."

"I've got the money. I'll pay you double."

Mrs. Star rubbed her hands again, turning the remaining bits of dough into little cylinders. Bella watched them drop onto the main mass of white paste, attaching themselves to it in such a way that they stuck up like little bits of hair. Suddenly she didn't feel so keen upon the bread—there was also the sickly smell that one sometimes found in bakeries—but Mrs. Star had decided that here was a bargain worth making.

"Thricefold. Three times."

"That's ridiculous," said Bella. But the initiative had already passed to the vendor. Bella felt herself reaching for her purse. She put out the coins on the counter. Mrs. Star fetched a long iron spatula, and pulled a loaf out of the oven. The deal was done.

On the way home, Bella held the warm, wrapped bundle against her, and felt better for it, in spite of the extortionate price. She went into the kitchen immediately, unwrapped the loaf from its paper, and cut a slice. It was still warm. There was no butter in the larder (that was now five bob a pound), but there was some pear preserve from Grimble's orchard; she spread it on the slice, and lifted it to her lips.

She had taken only one bite when her father came into the kitchen.

"What have we got here?" he said.

"Just having a snack." Her mouth was full, and the words came out all jumbled.

"And where did you get that loaf?" He pointed at the offending article, where it sat on the table—crumbs, bread knife and wrapping papers lying around, giving it the appearance of something out of a painting.

"Star's," said Bella, reddening.

"We've got no coupons . . . I suppose they made you pay over the odds?"

Bella nodded.

"How much?"

She whispered the sum. He walked over and, taking her by the shoulders, shook her.

"Just because there's a siege on, it doesn't mean we can go out spending money like lords. All these officers—they're not paying their bills too swiftly, you know."

Bella swallowed, and freed herself from his grasp. "Father! It wasn't that much!"

And then she burst into tears. He looked ashamed then, standing there with his hands at his sides.

"Ah, come on now, come on, I'm sorry . . ." He reached out for her and took her in his arms, gently this time, patting her back.

Leo Kiernan briefly held his daughter in his arms, allowing her sobs to subside, absorbing them in his own body. Then he released her.

"All right now?"

"Yes." Bella looked at the half-eaten crescent of bread on the table, smeared with amber-coloured preserve.

Her father smiled. "You might as well finish it up then. I'd better get back to the bar. It's quiet in there. Why don't you go up to your room?"

Bella did eat the rest of the slice, but it tasted bad, and made her stomach feel sour; so sour, in fact, that she vomited later on in the evening—an experience which made the whole enterprise seem all the more pointless, foolish and unpleasant. Still, she wouldn't have thought anything of it except that when Jane ate some of the bread the next day, she too was sick. It had evidently been spoiled.

The Kiernan family were not the only inhabitants of Ladysmith worrying about food. The rumour that those at Intombi Camp were eating better than those in town (untrue, as it happened) had made the neutral camp an all the more attractive destination to those not committed to the defence of the town; a faction which (as it also happened) included many who had shouted loudly at the public meeting against self-imposed exile. Flight to Intombi was now a possibility of which many non-combatants availed themselves. There were so many wounded to be conveyed there after the ceasefire had ended, and so many civilians whose patriotism had wilted, that Joubert (to his credit) had now agreed to let a train go out twice weekly. It was one of the conditions of civilian sojourn at Intombi that able-bodied people should help care for the wounded. Many were panic-stricken, however, so Bella could not see how they would perform their duties. British prisoners of war and injured Boers were also being sent there from Joubert's camp, so all in all it was said to be quite a colourful location, with a queer fraternization between the two sides.

Some were calling this place "Fort Funk." It was a description that might actually have been applied to Ladysmith itself: everything was now mortgaged to fear in the town. Rumour was the interest attached to this debt of fear, and it was rising at a rate which would have pleased a banker: Buller's army was on its way, it had left Durban, it was at Frere, it was not, it would be here tomorrow—all of this exacerbated by the refusal of the military powers to release any proper information.

It was on account of this that Nevinson, Steevens and Mac-Donald, and the many other correspondents immured in Ladysmith, established a newspaper or, more properly, "news sheet" under the title *The Ladysmith Lyre.* As Steevens wrote in the prospectus for this new venture, the purpose of the *Lyre* was "to supply a long-felt want. What you want in a besieged town, cut off from the world, is news which you can absolutely rely on as false. The rumours that pass from tongue to tongue may, for all we know, be occasionally true. Our news we guarantee to be false. In the collection and preparation of falsehoods we shall spare no effort and no expense. It is enough for us that Ladysmith wants stories; it shall have them."

13

"I've got a story for you," said Foster. "Funny thing that happened in our battery the other day. I wasn't there but I had it from Reynolds Sharp."

"Go on then."

"Our lads . . ." Foster kept bursting into laughter. "Our lads . . . were manning the trenches and one of them vaulted—over the parapet and . . . impaled himself on his own bayonet."

"No!" said Tom, disbelievingly.

"On God's honour. It went right into his arse up to the hilt. The sick orderly reported it as 'Bayonet passed through port cheek of backside'!"

Their laughter could be heard across the other side of the square—until a deeper sound covered it.

"Sounds like thunder," said Tom, as his chuckles subsided.

"It's shells, you dullard," Foster countered. "Maybe Buller is nearer than we think."

"Definitely thunder."

The two of them kept up this discussion as they approached the Royal, where they had an appointment with the Kiernan sisters—kept it up until a forty-pound shell from a six-inch gun settled it, falling about twenty yards in front of them, and killing a mounted orderly from the 5th Lancers. Foster and Tom were thrown to the ground, the latter's temple being scratched by a fragment of shrapnel.

Tom looked up. He could feel blood trickling down on his face. Through the smoke, he could see the orderly's lance quivering where it had stuck into its owner's back, having been driven into the air by the force of the explosion. It was a disgusting sight.

He heard Foster's voice beside him. "Are you all right?"

Tom scrambled to his feet, holding his sleeve to his bleeding temple, which was also burning hot. "Just a scratch, I think."

Foster came close and inspected it. "You'll be all right. It's more of a scorch really."

"Look, there it is." Tom pointed at a shard of metal lying on the ground near by, and reached down to pick it up.

"Don't!" cried Foster, but it was too late.

"Ow!" yelped Tom and instantly dropped the fragment, which was still stove-hot. Now he had a badly blistered thumb to add to his wound.

"That was a close business," said Foster as they continued their journey, stepping round a group of coolies gathering up the orderly's corpse into a blanket.

"Well, at least it answers the question of the thunder."

"Wasn't Buller, though."

"Uh-uh," said Tom, blowing on his thumb. "Johnny Boer."

They passed under the portals of the Royal in silence, presenting Jane and Bella with a hunted, haggard look when they came through to the bar—Tom proudly clutching Foster's handkerchief to his throbbing temple.

"What happened?" cried Bella, running up to him.

"I got a nick."

"Let me see."

"It's fine."

"I insist."

She lifted away the handkerchief and saw where the splinter had gashed him. "It needs bathing."

"No, it doesn't."

Bella's will prevailed and Tom was taken upstairs to be cared for, while Jane stayed behind the bar, talking to the bluejacket. The lunchtime rush had not yet begun, and it was still quiet.

Up in the sisters' room, Bella and Tom sat on the bed. She dabbed at the gash with a fresh handkerchief dipped in disinfectant and, true to the time-honoured form of such incidents, he winced dramatically each time she touched it.

"Don't be a baby."

"It really does hurt."

Bella raised her eyebrows and gave the dark-haired soldier a quizzical look. He suddenly leaned across towards her and, pausing to catch only the smallest encouragement from her gaze, kissed her on the mouth. Allowing his lips to rest upon hers for only the briefest moment, Bella drew back.

"I couldn't help it," Tom explained, giving her a look that was both innocent and amusing. "It's the concussion." Bella's only slightly put-on expression of affront faded away. Tom leaned forward again, but she put the flat of her hand on his tunic.

"This is not good behaviour, Trooper Barnes. And look, you've dripped on the bed."

On the white wick bedspread was a small spot of Tom Barnes's blood.

"I'll never get that out," Bella said. "Come on, let me put a dressing on it before you make any more mess."

Making him hold the disinfectant-soaked cloth to his temple, she got up and went to a chest of drawers. As she was looking inside for some lint, there was a knock on the door.

"Bella?"

The young woman looked anxiously at Tom.

"Bella? Are you there? It's time you were downstairs. People are coming in."

"Yes, Father," she said, in a strained voice. "I'm just on my way."

"Well, hurry up then. We've still got a business to run, war or no war."

They listened in silence as Mr. Kiernan walked along the corridor and clumped down the great bare staircase of paternal duty.

"That was close," said Bella. "I thought he was going to come in. It would have put him in one of his moods."

"So what if he had? It's not as if you were doing anything wrong—in fact, tending a wounded soldier is surely a sign of a good conscience."

"You don't understand. I mean, he wouldn't understand. He wouldn't approve—of a man being in my room. Come on, let me finish. I better hurry down. You follow later."

Once she had applied the dressing, Bella left Tom in the room, and went downstairs, to be greeted by the half-worried, half-naughty, blonde-framed expression of her sister.

"All right?"

Bella nodded, and picked up a couple of empty glasses.

"I tried to put him off," Jane whispered, looking sidelong at their father. "Where's Tom?"

"Coming down."

Tom Barnes was at that very moment making his appearance, walking down the uncarpeted, heavy-banistered stairs as unobtrusively as he could. But it was no good. Mr. Kiernan saw him and, lifting up the hatch in the bar, strode over to confront him.

"What have you been doing up there? You're not a guest, if I'm not mistaken."

Tom paused, and leaned against the banister with a cocky air.

"No, sir. Just looking."

"And what would you have been looking for, in God's name, upstairs in my hotel?"

"The hand of beauty, sir, to ease my pains."

"What the hell do you mean?" The Irishman's face was getting red. "I've seen you before round here, haven't I? Talking to my daughters, is that what you imply?"

"I have paid them my compliments, sir, it is true."

"I suppose that's your idea of a joke? Well, I don't find it very amusing."

Tom looked at his feet on the stairway.

"I didn't mean to be insolent, sir, I just find myself embarrassed."

Bella came up and touched her father's arm. But he ignored her, keeping his angry gaze fixed on Tom Barnes.

"Oh! Bella, is it?"

"Let me explain," intervened Bella, in agitated fashion.

"Very well then," he said, turning to her. "Explain."

"Before you were here, Trooper Barnes came in with a wound. You see the dressing. It was an emergency. I put it on for him."

"What? Upstairs?"

"Yes, Father."

"I see."

"Mr. Kiernan," said Tom from his station. "I am sorry if you misunderstood me—my remark, I mean—I was trying to pay you a compliment on the beauty as well as the kindness of Miss Bella here. I have acted entirely with honour."

This show of respect mollified Mr. Kiernan a little. He nodded slowly. "I should think so. You better come down." With that he went back to the bar, and Bella walked over with Tom to where Herbert was sitting.

"That was silly," she said. "You shouldn't have riled him."

"I didn't mean to. I was trying to say how beautiful you were."

"Well, don't," said Bella. "I'm not, anyway."

"You will still let me see you, won't you?"

She looked into his eyes and then, over his shoulder, at her father regarding them.

"No," she said. "I don't think it's a good idea."

That night, Bella was embarrassed about the bloodstain on her bed. Jane teased her about it, and when Bella slept, she dreamed an awful dream in which her blood and the blood of British soldiers mixed in dreadful fashion. The soldiery appeared in the figure of Tom Barnes, and the image of his body, mashed to pulp by a Boer shell, prompted her to cry aloud, waking her sister—who reached across and shook her.

"It means you love him," Jane mumbled through the darkness, when the dream was related; and Bella thought she might be right, and felt sick at heart as she tried to sleep again.

In the morning she woke not to the sound of shellfire but to the glow of the Natal sunshine which, on good days, would strengthen until noon, when even the scorpions would decide that shade must be found. The sun, and the sight of the gleaming, though much depleted, rows of vegetables in the kitchen garden—as she dressed, she could see the Zulu woman gathering produce for the day's meals—filled her with hope and excitement, erasing the previous day's worries and the night's ghastly dream. As she ate her breakfast, she determined that she would go over to Tom's camp and tell him that she did want to see him after all. She asked Jane if she would come with her.

"Are you sure it's sensible?" queried her sister. "It might cause a bit of a stir, two young women going into an army camp."

"We'll take them some food," said Bella, thinking of Nandi among the vegetables.

"Father won't like it."

"He won't miss a few potatoes."

So it was that the two Kiernan sisters, Bella carrying a basket on her arm, made their way over to Green Horse Valley. They approached the lines of white bell tents with some trepidation, inquiring after Trooper Barnes from a young, fresh-faced sentry. Sitting on a fallen tree at the perimeter, he couldn't have been more than seventeen.

"Barnes? He's one of Lieutenant Norris's men, isn't he? I think they are out on a job, but his tent's in line seven. What you got in there, ladies?"

With a twinkle in her eye, Bella lifted back the muslin covering of her basket.

"Potatoes!" exclaimed the sentry-boy. "We haven't seen much of them. Or of much else."

His face suddenly became older, craftier. "Say, I've got my billy here. Want some tea?"

"I am afraid we are engaged, young man," said Jane, with a condescending smile.

The two sisters linked arms and began to walk off.

"Wait!" shouted the boy. "At least give us a spud or two."

"We'd better," said Bella, rolling her eyes.

She picked a potato out of the basket and tossed it to the sentry, who—encumbered by his rifle—fluffed catching it, and then went down on his hands and knees to look for it as it rolled beneath the tree he had been sitting on. The sisters giggled, and walked on into the middle of the camp, where soldiers passed them astonished, and then lascivious looks. When they came to line seven, they stopped outside the first tent.

"Excuse me," said Bella, loudly. "Is there anyone in there?"

A face, covered in shaving lather, poked out of the flaps. "Bloody hell!" said the face's owner on seeing them.

"Sorry to disturb you," said Jane, sweetly. "We are looking for Trooper Barnes's tent."

"Three down," said the lather-covered man, bewildered by this female visitation.

Tom's tent mate was just as surprised to see them. "Well! I'm afraid he's not here. He's on a cutting-out expedition, see. Can I give him a message?"

"We brought these," said Bella, kneeling down in front of the tent and unpacking her basket.

"That's a boon," said the bewhiskered soldier. "Thank you, thank you very much, ladies."

"Could you tell him that I called?" said Bella.

"You must be the Bella he's been talking about."

Bella blushed. "That's right. Just tell him he would be welcome at the hotel."

"I will do," said the man. "I most certainly will."

On the way back, the sisters met Mr. Steevens, the famous correspondent, and after having introduced himself he took them up onto a bluff to watch the fighting.

"It will be safe today, as the Boers have left off shelling the town. They are training their guns on the Green Horse's cutting-out expedition."

He lent them his spyglass. Bella saw below her, careless of formation and galloping in an untidy ruck, a company of Green Horse, riding against the Boer lines. Shells were bursting around them in the pan of dust.

"My God," said Bella. "They are riding right into it."

Bella fancied she could see Tom Barnes among the riders, a little way apart along with another horseman. There were shells falling all around, like apples on a windy day. One burst between the two riders, and she gave a gasp.

"They must be killed," she whispered to Jane, and let the glass fall to her breast. Her stomach turned at the thought of it, and then she looked again. Only smoke, down there on the plain, grey smoke and grey dust. It was hard to tell the difference.

"Who are you worrying about?" asked Steevens, who looked a little grey himself to Bella's mind.

"We thought it might be Trooper Barnes down there," she explained.

"Is he your beau, then?" enquired the correspondent.

He reached over for the spyglass.

"Oh no," said Bella, a little too forcefully.

"You can't tell at this distance," said Steevens, his eye glued to the instrument. "Who it is, I mean. Anyway, I think they've got through all right, whoever they are."

He handed the spyglass back to her. Bella looked again. The curtain of smoke and dust had lifted, and the two cavalrymen were emerging from the pall unscathed. They watched for a little longer and then, leaving Steevens on the bluff, the young women took the long road home, through Grimble's orchard. On the way, to fill her empty basket, Bella picked some mignonette and wild roses from between the rows. She felt exhilarated. The trip to the men's camp, the sight of battle in the spyglass, the whole siege, it was all beginning to open up inside her in an entirely unexpected way. It was quite the strangest sensation, a mood of anticipated change that affected her very nerves and fibres, its modulations humming in her toes and fingers, in her breasts and the lobes of her ears.

Some things did not change, however. When they got back home, Father was in the kitchen, supervising the preparations for that evening's dinner. Everyone, from General White to the lowliest guest, was to have half portions, and hearing this decree Bella felt guilty about having taken the potatoes to the camp. She went to bed fearful that her father might find out that she had done so, only to have her worries exacerbated by a frightful night of shelling.

The Boers were obviously hoping to catch up on the day's lost work.

14

In the correspondents' cottage the following morning, the fact or otherwise of a night bombardment was disputed ground, as hotly contested as Ladysmith itself. Over breakfast, Steevens—who wasn't feeling well—was maintaining that there had been shelling during the night.

"Thud—thud—thud—ten or a dozen, I should say."

But his Australian colleague was having none of it. "You were dreaming. There was no shelling last night."

"There was. Say, Nevinson, shall we run a survey in the *Lyre* on the preponderance of imaginary shellfire in these days of strife? If MacDonald is right, I'm surely not the only one suffering from this condition."

Nevinson shrugged. "So far as the success of that paper goes, the more real shelling the better. When I took a few copies to some of the outlying troops last week, they were happy as sandboys. I think people will read anything if they've been shut up for a month under bombardment."

"They do lap it up, don't they?" said Steevens. "What do you think, though? We could write a spoof about how shellfire affects the imagination."

"It has certainly affected yours," said MacDonald crossly. "No shells fell last night. I'm a light sleeper, and would have woken immediately."

"Well, last night you must have had a thick head. There was shelling, I tell you."

Leaving them to their bickering, Nevinson got up from the table and went for a stroll. It was a beautiful, bright day and the outskirts of the town, with their fruit trees and syringas, were rather pretty. One large orchard of pears, however, had been dreadfully devastated by shellfire. All over the ground were smashed branches and splinters of wood. Fallen pears lay among the broken pieces. Some were still whole, but most were bruised and pulpy. Sitting in the middle of it, on the trunk of an overturned tree, was the owner. Nevinson recognized him as William Grimble, the farmer who had spoken at the Town Hall meeting. He had a basket full of fruit at his feet, evidently having been collecting it up.

"Ah, you," he said, a little sourly, on looking up as Nevinson entered the glade. "I hope you are going to write something down about what we townsfolk are suffering here."

"Well, the censors don't let me get much of that nature out. I see you've been under a bit of a hurricane here."

"Nothing compared with what has happened to my other orchard. General White, in his wisdom, has ordered it chopped up for fire-wood."

"That's a blow."

"Of course it's a blow! But what annoys me most is how pointless the whole thing is; however many shells they throw at us the rebels will never get possession of the place. If General White wasn't such a coward, we'd get out there and give them a hiding."

"I'm sure he has considered that option," said Nevinson, with a conciliatory smile. "And how many lives it would cost."

"This grove used to bring me in £25 a year, and the other twice as much."

"Send a bill to the Boers."

"Send a bill to our own army more like. One hundred thousand would not compensate us for the damage British troops have wrought on this town. They have taken our houses and property and knocked them about; they have drawn Boer shells into our streets; they're now telling me they want this fruit, my fruit, for provisions. Well, I'm going to take away as much as I can for myself. They call it martial law but to me it seems more like tyranny. I'm damn sure the Boers wouldn't have robbed us so blindly."

He reached out for another half-ruined pear and dropped it into the basket. "And if we do ever get out of here, I'll wager the compensation for it all will be but one per cent of the actual damage. I'm not convinced we will, anyway. Our so-called victories don't seem to amount to much."

"Cheer up," said Nevinson. "I'm sure Buller will be here soon, with a whole army. He said they would be in Pretoria within a month."

"Did he? Well, that's true enough. Many of them are already there—as prisoners of war!"

"Don't you think you are being a little too pessimistic?"

"You haven't seen as much life as I have, young man. I think we're going to be shut up in here for quite a while. It's no way for a mighty nation to be carrying on a war."

Realizing that they weren't going to see eye to eye on the matter, Nevinson smiled at him again, raised his hand slightly to say goodbye, and continued on his stroll. His nostrils were full of the smell of broken fruit. It made him hungry. The man could at least have offered him a pear, to see him on his journey.

The path wound through more orchards and then broke out into a space by the river, which it then ran alongside. The Klip took a tortuous course through the town and its environs, and the bank in parts was fairly high. It was so where he was walking, falling sharply away to the water. Here and there, poking up out of rushes and marsh grass, camel thorns struggled to gain a foothold in the inhospitable soil. Many of these bankside trees were hung with the oval, basket-like nests of weaver birds. Nevinson paused awhile, watching the small birds flit in and out of the little holes that gave entrance to their curious houses. As he watched, he realized he could hear a noise: not the birds, not the sound of the running water, nor the distant rumble of gunfire, but that of a great number of human voices, in conjunction with the kind of clanking busy-ness that betokened repetitive physical labour.

He followed in the direction of the sound until, rounding a corner, he came upon a scene that might have been out of Dante: several hundred men digging furiously at the clay bank—men of all colours and walks of life, from natives to town worthies, from lowly privates to the type of officer who, clearly, had rarely dirtied his hands in this way before. And they were dirty, all of them: many had stripped off their shirts and the red clay stuck to them like paint, giving them the warlike appearance of the American Indian.

The diggers wielded picks and spades and the like, and everywhere about lay the great stacks of wood that would be used for buttressing the caves. Nevinson recognized some familiar faces in the mêlée: Farquhar, the mayor, who gave him a weary smile and lifted up his spade in acknowledgement; Willie Maud, the war artist, who had exchanged his brush for a shovel; even the Greenacre boy, whom he had seen rushing about the town, was struggling to heft a pickaxe. Operations were being directed by one of the uitlander miners.

Behind the bankside fortifications were other defences: forts within forts known as sangars, that is to say circles of piled-up rocks buttressed with sand-filled mealie bags, cases of corned beef and—pity to regard—the personal bags and boxes of the soldiers. Already the white ant, servant of Joubert, was chewing his way through these.

He noticed Torres, the barber, among the diggers. Stripped to the waist, the Portuguese was throwing his spade's edge at the red clay with such ferocity that he might have been driving a bayonet into a man's chest. The muscles of his bare olive chest and back stood out clearly above his trousers, the legs of which were tucked into tall boots that might have been a cavalryman's, save that they were jet-black instead of regulation brown. Although they were now mostly brown, or red at any rate, being covered with wild stripes of clay.

Smelling perfume beside him, Nevinson realized that he was not the only spectator. He turned, and saw standing beside him a young woman with short dark hair and the kind of light cotton dress which a rigorous eye would have deemed too informal for walking out; but this was siege time, he reflected, and all conventions were falling away.

"Hullo," she said, smiling at him—she had bright, even teeth, which contrasted sharply with her well-tanned skin. "Come to join the troglodytes?"

"Just an observer . . . though I suspect we might all be down here soon."

"I very much hope not," she said. "I'm Bella Kiernan, by the way."

Nevinson made an indistinct gesture, some semblance of a bow, with his head.

"I have seen you in the hotel, miss. My friend, George Steevens, mentioned that he met you yesterday."

"He was most kind," said Bella.

Bobby Greenacre ran over to them. "Have you heard what happened to Mr. Torres?" cried the boy, panting.

"No," said Bella. "What?"

They both looked at the barber.

"He's been bombed out."

They looked again. As they watched, Torres dropped his spade and, picking up his white shirt from where it hung over a wooden post, wiped his face with it.

"Poor man," said Nevinson. "I went in to him for a haircut only recently."

"Well, you were lucky, mister," said Bobby Greenacre. "The chair was blown to pieces."

The boy scampered off, back to the diggings.

"It's just excitement for them, isn't it?" said Nevinson.

Nodding her head, Bella looked at the barber again; she found herself raising her hand and giving him a little wave. Seeing he was observed, Torres began to make his way over to them, jacket and shirt flung over his bare shoulder, sweat making runnels down his muddied torso.

"I heard your dreadful news," called Bella over the din. "I'm sorry."

"Bad luck," said Nevinson, shaking his head as the man approached them.

Giving a sad smile, the barber kicked a rock with his tall boot. "I have lost everything."

"The chair," said Nevinson, sympathetically. "I heard."

"My best leather one, and all of my jars and much else besides."

Nevinson saw the girl from the hotel instinctively reach out to touch the barber's arm, and then draw back suddenly, as if shocked by its glistening nakedness. He watched her lift the hand to her mouth, realizing that she had overstepped some bound or other. It was a picture that stuck with him: the girl's lips, the man's arm, the eyes of both meeting in recognition that something out of the ordinary had taken place.

15

Things, Nevinson noted in his journal, are getting worse. The sentiment was mainly prompted by Steevens having taken to his bed with a bout of fever. It was not just his friend, though. Everywhere in the town, the signs of destruction and decline were beginning to show, as shelling and disease took their toll. In the month or so since the telegraph wires had been cut, the shelling had increased dramatically in intensity. By December 5, nearly 3,500 cylinders of explosive iron had been hurled at a patch of ground not measuring three miles each way. The more complete the isolation, the harder fell the bombardment. The whirr of shells had become more familiar a noise than any other, and the clamour of explosion was fearfully echoed, or presaged, by unexpected sounds: a dropped fork in the dining room of the Royal, for instance, would raise a gasp from every table. Battery followed battery, and worst of all was the terrible shrapnel, the iron rain.

The contents of these shrapnel shells, either circlets of metal—lightly welded so as to fly apart easily on the explosion—or canisters full of sharp-edged factory dies, ripped through the human frame, tearing through bone and sinew to make horrible wounds that healed, if at all, with much more difficulty than the puncture of a Mauser bullet or a blunt explosive amputation.

Only the other day, a shell had burst next to Nevinson himself and another correspondent, the artist Willie Maud, while they were riding the perimeter. Their horses had plunged wildly, but the two men had simply resumed their conversation once the mounts had calmed down, as if nothing had happened.

Others were not so lucky. The Boer gunners calculated their ranges and elevations very nicely, and when an officer of the Dublin

Fusiliers had his leg taken clean off in the main street, as if by a butcher's cleaver, it was said to be in reprisal for a successful raid he had made the previous week. So it went on, the shrapnel scarring a wall here, the heavy shells embedding themselves in an earthwork there. The cycle of events had a Sisyphean, ever-present quality to it.

Nevinson tried to explain how, with the smaller guns, like that on Umbulwana, the shell travelled more swiftly than the sound. In the case of Long Tom, emplaced on Pepworth Hill, the report was heard first, then the whirring howl, and then the explosion. *PONG!—s—ss—sst—ssst—sssst—Z—WOUF!* And then a cloud of red dust, a burst of shrapnel a few yards further on and (in all likelihood) a death. Before all this, a puff of smoke high up in the circle of hills—but be still, it probably is too late to move, and you may move, in any case, into the line of fire rather than out of it.

The mood of the townsfolk was changing. At first there had been consternation and despair and, among some, that tendency to wild laughter which was a sign of siege madness. Now many were quiet and submissive, as if they had become accustomed, if not indifferent, to the danger. And yet precautions were still being taken. Tom's regiment had been covering their white tents with mud to make them khaki-coloured. More holes had been dug for shelled-out civilians. Archdeacon Barker had prayed that the Lord "Guide the shells into scrub places," and sometimes He had, producing a religious feeling in the town among others than the faithful, chief of whose number was Mrs. Frinton.

But the most widespread feeling was one of gloom. With good reason—enteric fever and dysentery were beginning to take hold among troops and civilians, while food, fodder and ammunition were running low. It was difficult to buy anything at the semi-official sales of produce. Potatoes were one-and-six a pound, and milk had long since been reserved for the sick and wounded. As for eggs, they were half a guinea a dozen. Butter, tinned meats, jam—all gone. The quality of the food was also deteriorating: beef now came from trek ox, tough as boots even after hours of boiling; bread was now being baked, in the Stars' establishment, with laundry starch as the thickening agent. It was horrible stuff, this "siege bread."

One consequence of the adulterated bread was that, in search of a full belly, many whites were taking to hard biscuit or to the native staple, mealie meal, which could be made into a kind of porridge. It was not just bread, however. The ingredients of every dish became questionable, as rumours circulated about glue and hair oil being put into stews.

The cavalry's thousands of horses were also suffering: bedding hay was now used as fodder, and pure dust as bedding. There was talk of these poor, half-fed beasts having to be destroyed. Many had already been turned loose on the veld, to be promptly rounded up by the Boers.

Water, too, was scarce: the Klip had become discoloured and soup-like owing to the number of people camped on its banks; it was poison to drink from this torrent of filth, and yet people did. So even though thirst, of which there was plenty, could be slaked, the slaking always carried the danger of disease. Flies were another hazard, their onslaught only leaving off in the frequent heavy rainstorms, which then brought out large, lumbering mosquitoes at night. The rain, accompanied by stupendous thunder, was a particular curse. This deluge came at least weekly. Afterwards, the main street of Ladysmith was like a ploughed field (or rice pudding, as Steevens had once called it), churned up by the heavy wheels of guns in transit and the constant traffic of horses. The quagmire would then dry out, turning into a deeply rutted expanse which, through half-closed eyes, could pass for the surface of the moon.

Indeed, remembering that the site of Ladysmith was said to have been a lagoon or lake in bygone ages (thereby becoming a hollow amid hills and difficult to defend), Nevinson was able to imagine himself an intelligent agent unaccountably transported back to the primeval sludge, man's first slime. Take any poor Tommy, out at his picket on the bare hillside or rocky kloof, either blistering in 104-degree heat or shivering under his waterproof sheet, and he could easily believe it so. But civilization was insistent. Unshorn and reeking, the miserable soldier would hum a music-hall tune, think of his girl, and set his woollen cap more firmly on his head. This for a shilling a day. And the Queen, of course.

On hot days, a wild west wind, coming up from the deserted plain of the old camp Nevinson had surveyed all those weeks ago, blew right through the town. It carried dry filth on its wings in a long yellow cloud. The street acted like a tunnel and—as he noted with horror—most of the muck seemed to end up in the emergency hospital in the Town Hall, where it fell upon wounds, dressings and surgical instruments in a noxious layer, making the extraction of bullets, the staunching of blood, and the amputation of limbs more liable than ever to infection. Through it all, swamping even the smell of iodoform, persisted the stink of diarrhoea and gangrene, forcing the white-aproned wound-dressers to hold handkerchiefs to their noses.

So it went on. The shelling had become so constant and familiar a companion that, as the correspondent rather guiltily admitted to himself, he missed it on quiet days, craving the awful excitement. Then the bombardment would build up again, and the next three days would bring a barrage of shells. Night shelling had now become common, and on bad nights it was not unusual to see people rushing about the streets in their bedclothes, weirdly lit up by the orange flashes of gunfire.

As the siege continued through the first month and into early December, there was more contact with the Boers: military messengers went between the two lines, carrying white flags. Men from opposing sides, protected by their forts, had shouted conversations. Boer medical orderlies came into the town for some chlorodyne (they too were suffering from dysentery); and were given it, too, though many thought this beyond the duties of even a gentlemanly war.

And yet, at the same time, there were also occasional sorties against the enemy. In one instance a big gun was destroyed, on "Surprise Hill," as it had been named. Gunner Foster had been on this expedition, kitting up with other artillerymen and engineers in the dead of night with forage caps and light boots, rifles and revolvers, and equipment to spike the guns. Overpowering the sleepy Boer guards, some of whom were bayoneted, the raiders had exploded the barrel by stuffing it with gun-cotton, and removed the breech block—which now sat on a table in the mess of the Imperial Light Horse, receptacle for a bunch of flowers.

It was a good trophy, but as there were now several Long Toms ranged on Ladysmith, it could not be said that Long Tom had been vanquished, not to speak of the lesser siege guns, field guns, pompoms and ranks of unpleasantly whining Mausers which still surrounded the town. Yet the destruction of the big gun was news and Nevinson was determined that it should get back to his paper. The heliograph station had now been set on the round shoulder of Weenen and from it to Ladysmith and back the instrument would wink, weather permitting—and military priorities permitting. At present Major Mott, who as censor presided over the heliograph, allowed correspondents to send only thirty words per week, which was nothing like enough to satisfy the hungry reading public, not to mention the colleagues whom Nevinson and the others knew were awaiting their despatches back in London.

Besides, today was a dull day, overcast and showery. The device would not work under such a curtain of weeping cloud, so Nevinson had remained in the cottage, writing up his journal. He was alone—MacDonald was out with patrols, and Steevens was still upstairs in bed—and would have been enjoying his own company, except that he desperately craved a drink (too expensive) and was ravenously hungry (there was nothing in the house, and they weren't due anything more from the Commissariat till the morrow). Still, be thankful for small mercies, he thought. At least the corrugated iron roof was not roasting above, as it often was; though every now and then a little piece of stray shrapnel, or a spent bullet falling from on high, rattled down it into the gutter.

It was ironic, he reflected, that although Ladysmith was now festooned with wires from the new field telephones that linked the outposts to General White's headquarters, so far as communication with the outside world was concerned, they might as well be in the Dark Ages.

So it was back to pen and paper, like the monks of old. He put into his notebook an amusing item about Lieutenant Norris, Tom Barnes's officer, who had been lecturing his men on the futility of ducking— "When you hear it, it's actually passed, so ducking is quite useless"— and at that moment a shell had come over, and he had ducked. Tom Barnes had burst out laughing, and been reprimanded by the embarrassed lieutenant.

Hunched over the page, Nevinson set down descriptions of men suffering from typhoid fever—how they raved and how their lost eyes stared into the distance above one's head. He tried to reproduce the dual experience of men and women waiting for both shellfire and relief—smoking, reading, sewing, knitting, playing cards or chess, but above all waiting—how it tried their minds in a fashion that was rather intriguing, weighing them down with threatful expectancy, buoying them up with hopeful anticipation.

He drew word pictures of the Boer guards on Surprise Hill, of the bayonets being driven through their chests, with their cautious challenge—*Wie kom dar?*—hardly formed on their lips. He wrote "The Story of a Sortie" in the margin, as a possible title for a chapter on this subject in some projected book (when this is all over!), and then crossed it out again.

He related the tale of how one night a spare locomotive was sent out, driverless and at full speed, on the intact line leading towards the Boer junction at nearby Harrismith, with the intention of smashing up the Boer engine sitting in the station there; and how it dashed off the rails at a curve and, fizzling itself cold, became a welcome addition to General Joubert's stores.

He told the curious story of how Mr. Lynch, who along with Steevens had been a correspondent in the war in Cuba the previous year, had appeared to lose his head. How he rode a grey called Kruger, one side of which had been dyed khaki with Condy's fluid (for camouflage, rather than fashion) and the other left white for want of dye. How this reckless man had interpreted the journalistic ethic of transmitting news with a literalism and severity unknown on Fleet Street, riding off into the veld with but two things in his pockets: a copy of the *Ladysmith Lyre,* and a rare bottle of whisky. The latter was a present for Joubert, the former he aimed to exchange for any news the Boers might have. He had not been seen since.

As a matter of fact, in the days before he had taken to his bed, Steevens had made a pair with Lynch through his riding of a dapple grey, which made him too a conspicuous mark and the object of curses from soldiers when he rode by them. "Very handsome and showy to look at," as MacDonald had said, "but a danger to your person, I reckon." The old army hands had marvelled that he was not hit. But now he was down with enteric.

Nevinson related too how Mr. Grimble had continued to plough his fields near the racecourse, he and his team quite indifferent to the war—until the Boers began to shell him deliberately, following him up and down the field. It was the fact that the shells ploughed up the earth all wrong that really got Grimble's goat, rather than the danger to his person. Yet still he drove his plough on.

And many other incidents, accidents and realities Nevinson committed to his notebook. Mainly ennui and illness and hunger, enlivened only (if he could be pardoned the paradox) by sudden death. Here came the tragic note: the sadness of the nightly burials, at which the lanterns gleamed on the white crosses, and the bodies, of soldiers and civilians alike, were slipped into their graves with pauper's dignity. Last night a shell had fallen nearby as the burial party was carrying the body. They dropped it and fell to the ground; and then, once they were certain—though of course they never could be—that another shell would not follow in the same course, continued with their depressing errand.

The effect of such events as these upon all in the town was to change their very nature. Even a fellow like MacDonald, with strong opinions, was forced to alter his outlook.

"I've seen horrible things today," he said to Nevinson on coming in that evening. "This war is different, isn't it? Without bands and flags and all that glitter and circumstance, it's just plain killing. There's no redemption in it."

Nevinson was shocked at such a swerve in the character of his house mate. But then MacDonald had spoiled it by reverting to cynical type. "The loss in artistic effect is enormous," he sniggered.

Nevinson told Steevens of this as they sat on the veranda later that night, smoking their pipes. Against doctor's advice, the sick *Mail* man had come downstairs, determined not to let his illness get the better of him.

"The important thing," Steevens said in his slow, trenchant voice as they discussed the war, "is that we are learning lessons every day from the Boer. We are getting to know his game, and learning to play it ourselves."

16

"Play it yourself then, if you're so good."

Tom gathered up the cards and handed them to Bob. He had been playing Patience outside the bell tent, but his friend's interfering advice, combined with his own ineptitude, had finally proved too much.

"No thanks," said Bob. "I just wanted to see you get it right."

They were not the only two companions getting on each other's nerves. All around the camp, the waiting was wearing people down. The lack of beer played some part in this, as did the constant threat of fever and shell, but mostly it was the lack of action. Many were all for rushing the Boers and being done with it, whatever the cost.

"We've got exercise soon, anyway," Bob said. "Let's go up there now. Then we won't have to queue."

Tom didn't reply. He watched his friend pick up his saddle and other tack and hoist them onto his shoulder. Then, sighing, he did the same and followed Bob over to the compound in which the horses were kept.

He hung the saddle and bridle on the wooden fence and looked for Bashful in the swirling mass of brown horseflesh. Eventually, he picked out the blaze of white down his mount's nose, and whistled: a particular, three-tone melody that the horse already knew as his. Whinnying with delight, Bashful came over. It cheered Tom to see him, and he smiled at the horse as if he were an old friend, and patted his neck. The horse's long eyelashes were beautiful, he thought. Balancing on the lower rung of the wooden fence, he draped the reins over the horse's neck and slipped the bridle on—Bashful standing there calmly all the while—then slung the saddle over its back. He then got down and stooped beneath the horse to tighten the girth.

Finally, when it was all done, he climbed back onto the fence and took the saddle. By this time Bob had also mounted, and the two of them guided their horses through the crowd to the gate and waited there until the guard let them out. Then over to the open ground where the exercise would take place. This business had become part of Ladysmith routine. As the siege had progressed, and cutting-out expeditions become more infrequent, the horses had had to be exercised within the town thrice weekly. It was a complex task, involving a couple of hundred beasts trotting in concentric circles over a small area.

Lieutenant Norris, on marshal duty, was supposed to make sure that the exercise ran smoothly. Of course, thought Tom, he will make a mess of it as usual, but in fact the Lieutenant was surprisingly efficient today. If the man in the war balloon had been watching the Green Horse on exercise, what he would have seen would have looked much like a ballet or a Morris dance: the lines of mounted men weaving in and out of each other in perfect harmony, all bobbing up and down in time with the beat of hoofs and the tinkle of bit and curb chain. In the centre of it all was Norris, stationary on his own horse, signalling when the leader of each line of men should make his turn.

"Appeals to his sense of order, this," said Bob, who was trotting in front of Tom, his elegant seat on a horse belying his ungainly frame.

"He'd have us running round in rings without horses if he could."

Norris, spotting them chatting, waved his baton at them from the centre of the ring. "Quiet there, Barnes. No time for gossiping."

The Lieutenant's voice was drowned by the insistent whirr of a shell, courtesy of the *Staats Artillerie*. Obviously meant for him, it went wide and pitched a few feet away from Tom and Bashful. The horse reared, and Tom was thrown clear. In the air, all he could think about was the smell of death, and he readied himself for the bigger blast. This is my end, he thought, but no explosion came, only a wild neighing and a tumbled vision of plunging horses and men. Tom fell to the ground.

As he lay there, horses and men began to get to their feet, the former throwing themselves upright in their paroxysmic way, the latter rising more slowly, brushing down their clothes. Tom, dazed, sat up in the dust. He reached for his ankle. It was already swelling up in the tight cavalry boot. All around, amid the slowly ebbing noise of horses, was the quieter whisper of men, thanking their lucky stars. Somewhere, a little way away, he could hear something being read out. And then laughter.

Bob came over, walking his horse. "You get a knock, mate?"

"Twisted ankle. Must have been a dud."

"Uh-uh. No charge. There was a note tied to it with string. To Norris. Someone's just read it out."

"Saying what?"

"'The circus has left town, and you left your top hat in your tent'!"

Tom grunted and, taking Bob's proffered hand, winced as he tried to put weight on his ankle.

"Reckon exercise will be cancelled today," said his friend, and they began to walk towards the perimeter of the parade ring, with Bob's horse ambling along behind them.

"Christ," exclaimed Tom. "Bashful. I forgot him."

Fearful that his mount had been injured, he turned back quickly to look at the untangling crowd of men and horses, to see where he was. But Bashful was already trotting towards them.

Tom took the rein. "I'd say he was grinning, if a horse could do such a thing."

"They can," said Bob. "I was reading it in one of my magazines. There's a fellow back home's published a book on the expressions of animals. It had diagrams. Pictures—of dogs and monkeys. Horses too."

"I bet there were no sheep. I've never seen a sheep that didn't look stupid."

"No, there weren't any sheep. But it said we're just like them."

"What do you mean?"

"It said humans make the same faces." Bob bared his teeth in imitation of an animal.

Tom snorted in derision, and pointed to an African woman with a basket of yellow corn on her head. "Them, maybe. Not us."

17

After all they had been through—after the rout from Goli, the procession of refugees from that place of gold, after the disappearance of her husband, and their first, awful weeks in a closed-up Ladysmith looking for work and food—Wellington did this. *Mntanami, mntanami . . .*

The ragged, careworn figure of Nandi Maseku was squatting outside the back door of the Royal Hotel, grinding maize with a large pestle and mortar. This was the wages the young mama, Miss Bella, had promised her in recompense for working in the kitchen and gardens of the hotel, together with lodging in the servants' quarters. Though Nandi's thoughts turned constantly to Muhle and his fate—wherever he was, outside the perimeter—she had been feeling a little less anxious, until now.

When Wellington had told her that he intended to become a message-runner, having been offered the colossal sum of £20 for each journey, she hadn't at first grasped what it involved. Then, later that night, when her son had explained, she had broken down.

"How can you do this?" she had cried, taking him by the shirt. "I am already worried enough about your father, without you endangering yourself in this way."

"Mother, it is better this way. I will be able to get more food from the bush, and the money will help us greatly when this siege is over."

"We don't know when it will be over. We don't know what has happened to your father."

"Father will be all right. He is strong and clever. I may be able to find him, while I am on my journey."

"I forbid you to go."

But he had gone, leaving before dawn, or rather in the very moment that the soft grey light of the moon began to ease away. She had watched him put the message packet into his trousers, felt his kiss upon her cheek, and seen his slight figure jog towards the orchards and, quickly becoming indistinct in the strange light, disappear among the trees. And now nearly a whole day had passed. She looked out at the hills around the town. The cloud lay low today, covering the table of Bulwan like a cloth, and mixing with the smoke of the Boer guns, which thundered still.

Somewhere, out there, were all that she loved, husband and son. She suddenly felt very angry about this white man's war, and she pounded the maize all the harder. She thought of what might be happening to either of them, especially to Wellington: the sudden crack of a bullet, and him thrown down in the grass, bloodied. *Mntanami,* she whispered again, and salt tears fell into the coarse meal, *mntanami*—my child, my child.

She began to sing softly to herself, beguiling the tedium of the task with the chant, repeating the words over and over again. Very soon, the maize-grinding went with a swing, comfort and healing coming into her from the words and their rhythm, coming into her like a glow.

And then she stopped and, worried again, looked into the *ukhamba,* the bowl, and saw *unokufa,* death: saw Wellington shot in the head as he ran. Saw it in her own head. Filled once again with anxiety, she put down the heavy, four-foot pestle and went into the servants' quarters. It was dark inside, and as her eyes adjusted after the harsh sunlight it took her a little time to find what she was looking for. She finally laid hands on a long-stemmed object made of white clay. Filling it with rough tobacco, and adding a pinch of dagga, the strong Zulu marijuana, she sat down on the packed-earth floor, lit the pipe, drew on it deeply, and tried to forget.

Sengiyokholwa-ke . . . I shall believe, I shall believe you have died only when *inqomfi,* the lark, hovers over my head in the evil omen of my people. Only then. So thought Wellington as he ran through the ruffling quilts of grass, ducking down, skulking like a bandit in his own country. His father's country, whose milch-cows the sons of the white men had sucked dry since the time of Cetewayo. Not till the lark rose above him would he believe his father was dead. As he ran, his eyes slanted everywhere, looking for a sign. This precious packet, nestling in his groin, would be as nothing in a trade for such a sign. He knew how to look out for them, his father had taught him the markings on trees and in the dust that betokened a message.

There were other things to look out for. All across the paths and byways, the Boers had laid bell wires to alert them to movement: one was placed closed to the ground, the other at head height. He had to move carefully, as looking out for one meant that you could easily strike another. Yet he kept up his pace.

After about two miles he became breathless and halted. He wanted, in any case, to check his burden was not soaked. He had had to make a pipe of reeds to cross under the water at a place where there was a Boer guard, a young man with a rifle who, in spite of his lack of beard, was no less frightening to Wellington than the *tokoloshe*, the water kelpie of legend that aided witches and resembled a hairy giant. Most of the Boers were like that, it seemed to him, and maybe this one—whose pale blue eyes had not seen him as he had insinuated himself into the river and crept across—was just a shape-changer. He hoped the oilskin cloth which the white man had wrapped around his bundle of paper had given adequate protection during the crossing. He looked. Yes, it was so.

He lay down in the fields of Bulwan, the great hill, and rested then. And prayed, as he lay there—low, like a dassie, among the yellow grasses—that Nomkhubulwana, goddess of rain and harvests, would send a great storm to wash this battle from her hair. Then they could return to their kraal. He had never been there, having grown up in Goli, Johannesburg, the place of the mines, but his father had told him how he longed for the smell of goat roasting over wood, the sound of the women chattering in their huts, the girls with calabashes on their heads, and all around the bounty of Zululand, the ripening fields of millet, the melons and berries and pumpkins that were his birthright.

But there were other bounties. Below him he could see the railway track, which Boer—Mzondwase, the Hated One—and British—Khalisile, the Causer of Tears—had fought over; and he wondered if, one day, these things of iron would be the slaves of black men rather than Kwini Vittoria. With this thought in his head, he slept a while, knowing that he would have to wait till nightfall now, if he was to continue his journey unhindered by the Boer sentries. Slept, yes, but like a hare, with one eye unclosed. Slept in the sun in a dell of Bulwan, while around him crickets chirruped, millipedes made their epoch-long progress up stalk and across leaf, and doves and finches sang their song.

Nearby, but not near enough, Muhle lay in his hut of straw and thought of other huts: the wattle-and-daub ones the Dutch had first made when they came to the country, the huts of which Shaka, the great king, had said to his brothers Dingaan and Mhlanga: "You think you will rule this country, but I see the coming of the swallows who build with mud, and they will become your masters." And so it had proved, and now he lay here imprisoned. But his ankle was healing, becoming stronger, and soon he would creep like a lizard out of this camp.

Sterkx had continued to be kind to him, but he saw less of the good doctor now; since the shelling had begun, the Dutchman had been busy at his wagon, tending to the injured. The worst casualties were from the new explosive the English were using, lyddite, the yellow-and-green fumes of which burned the chest and throat. This, and the moment when General Buller would launch his long-expected attempt to ford the Tugela River and break through to relieve Ladysmith, was the talk of the camp.

But there was other talk. There was talk going on outside Muhle's hut right there and then. Through the opening, a few yards away, he could just see two Boers squatting down, sharing a pipe. But they weren't Boers, they were talking English—an English that Muhle recognized as having the same queer singing tones as that of the prisoners taken at Nicholson's Nek a few weeks earlier.

"We got one of our boys in the town, hugger-mugger. Not a gas man, but a solid fellow all the same, and doing mighty work. I knew him back in the early days of the Brotherhood."

"Is that a fact, Major MacBride?" said the other. "Well, we'll jolly him up with a sup then, when we get in there. How long so, do you reckon?"

"Inside of a month. We'll have Christmas Mass said in Ladysmith this year, sure as eggs, and we'll go on the Wren too."

Then the man called MacBride stood up, and started to sing:

> *The wren, the wren, the king of all birds,*
> *On Saint Stephen's Day he was caught in the furze . . .*

And the other joined in:

> *Up with the kettle and down with the pan . . .*
> *And give us a copper to bury the wren.*

They went off, laughing and slapping each other on the back. Perhaps all white men, thought Muhle as the figures were obscured by the edge of the opening, are just plain mad.

The following morning, he saw the same two men involved in a commotion, along with some others of their brigade. The noise of it had woken him up, making him glance up from his bed. Through the gap, he focused on white hands and faces, and something—what? It was a black face, a thin body, he saw there in the middle of the group of white men just a little way across the camp: the recognition came not to his sleepy eyes, though, but to the pit of his stomach . . . it was Wellington. They were cuffing him and throwing him from one side of the group to the other. Muhle didn't stop to think. With a cry, he leaped up from his straw bed and, reaching for his crutches, lurched towards the group of men as fast as he could. When he reached the edge of the circle, he saw his son had fallen to the ground, and that one of the men was kicking him in the ribs and back with his heavy boots. The man called MacBride was leafing through a packet of papers.

Muhle burst into the circle. "Stop!"

The white men looked astonished, and the one in the middle left off kicking.

"What's this then?" he said. "Are we taking orders from the likes of ye now?"

At his feet, Wellington lay curled in a ball, moaning. Muhle tried to move forward on his crutches, but felt the hands of one of the white men grabbing his collar.

"Are you in with him too, then? Is that it?"

"I don't know what you mean," Muhle said, trembling. He pointed with the crutch. "He is my son! Why are you beating him?"

MacBride came forward, with the papers in his hand. "He is in the service of the English. We found him going through our lines in the night, with these papers."

Muhle looked down at Wellington. He had sat up now, and was holding his stomach.

"Is this true?" Muhle said.

Wellington nodded miserably. Muhle turned to MacBride. "Please, let him go. He is too young; the English must have forced him."

"I don't think so. He'll be shot like all the other spies."

Two of the other men reached down and grasped Wellington under the arms. Muhle dropped one crutch and pulled at the sleeve of the man with the papers.

"No!"

"Father . . ."

Muhle saw Wellington struggle in the arms of the white men. With a roar he ran at them. One of them laughed and, planting his hand four square in Muhle's chest, pushed him over. They lifted Wellington up. From the ground, Muhle saw his son's thin legs kicking out. He was helpless; no, here was his crutch. Sitting up, he thrust it into the groin of MacBride.

"Jesus!" shouted the Irishman, doubling over and dropping the packet.

The papers scattered, some of them falling into Muhle's lap. Almost purple with rage, MacBride drew his revolver and shot the Zulu in the thigh. At such close quarters the report was impossibly loud, and the force of the bullet hit him like a hammer. Muhle shrieked and clutched at his leg; and then the pain started, a searing sensation that circled outward from the centre of the wound and then enveloped him, leaving him teetering on the edge of consciousness. Suddenly, all he was aware of was the warm wetness on his hands.

The rest of it he could only recall vaguely, or heard later from the doctor as he lay delirious with pain: Sterkx himself coming over and falling into an argument with Major MacBride's Irishmen . . . The doctor demanding by what right they would make the execution . . . Joubert being summoned and the case being put before him . . . Sterkx cutting away some of his trouser leg and applying a tourniquet . . .

18

The Biographer sipped a scalding cup of black tea outside his tent, and looked about him. Estcourt at dusk: a mean little town of two or three hundred corrugated-iron houses. The drift of dust and dirt to which the place amounted was quickly becoming hidden by night. A portion of Buller's army was now at the town, having driven the Boers further up the line. Atkins and Churchill had been here for a week or so, but the latter had now gone and got himself captured in a foolish incident in which the Boers had ambushed and derailed an armoured train. Only days before, he had been mocking the name of the thing, laughing at the idea of "a locomotive disguised as a knight-errant" and now it had proved the instrument of his imprisonment. Reports said that he had conducted himself heroically in trying to resist the capture of the train, however, and his case had been taken up with gusto by the remaining correspondents. He was said to be in gaol in Pretoria. The Biographer couldn't quite summon up the fervour with which everyone else was bruiting the ignominy of Churchill's situation, and felt that it served him right. Then he chided himself for allowing such an ungracious thought to pass through his head.

From a professional point of view, it was a shame that the train had been captured. With the use of the engine and a flat car, Biograph panorama runs of the camp and columns on the move had been proving very effective—in spite of there being some danger of vibration, owing to the car's want of decent springs. But another engine was being brought up. Soon, he hoped, there would be real action to photograph in any case. The Boers were only five miles away, and the guns around Ladysmith could be clearly heard. Now, taking advantage of the ripening darkness, the signallers were streaking the sky with searchlights, making dots and dashes against the horizon. The signal light here was powered by a dynamo and consisted of a fifteen-inch mirror and a slatted shutter worked by a lever. It threw a great, epic beam into the sky; the one at Ladysmith was less advanced and sent out much feebler signals. Last night, the Biographer had stayed up too late trying to decipher them, but the intricacies of the code and the faintness of the beam made it impossible. Determined not to make the same mistake tonight, he turned in to get some sleep.

The noise of the new train woke him in the morning. Summoning the Zulu rickshaw runner, whom he had taken on as a servant back at the Cape, he loaded the cart and made preparations to travel to Frere: the end of the line since the Boers had blown up the bridge over the Tugela, thus preventing further rail traffic towards Ladysmith and beyond. With great difficulty, the cart was levered onto an open truck and lashed down. The ride was an exciting one, and the Biographer found himself, at every turn of the track, expecting to suffer the same fate as Churchill, but the journey passed off without mishap.

Frere was much busier than Estcourt: as far as the eye could see were tents and soldiers. Many were concerned with the repair of the broken bridge, in which labour they were helped invaluably by hundreds of Africans, who chanted rhythmically to keep time as they worked. To the Biographer it seemed a natural scene to record, but when he unloaded the equipment and set the big iron tripod in position, the natives stopped working, thus depriving him of the very movement the Biograph was uniquely qualified to register. He was none too pleased, and nor was the sapper officer in charge of the work, who sent him away in disgrace for holding up proceedings.

Instead, he contented himself with filming some troopers as they ate their lunch—if the leathery, indestructible trek ox they were consuming could be favoured with such a name. Among them was Perry Barnes, and he and his mates were much taken with the Biograph.

"Hey, Perry, come and see your face," said one. "There's a looking-glass in this here machine."

The young farrier regarded his unshaven, sunburned face in the mirror of the camera's distance finder.

"What would Mother think of me now?" he said, and laughed.

The company kindly shared their food with the Biographer who, not being attached to any particular regiment, was having great difficulties in this regard—not that anyone was eating particularly well, the lines of supply being both irregular and badly organized. As Perry

Barnes said mournfully, "We might just as well be under siege ourselves."

The Biographer had been reduced to foraging in abandoned Boer farms. In one looted house he had found a half-eaten joint of beef and some bread and jam. This had proved a great feast, although its grandeur was much undone by the state of the place. It had been discovered that the men of the house had gone off to join the enemy, so the troopers had taken violent revenge, sending the wife and daughter off the place while they smashed it up. Each room was littered with torn books and letters and the glass of broken pictures. Some of the soldiers had defecated in corners of the house, with the result that there were flies everywhere. But the Biographer was so hungry that he had eaten the food nonetheless.

Otherwise, he was forced to subsist on the same mealie meal that his Zulu ate every day. As for water, every drop in the camp was guarded, and he had to send the Zulu two miles to fill his water bucket each morning. Often he would return with the bucket empty, having been stopped by soldiers on the way, who took advantage of his being a native and drank the water, ignoring his protestations.

This business of securing grub for man and beast, and fetching water for the same, got very much in the way of photography, as did the constant interruption of sentries asking for passes. "Halt! Who goes there?" the cry would come, and he would reply, "Friend," and then give the password, which was "Aldershot," and show his pass. To his great irritation, the Biographer discovered that the petition signed by Buller was not good for passing between stations. He had to get other, more detailed passes for this purpose, such was the worry about spies. Perry Barnes afforded him every assistance in his dealings with the army in this matter, and as the column waited for the order to advance, via Colenso, on Ladysmith the two of them became friends.

The order never seemed to come and they were left with a deal of time on their hands. One afternoon, after going out on a sortie with units from Lord Dundonald's cavalry brigade, the Biographer was lying in his tent, too exhausted to do anything except read. He heard a slight scratching sound, and on looking up saw an immense tarantula crawling across the canvas. With a yell he leapt up and dealt it a crushing blow with his book. It fell down stunned, and disappeared among the bedding and equipment. The Biographer's shout alerted the Zulu and Barnes, and it was only after much turning up of linen and clothing in the tent that the creature was found—lurking under the Biographer's satchel. Seeing it there, twirling its hairy pedipalps, it struck the Biographer that the tarantula would make a good picture in close-up. He suggested this to Barnes, and the brave farmer's son held the spider down with the flap of the satchel while the Biographer fetched a bottle in which to imprison it.

"Tell you what, sir," said Barnes afterwards, as the two of them regarded the creature scurrying about in the bottle. "If you got yourself a scorpion you could put the two of them together and take a picture of a duel."

In spite of the fright he had had, the Biographer thought this a good idea, and the word was put around camp that he wanted to make a collection of fearsome insects. By that time the next afternoon, there had been brought to him two trapdoor spiders, another tarantula, a fair-sized scorpion, two small, flat, black-headed snakes and a large number of common centipedes. Sometimes they came in bottles, but most often the specimens were proffered between the ends of two sticks, held by a cheerful soldier exclaiming, "We heard you were collecting these things."

News of the pet picture spread through the camp and the day for which it was arranged saw a large enthusiastic audience gathered round a table covered with a sheet. It was mooted that a battle en masse would provide the greatest entertainment, but the Biographer thought it would be better to have just two contestants, thereby enabling him to focus on them closely—which image, he hoped, would be enlarged to mythic proportions when presented on a large screen. The first bout was between the scorpion and one of the tarantulas, which were decanted amid cheers from the surrounding soldiery. Nothing occurred to begin with, as the gladiators just remained motionless at each end of the table; but with the aid of a poking stick they warmed to their work, to the effect that the scorpion was devoured entire and the tarantula greatly increased in size.

The next set-to, between a snake and the rotund tarantula, was not so successful, since the reptile simply slid off the edge of the table and moved quickly across the ground, causing consternation among the audience before it disappeared into some grass. A search was made, but the desire for entertainment being greater than the concern for safety, another battle was clamoured for and prepared, this time between the two trapdoor spiders. They obliged most heartily, displaying satisfactory cannibalistic tendencies and issuing noxious yellow fluid from their wounds.

The daily fights became a feature of camp life, until the Biographer sickened of them, and took to refusing the tide of creatures that was brought to his tent—except for a kitten that had been found in a deserted Zulu kraal. Her antics provided great pleasure during the long wait for the order to advance, and fearful of losing her the Biographer made her a collar and wrote on it: "Biograph is my name. Please take me home."

Human voices were saying much the same; or, at least, let battle commence and this quarrel be sorted. The weeks passed—until, at long last, the order came. Under a broiling sun, the column finally moved up to Colenso and the big guns began firing at the Boers. Smoke and yellow-green lyddite fumes obscured the kopjes—and the enemy—from view. Many good shots of the effects of recoil and concussion were taken, but owing to the haze and dust it was impossible to focus the lens properly on anything far away. One single sequence—of a great column of earth, stones and men going up in the air—was taken, however, and this pleased the Biographer greatly. However, the deadly fire sent back by Boer sharpshooters and quick-firing guns soon began to cause great discomfort, with some wounded men being forced to tear at the earth to hide their heads from bullets. Still the British troops tried to batter a passage across the river, fighting their way to the south bank, there to be forced to take cover from the withering fire. Some even got across, wading with their rifles above their heads, but those who were not shot down were driven back.

The battle turned, and seemed to be going the Boers' way. Some guns up ahead were lost to them. Buller himself rode up the lines. The advance crawled forward, seeming to achieve nothing except allow the Boer artillery to burst closer to the Biographer's cart, which was situated among the Red Cross wagons at the rear of the column. Suddenly, the British forces seemed to be in crisis. It appeared they had walked into a trap, made by Boers they could not see, never mind kill. Even Buller himself was put in danger, his staff surgeon being killed beside him and a piece of the shell casing bruising his own side. He just sat down on the ground and ate some sandwiches, to the Biographer seeming the very picture of a broken man.

At one stage, a shell exploded right in the middle of the ambulances. The effect of this was to prick the Biographer's conscience, and he went to help with the wounded. Their gasps and groans curdled his blood: many had been shot through the head or stomach. While doing what he could for them, he discovered Gandhi and his Indian friends—the "body-snatchers" as Perry called them—to be among those carrying the injured men away to field hospitals, or down to the train for transport back to the general hospital tents.

"Come on you," shouted the Indian, looking entirely different in his khaki uniform. "We need as many hands as we can get. Why don't you help me carry this fellow?"

"Very well," replied the Biographer meekly, and bent down to pick up the broom-handle ends of the stretcher. The occupant's face had been torn by shrapnel; even to a close friend or relative he would have been unrecognizable. Only his mouth was visible, under a mask of oozing blood. Every now and then, as the two men jogged with the stretcher, the mouth opened and a low moan emerged from its white-toothed, red-flanged aperture. The sight and sound of it was almost too much for the Biographer to bear.

"This is hardly biographing," he huffed, to Gandhi's back.

"It is true suffering and misery," came the serene voice, seemingly untroubled by breathlessness. "And do not believe that the Boers are suffering any less. I have been on the battlefield and seen it for myself. It is because of such things that I have resolved my metaphysic."

"What?"

"In my language it is called *satyagraha*, which is the opposite of force and imperialism. It means truth-fervour, or the conquest of one's adversary by suffering in one's own person."

The Biographer could not believe that even this sage, unearthly-seeming man was saying such things, at such a time. "Well, you are hardly doing that now, satya-whatever, are you?" he said, snidely. "Helping the British Army."

"In spite of my opposition to the Empire, I still believe in the British Constitution," said the wise-sounding voice. "I would vie with any Englishman in loyalty to the throne. But this is not really about that. It is about the saving of life, and the ending of all violence. Anyway . . . enough. We are here."

They had reached the field hospital. The man was taken inside a tent for his wounds to be dressed, in which task the Biographer watched Gandhi assisting the surgeon with great care and attention. Afterwards, with bandages over all parts of his face except for his mouth and two small holes for his nose, the man looked like a mummy. Still the slow, low moans came out of that disembodied mouth, even when Gandhi tried to feed him some Bovril through it, with the effect that the warm brown liquid bubbled horribly back.

"I doubt he will survive," he said to the Biographer, quietly. "I believe that a piece of shell has opened up his brain."

The Biographer went outside to be sick. On coming back in, he found the Indian recording the soldier's injuries in a ledger and writing down his name from the tag on a cord round his neck.

"My, but you are a strange revolutionary," he said.

Gandhi looked up at him briefly, but said nothing and continued with his note taking.

In the morning, an armistice was called to allow the two sides to gather up their dead. The Biographer went onto the field with his cart, and what he saw was harrowing: everywhere were men—dead men and the pieces of men, their khaki stained, soaked with blood, and their faces black and swollen from the sun. Between the human corpses lay those of horses and mules, their sides opened up to reveal cleaved bone, ripped flesh and marbled layers of fat. Already great swarms of flies hung over the place, and to protect himself the Biographer tied over his face a sieve he had found in one of the looted Boer houses. This beekeeper's mask did not prevent the smell, however, which was terrible, especially that of the mules, which seemed to become rank quicker than anything else; and the mask had to be taken off whenever he wanted to film. This he did, albeit with little satisfaction, since he suspected such horrors as filled his lens could never be shown to the British public.

The news, if not the images, did become public property. That week, there had been other battles, at Stormberg and Magersfontein, and together with casualties from Colenso, the butcher's bill came to over three thousand. Britain had never seen the like, and this humiliating Black Week, as it became known, produced great displays of patriotism and indignation at home. As each tragic episode in the drama of the relief of Ladysmith unfolded, a sort of madness seized people, and there was a rush to join the army. The other colonies contributed millions of pounds to the war effort, as well as more than forty thousand volunteers, frightened by the constant stream of bad news and the support for the Boers shown by Germany, Russia and France.

Chief among this bad news was the message that the dispirited Buller was reported to have heliographed into Ladysmith:

> I tried Colenso yesterday, but failed. The enemy is too strong for my force, except with siege operations, which will take one full month to prepare. Can you last so long? If not, how many days can you give me to take up defensive position, after which I suggest your firing away as much ammunition as you can, and making the best terms you can. I can remain here if you have alternative suggestions, but unaided I cannot break in . . . Whatever happens, recollect to burn your cipher and decipher and code books and any deciphered messages.

It was the time of the popular press, and every day the papers were full of "the news from the Cape." Even in the rural seclusion of the Barnes family's Warwickshire farm, the minutest details of the campaign were discussed and analysed. Lizzie and the rest of the family waited for letters from the two brothers and, receiving them, saw beyond the shrieking stories of, on the one hand, the heroic defenders of Ladysmith and, on the other, the town's blundering relievers.

19

57109 Trooper Barnes, P.,
Green Horse,
Military Camp No 2,
Frere,
Natal.

December 17, 1899

Dear Lizzie,

I think it is your turn to get a letter from me. I was wondering how it was I didn't get a letter from you when your parcel and postcard of General Buller arrived: they are very quick to print them nowadays, aren't they? Thank you for the handkerchiefs and the chocolate, although the latter was badly crushed—which I know is not your fault.

Sorry I have not written earlier but we have had a hard battle near here recently. You will no doubt have seen from accounts in the papers that we have been doing a good deal of fighting. At this place, Colenso, our men have been lying all over the field, and one squadron alone had over 50 horses killed. I can only say I don't want another lot like it. One man had his thigh broke. The Indian stretcher-bearers have been doing sterling work.

Some of our men were captured in this last action, and then released to wander on the veld. The Boers strip all of them perfectly naked, as they are short of clothes. It also serves their turn, as in dressing exactly like us, they are continually decoying the chaps into their traps. They have a nasty habit of creeping up under cover of trees, nearly all big mimosas, and hiding under the branches. So we have had to cut them all down, which makes Africa a less pretty place than it was before.

Answering your questions,

1) *My health is good and temper fairly decent.*

2) *No such luck as being home for Xmas. Shall most likely be in Ladysmith with Tom—or just outside, unless things speed up. I hope he is all right; I tried to get a helio message through to him the other day, but I don't know if I succeeded.*

3) *The plenty to eat consists 1/2 lb trek ox that has been knocked up drawing bully after us—1/4 lb bully consisting of every imaginable kind of meat, 1/4 lb of jam, and 4 biscuits per diem. The only vegetables to be had are hard green peas, of which I have had a feed.*

When there are no biscuits they dish us out with 1 lb flour instead. We make what we call fat cakes. Mix the flour and water into a paste and then fry it in fat. I am afraid you would suffer from indigestion if you ate any, as they are a trifle heavy.

I am glad to hear you have better potato crops than the corn or hay crops were. I suppose the ploughs are busy now. By the way, I saw Father's advertisement in the B'ham Mail *for a cowman, so you see it gets over a very wide area and you may have a darkie answering it.*

It is terribly hot out here now and we get some terrific thunder storms every few days. There is a fellow here with a camera, and he took a picture of me soaked from head to toe. Sometimes if caught out in such storms we are served a ration of rum to stop us getting stiff, but not often enough, I am sad to say. There is also hail, the stones a tremendous size, many of them as big as hens' eggs. Although the days are hot, the nights are awfully cold, I should point out. There was a total eclipse of the moon last night. I haven't had such a good view before. The cameraman filmed that, too.

Our squad has been without soap for several days but relief has come at last: I hope poor Tom is soon able to say the same.

We have been paid £2 today, and another of our fellows has died of enteric.

I bet Arthur enjoyed himself at the Farmer's Club party. Does Wilcox still visit you? I will send you some Kruger coins as your Xmas present, when I can get a chance to do so. Things are looking rather blue for the season, but I will do my best to enjoy myself. Now we are just waiting to force the Tugela and get through to Tom and Ladysmith. I will close now as the candle gutters on the tobacco tin, and lay down my weary limbs to rest.

Your affectionate brother,

Perry

p.s. You say in your card that you are copying down my letters and Tom's into a notebook for posterity. Well, I must be careful what I write, or it might rise up and strike me!

20

Nevinson was depressed, and his depression took the form of a lid opening in the top of his head and the dark of the night sky funnelling down into the hole. He could feel it going through him, like a stain on blotting paper. It had a chemical quality to it, what he was feeling, but he knew that was nonsense. It was purely a matter of cause and effect. The reason? The reason had to do with ink, too. The despatch he had sent out with the boy Wellington had just come back into town—part of a larger bag sent in by the Boers, together with General Joubert's compliments. The messages had all been opened, and in some cases defaced with obscene messages. Someone had crept up to a sangar on the outer perimeter and cheekily tossed the sack over. It had hit the sentry on the head.

There was no sign of the oilskin wrapper of his own packet, only its paper contents. These were slightly bloodstained, suggesting the boy had been shot, but it was possible—he studied the brown-red smears as if they were ancient texts—that this had rubbed off from one of the other letters. These included much earlier despatches of his own, as well as ones from Steevens and MacDonald. All were shuffled up together, according to Major Mott (who was furious), having clearly been read carefully from the point of view of intelligence as well as that of sport. Letters were returned to their senders, causing great irritation and distress. When, on top of this, news of Colenso and the other defeats of Black Week filtered through, along with the story of Buller's heliograph signal (which General White, to his credit, ignored), the morale of the beleaguered town declined still further.

But it was the fate of his runner that was Nevinson's main concern. Standing there in the night air, he grimaced at the memory of the boy's angular face, and felt an overwhelming sadness. Now he would have the unpleasant task of selecting another victim to sacrifice on the altar of journalism. He had spent the day interviewing soldiers, and many of them had seemed disheartened too. Everybody was sick of the siege. And dying of it as—hour by hour—the casualties mounted. Today he had seen a Dr. Stark from Torquay lose a leg on the front porch of the Royal, spattering the steps horribly with blood: he had died on the operating table an hour later.

Tonight, as he stood in the moonlight outside the same place—its steps and veranda freshly mopped—he saw Mr. Kiernan, the owner, come out; he had a haversack on his back, out of which poked a long brass telescope. Kiernan gave him a dark look as he passed, and Nevinson wondered where he was off to. There was a founder's-day party that night for the Carbineers—he had already seen Grimble go in—and he thought the hotelier would have been busy.

He sat down on a low wall opposite the Royal. Save for the chatter from the dining room, the flutter of bats' wings, and the occasional stamp of a horse's hoof, the town was quiet that night. There had been no shelling. In the middle of the deserted street he could just make out the dark little islands of horse dung that were now everywhere in Ladysmith. There was simply not enough room in the town for so much livestock. The numbers encouraged disease—the incidence of enteric was increasing daily. Steevens, who was no better, was at least now keeping to his bed. If he grew any worse they would have to get a nurse for him, or send him to the hospital.

One of the main causes of enteric was the animal waste that had tainted the town's water supply. This and the dire lack of forage led Nevinson to expect that many of the animals would be slaughtered if the siege lasted much longer. There was talk of horseflesh becoming the main source of meat. Where, he wondered, had the Carbineers got the means of their feast? Decent food was becoming impossible to lay hold of.

He looked up at the sky. Every now and then he could see the flash of the night signal, which Major Mott had engineered to shine on the clouds by means of a searchlight and a Venetian blind. The message went out and then the reply would come back, calling "Ladysmith" three times in plain Morse, and then going into cipher before ending "Buller, Maritzburg."

But the Major was not the only man to have been organizing signalling in recent weeks. There was some suspicion the Boers might have been sending the day signal as a decoy (three copies of a cipher had been lost at Dundee). Furthermore, one of the mountain battery was to be hanged tomorrow for signalling to the enemy, and a Cape Coloured muleteer had been shot by a sentry in the very act of sending details of British movements. Others had been suspected of signalling from lighted windows at night. Several of these traitors had already been hanged or shot, but some had slipped the net. A man named Oscar Meyer, known to have Boer sympathies, had hidden in Ladysmith for three whole weeks. Realizing the hunt for him was likely to be successful at some point, he had stolen a horse and saddle and tricked a sentry at the furthest outpost by wearing a helmet wound with the blue and white puggaree of the Guides. Employing some melodramatic business involving the search for a non-existent pass, he had suddenly spurred his horse at full speed towards the Boer lines across the veld.

The lookout for spies had its nastier side. Every day, another "shady character" was arrested in the town. Nevinson suspected that many of these Russians, French and Germans were entirely innocent. Together with the Dutch prisoners proper, they were being kept in the compound of the Dopper Church. Surrounded by a wire fence, it was a curious place these days, full of a cosmopolitan crowd of European faces. Whenever Boer prisoners were brought in, the Africans in the town would shout *Upi pass? Upi pass?* at them— "Where's your pass? Where's your pass?"—mocking them with the same question that the Boer authorities habitually put to natives working in the mines.

Up in the hills, Nevinson could see the watch fires of the Boer camps. To his left, suspended in the sky, was the dark shape of one of the British observation balloons, from which the fan of a searchlight intermittently swept across the outer defences. He felt sorry for the fellows who had to spend the night in it, always running the risk that the Boers would take a pot-shot at them, although the balloons had so far proved out of range. His gaze followed the dim outline of the mooring rope down to its anchor point, and then along the kerb until he was looking at the frontage of the Royal Hotel again, its dining-room window displaying the tableau of a mighty army at play: the

Carbineers' party. He saw Mr. Grimble standing in front of a tureen, ladling—if he was not mistaken—pears in red wine into bowls. Evidently this was such a special treat that the fruit-grower had insisted on serving his fellow officers himself. Where had those buggers got wine from?

The soaked fruit made Nevinson think of wounds: the doctor from Torquay who had suffered on this very stoep. He raised his eyes from the scene, and looked up and down the calm and innocent facade of the hotel, one golden square after another; he looked—and saw in the tableau death, only death.

21

Bella rubbed the pane with a soapy cloth. The gable end of the hotel, the other side from where she was, had received a glancing blow from a shell during the bombardment that had killed Dr. Stark yesterday. How horrible that had been: she had asked the Zulu woman to clean up the mess, not being able to face it herself. The damage incurred by the hotel was negligible, but dust and muck from the injured brick-work, blown through by the wind, had lodged in the corners of the window casements on the top floor. How, she wondered, had it got under the doors? It must have been the force of the blast. Father had said clean it, clean it all. But it stuck to the glass, smearing as she rubbed.

Now it was coming up to six o'clock and she was tired. She stopped for a moment and sighed, resenting the burden of the extra chores the siege had provoked. As if it wasn't objectionable enough having hot lumps of iron pelted at you each day! She looked at the window, where the red brick dust had now dissolved in her soapy, greasy water and transformed itself into something with the consistency of paint. All she could see was her own reflection, distorted by the marks left by her cloth. She was at the top of the hotel now, having done all the other windows, and her back was aching from carrying the buckets. Not just up the stairs, either. The town's waterworks having been destroyed, she had to bring water all the way from the river. She had remonstrated with Father about the foolishness of this, but he had been insistent.

This room, they called it the Star Room, was where Father kept his astronomy equipment. A great pile of the stuff—brass telescopes and compasses, charts rolled up and tied with purple ribbons, a globe—lay on a big desk to her left. On the right was a large clock, and next to it, on a smaller desk, the workings of two other clocks: gears and springs and faces with the hands missing. What a queer idea that was, she thought—faces with the hands missing! But pride of place, astronomically speaking at any rate, went to the painted description of the sky at night which covered the curved ceiling of the room, and gave it its name. They were all here—Betelgeuse, Saturn, the Pleiades, the cluster in the sword-handle of Perseus—and Father had taught Jane and her the names of each. The difficulty was, it was not a southern-hemisphere map and showed stars which, in the real night sky above Ladysmith, she could never see.

She looked down. On the smaller desk, next to the dismantled clocks, stood a photograph in a tin frame: their mother, dressed in black, holding little Bella in her arms, Father next to her. How many times she had tried to remember this moment, this single recorded moment of contact with Cathleen Kiernan, but all she could muster was a vague sense of absence. This made her feel guilty, even though she knew it was silly that she should feel guilty that her mother, two years after giving birth to her, should have died while being delivered of Jane. Strangely, little Bella looked older than two in the picture; but Father never elaborated on the subject of their mother, even though she and Jane had pressed him to do so.

Both of them believed that his recurrent black moods were on account of their mother's death, which had taken place back in Ireland and which, along with the harshness of life there at that time, had led Leo Kiernan to bring his two young daughters out to South Africa. Of the rest of the family they knew little, except that their father once had a brother. He had died too, Father had said. Both the sisters wished he would be more forthcoming about that part of his life. It was hard for them to accept, when they thought about the past, that there was nothing there: but Father just kept silent when they asked him, or stood up and went into another room. Sometimes Bella wondered if there was a secret in the family.

She picked up the picture in its tin frame. Even when he was in his darkest moods, as he had been all this day, Bella felt sorry for Father. She was old enough to realize how hard it must have been for him to make the journey from Ireland, still more bring them up in these inhospitable environs. Well, mostly that had been done by a string of Zulu nannies. Now, whenever she thought of her mother, a black face came into Bella's mind, rather than that of the woman whose frozen image she was holding in her hand. It was a composite black face, though, because the nannies—actually they called them ayahs, after the Indian fashion—always left after a while. Father drove them too hard. He was always shouting at them, not out of anger, as Bella saw it, but out of guilt. She could see this clear, how after sweating late into the night at the bar, he woke every morning to the soul-searching realization that his "two little darlin's," as he called them, had no mother. He was thought strange by the town for not remarrying; she had heard the conversations, but something else she saw clearly also: Father had loved Cathleen Kiernan, this . . . that distant figment, with all his heart. He just was not the sort of man to take another woman.

One result of the string of nannies was that both she and Jane spoke fluent Zulu, or "Kaffir," as most of the townsfolk called it. This was actually quite useful. She had recently taken on a new maid and boy for the hotel. The pair, a mother and son, spoke only a little English. The previous servants, like many of the Africans and Indians, had fled or been sent out of the town when the siege began. Some of the bigger shops, which before had up to fifty natives on their books, now had only one or two.

But the Boers had lately begun forcing in upon them hundreds of native refugees from the north; as they were here, Bella had reasoned, the hotel might as well make use of one or two of them. Father had grumbled about the cost but had eventually agreed that Nandi and Wellington—as they were called—should join the staff for the duration of the siege; which, as everyone had thought, would only be a couple of weeks. After all, when the relief column had begun its march in earnest, it had only been twenty-five miles away. But now, she thought, we have been shut up for nearly a month. Food was running low. They were being issued daily rations by the military commissariat—tooth-breaking biscuits, bully beef and other horrible stuff—and the hotel menu had become as regular a text as the Bible; they were lucky to have the vegetable garden to supplement it.

Father had been in a reasonably placid mood when he had agreed to take on their new employees. This was a relief, since he and Bella had had some bitter arguments in the weeks preceding the siege. She had wanted—still wanted now, as she dusted the glass cabinet in which his astronomy books were ranged—to go away and get some further schooling; and then, as she had explained to Jane, meet a different stamp of husband than those offered by the careful tradesmen and brawny pioneers of Ladysmith. She had thought maybe the Cape, or even Britain. This last suggestion had met with her father's extreme displeasure. His refusal even to countenance the possibility of such a move saddened her greatly. How she longed to go to London and see everything! Really, the isolation of this siege was just another wall around her. Some days, she felt like an egg waiting to be cracked.

Bella's thoughts—half-formed, as idling as the Klip River—were interrupted by the unearthly moan of a shell. She looked out of the window, which was still emblazoned with roundels of scum from her efforts at cleaning it, and caught a glimpse of flame. Earlier in the day she had seen a man take the blast of a shell full in his back. There was a time when she would have run down to help him—pointlessly, since he had clearly been killed—but after a month of ceaseless bombardment she had learned to look on death and injury with disregard.

What a time it had been, since the first shell had fallen. At first, all shops and businesses, including the Royal, had closed, but within a day or two they were open again, each remaining so until its proprietors had nothing left to sell. The railway had stopped that day too, and many women and children had left on the last train to Pietermaritzburg. She and Jane had laid in a stock of provisions—biscuits, sugar, rice, mealie meal, tinned meat—enough for a few weeks. Father had then told them to go back and duplicate it, "in case we are shut in for a month or two."

But all that had run out now. Bella felt hungry nearly all of the time. She wanted nothing so much as a bit of meat—a slice of ham, or some brawn. But all there was to have was boiled trek ox, which didn't seem to yield any sustenance at all. Now that food was being distributed by the military, and soldiers stood behind the counters at the shops, every item had to be accounted for—even clothing.

How many shells had fallen during the first month? She didn't know, she knew only that the Town Hall was full of wounded soldiers and civilians. Anyone who had been bombed out—like Torres—had gone down to the Klip and dug himself a hole there for protection. The soft ground of the riverbank helped absorb the shell blast and shrapnel.

She thought some more about Torres, how she had accidentally tasted him when she had lifted her hand to her face after touching his perspiring arm at the diggings. How slippery his arm had been. Like a fish.

Then another shell went off and she considered them, the Boers, and another man the siege had brought into her orbit. They were cunning as well as patient, the Dutch. For it was from Tom Barnes, who in spite of being warned off by Father had taken to dropping in to the hotel frequently, that she had learned how the Boers had hoisted a white flag so they could repair one of their guns.

And I too, she thought, have hoisted a white flag. For over the first month of investment, love—so Bella fancied—had worked its artful process on her and Tom. Their subtle manoeuvres of attack and counter-attack, as they glimpsed each other round the town and over tea at the hotel, had become plain to each; and yet there had been just as much complicated deployment of gesture and look and tone of voice to ward each other off.

So there was defence as well as attack. The generals, White and Joubert, were children by comparison, in the ways they disposed their forces. Yet in the manner of these things, the ebb and flow of hot looks and cold looks, compliment and mild disparagement, had become one and the same. Yes, Tom Barnes and Bella Kiernan could fairly be said to be courting. Although only that one kiss had passed between them, her sister had taken to referring to him as "Long Tom," and complaining that her own suitor, the bluejacket Foster, was thereby bound to play the part of "Puffing Billy," as one of the smaller Boer guns was known.

These were sisters' secrets, but even so Bella burned at the thought of them . . . it was Jane's fault; if she didn't talk like that, such thoughts wouldn't be entertained. And yet they came all the same, persistent as Boer shellfire from somewhere deep inside. She'd need—what did they call those protective forts?—a sangar to stop them. Without it, as she rubbed and dusted and thought about these things, every circular movement now seemed to describe some other story: its ending, the furthest ripple of its pebble in a pond, being that life with Tom—Durban maybe, the Cape, England! And a house, a garden, children . . . some place where the rippling stopped and all was a quiet peace that went on for ever.

Bella picked up the buckets and walked towards the door. It was time she went to join Jane behind the bar. The intrusion of humdrum duty upon her dreaminess made her cynical where, seconds before, she had been rhapsodic; maybe the whole thing was a silly notion, a function of siege time. For when it ended, however it ended, Tom would be gone; and anyway, in spite of her picket-fence dreams, she was clever enough—indeed I am, she thought—to see faults in him, a clumsy, impetuous quality among them, faults that gave her pause, faults that with every step she took downstairs, a bucket in each hand, made her reconsider the matter of romance, faults that by the time she got to the bottom of the stairs (these, of course, were the back stairs, not the grander ones upon which Tom had encountered her father), yes, by the time she had got to the bottom of the back stairs and opened the door to the scullery, had decided her that she would take it slowly, this half-considered, evanescent thing she thought of as love.

On coming from the scullery into the bar, she found Major Mott on the point of launching into a discussion with her father, who was busy drying a row of glasses.

"Mr. Kiernan," the Major said. "I have a proposal for you."

"What's that then?"

"Well, as you know, the various military contingents in the town have been finding themselves healthy leisure activities with which to while away the time when they are not on duty. You know, whist drives, mule gymkhanas, football . . ."

"I do," said her father. He pushed his cloth inside a glass. "So?"

"Well, General White has asked me to devise some sport which would involve the townsfolk in conjunction with the soldiery, as a boost to morale."

"How do you reckon I can help you, Major?"

"I thought perhaps we'd have a game of cricket. Colonial Born versus the Mother Country? How does that sound?"

"I don't know much about cricket, Major. As an Irishman, you understand. Now hurling, I'd be on for that. The fastest game on grass."

"Well . . . it is a little specialized. Seriously, though, what do you think?"

The conversation between the two men had created some interest, and a small group had gathered around them.

"It seems a slightly arbitrary division," said Kiernan. "Considering we are all in the same boat." He looked round the room. "Wouldn't Bearded versus Beardless be a better bet? Or Smokers versus Non-Smokers? Or what about Handsomes versus Uglies?"

Bella smiled as she watched him tease the Major. She loved him dearly when the playful side of his nature came to the surface. Unbidden, the picture came into her head of something turned up in the diggings at the Klip: a clay pot or bone-handled tool, or some other artefact from long ago. A time when her father was happy—that seemed just as distant.

"Really, Mr. Kiernan, I think the original distinction was more suitable. Will you captain?"

"I can hardly play the game, Major. Besides, isn't there someone else more suitable?"

"I think not," said a voice. It was a frail one, rather high, certainly not the Major's. The two men turned round, and saw the stiff figure of General White, together with Colonel Hamilton and one or two others of the senior staff.

"Yes," said the General. "I think you'd be just the chap to lead a team, Mr. Kiernan. After all, the Royal is the centre of the community in Ladysmith, the very hub."

"But I'm no good, sir," said the Irishman, suddenly hapless.

"Nonsense, man, you'll acquit yourself well, of that I am sure. As will all involved. Just what we need to perk things up round here—a manly impulse towards recreation. Courage, patience, endurance, courtesy, control . . . these are the virtues of cricket and these are the virtues of the Empire too. So, go to it. Mott, arrange the match for a Sunday."

"Very well, sir," said the Major, as White and his entourage swept to a table in the dining room.

"Looks like you're landed with it, Father," said Bella, smiling.

"Indeed it does."

22

Nevinson was sitting on Steevens's sickbed, telling him the story of his day. He was trying to take his friend's mind off the fever which, in the last four weeks, had grasped and released him like an uncertain lover.

"Two pieces of good fortune came to me today, almost at an instant. The first concerned my own life. I had gone down to the river with Willie Maud, aiming to show him a quiet place for sketching the whole view of the town in peace. He had taken his sketchbook out and I was standing there watching some Zulus bathing—soaping themselves white, they were—when a shell whiffled over us. We didn't take much notice at first, and neither did the horses: they stood there drinking like the orphan lamb. Then suddenly the water was alive with shreds of iron. My hat was knocked off, and the horses were jumping around like hell's imps. Maud shouted: 'Are you killed?' I said: 'I don't think so. Are you?' It was a near thing, George, I can tell you."

Wearing pyjamas, Steevens was sat up in the bed, packing his pipe. A notebook lay on the sheet over his lap.

"Mmm. And what was the other?"

"Well, once I had lashed my horse back—there is nothing like shellfire for giving lessons in horsemanship—and retrieved my broken hat, my eye fell upon the Zulus. They were mostly women."

"Steamy," interrupted Steevens, and chuckled.

"One of them—she skivvies at the Royal, I think—is, or was as I thought, the mother of my latest runner. I had given him up for dead, on account of the return of the bloodstained packet—I told you about it—but then I see this round black head surfacing from the water. And by Jove it's him, it's my dead runner taking a wash after his exertions. So I leave Maud to his sketchbook and go over to ask the lad what he's about. He tells me the Boers let him go on Joubert's orders; the old fox had ordered him to bring the letters back into town, to put the wind up us and show us we've no chance. But the poor boy was so scared of getting into trouble with our lot—the Dutchmen roughed him up—that he just slung it over the edge of a sangar. His mama is very happy to have him back, but they're both a bit glum because it turns out the father is in the Boer camp."

"There must be a lot of them," said Steevens, putting aside his pipe. "Damn thing won't draw."

"What?"

"There must be a lot of African families split on either side."

"Yes, and many a European one, too. I went into the Dopper Church today, where they've got the prisoners, to talk to a Jew called Blok. He had a farm up by the border of Portuguese East Africa, but the Boers pressganged him to join their army, so he had to leave his wife behind. But it turned out he couldn't really ride or shoot or live on biltong, and could only talk Russian, which is a useless accomplishment in a Boer commando, so they sent him into our camp."

"Joubert's still up to that trick, is he? Dumping them on us to eat our rations? I remember, at the start, seeing all the Indians he sent us as a present."

"Yes, the same old line," said Nevinson. "There's something a little medieval about it, in my opinion—sending a crowd of hungry noncombatants into an invested town. Our lot have sentenced one poor coolie to death, just for stealing a goat."

"Medieval? It's more ancient than that, even. Sieges are out of date. In the days of Troy, to be besieged or besieger was the natural lot of man; to give ten years at a stretch to it, why, it was all in a life's work; there was nothing else to do."

Nevinson laughed, even though he suspected his friend's fever was taking hold of him again.

"In the old days," continued Steevens, "when a great victory was gained one year, and a fast frigate arrived with news the next, a man still had leisure in his life for a year's siege now and again."

The other correspondent laughed again, but he could see the sheen of sweat gathering on Steevens's brow as he grew more excitable.

"But to the man of 1899—excuse me, inclining to 1900—with five editions of the evening papers every day, a siege is a thousandfold a hardship. We make it a grievance nowadays if we are a day behind the news—news that concerns us not at all!"

"Oh, that reminds me," said Nevinson. "I've got a paper for you."

He went through to his room and fetched it. When he came back in, Steevens was standing over his washbowl with his head in the water. Nevinson stood behind him, holding the paper, until Steevens pulled his head out of the water and shook it, like a dog. Nevinson was disgusted to see how stained and yellowed were the bottoms of his friend's pyjamas.

"I say, George, are you all right?"

Steevens rubbed his face with the hand towel and let out a burst of breath. "Yes, just feeling a bit faint. Thought the application of some cold water might help. Though it's tepid, of course. God, this business is an unredeemed curse. Dismal! Weary, stale, flat, unprofitable, the whole thing . . ."

He got back into bed, the tendrils of damp hair round his greenish face giving him, to Nevinson's mind, a slightly Medusa-like air.

"Dismal!" repeated Steevens. "For my part, I feel it will never end. Henry, I now know exactly how a fly in a beer bottle feels."

He did look awful, thought Nevinson, handing him the paper. "How's your book going?" he asked, trying to take his mind off his gloomy thoughts.

"Just a dull diary now. I've abandoned my new monologues of the dead. I haven't the heart for them. Someone else can write the bloody things. I've lost my edge. I feel like a monk without a vocation. I'm just going to carry on writing the diary, and then when we're still here in twenty years' time, dropping off one by one from old age, I will wrap it up in a Red Cross flag and bury it under the tree outside."

He threw the notebook onto the floor and snapped open the newspaper that Nevinson had given him. "And then, in the enlightened year 1999, after antiquarians have come to dig up the forgotten towns of Natal and discovered it, the unnumbered readers of the *Daily Mail* will know what a siege and bombardment was really like!"

The wildness of Steevens's imagination was almost frightening to Nevinson; he felt helpless in front of it, and saw nothing to do but retire and let his friend calm down in his own time.

"I'll leave you to the paper then, George," he said, mildly. "Go and write up my own reports. Bang on the wall if there's anything you want."

"Hold up," said Steevens. "The bloody Boers have captured Winston Churchill. Something to do with an armoured train. I can't believe it. He seemed to have so much promise. What a blow. It's all so pointless and stupid."

"Do you know him?"

"I suppose you could call us friends. We met in the Sudan, with Kitchener's expedition . . . had dinner together on the Nile. Then I bumped into him at a junction in India, when he was stationed there and I was reporting. In fact, we always seemed to run into each other in transit. We were together for five days once on a boat in the Mediterranean, and for two on an express on the Continent. I gave him some help with the proofs for his book on the River War. His prose used to be rather heavy—not the modern style—but it's getting better. He came for a long Sunday lunch once at my house in Merton, too. He has great plans in politics, you know . . . but I suppose those are all done for now. It's a shame. He could have gone far."

"We could all go far if we had a family name to give us a leg up," said Nevinson, to whom Churchill's politics were anathema. "He is simply fulfilling the self-perpetuating myth of the Spencers, Marlboroughs and whatever other grandees inhabit his blood."

Steevens laughed. "You'll be throwing bombs next. And you won't need to, that's the funny thing. The old order is changing anyway, regardless of what you and your anarchist friends think. There are new names about, and new myths to go with them. Look at millionaires like Lipton. He invented himself. He may be vulgar, his advertising methods may border on the dishonest, but you have to admire the man's energy. He is opening a grocery store a week nowadays, here and in America."

"Stop," said Nevinson. "Please. The mere thought of a slice of Lipton ham would drive me to distraction."

23

The pain and smell from his wounded leg were appalling. Having been on the point of recovering from a fractured ankle, Muhle Maseku was now back in his hut, nursing the bullet wound in his thigh. Truly, the gods were not on his side. Doctor Sterkx, whom he had to thank for Wellington's escape from execution, had told him he was very lucky the bone had not been shattered. The bullet had passed straight through the flesh, causing most damage on its exit at the back of the thigh, ripping through sinew and muscle before embedding itself in the ground.

Sterkx had dressed the wound, but could not spare any medicine for the pain. It rendered Muhle almost unable to think, but all the time he hung on to one thing: as he had lain on the blood-soaked ground after Major MacBride had shot him, half-listening to the discussion between Joubert, Sterkx and the Major about Wellington's fate, he had realized that if Wellington was to be freed, he ought somehow to communicate to his son a place where they could make a rendezvous. He could see Wellington a little way away, struggling between two of MacBride's men, but every time he himself had tried to sit up, another of the men had kicked him back down.

His mind had raced. He had to find some way to fix a location in Wellington's mind. But neither of them knew the area well and this, with the added disadvantage that everywhere was crawling with Boer sentries, made the task almost impossible. Just as they were about to take Wellington away, to send him back to Ladysmith, it had come to him.

"I will meet you at the isivivane," he had shouted out in Zulu, from beneath the white man's boot.

From across the camp had come Wellington's answering voice. "At the isivivane, Father."

And then another voice. "Shut up, kaffir."

All this Muhle rehearsed as he lay—once more—in this damned hut. The *isivivane:* the reference was to the "lucky" heap of stones placed at the edge of a path as it entered strange territory. There would have been many such piles in the area, but at least it narrowed things down a little. Now all he had to do was escape from the Boer camp himself and that, he knew, was no easy task, especially with a wounded leg. He toyed with the idea of asking Sterkx for help, but reckoned that although the good doctor might be prepared to save a life, he would never do something that might be conceived of as betrayal. Unless . . . unless . . . Sterkx had mentioned that his wife was a prisoner in Ladysmith: if Muhle promised to get a message to her, perhaps the doctor would help him.

He put it to Sterkx when he came in to look at his dressing, which was soaked and stained with an ominous discharge.

"Doctor, first of all I wish to thank you for saving the life of my son. For this I am eternally in your debt."

Bending over him, Sterkx shrugged. "It was the right thing to do. Too many people are being killed in this unnecessary business."

"I have a proposal for you," said Muhle.

"Oh yes?"

"I want you to help me escape from the camp. All I ask is that you provide me with some food and water."

Sterkx squatted down and pulled the new bandage tight round Muhle's thigh. The Zulu gasped.

"I assume you are joking," said the Boer. "You can hardly move, your leg is badly infected. In any case, it would be a treasonous act on my part. I could get myself shot."

"What I am offering you," explained Muhle, "is the chance to send a message to your wife. I have to get into Ladysmith to find my family, and once I am inside I will do my best to help her."

In the gloom of the hut, the doctor's eyes lit up. "You think you could?" But as soon as he had spoken the words, his enthusiasm dimmed. "It would be madness. I do not think you could get there."

"I have to," said Muhle. "I will just rot away to death if I lie here. Please, you must help me. I will not forget my promise."

Sterkx straightened up. "I will think about it."

"You are a good man," said Muhle, as the doctor made his way to the door.

"All I said was that I would think about it."

A silhouette in the light, the outline of his hat and beard clearly defined, Sterkx looked back at the injured African, let out an explosive sigh, then ducked out of the doorway.

24

Does agreement to an assignation amount to submission? This—although she wouldn't have put it like that, not exactly—was a question that concerned Bella greatly during the following day. In the morning, Tom stopped by the entrance of the Royal and asked if she would walk out with him that evening, once he had come off duty.

Shaded from the sunlight, she had stood without moving on the stoep, and then said, in neutral tones, "Very well."

He'd flashed her a grateful smile. "Five o'clock then?"

"Yes," she had said, and glanced down, avoiding his eyes.

She knew, she thought, that she liked him, and realized also, from his tone and from his eager looks, that she was admired in her turn. But all day she worried at the notion of it, and was filled with a mixture of apprehension and desire by the thought that he might make some advance. What should she do if he did? Jane had already succumbed to Herbert Foster's overtures and, one night after the bar had closed, and Father was out on the hills with his telescopes, had fallen into an embrace with him in the scullery.

So it was a sweet, satisfying anticipation, mixed with worry, that filled Bella's heart when Trooper Barnes called for her late that afternoon. He looked very smart in his khaki uniform, his belt and shoulder strap polished a deep chestnut, his green eyes twinkling, and his dark hair well combed.

"Where would you like to go?" he asked, as they stepped out into the main street.

"I don't know," she answered, and in that moment saw exactly how it would be. Where was there to go in Ladysmith, after all?

"Well, it's you that lives here."

Bella thought this reply a little uncouth, and said nothing.

"How about the orchard?" Tom asked, taking her arm.

"All right then," she said, conscious of what people would think at the sight of her on a soldier's arm. She imagined Mrs. Frinton pursing her lips.

They manoeuvred their way up the main street, between carts and limbers and the ever-present coolies, sitting on their heels by the kerb.

"That was Rashid, Foster's shell carrier," Tom said, as they passed one. "He's a good little fellow. Brave as a terrier."

Bella looked back at the man, thinking of Jane and her gunner. Clad in nothing but a loincloth, the Indian was using his hand to spoon rice into his mouth from a tin billy. He was utterly concentrated on the task, and had seemed not to notice them.

"I wonder how they feel," she said.

"Who?"

"Them, and the kaffirs. About being boxed in like this, I mean."

"No different from us, I should say."

"But it's nothing to do with them. They're just innocent bystanders."

"Sitters," said Tom, and chuckled. "Well, they are subjects of the Empire, love."

She flinched at him using the word. He hadn't earned the right.

"Some of them are here under contract," Tom continued.

"Indenture," Bella said. "It's not the same. Indeed, it's only a small degree away from slavery."

Tom rubbed her on the back. "You're a smart puss, aren't you?"

They had reached the fringes of the orchard. "Come on, race you to the trees!" he said, and set off at a sprint.

Silly, she thought, then gathered up her skirts and ran after him. The light was different under the foliage, not just greener but dappled with all sorts of colours.

"Come on," shouted Tom, ahead of her.

She ran on. It became difficult. Fronds of leaf brushed her face, trunks suddenly appeared where she had thought there were none, and the ground was uneven; not to speak of the branches that lay around, waiting like traps to trip her. She didn't stumble, however, but ran on, and was soon with him in a more open place, where the grass grew long and the evening sunlight was beginning to fall. It was beautiful and, as she caught her breath, Bella almost forgot that she was shut up in Ladysmith, with its ugliness of mud and dust and cow dung and shellfire—forgot too her companion's silliness, his clumsy bravado and casual Empire spirit. She had never been very close to men before, not alone, but she had seen how they were. Watched them while working at the bar, her sober eyes searching their drunken ones, watched how they held themselves, walked, sat down. Listened to what they said. Learned how even the tenderest moment, the sweetest thing, was always in danger of being buried in brag and bluster.

Her heart was beating hard. Tom had unbuttoned his tunic and the top of his shirt and was lying on the grass. She could see the dark hairs of his chest poking out. The warm evening sun was casting long shadows, and all around was a murmurous hush, a fierce calm. She felt an expectant sensation kindling in her stomach, a curious feeling at once tense and relaxed. You don't have to do anything, she told herself as she knelt down beside him. But she wanted to know. She wanted to know what he, what any of them, looked like underneath the army clothes, what he felt like, smelled like. She was older than her sister, after all. So she was businesslike, brisk even, and acted as if she knew what she was doing when she leant across from her kneeling position and kissed him. He responded keenly, too keenly, opening his mouth. She pushed him back on the ground, her hand full on his chest. The breath went out of him and he gave a little gasp. She leant over again and kissed him softly, to the side of his mouth. She felt his eyelids flutter against her forehead. Then he sat up, and swung her round in the crook of his arm; so that, in one movement, she was almost beneath him. She felt his mouth on hers, working at it, softly at first and then harder. It was like nothing she had ever experienced before. The nearest thing she could think of was eating oranges and yet, as she looked above, what she could see were pears. Pears! Great green bundles of them, hanging in the sky.

She closed her eyes, and as he—kneeling between her petticoated legs now—unbuttoned her blouse, said to herself, to her own mind, oranges, pears, oranges, pears . . . and then giggled out loud in embarrassment at her ludicrous train of thought, as if there had been someone listening inside her head.

"What?" said the voice above her, crossly. Tom must have thought she was laughing at him.

"Nothing," she said, and reached out and grasped his hovering wrist.

He pushed her hand down. She felt the grass imprint upon the back of it and then he was kissing her again, more gently this time, so gently she could feel his pulse upon her lips. His hand moved down—allowing hers to spring up limply, like a cat's paw, behind her head—and his palm began to rub her breast in a slow, circular movement. She didn't want it to become too rhythmic, too geometric. She liked the vagueness of it, the casual way of it, and she liked the way the weight of his body was upon her, the hardness of him on her chest, even where his metal buttons dug into her.

She shifted under him a little, and then he moved further over her, so that his thigh fell between hers. As they kissed, he pushed against her a little with his thigh, and she felt herself pressing back accordingly. Then he stopped kissing her, and put his head in his free hand, looking at her from the side while his other hand touched her face and her hair and lips—questioningly, like a schoolboy with a pet. She turned to look at him.

His expression appeared terribly serious at first and then, as she stared frankly back at him—so close—he looked ashamed.

"You look a bit bashful, Trooper Barnes," she said coolly, and smiled.

"That's strange," he said.

"Why?"

"I've got a horse called Bashful."

"That's a funny name for a horse," she said.

"Maybe."

She looked around. It was nearly dark now. The shadows on the grass looked like leopard spots, and it was hard to tell whether it was dapples of light she was looking at now or patches of night.

"What if someone sees us? They could easily . . ."

Before she could finish, her words were swallowed up by his mouth coming down on hers again. It was a kind of peck except that his lips opened in the instant and gave hers a fillip, before pattering over her cheeks and her eyelids and the tip of her nose. She shivered a little, and then felt his hand go inside her blouse, tracing the edge of her corset with a finger. Another button was undone, and another, and then he began to stroke her breasts through the fabric, stroke them with that same half-directed, half-careless intensity. Was this what it was always like? Did they always pretend that it was all somehow happening by accident?

The question went out of her head as she felt him try to unhook her stays. She turned to help him, and then felt herself swell as the tightness went away, and suddenly she didn't care whether anyone saw them. Now he was pulling up her knees, his fingers scooping the soft flesh behind, above the tops of her calf-high boots. Her outer skirt fell down about her waist, and then his hands were beneath her petticoat, raising it like two white alps in the fleeing light. He flung it up—she felt the blow of it on her wet mouth—and then his mouth, his tongue, was probing at her through her underwear. She gave a little sob at the shock of it, feeling every lineament of the cloth's weave. It was almost painful in being so particular, but she didn't want it to stop all the same, especially in the moments when—and they were unpredictable, save that he was learning, gauging the rightness of it from her reaction—he touched her in such a way . . . She closed her eyes and willed it to go on for ever, to go on till morning came down through the tops of the trees, moving stealthily between the leaves. She was a leaf herself now, waving, hoping to fall . . .

Bella felt hands either side of her, tugging at her underwear.

"You mustn't," she said, tensing.

Full of regret, she sat up, her legs apart with him kneeling between them. To keep her balance, she was forced to throw her arms around his neck. This pulled him down onto her, and then he slumped to one side, breathing heavily. She could feel him pressing against her through his breeches. Determined to distract him, yet still half-full of exploring zeal, she snaked down a hand. Tom moaned, and rolled over on to his back. She rubbed against the straining tip of him, using the palm of her hand as he had done upon her breast.

"Like this," he whispered, shaking his head, and at first she didn't understand that it was an instruction, not an expression of pleasure.

He reached down and moved her hand aside, and with a quick movement undid his belt and the top button of his breeches. Almost reluctantly, Bella pushed her hand into the gap—felt the fleshy top of him, warm underneath her palm, astonishingly warm, and softly textured. That velvetiness of skin was more striking to her than the prodding, hard way the thing pushed up against her hand. Tom put his own hand on top of hers and moved it up and down, and then undid some more buttons, until he sprung free.

Long Tom!

She smiled at her own thought, and in the consciousness of it gripped him more firmly. Moving her hand up and down the stock of him, she could feel a long, arcing vein under her fingers. Or was it a muscle? Every now and then it twitched a little. She noticed quickly that Tom moved about and made small, breathy noises at the beginning and end of each movement of her hand. The fascination was in the pure mechanism of it; she felt like an engineer, one surprised by some chance discovery in the field of iron bridge building, or steam. She was even more surprised when Tom released a sharper breath than all the previous ones, kicked out his legs, and a small, wet frog landed on her bare arm.

25

"Frogs!"

Herbert Foster swore as the Boer shell buried itself in the earth breastwork beneath his emplacement on Junction Hill, making the whole thing shake. The redoubt was more like a conning tower than a sandbag epaulement, they had built it so tall—shoulder-high and six foot thick, with the Armstrong sticking out at forty-five degrees and the Maxim trained point blank. But Long Tom was getting the better of the exchange . . .

"Bloody Frogs! Bloody Huns! Bloody Irish! If they weren't all fighting with them, then we might have a chance."

No one was listening, and even if they had been they could not have heard him over the noise of battery and counter-battery fire. But he was not really addressing his remarks to anyone in particular, just expressing his frustration at the good aim of the gunners of the *Staats Artillerie.*

The reference to the French was based on little more than the fact that some of the Boer guns were made by a French company (thus supplementing the Kaiser's Krupps), and the imprecation upon the Irish was a consequence of the discovery that the Boers, like the British, had their own Irish brigade—"full of paddywacks with a grievance" as Foster put it—whose second-in-command was a renegade nationalist politician called MacBride. News of the existence of this brigade had already caused some tension in the ranks, being the cause of a brawl between a man of the Leicesters and a sergeant of the Dublin Fusiliers, who resented his loyalty to the Crown being called into question. The man got a double beating, first from the sergeant, and then from the provosts, on account of his having struck a superior.

But there were larger quarrels, ones in which such discriminations counted for naught. The big guns on Umbulwana and Pepworth Hill had kept up their racket all week, making no distinction between famous or ordinary human beings, or for that matter between human beings and animals. Lord Dufferin, Dr. Jameson (of "Jameson Raid" notoriety) and Colonel Frank Rhodes (brother of Cecil) were disturbed by a shell while sitting for a photograph. Another mule of Rashid, carrier to Gunner Foster, had been disembowelled at the naval gunpit, and now he had to carry the shells himself.

It was not all one way, not by any means. Foster's Armstrong was roaring like a bullock today. It searched the country for Dutch blood, as if in revenge for the ill-fated mule.

"A Boer name on every round," Foster would say, and spit, as Rashid staggered over with the heavy shell in his arms.

This utterance would be made from a low shelf beneath the parapet, upon which Foster would sit down between firings to smoke his cigar. Rashid, even without his beast of burden, was so quick with the shells that he hardly had time for more than a couple of puffs before he had to be up taking the shells in and supervising the firing. The consequence of this was—albeit hard to distinguish amid the mazy hell of a gun position in action—a pretty little counterpoint of bluish smoke: the big puff of the Armstrong, the little one of Foster's cigar.

Apart from technical details to do with aim and elevation, the question of where the shells were actually going was hardly entertained. Whenever he tried to think about the other side, an awful blankness descended upon Foster. They were just—the enemy. It could not be otherwise, for to extend any particularity towards them made the job impossible. Humanity lived on this side of the gun, began and ended within the confines of Ladysmith—and, like others, he was quite happy to exclude the Africans and Indians from that compass.

Not everyone thought like this. In the quiet of the night, that sturdy freethinker, Nevinson of the *Daily Chronicle*, thought about the black families he had seen on the way up here, as the rumour of war swept across the country. Thought, too, about the Dutch women and children being rounded up and brought in by British soldiers from farms close to Ladysmith. Most had escaped under the protection of their menfolk, but perhaps twenty or thirty of these fatherless families had been locked up in the Dopper Church, along with those long-standing Afrikaner inhabitants of Ladysmith who had not gone out to join the rebel armies, and the new "shady characters." Even in many of the Dutch cases—such as that of one Heer De Vries, a long-beard of ancient years—it was clear that such people could pose no threat to the security of Ladysmith, but the order had been given by General White and that was that.

Behind their wire fence, the prisoners made a pitiful sight when they came out to exercise each day. There were now, reflected Nevinson, so many enclosures and fortifications in and around the town, from the Klip earthworks and the sangars of the outer defences to the merest piling up of sandbags around a cottage window, that seen from above (as he supposed the men in the observation balloons saw it), it must have appeared a near-impregnable series of plots and snares. But although Ladysmith now had something of the Great Wall of China about it, there were many gaps, and the fortifications were far from impenetrable. On balance, it was fear of bristling bayonets that prevented the Boers from simply storming the place, rather than the crudely built demi-lunes, hornworks and ravelins of the town's hastily erected defences. All that traditional siegecraft and geometrical deviousness became irrelevant when the shells came whistling over: that demanded fortification of a different type—getting as low as possible in a cushioned hole, walling yourself in on top as well as at the sides. And everyone, all the town and garrison, was doing it, covering themselves in layer after layer of earth and stone, hoping that the layers underneath, those of skin and flesh and skeleton, would stay unharmed.

"It's as if we are all protecting some dreadful secret," he said to Steevens on his nightly visit to the sick man.

Enteric was taking its toll. Steevens had been sweating heavily all day, soaking the sheets, and the room smelt of diarrhoea. But he maintained his customary cheerfulness and wit.

"I know what you mean," he replied from his pillow. "We should all be shaking hands and sharing cups of tea with the Boers, telling them our innermost thoughts. Perhaps even building a new world order with them, circling outwards from the Cape, as Rhodes thinks we should. What a load of rot. Imagine it, the connection of good Afrikaner stock with British brains. He reckons he would conquer the world by that kind of admixture. To my mind, it seems a very dangerous kind of thinking. Talking of which—I've got some bits and pieces for the *Lyre,* if you might take them down to the office."

Steevens gathered a sheaf of papers from the bedside table and handed them to Nevinson.

"And if, by any miracle of fate, you lay your hands on another paper from outside, I'd give my right arm for it."

"I'll ask about, and see if any of the runners has brought one in," said Nevinson. "Probably be weeks old again, though."

"Better than nothing."

"Anything else you want?"

"Dancing girls," said Steevens loudly. "My own troupe. And a box of Turkish delight!"

His drolleries, reflected Nevinson as he went next door to his own room, were becoming more extravagant by the day. Perhaps it was the fever. He prepared himself for bed and then settled down to peruse Steevens's contributions to the *Lyre.*

THE SITUATION
The situation is unchanged.

NEWS
There is no news.

THE CONVENT
The Convent is evacuated. Nun there.

THE DIARY OF A CITIZEN
NOV. 14. General Buller has twice been seen in Ladysmith, disguised as a kaffir. His force is entrenched behind Bulwan. Hurrah!
NOV. 20. HMS *Powerful* ran aground in attempting to steam up the Klip. Feared total loss.
NOV. 21. Hear on good authority that gunner of Long Tom is Captain Dreyfus.
NOV. 22. Dreyfus rumour confirmed.

NEW SONGS
"Oft in the Stilly Night"
Boer Artillery Chorus

"Over the Hills and Far Away"
Relief Column Chorus

They're after me, they're after me,
To capture me is everyone's desire;
They're after me, they're after me,
I'm the individual they require.

By Colonel Rhodes, on account of the Boer shells which follow him
however often he changes his residence.

SKILL COMPETITION

A bottle of anchovies will be awarded to sender of first opened solu-
tion of this competition: "Name date of relief of Ladysmith."
Generals and inhabitants of Ladysmith who say "Ja" instead of "Yes"
will be disqualified as possessing exceptional sources of information.
Send answers, with small bottle of beer enclosed, to Puzzle Editor,
Ladysmith Lyre.

WHERE TO SPEND A HAPPY DAY

To the Ladies of Pretoria: Messrs. Kook and Son beg to announce a
personally conducted tour, Saturday to Monday, to witness the Siege
of Ladysmith. Full view of the enemy guaranteed. Tea and shrimps
(direct from Durban) on the train. Four-in-hand ox wagon direct
from Modder Spruit to Bulwan. Fare 15s. return. One guinea if Long
Tom is in action.

FRAGMENT OF A POEM

(found in a hole in the ground)
A pipe of Boer tobacco 'neath the blue,
A tin of meat, a bottle, and a few
Choice magazines like *Harmsworth's* or *The Strand*—
I sometimes think war has its blessings too.

26

On the day of the cricket match, a strange silence hung above the beleaguered town. Talk of a truce had been heard around Ladysmith and (so the spies said) behind the Boer lines as well. At any rate— thanks in no small part to the counter-battery fire of the naval guns, like that of Foster and his team, carted in from HMS *Powerful*—the Boer firing had slackened. A collective sense of relief had spread through the garrison and townsfolk. The quartermaster felt it, to the extent of issuing several barrels of stockfish for general use; the press corps felt it; two sisters sitting in deck chairs under some blue-gums by the edge of the pitch felt it.

The band of the Leicesters played the game in, mostly with tuba and trombone. A large crowd of Ladysmithites and assorted military were there to watch, though not all from the same vantage point. The soldiers, for propriety's sake, had been ordered to keep on the opposite side of the pitch to the ladies. Near to Bella and Jane was a large white tent which had been brought in from the cavalry lines to serve as a refreshment stall: cordials were on offer, along with sandwiches filled with cucumber and stockfish paste. Two large bowls of pears stood on a trestle table outside, covered with muslin fly-guards.

The pitch itself was a stretch of coarse grass on the outskirts of town. It wasn't, as many of the cricketers remarked, a good wicket, being hard and bumpy. The outfield was so overgrown with elephant grass that it could indeed have concealed an elephant, never mind a withered lump of leather. All seemed set to enjoy themselves in fair measure—given good weather grace of the Umpire in the Sky and, more important still, a quiet, shell-free sky, grace of Long Tom. A stake of a case of champagne, one of few remaining in the town, had been raised for the game.

The sisters watched their father walk out for the toss. Against his will, against his better judgement, against, for that matter, fact (unless Ireland were to be called a colony), he was captain of the Colonial Born . . . Lieutenant Norris, wearing a hideous parti-coloured silk cap, was captain of the Mother Country. "You call this a ball?" he said to the hotel-keeper, holding it between thumb and forefinger, with a queer look on his face.

"You're not at Lords now, sir," Kiernan replied, piqued. "In the Colonies, Lieutenant, we have to make do."

The Mother Country won the toss, and elected to bat.

"Why are we going in first?" asked a drummer boy of Hussars, who though he had played many good games for his school, had not been given a place in the team.

"Because both science and cricketing lore tell us," said Major Mott, "that a bad wicket is likely further to deteriorate over time."

The Major was talking through his sea-lion moustache, but he was right all the same. The match started at twelve and, with old Sol sending down—through a cloudless, noonday sky more devilish than heavenly—the kind of rays that would penetrate even Lieutenant Norris's cap, the few remaining stalks of grass on the crease were soon shrivelling. There were actually not many proper cricket caps to be seen; indeed, all manner of uniform was on display—one full set only of virginal white flannel, plus large displays of khaki fatigues (on the one side) and of shirtsleeves and braces (the other). Mr. Star was wearing a straw boater but pride of place went to Mr. Grimble, who— being a man of some vanity—had arrayed himself in tails, top hat and stiff collar, à la Alfred Mynn, the famous cricketer.

He must be boiling up, Bella thought. She took a handkerchief out of her sleeve and wiped her forehead. Round about her and her sister was gathered a fair proportion of Ladysmith's population, including Mrs. Frinton—who was presiding over a vat of home-made lemonade in the shade of the tent—and a noisy Bobby Greenacre. The latter was another enthusiastic young aspirant to cricket honours who had not been permitted to play.

On the other side of the pitch, Major Mott was busy explaining to the drummer boy of the Hussars that cricket was significant because it was a metaphor for life, its regular rhythms and sudden, surprising changes imitating the very phases of existence. This, he said, was why it was most important to watch the match closely.

On the near side, Bella and Jane were not looking at the match, but through it—beyond the scattered figures, beyond Major Mott and the little drummer boy—to a patch of grass where two Mother Country batsmen, Barnes and Foster, awaited their chance of glory. The two men were practising their catching, throwing the ball in high looping curves against the sunlight.

"I do hope they come in soon," said Jane. "Goodness, they're throwing it up a long way. They must have strong wrists."

Then she laughed.

"Janey," said Bella reprovingly, then laughed herself.

A couple of Imperial Light Horse were keeping score on roughly chalked blackboards, while Henry Nevinson, the journalist, was acting as chief umpire. This was assented to by the opposing teams mainly because of his supposedly neutral status, but also on the strength of his knowing W. G. Grace, who had sometimes signed his names to the charity-seeking letters sent out from Toynbee Hall when Nevinson worked there. What a fine specimen of man he was, the Champion. The journalist remembered writing in his diary of the great cricketing doctor, "and all his powers spent on knocking balls about! What might he not have done a thousand years ago!"

Initial progress at Ladysmith seemed (as Nevinson further observed) a thousandfold slower than if W.G. had been on the pitch. Messrs. Greenacre and Grimble opened the Colonial Born bowling. At first both bowled too short and were ruthlessly cut and pulled. Once they steadied down, they took a wicket apiece, and thereafter Mother Country wickets began to fall. Mr. Star, the baker, surprised everyone with a great catch, picking a skimming ball out of the air as if he had known, a few seconds before, where it was going to be. At fifty-six for four, Tom Barnes came in and, easy and alert at the wicket, began to forge a useful partnership with Herbert Foster. The latter was frail and sensitive, a little awkward in his movements, but he gave the Colonials beans: his highlight was a six into the blue-gums, off a ball by Mr. Kiernan. The same bowler, however, finally caused his downfall, with a smart caught and bowled. Barnes went out through a copybook l.b.w. and the tail was then mopped up, leaving a final target of one hundred and fifty-three runs.

"I told you I was feeling lucky," said Foster during the break.

The drummer boy of the Hussars had been sent over to collect trays of food and drink from Mrs. Frinton, and now the two men were lying on the grass, a little away from the rest of the team. Tom finished his mouthful of fish-paste sandwich.

"It's not luck," he said. "It's all worked out, up there."

He lay back on the grass and looked up into the sky: the hard, hot blue of the first innings had softened, and now a few large white galleons were beginning to sail over from the crest of the Drakensberg.

"You reckon?" queried Foster, as if it were a matter of little import.

"All shall be revealed before stumps are pulled," said Tom, with mock solemnity. He turned his head to where Jane and Bella were sitting, on the opposite side of the pitch. He thought he could hear them laughing, or maybe it was just in his head, this engaging giggle of young girls. "Not fair, this no-association rule, considering."

"Considering what?"

"Considering that even the pluckiest fellow needs the comfort of womankind. We're under fire, after all."

Foster sat up and rubbed his elbow. "Hardly," he said. "I mean, we're not now, are we?"

"Looks like we are." Tom nodded in the direction of Lieutenant Norris, who was irritatedly beckoning them over for a bracing talk.

Once the break was over, the correspondent-umpire took up his position and watched with a cold eye. Mr. Grimble opened the account for the Colonial Born, strutting out in his long coat like a peacock. The impression was marred only by his carrying of the bat over his shoulder. Off the very first ball (unidentified bowler) he gave a chance to Major Mott at square leg, but it was not held. The Mother Country supporters groaned with disappointment.

Foster was keeping wicket, cheroot between his lips, and Tom Barnes next to bowl. He proceeded to deliver three overs of hostile inswingers, one delivery cracking Mr. Grimble on the ankle.

"That was a bit quick," said Nevinson to Barnes, censoriously.

"It's my style."

Kneeling, his coattails spread on the crease like a bridal gown, Mr. Grimble inspected his bruised ankle. There was then some talk of a runner being called for, but the farmer decided in the end to persevere, to a chorus of bravos. To give him his due, he proved a stayer, persisting while other Colonial Born batsmen came and went.

Star the baker, walking out, announced: "I mean to lay on the wood."

He returned without scoring, saying the wicket was untrue.

By the time it was Leo Kiernan's turn to pad up, the Colonial Born were falling like dead men, six dismissed in the first eight overs.

"I'll stop this rot," he said to Bella as he strode out to join Mr. Grimble, hefting the bat in his hand. "Good God, this must weigh four pounds. And it looks like the kaffir's dog has been at it."

By now, Tom having ceased bowling, Bella was beginning to lose interest. But she supposed she ought to see how Father got on.

"He is taking it all very seriously," she said to Jane, beside her.

"Of course he is. I hope Herbert doesn't stump him out, or else he will never like him."

"He probably won't ever anyway."

"He'll come round—more than he will with Tom anyway, since he was so rude."

They fell silent, concentrating on the figures as they moved about on the carpet of yellowing veld. Although Father didn't look like the hero to redeem the score, he acquitted himself well. The first ball came and he blocked it stoutly. Then the second—and then an ostrich, which had been brought into town for meat, ran out over the pitch. Play was suspended for ten minutes or so while they tried to catch it. Everybody rushed about in circles, and Father collided with Mr. Grimble, whose top hat fell off.

As she watched the ostrich run about, jerking its neck hither and thither, Bella was reminded of a story she had once heard: how, when hunting the outlandish birds, the Bushmen who lived around here long ago would dress up in feathers and go into the middle of a flock to shoot them with poisoned arrows, maintaining the illusion of being ostriches even as they killed them. Not far outside the town was a Bushman cave with paintings in it that she and Jane had once explored, but the paintings did not show that scene. Perhaps it was just a tall tale.

Finally, play resumed. Bella reached down for the glass next to the deck chair and took a sip of lemonade. The taste reminded her of childhood, stirring faint memories of her mother which, together with the comforting murmur of the game, made her feel dreamy.

She tried to concentrate on the game. It was quite soothing to watch. Most of the time, it seemed to her, people didn't seem to be doing anything, just loafing about, lost in their own reflections, alone with their thoughts. Some, like Foster, were smoking and some even had their hands in their pockets.

The bowlers changed. Mr. Grimble hit the ball in the air past square leg, narrowly missing being caught by Major Mott. The ball rolled under the rope close to her. She wondered whether to get up and throw it in, but then the Major trundled past her, his moustache jiggling up and down. It really was very large, in the handlebar style, and as the Major threw in, Bella wondered whether children liked to ask him if they could pull it, to see if it was real. She could hardly resist the inclination herself.

Moustaches apart, the drowsy sounds of the game were the things most present in Bella's head—the applause, the clicks and thumps, the shouted appeals, "Well played!" and "Yes! No! Get back!"—which, in their mixed-up totality, made the whole thing all the more soporific. Other sounds too, that weren't properly part of it, contributed to the somnolent effect: the cooing of collared doves in the blue-gums; the clank of Mrs. Frinton's ladle in the lemonade vat; the snuffling of a cavalryman's charger that had been tied to a guy-rope of the tent and—these last were not peaceful, that had to be conceded—the croak of a pair of ravens nesting in a nearby outcrop of rock, their intimation of death punctuating an all-too-lively repetitive tapping of ball on bat.

That came from Bobby Greenacre, showing off how long he could keep the ball bouncing on the bat. He was behind Bella, and every time the ball fell to the ground he exclaimed in disappointment.

"Shouldn't you be over with the men?" she said over her shoulder.

"Oh! You've ruined my concentration," he replied, coming round in front of her.

"Sorry, Bobby," said Bella, wearily.

He retrieved the ball from where it had rolled under a tent flap and began bouncing it on the bat again.

"But I suppose you're right, Miss Kiernan," he said at length. With that he set off along the edge of the pitch, still bouncing the ball as he walked, dancing from side to side to keep it going.

"He's so annoying," said Jane, getting up to fetch a pear from the table nearby.

"Want one?"

"Please."

Bella watched the Greenacre boy make his way to the military supporters and begin his own private game with the drummer boy, who
bowled to him along the perimeter. Jane came back, handed a pear to
Bella, and sat down on the chair's striped canvas.

"He's just enjoying himself," Bella said. "It must be strange, all
this, if you're a child."

"Strange for all of us. Look at Herbert in all his kit."

Bella bit into the pear, looked out at Foster crouched down at the
wicket, and then beyond—through the crisscrossed figures in the
bright light—at the two young hopefuls. Mostly Bobby seemed to be
missing the drummer boy's hard-flung balls, but he did get a fair
knock at one, and out it went into the pitch proper, to hit Major Mott
in the ribs.

"You're right, he is annoying," said Bella, as Bobby ran out to
retrieve the rogue ball.

Out in the slips, Tom Barnes was annoyed too, for three reasons.
Firstly because he wasn't bowling. Secondly because he had just
missed an edge from Bella's father. Too fast, it had caught him on the
thumbnail, which was now swelling up. The thumb was the same one
which had been blistered by the piece of hot shell he had picked up,
and was consequently very painful. The third reason was that he
didn't respect his captain. Tom played a lot of cricket for the village at
home. In his view Lieutenant Norris hadn't disposed his fielders cor-
rectly—they were out too deep—and, like all bad captains, was bowling too much himself.

"That's gone for four at least," he muttered to no one in particular
as a ball was lifted into deep mid-off. "We are too many on the on
side."

"Tell the cap to move someone over," said Foster, crouched in his
wicket-keeper's position.

"I can't," said Tom. "He's in my unit."

"Bugger!" cried out Foster. "Bugger!" He straightened and began
to jump around. "My smoke's gone down my pad!"

He continued leaping like a dervish. Tom laughed, until the gunner finally extricated the still-glowing cheroot from between pad and
leg. At the other end, Norris was standing hand on hip, waiting for
the keeper to sort himself out.

They settled down to concentrate on the next ball. As if he had sensed the mounting unease of the team (they had been positive at first, but now progress was slowing and collective doubts were setting in), Norris had begun to vary his line, this time delivering a ball that sent Grimble's off-stump sideways.

"How's that?" went up the chorus, and at the other end the dour figure of Nevinson gave the sign. Norris beamed.

"That was a flyer, I have to admit," remarked Foster, as he collected up the ball in his keeper's glove and tossed it back up the pitch.

"Not bad," said Tom, wishing that it was his turn. He looked into the unkempt outfield, and then round to the tent, with its crowd of women—among them Bella—and then her father, damn him, swept a high, ballooning ball for six, sending it sailing over the blue-gums, just as Foster had in the previous innings. The Ladysmith supporters cheered hysterically, leaping up and down, though Bella, upon whom Tom kept his eye fixed, didn't stir from her chair. He wondered whether that was slightly unnatural. The triumphant batsman was her father, after all, even if he was a bit of a grouch.

In fact, Bella had been concentrating on something high above her father's head. She thought she had seen movement around the spinney, high in the hills, where the Boers kept one of their heavy Krupp guns. She mentioned it to Jane, but her sister pooh-poohed her fears.

"Oh, they won't shell us on the Sabbath. They're Christians and gentlemen, even if they are Boers. Anyway, they're probably enjoying the game through their field glasses."

"Boers don't understand cricket, sis. Well, neither do I actually."

"Nor me. Look, your Tom's back on bowling."

The tumble of Colonial Born wickets seemed to have halted at the lower end of the batting order, and the tag-end batsmen were making a good fist of it. With the mounting runs came further disillusion among the Mother Country. Even Norris conceded that they needed to make something happen, and with some urging from Foster allowed Tom Barnes to take the ball.

So it was that the mysterious controlling force of destiny (which struck Bella as rather fortuitous) decreed that Tom should be bowling to Father, while Foster crouched behind, alert and expectant, his wicket-keeper's gloves, pads and leather helmet as armour-like as the accoutrements of a medieval knight. And yet she should not have thought these an encumbrance, if Foster's handling of the next ball was anything to go by.

Bella watched Tom pace out, turn, run back to the crease and let fly. A scorcher, it first made Father jerk back, so that the cap fell off to reveal his red hair, and then—passing high above the off stump—caused Foster to leap acrobatically to the right as he enclosed the ball in his capacious glove. The cries of triumph of Mother Country supporters rose in unison as the gunner rolled to one side and clambered to his feet. But did they anticipate the facts? Had ball touched bat, or not? As Foster made his appeal, all eyes were on Nevinson, waiting for movement.

But that grave adjudicator gave only a stern compression of his brow, keeping his hands firmly behind his back. The next ball he called over, and the loose pattern of fielders broke up as they moved across the pitch to take up their new positions.

Now Norris was bowling again, and it was here that the balance of the game swung. In spite of Mother Country worries, at sixty-two for seven it had looked—to Nevinson's impartial eye—as if the Colonial Born were on the rack. But then in came Mr. Greenacre, who was careful but productive. This new batsman's fruitful caution would, in combination with further flamboyant striking by Mr. Kiernan, see the Ladysmithites home. Or so Nevinson believed.

Even the weather seemed to change in those closing stages. As the day declined, a sluggish draught of wind blew away the vibrating heat and broke up the large, isolated clouds that had been floating across from the Drakensberg. Their luxury liners and heavily laden men-o'-war now disintegrated into a flotilla of lesser craft—steam packets, skiffs and wherries, cutters. As each fragment of cloud eased imperceptibly away, the overall effect was to increase the shade over the pitch, and an air of coolness descended upon the players. A resounding crack alerted Nevinson to Kiernan taking a four off his leg stump. He only caught the end of the stroke. Rather outlandish, but effective. The next ball, though, the correspondent gave Greenacre out l.b.w., reflecting that caution can sometimes let you down . . .

It fell to another batsman to help Leo Kiernan round things off. With the Colonial Born needing one run to win, and their father himself needing a six to reach his own fifty, even Jane and Bella were on tenterhooks. Then, just as the bowler was running up, Bella happened to look up at the hills again.

She understood at once the significance of what she saw: in the middle of the spinney, a puff of white smoke, a noise like a gong, and then—too soon, too soon—a hissing sound. Norris stopped dead in the middle of his run-up, Father's bat froze at the end of his arms as if it was part of them; others scattered, still not wise to the rule of keeping still. Tom and Foster, wise heads, kept their positions. Foster, to his credit, moved not an inch, maintaining his keeper's crouch perfectly as, out of the cloudless sky above the pitch, the canister burst like a seed head.

The iron cascaded down.

Astonishingly, as it appeared in the quiet afterwards, there seemed to be no casualties among players or spectators. Worst off were the blue-gum trees, which, rained upon by searing metal, sputtered and glowed.

"My God," whispered Jane, "that was lucky."

Bella's throat was too dry to speak; she looked up at the sky again, as if for another shell, and saw only the golden fizz of the gum trees.

On the field, the cricketers slowly regathered, resuming their positions. No earthly power would prevent the conclusion of the game: the Colonial Born, the Mother Country, the Empire itself was at one in this. Men near the wicket kicked glowing splinters of steel into the outfield.

Bella heard Father's voice ring across the pitch. "Come on, let's finish it, I've got a fifty to make. The end is close at hand!"

A dry, crackling laugh rustled across the pitch. Major Mott's it was, and then everyone, nearly, was laughing with the blessed relief of it all. Norris walked back to his scuff mark, ready to bowl again: that last ball that would come, six or no six, siege or no siege. Tom readied himself in the slips, glancing at Foster. What a brick, Tom thought. The keeper was still crouching in his position, his pads erect, gloved hands out. He hadn't moved a muscle—although he looked a trifle pale. But then they all did.

"Ready then, Herbert?" Tom said affectionately. He'd never used that forename before, not knowing Foster very well, but what they'd just been through brought all those men closer together. The keeper made no reply. He was concentrating, his eye trained on the line of Norris's vicious outswing.

Leo Kiernan swung for his six, missed. The ball hit Foster chest-on. He fell over to one side. Tom sighed with relief. The Mother

Country had won. Then he heard a strange noise, like the first sound—the very first, that is almost not to be heard—of a kettle coming to the boil: Foster's mouth, the breath coming out of.

"I say, are you all right?" Tom leaned down over the wicket-keeper, whose knees were drawn up uncomfortably into his belly.

"Winded, is he?" asked Kiernan, leaning on his bat.

Tom saw how Foster's lips, still whistling, were blue; how the leather helmet was ripped at the very crown of the head where a small piece of shrapnel, plunging downwards, had passed through his skull. For Foster, who died none the wiser, the last-but-one-ball had also been the last. Tom looked at Kiernan, whose eyes were popping, and then over to Bella and Jane. The latter had got up out of her deck chair and was running towards them. As she ran, her dress was rippling. Behind her, fanned by the wind, a tall curtain of flame gathered in the blasted trees.

The Tower

27

Bella looked for her mirror, opening drawers and pulling aside curtains. She couldn't understand it. The thing seemed to have disappeared. She soon abandoned the search, however. There were more important things to worry about. For the second night running, she climbed into bed with her sister. The first night, Jane's sobbing had been quiet: convulsive and rapid, but quiet. Tonight the sobs were just as regular, except that they were broken with involuntary cries and shudders. These cries were much louder than the sobbing and had a raw quality to them: something of an animal caught in a trap. Bella held her close, cupping her with her own body, so that the heat of their skins interpenetrated their nightgowns.

In the middle of the night, Bella woke to find Jane smoking a kaffir pipe on the window seat, her legs gathered up beneath her on the warped wood.

"Janey," she exclaimed. "Come back to bed."

"I'm all right. Leave me."

The room was full of sweetly scented smoke.

"Where did you get that thing?" asked Bella.

"The Zulu woman. Nandi . . . she saw me crying, and said it would help."

"You shouldn't."

"Leave me."

Bella thought it was best to do so. Maybe the pipe would help. Whenever she had pressed Jane in any way since Foster's death, it had resulted in tears, so now she thought it sensible to let her be. She tried to watch over her for a while—sitting there wide-eyed in the window, amid plumes of smoke shot through with moonlight—but then sleep won the battle.

In the morning, Jane was still at the window. Bella got up quickly and rushed to her. An ember from the pipe had burned a hole in her gown. There were dabs of ash on the fabric and on the skin of her breasts. Her eyes were hollow and vacant.

"Jane . . . ," Bella said, in a tone somewhere between reproach and concern, and took her by the shoulders. Her sister slumped into her arms and whimpered. Bella helped her back to the bed, and pulled the covers over her. She sat there stroking her hair for a while, and then, when it seemed she was asleep, dressed and went downstairs to make her some breakfast.

Her father was in the kitchen. "How's Jane?" he said.

"Not good. She didn't sleep."

"Should I go and see her?"

"Best not now. I think she's gone off."

"Do you reckon we should get a doctor?"

"Maybe. I don't know if it would help. She has become locked up in herself. Let's see how she does today."

Bella made up a tray of bread (there was no jam or butter now), mealie porridge and tea without milk, adding to the last the final shakings of the sugar bag, and took it upstairs. Jane was awake again, sitting up in bed and staring straight in front of her.

"You must eat, Janey."

She shook her head.

"Please." Bella held out the cup of tea.

Jane took it, and sipped. And then put it down. Bella picked up the mealies bowl and began to spoon the grey porridge into her sister's slack mouth. It was dreadfully slow. Every now and then Jane turned her head, and a dribble of porridge came out of the side of her mouth. Bella fetched a handkerchief from the chest of drawers and wiped Jane's face. Spoon. Then more tea. And the bread. Finally it was finished.

"Good," Bella said, rubbing Jane's arm.

Then a shell went off nearby, and Ladysmith's guns began to return fire. Jane lifted both her hands to her face and started screaming, throwing the tray to the floor and kicking out her legs like an infant. Bella climbed onto the bed and pulled her close, gathering her like a ball and holding her tight until the thrashing stopped. Still the guns rumbled and roared, and after every sound Jane started gasping hoarsely. Bella held her, waited. Slowly her sister relaxed, and then, with a regular moaning noise, fell into some sort of sleep. Bella gathered up the scattered breakfast things and carried the tray downstairs.

Later, when Bella went up to check on Jane again, she found her sitting naked in a corner of the room. She was shivering, in spite of the heat outside. She had also been sick, and there was vomit on the bedclothes. When Bella tried to pick her up, reaching under her arms, she just let her weight go dead. The elder girl squatted down next to her.

"Help me, Janey. Don't be like this."

No reply. Her sister's face, that face which she knew as well as her own, registered no expression—just stared through her. Bella looked back, and shook her head. Outside, the sound of shellfire came again. She put her hands over Jane's ears.

Once the bombardment had ceased, Bella went out onto the landing to fetch fresh bedclothes from the cupboard. Returning with a bundle she found her sister lying on her front on the floor, with her arms out. Her temple and one ear were flat against the boards, as if she were listening for something. Dropping her bundle on the floor, Bella picked out a blanket and laid it over the prone figure of her sister. She then removed the soiled bedclothes and took them through to the bathroom. No water to clean them with. She remade the bed with fresh linen and with great difficulty half heaved, half cajoled Jane back into it.

This was no good, they would have to get her a doctor . . . Or take her down to Intombi, where the nuns could give her proper care. She, Bella, would go too; Father would just have to manage in the hotel on his own. Nandi could help. She went downstairs to the bar to tell him.

It was an ordinary evening at the Royal Hotel—an ordinary evening in siege time, that is, which is different from ordinary time. Expectancy hung over everything. Critical but chronic, specific but elastic, this expectancy was the pervasive, overwhelming condition. It was the element in which townsfolk and garrison existed, but it was also as elusive as the will-o'-the-wisp. For like the lamps above the Royal's dining tables, which could be moved lower or higher by means of a pulley (according to the number and relative intimacy of the diners), expectancy was governed by the day, the hour, the minute at which the relief column would arrive. Hope abolished being an impossible and unpatriotic condition, as news of the approach of General Buller came, went and returned, hope deferred became the only constant note.

Yet, if truth be told, there were other constants, even if they appeared to belong to another era—a lost, machineless time of troubadours and old-style crafts, romance and derring-do. Ironically enough, it was a machine that evoked these sentiments among the company at the Royal that night, as they ate their meagre dinners— the musical box, playing through its customary roster of songs and tunes: "The Lincolnshire Poacher," "The March of the Cameron Men," "The Old Folks at Home". . .

It was during this last that a shell spun through the slates of the roof and exploded in the hallway outside the dining room. The bar filled with acrid smoke within seconds. Bella had hardly time to take cover before another shell-burst ripped through the building—from below, as it seemed, entering the window of a cellar room directly beneath the main dining room. The floor collapsed, then a wall. The tables were swept clear of everything, and she saw her father blown from his stool at the edge of the bar; he seemed to be flung halfway across the room. Bottles flew off the shelves and exploded on the floor. Aware only of a tearing sound and the terrible fumes filling her lungs, Bella was tumbled down by the blast and, receiving a violent blow on the side of the head, lost consciousness.

Very quickly afterwards, as a vast volume of smoke and dust billowed out of the broken doors and smashed windows, came a shocked silence—punctured only by the moaning of the injured, the sound of falling plaster, and the eerie continuance of the musical box, playing on regardless: *There's where my heart is turning ever, There's where the old folks stay* . . .

28

The tune woke her, played again in the machine of her head. Also a violent image . . . crashing debris . . . Father flying through the air. She wasn't sure whether she was awake or sleeping. Yes, awake: in the emergency hospital at the Town Hall. High ceiling. Her father was sitting on the bed, holding her hand. Beneath a bandage, her temple was hurting. Realizing that her father, too, had a wound—a long, raw gash down his cheek—she started to cry.

"It's all right," her father said, "it's all right."

"What happened? Your face . . ."

"A shell hit the hotel. I got knocked off my stool—this is just from a glass splinter—and you banged your head on a table."

Bella lay on the bed absorbing this information; then, realizing something was missing, sat bolt upright.

"Where's Janey? Is she hurt?" She threw off the bedclothes and tried to get out. Her father pressed her down.

"It's all right. Calm down. She's not hurt. Not injured, anyway. She has been taken to Intombi."

"No. She can't go on her own. I must go."

"You can't. The Boers won't let anyone through unless they are clearly ill."

As Bella considered this (had Jane got so bad that even the Boer guards on the railway line could see she was suffering?), she slowly became aware of her surroundings. All around her, on beds and on stretchers set down on the floor, lay wounded soldiers and civilians. Many were mumbling quietly to themselves. The only other noise was that of the nurses' shoes clacking on the tiles.

Bella looked back at her father, accusingly.

"Why did you let her go? She can't look after herself."

"A nurse has gone with her."

Bella's temple started to throb. She put up her hand and felt a dressing, and underneath it a large, tender lump. She looked at her father's florid, wounded face. There were tears running down his cheeks, into the open gash. He reached over and took her in his arms.

"The hotel is destroyed," he said, into her shoulder.

Later that day, when she was strong enough to get up, Bella went with their father to see for herself. It was true. The roof was crashed in, right in the middle, and all three levels had suffered considerable damage. Much of the flooring of the bar and dining room had been ripped up and was jammed through the ceiling, boards sticking up bizarrely into the bedrooms above. Doors had been torn off their hinges, bottles, crockery and the glass of pictures reduced to powder. The only room left unscathed was the Star Room, where she saw that Father had laid out a bedroll. Everywhere else, there were fragments of metal, splinters of wood, and chunks of masonry and plaster. Her clothes and belongings, spilled from her wardrobes and drawers and flung about, had mainly been ruined. Seeing the devastation, Bella burst into tears again.

"Come on," said Father, putting his arm round her. "Gather up what you can. I've managed to get a place for you by the river, with Mrs. Frinton. Her cottage has been shelled too."

"In those tunnels? I'm not going there. Why can't I stay here with you?"

"You must. It'll be safer. There is a separate set of tunnels for women and children now."

"I don't want to."

He took her by the shoulders, and then pulled her to him. "Don't argue. You will be protected from the bombs there, and that is the most important thing."

Clutching each other, they stood for a few minutes in the ruins like that, and as her father pressed her against his chest, Bella felt closer to him than she had ever before. She wept again, but these were happier tears.

"Come on now," he said, after a while. Seeing she had no choice, Bella climbed into her blasted room and, turning over smashed pieces of wood and brick, picked out some clothes and other belongings. All were covered with dust and soot, and she had to shake them before putting them into a battered suitcase.

"Take some bedding, too," said her father from the doorway.

"I won't have room."

"I'll carry it. You'll need something for a groundsheet as well."

A groundsheet! The very thought of it made Bella shudder with horror.

It was nearly dusk when they reached the Klip earthworks, though it was still light enough for Bella to see that she needn't have bothered shaking her clothes. The area outside the entrances was a sea of mud and puddles, and out of the caves and holes peered a number of dishevelled women. Father led her towards a small yellow flame over which Mrs. Frinton was attempting to coax some warmth into a billy of murky water.

"So you are here," said the widow. "Just in time for tea—though I am afraid it will taste horrible."

She took the billy off the tripod above the fire. "I'll show you your room, as we are styling them."

The old woman picked up a hurricane lamp and bent down to enter one of the holes, the sides of which were shored up by fat sandbags and roughly shaped wooden posts. Bella and her father followed. Even by the meagre light, she could see that she had entered some kind of labyrinth. Steps, corridors, thresholds: the tunnel spread out into a network of side vaults and chambers, from each of which Bella could hear the voices of women and children, and here and there caught a glimpse of lamplight, or heard the clank of a bucket.

"Here we are," said Mrs. Frinton, stooping. "You're lucky, you got the last pallet. They've run out of wood now."

She gestured into a narrow chamber that smelt of newly turned earth. There was also a sweeter smell, like that of fields in summer. Thick wooden pillars held up the roof beams, which were made of old railway sleepers. The roof and walls were bales of hay—which accounted for the other smell.

"Three trusses thick," said Mrs. Frinton, bouncing her little fist against one of the hay walls. "Though I won't be surprised if they come and take it away for the horses soon."

Bella stepped inside, feeling her father behind her, with his bundle of bedding and tarpaulin.

"I'd better put the groundsheet down first," he said.

She stood aside to let him go in and then, once he was finished, went mutely inside to put her suitcase at the foot of the roughly made slats of wood that were now her bed.

"There's a lamp hanging at the head," said Mrs. Frinton from outside.

"I've got a match," said Bella's father.

He came through into the chamber with her, on the other side of the pallet, and bent close over the lamp, striking the match several times before he was able to light it. When it was finally done, his face and hair brightened in the glow.

He looked at her across the pallet. "You'll be safe here, my love. And it will be over soon. You will manage, won't you?"

"Of course she'll manage," said Mrs. Frinton brusquely. "There's lots of us managing here. The townies soon fit in. To begin with, why don't you come up and have that cup of tea?"

Bella followed them out, and squatted down next to the fire as Mrs. Frinton put the billy back on.

"So what are you going to do now, Mr. Kiernan?" said the widow. "With the hotel bombed? It must be a blow."

"Yes," said Bella's father, quietly. "A blow. It is certainly that, though it is Jane's situation I am most worried about."

"She'll mend," said the widow. "She's young enough and strong enough."

Shivering with the cold, Bella felt distant from them both, even though she shared her father's worries about Jane. How different he was now, in crisis, how much more thoughtful; what would it be like when things got back to normal? If they got back to normal. She heard his voice. "I suppose I'll spend my time rebuilding what I can. And then there's the town council. There's still work to do there. My personal view is that we should get all you women and children out to Intombi, make a deal with the Boers. It isn't right that you should have to live like this."

They talked on a little longer, and then her father got up to go. Bidding her goodbye, he told Bella that she should not come up into the town except in an emergency. "I don't want another daughter falling ill," he said. "Or being exposed to shellfire."

29

Emerging in the morning, after an uncomfortable night, Bella shook hay and earth from her hair and petticoats. Now she could get a clearer view of her surroundings. The sun was out—was getting very hot, in fact—and the pools of water outside the earthworks were quickly drying up. There were, she noticed, tunnel entrances all along the bank of the river now, far more than on her previous visit, and a little further along she could see the men's area, where among those sitting down to their breakfast she spotted the distinctive figure of the barber, Torres.

"We've had a delivery."

Mrs. Frinton's voice. Bella turned round to see the widow removing various items from a flour sack.

"Siege bread, tinned meat, a few potatoes, a little bit of tea . . . we're all on army rations down here now. We've got some chickens and a cow over the other side, though, and sometimes I can get a few eggs and a drop of milk. Just bread for breakfast today, though, I'm afraid. Oh for some bacon . . ."

Handing her two small, grey rolls, Mrs. Frinton went down to the river's edge to get water for the billy. Bella looked about: at women cooking or washing their clothes in tin buckets; at mothers rubbing their children's mud-covered faces with the corners of their gowns. Many of these women, she thought, had a hunted look about them. Father was right: they should all have gone to Intombi while they had the chance.

Mrs. Frinton came back, and they began to eat their breakfast while waiting for the water to boil.

"You will find life here depends entirely on the level of shelling," said the widow. Bella nodded; it was obvious, after all, the same in the whole of Ladysmith.

"I do a lot of sewing," said Mrs. Frinton brightly, as she stirred the tea leaves in the billy. "We have a circle." The younger woman smiled in answer—deceptively, as she hated sewing, always pricking her finger.

Useful work seemed to be on the widow's mind, for she gestured up the bank, in the direction of the male tunnels. "The men go fishing, mostly: for eels in the river. They throw long handlines in."

"Eels? They eat them?"

"Of course. They are all right, if you can find a little oil and salt to go with them."

Bella chewed on her roll, which tasted like cardboard, and looked down at the river. The surroundings could, she supposed, be called pretty: there was whispering bankside vegetation all around, from which starry kingfishers and dun-coloured water rats went to and fro, and the sky above was a radiant blue. But the water itself was filthy, a yellow streak. And everywhere was the smell of excrement, everywhere the greenish dollops and crusts of horse, mule and ox dung—all the livestock in Ladysmith was watered at the Klip now. She looked at her tea, convinced it had a strong smell of the stable. Maybe she was just smelling the hay on herself.

"Is it safe, this water?"

Mrs. Frinton made an expression of helplessness. "Stiff with typhoid, probably, unless you boil it. But we have, so that's that."

Bella looked at her cup again, but was saved a decision on whether to drink any more of it by the yowling, screeching sound of a shell. All of a sudden, there was a general commotion around the riverbank as everyone gathered up what they could and dashed back into the tunnels. On the way in, Bella tripped on the corner of a mattress someone had pulled out into the main gallery, and fell flat on her face in the mud.

As a consequence, she spent the first morning of her new life curled up on her pallet. She had cleaned herself as best she could, but still felt grubby and despondent and unwilling to meet the world. She thought about Jane, trying to imagine her sister's rosy, healthy-looking face—the face of before—as if by doing so she could bring it back. She thought about Tom Barnes, too, his dark hair and the buttons and belt on his uniform; she wondered if she would see him again soon. And she thought about her father, and the odd change that the bombing of the hotel had wrought in him. All the while she could hear the roar of shell and, if one came near, feel the walls of the shelter shift and sway. When that happened, her heart beat hard, and her breath grew short. She tried to shoo away the idea of being trapped in there, of the beams falling and then a ton of smothering earth . . . She dreaded to think further. Besides, hadn't Mrs. Frinton said the tunnels had been built by the best mining engineers out of the Rand, and could withstand the heaviest bombardment?

By noon, the shelling had eased. At lunchtime, the widow came to get her, peering through the gloom.

"You can't stay in there the whole time. What we usually do is gather together in the main entrance, and talk. I've got a spare chair you can sit on."

Bella went out, to join her and the small group of other ladies sitting in the gallery at the opening of the tunnels. They had spread a tarpaulin out on the dirt, and covered it with pillows and eiderdowns. Most, as Mrs. Frinton had said, were sewing; others were playing cards or reading. Lunch was potato soup with more of the grey rolls: the potatoes must have been near rotten, because the soup tasted awful. Already feeling queasy, when Bella saw a drawn and haggard woman chewing up mouthfuls of roll and then putting the wet, softened pieces into her baby's mouth, she had to run out and be sick.

Clamping her hand over her own mouth, Bella ran round the back of the bank into which the shelter was dug. As she was finishing, she became aware that she was being observed. A bare-chested man was standing at the back of the men's shelter, with his foot on the blade of a spade. He waved. She recognized the tall, slender figure as that of Torres. He beckoned her over.

"Hello," said the Portuguese, when she reached him. "I saw you vomiting. I would have come to you but, you know, the rules . . . Do you have enteric?"

"No, it's nothing," said Bella, embarrassed at his directness. "Just the combination of nerves and some rotten vegetables."

"Well, you must be careful, as there is much disease here. It's nice to see you, although I am sorry to hear about the hotel."

"I suppose we must suffer like everyone," said Bella. "It was only a matter of time, anyway. They will get all the big buildings in the end." She realized she was blushing, partly on account of his having seen her being sick; partly because his bare chest and spade reminded her of their encounter on her previous visit. Something was different this time, she noticed. He had a tattoo on his arm.

"What are you doing?" she said, her eyes trying to make out the legend incorporated in the tattoo.

"You will see," he replied, and dug down further into the soil of the bank.

She watched him bend over the spade. When he levered up clods of earth, the muscles of his back stood out sharply.

"Come on," she said, a little coquettishly. "Tell me."

He threw down the spade and, crouching by the hole, reached into it. "It's gardening, Ladysmith style." Pushing and pulling at something in the ground, he eventually tugged out a large fragment of shell, a great chunk of blackened iron.

"Oh, I see," said Bella. She had heard that soldiers and people in the town were gathering up these things as mementoes. The poor drummer boy of the Hussars had been blinded when he tried to knock the fuse out of one of these treasures with a hammer. He was an awfully stupid and awfully unmilitary drummer boy, Major Mott had said; and a lucky one too—if the main charge had not been defective, the Major said, the boy would have been atomized.

"Be careful," she said, recalling the incident, and taking a step back.

"Don't be afraid. It is only a broken-off piece. All the detonation is gone."

"Still . . ."

"It fell only this morning, Miss Kiernan," said the barber, as if that were any guarantee of safety. Then, bowing, he presented it to her. "I would like you to accept it as a trophy, with my compliments."

Bella reached out and took the piece of metal. It was so heavy it made her hand drop with the weight.

"I can't carry it," she said. "You'll have to get me a lighter one."

Torres picked up his spade and, crooking his elbow, leant his tattooed arm on the handle. "I will get you a complete shell instead. A little one. What do they say? Pom-pom?"

"That would be nice. Though I don't know where I would put it." She moved closer to him. "What's that design on your arm?"

He held it out. "My Ladysmith tattoo."

She took his arm and read *Siege of Ladysmith, 1899,* beneath a picture of a wheeled gun.

"Who did it?"

"I did it myself. It is one of the things we barbers know. I have been doing it for many people in the tunnels. To pass the time. I will do you one, if you like."

"I couldn't," said Bella, abashed.

"It would be a pleasure," Torres countered. "I . . ."

He was interrupted by the whirr of a shell. Quickly taking her hand, he ran down with her to the men's shelter. As the guns began to roar once more, Bella found herself among a crowd of staring menfolk. Apart from smelling strongly of sweat and tobacco, and showing more evidence of card and chess playing, the men's gallery was much the same as her own: a cellar-like place with chairs and mattresses laid out on a tarpaulin for comfortable lounging. In the back, near the entrances to the individual tunnels, a smoky hurricane lamp gave out a sparse light. She crouched down between the barber and a wooden pillar, trying to make herself unobtrusive. But still they all just stared at her, the light from the lamp making the eyes of those in the rear shine eerily. They reminded her of the jackals and servals whose eyes could sometimes be seen at night on the edges of the town.

"Well," said a rough voice, "the dago has got himself a ride."

In a second Torres had the man by the throat and was grappling him to the ground. Other men in the gallery cheered and a space cleared around the wrestling men. A chair was tipped up, and as the two bodies turned over and over on the tarpaulin, she caught glimpses of Torres's brown face and of the unshaven one of the other man, whose lips were drawn back over his teeth like those of a cornered animal. Bella was frightened, and shocked by how quickly it had all happened. She thought of running away, but felt she could not leave Torres, who now seemed to be getting the worst of the fight. The other man had him pinned down. He was raising his fist. She knew she must do something.

So she cried out, as loud as she was able. The shrillness of it caught them unawares. The gallery fell suddenly silent, and the man on top of Torres—she did not recognize him, but from his heavy canvas clothes and steel helmet thought he must be one of the rough uitlander miners who had come down from Johannesburg—lowered his fist. At that instant another man in a helmet came over and pulled him off Torres, who got to his feet and dusted himself down.

All that could be heard was the booming of the guns outside.

Full of inquisitive silence, the men crowded round Bella, Torres and his antagonist. In closer proximity, she was again aware of how bad they all smelled.

"Apologize to Miss Kiernan," said Torres, his eyes blazing.

"It's all right," said Bella. "Please. Just stop fighting."

"No, he insulted you," exclaimed Torres. "He must apologize."

"Yes, tell the lady you are sorry," said someone else, and then suddenly everyone in the cave seemed to be on Torres's side. But the other man just spat on the ground, and retreated into the darkness.

Once the brouhaha had died down, the men spoiled Bella terribly, bringing her bits and pieces of food, as if to atone for the behaviour of their fellow. A tall man in an overcoat made a cup of tea and carried it over to her, taking great care not to spill it. One even fried up some slices of eel, but the greasy look of them turned her stomach and she had to refuse. Outside, all the while, Long Tom rattled and roared.

It was nearly four o'clock before there was a lull in the shelling and Torres was able to escort her back to the women's shelter.

"I am sorry about all that," he said, taking her arm casually and naturally. "I am afraid that some of these men are very uncouth."

"You shouldn't have tried to fight him. I think perhaps you are not so tough as some of those people."

"No doubt. But it was the honourable thing to do," said Torres. "You would not have respected me if I had not done so." They had reached the edge of the women's shelter. "Well," he said. "Here we are. I hope your next visit will be more pleasant."

He took her hand and kissed it in courtly fashion, before turning on his heel and heading back. Bella couldn't help smiling, and stood for a little while watching him as he strode in his tall boots across the broken earth.

When, that evening, Bella told Mrs. Frinton about the incident, the widow cluck-clucked and shook her head.

"Well, you shouldn't have gone there. You might have been . . . might have had advantage taken of you!"

"I had no choice—the shells."

"Well," said Mrs. Frinton. "Men are men, you know, just as shells are shells."

Bella could not agree. At no point in the encounter had she felt that her virtue was in danger.

"They are just like us, really," she ventured. "Only most of the time we don't realize it."

"That's a very newfangled view," said the widow. "It's not one I hold with myself. You or I wouldn't fight—not just brawling, I mean, we wouldn't be fighting this war. This—it's all men, just men. Believe you me, when we get to the Good Place, we will find many more women there than men."

Bella smiled to herself, and said nothing. Everyone else had gone to bed, and she and the widow were sitting up in the mouth of the cave, watching the night shelling. The town was now completely surrounded by Boer guns, but at night the shells seemed to be mostly pitched from behind them. Most of them were off target, and hit the rock ridge on the opposite side of the river, shattering into a thousand fiery splinters. In the darkness the curving sweep of these glowing fragments was a sight to see.

Eventually it grew too cold to sit up, and they retired. Wrapped up on her pallet, Bella felt sad and lonely. She could not sleep, and wasted the candle, letting it burn to no purpose. The closeness of the little cell bred anxiety. Her heart and lungs felt tight. She wanted to see her father. She wondered what had happened to Tom: she had not seen him since their intimate encounter, and was beginning to experience uncertainty about the vision of love—slow, spacious, unfolding—which she had attached to him. She thought about the barber, too, and other things. Disappointments . . . hopes . . . responsibilities. She realized, for instance, that she had left the new servants at the hotel without any instructions, and hoped Father was taking care of them. All these thoughts jumped around in her head, impish as the shadows cast by the candle.

Every now and then a shell fell near the shelter with a dull thud, making it vibrate, and she would pull her bedding more closely about her. All through the tunnels could be heard the gasps and murmurs of others who also were awake and fearful. The candle diminished. She kept thinking she should blow it out, but was unable to summon up the energy. Then it went out of its own accord.

Still she could not sleep. For one thing, it was freezing cold. Ladysmith above ground could get very nippy at night, in spite of scorching heat during the day. Down in the caves, the cold seemed to be powerfully amplified. The chill of the earthy air, the dampness coming up from the floor, seemed to seep not only into her bones but also into her mind, where she began to equate it with all the unsatisfactory elements of her world, both before and since the siege: Father's rigidity and moodiness, his deep inconsolability; Jane, ill and on her own at Intombi; Tom, once more; the loss of the hotel . . . She pressed her face into the pillow. Why would it all not go away? Why could she herself not go away—ship abroad under splendid purple clouds, leaving Father, even Jane, everyone, shaking handkerchiefs on a jetty?

As she turned from side to side and the night wore on, she tried to clear her mind of these foolish, troublesome images by building in it a wall; a wall around some empty space, her own to inhabit. She imagined this construction as something like a tower, at the top of which was a white-painted room with long, open views from its windows. As she eventually began to drift off, that was the picture she tried to keep in her head. Then, to her intense irritation, she found herself growing unsure whether the tower was not a troublesome picture in itself. The mental dwelling on it all made her yet more anxious, fearfully tightening lungs and heart once again, fending off sleep once more. But sleep she did, finally.

And so other nights and other mornings came. Life in the tunnels developed into a routine. Like everything else, it was governed by shellfire. The ear was deafened, then came a sinister silence. This would be the pattern of Bella's days and nights until Christmas. Explosion. Silence. Explosion. Silence. Explosion . . . It was hardly bearable. When the tunnel-dwellers had to come inside, the booms were quieter, and all around the catacomb could be heard the sound of plaintive murmuring:

"When will it end?"

"I never thought I would see myself like this."

"Mummy!"

"My God, I have no hope left in me."

Then the silence again. Outside for a breath of fresh air, or a drink of water, the only thing that would quell the hunger. And then only for a short while. As Mrs. Frinton had said, it was not a good idea to drink the tainted stuff without boiling it first: those who had been careless about this were going down with dysentery. Whenever she felt a twinge in her stomach, Bella dreaded that she was going down with it.

Mostly, this morbid fear of illness came at night, riding on the chill air she had grown to hate so much. She tried to steel herself into recognizing that all her feelings of dread, and the upset stomachs that went with them, were nothing but the expression of extreme discomfort—not the first signs of enteric fever, nor the early symptoms of an hysteric madness. But as she lay on her pallet the image of the tower kept coming back to her, so much so that she began to wonder if what she was imagining was not a tower at all, but a vastly magnified shell. She tried to understand her feelings, though with little success. One thing she knew, however. There was this wanting that persisted: a terrible emptiness of soul and heart, as she described it to herself. That sounded too grand. She didn't have the words. Yet it was how she felt.

So what did she want, exactly? She didn't know, though she had asked herself that question every one of those cold nights. Tom? Tom as her husband? Any husband? To be sure, the tunk-tunk of the banjo and the drone of the accordion from the men's tunnels sang that tune, or the possibility of it, each night. As indeed, in more raucous fashion, did the shouts accompanying a favourite card game, the roars of "Top of the house! Top of the house!" But she hadn't spoken to a man since the business with Torres, and the most she saw of the male sex was the flicker of a match as one of them lit his pipe or, from time to time, a great-coated sentry lumbering past, rigid with cold and drenched with wet.

Her frets and fancies seemed to come from so deep within that they frightened her, and some nights she thought she might be losing her mind. And then, one night, she realized. The tower was a prison, not a haven or somewhere from which to view her prospects of future happiness. Yes, the tower and the wanting were one and the same. It was just like the inside and outside of the siege. Accepting this, she said to herself: no more. Even as she said it, she was not convinced of the efficacy of this self-instruction—but it did give her a certain amount of satisfaction to be back in authority over her thoughts and feelings . . .

Nobody in true authority was taking much notice of the troglodytes. One afternoon, General White did come by with his staff, and leaned into Bella's tunnel.

"It's a fine tunnel, ladies," he said, taking off his hat. "But you won't need it long—there are three brigades coming." And then continued down the line of catacombs, like an Egyptologist inspecting a row of mummies.

Buller won't bring my home back, Bella thought, as she watched the old man limp along the bank. Nor will his three brigades. All her stuff, all the bits and pieces in her room: she must go back and retrieve them. But Father had said she should remain in the tunnels. She felt naked without her things; the barriers between her and the world were gone. All she had was a suitcase full of clothes covered in masonry dust. A woman in the tunnel next door was wearing some of them; everything was exchangeable for food now, and this woman had offered a tomato for a pair of woollen stockings of Bella's. She had not wanted to give them up, but the idea of a fresh vegetable had been too attractive to resist. There were almost none left in the town now, the Royal's and other vegetable gardens having been either shelled or simply stripped of everything edible.

Food, food: it was that which consumed them most, after the "mere fact" of shelling. Even bad food: the sour, acidic bread, the grey potatoes and stringy trek ox. Eating this stuff seemed to make the bad dreams worse. She tried to steel herself at night now. As she well knew already, you could get lost like that in the tunnels: one or two of the women had become properly hysterical, and had to be taken away to Intombi. She had toyed with the idea of pretending, so she could get through to see Jane. But the council would have to sign the pass. Father would know, and he would see that her application was refused.

She had not seen much of him. Every now and then he would come down, bringing some little offering of food—dried peas, an onion—in a paper bag, but otherwise it seemed he was busy with his work. He had been made a member of the Alien Persons Committee, which was vetting those civilians the army thought might be passing information to the Boers. It seemed that this had become a serious problem, for the Boer gunners had managed to pick out two of the main ammunition magazines. As these had been hidden, the deduction was made that information on their whereabouts had been transmitted from within the town. Said the widow: "The spies would have done better to tell them the location of the food stores." Food, again.

Bella thought of the kitchen in the hotel: the big range, the implements hanging from their hooks. All that stuff was useless now, when all that was available for cooking was a few sticks, a tiny flame and a pot of boiling water. It was as if they had gone back in time to a prehistoric era; it was as if they were real cave-dwellers now.

For Neanderthals, they got along well enough. Sometimes, in the outer gallery, the gloomy atmosphere lightened unaccountably, and they had a bit of a sing-song. One woman had a grey parrot, which at least provided much entertainment for the children: it had to be covered up during shelling, however, as otherwise it would get nervous and start to hop about and squawk.

There were incidents, of course. Another woman was hit by a shell as she was washing clothes, and bled to death before a doctor could be fetched. One day, a piece of the bank broke, and a section of the tunnels was flooded: everybody helped to bail it out, passing pots and buckets from hand to hand. Soldiers came to dam up the broken bank. Tom was among them, but though he waved, he appeared too busy to talk to her. That hurt her feelings. Had he abandoned her now? Left her to the underworld of the tunnels? Perhaps he really was just too busy. Bella thought about all this for some while, and in the end persuaded herself that she could accept his lack of attention. There were excuses: this was a siege, he was a soldier. In any case, her—she struggled for a word—encounter with him, and her already mixed feelings for him, seemed now to belong to another age: the time of the hotel. Now they were in the time of the tunnels, and everything was changed and distorted and full of upset. The only thing to look forward to was the dance that had been scheduled for Christmas Day. Bella had put aside a white blouse especially for it, and spent the long days in the catacombs dreaming of being whirled round by a khaki youth. The only thing was, he didn't have Tom's face. She was not sure whose face he had.

30

Office of Commissioner of Police,
Pretoria, 20th December 1899

Honourable Sir,

Herewith I send you 3 portraits of the prisoner of war, Winston Spencer Churchill, correspondent of the "Morning Post" of London, who ran away from the State Model School here presumably between the hours of 10 o'clock on the evening of 12th and 4 o'clock on the morning of the 13th inst. Further described as follows:—

> *Englishman, 25 years of age, about 5 feet 8 inches in height, medium build, stooping gait, fair complexion, reddish brown hair, almost invisible slight moustache, speaks through his nose, cannot give full expression of the letter "s," and does not speak a word of Dutch. Wore a suit of brown clothes, but not uniform—an ordinary suit of clothes.*

It is necessary to mention that the accompanying photograph is a copy of one taken most probably about 18 months ago. Be good enough to show the public (as far as possible) this photograph, and request your police and the burghers to keep a sharp lookout for the fugitive, and if he is identified to place him under arrest at once. Should anything important come to light with regard to the said prisoner I request that you will inform me of the same without delay.

> *I have the honour to be,*
> *Your obedient servant,*

The Honourable Resident Justice of the Peace

SCHWEIZER-RENECKE.

31

Bella was applying what little powder and rouge she had left, or had been able to borrow, when the shell landed—so close that pellets of earth stung her face. It was a horrible thing to happen to a young woman on Christmas Day, especially one who had been happily anticipating going to a dance. After the explosion she fell grovelling to the ground and for several hours afterwards could only murmur, "Not hurt, not hurt." Mrs. Frinton took her in her arms and comforted her before putting her to bed.

So passed Bella's Christmas morning. When her father came down to see her, he produced a letter from his jacket pocket and gave it to her.

"Happy Christmas, my love."

It was from Jane.

Intombi Camp,
December 23, 1899.

My dearest Bella and Papa,

You will be pleased to hear that I am now fully recovered from my hysterics. I suppose I ought to tell you my story. When I was got into the train, they put me on a mattress and I was fed milk and biscuits—the only milk I have had since I saw you, as that commodity has long since run out. The journey was short, but even in my distress I was surprised when we just stopped and had to jump down in the middle of the veld, there being no platform of course, only a barbed-wire fence, inside which were pitched a vast field of tents and marquees.

I was put in a corner of one of these marquees, along with many other patients, some so badly wounded that I am ashamed I took my place there. A soldier who had lost his arm gave me a cup of stout, as I was still crying and shouting. You know that I normally detest it, but in a few moments I fell asleep. In the morning, I got talking to him, and he touched his tunic pocket and said, "In case I kick the bucket, there are letters in here for my parents. I want you to have them." The next day, he was dead, from loss of blood. This is a horrible place for making friends and losing them. Crosses are being put up in a field next door for all those who die.

There are some good and kindly nurses here. Nurses Wall and Rounsel have been especially sweet to me, and since my recovery I have been helping them in their work—which activity has helped me while waiting for all this to end and get back to you. Mostly I make arrowroot tea and distribute food—and talk to the patients, though there is a rule here that only the most ill must be petted or spoiled. The groans and cries of those with bad wounds, echoing out over the camp during the night, are too dismal to describe.

So do not let the fact that my spirits are higher than when I was with you last, persuade you that this is a pleasant place. In the day the heat in the tents is intense, and there are many scorpions, tarantulas and centipedes to contend with. Lately I have been helping in the fever tent, which is filling more rapidly than the wounds tent where I first slept. Now that I am "helper" rather than "patient" I sleep in a small tent: as I write, if I look up at the white roof of it, I see that the outside is dotted with thousands of black flies. They are drawn by the diarrhoea of the enteric sufferers, which gets everywhere, thereby infecting others, including many of the nurses and helpers. It often seems a hopeless business. The place smells terribly, and there are almost no medicines. Hardly a day passes but someone dies.

The rain is a blessing in lowering the temperatures, although it brings its own hindrances, sometimes pouring in under the canvas and washing us out. One day, a boot floated out from under a bed! We have also been struck by lightning, Nurse Rounsel being knocked down by a splintered pole. We have had to put upturned soda-water bottles on the poles as lightning conductors.

Lately, rations have been very scarce. In respect of this, I must report that I have met a friend of ours—the young Zulu boy called

Wellington, who staggered into our camp one day with two heavy sacks of condensed milk and dropped exhausted on the ground. When he rose up, after we had wiped his face with cold water, he said, in Zulu, Pelindaba—*the end of the story*. Bit by bit he told us what had happened: how the Boers had sniped at him all the way between the town and us. One bullet was deflected by the cans on his back. He is very brave, and it is to him that I have given this letter for delivery to you.

I very much hope that I myself will be delivered to you shortly, in the bosom of General Buller's army: though his arrival has been so long promised and deferred that I am sick of hearing of it. Please both take care from shellfire.

I am,

Your most affectionate sister and daughter,

Jane Kiernan

p.s. I have drunk the dread Chevril, and to my surprise found it delicious and comforting, though the same cannot be said for the cow-heel jelly made from horse hoof, which is sickly and fermenting—it is also dyed mauve, I suppose as an encouragement.

32

Bella's shell was not the only one to fall on Christmas Day. Two others came in also. These did not explode, however, wooden plugs having been substituted for their fuses. On inspection, it turned out that they had been painted in the Free State colours and engraved "With the compliments of the season." One was empty, the other filled with plum pudding. Another practical joke—the last word in Boer humour—was played by a burgher who crept down to within range of Green Horse Valley and emptied the magazine of his Mauser into it, calling out, "A Merry Christmas, rooineks."

Dutch jokes excepted, the main presents exchanged at Christmas were mementoes of the bombardment. These now had a marketable value in the town. A ninety-pound shell, which must have cost the Boers about £35, would fetch £10 secondhand, which was a considerable sum. These were not the sort of presents likely to make the youngest among the besieged very happy, however, and a scheme was organized by Colonel Rhodes to entertain the two hundred and fifty or so children who remained in the town. Four big trees were erected in the auction rooms and decked with whatever decoration could be found. In the spirit of the Empire, the trees were labelled Great Britain, South Africa, Australia and Canada: they were, respectively, a pine, a thorn, a blue-gum and a fir.

Moreover, and even though it was 103 in the shade, a Father Christmas was contracted in the figure of Major Mott, who stalked round the town with branches of pine and a red cap covered with cotton-wool. When he came down to the Klip, the children poured out of the burrows by the riverbank and trooped up into town after him as though he were the Pied Piper.

The Natal Mounted Rifles organized a mounted band, swinging a pair of oil drums across the withers of a horse and making cymbals from the ends of kerosene tins. Other regiments celebrated the festive season in their own particular ways—with championship football and boxing matches, tugs-of-war, donkey derbies, and egg-and-spoon races, as the whim took them. The exigencies of the siege meant that mules were substituted for donkeys, and stones for eggs, but the enjoyment was not diminished.

That was the official version. Saving the matter of the Hamelin-like children, Christmas 1899 in Ladysmith was in fact characterized by people pretending to enjoy themselves. The lack of rich food and copious drink was keenly felt by all. The Green Horse had a very thin time of it, their experience of the festivities being among those described in a letter Tom Barnes wrote to his sister on New Year's Day.

67111 Tpr Barnes, T.
Green Horse Valley,
Ladysmith,
January 1, 1900.

Dear Lizzie,

So, Christmas and New Year have passed and we are still impris-oned in this hole. Rather a grim Xmas. We did get so far as making a pudding out of some stewed pears, but it was hardly splendid see-ing as it was cooked in our camp kettles and had no sugar in it—a foolish thing from start to finish. I had my last pipe afterwards: pre-cious little tobacco here now until Perry arrives. God speed him and save him from Boer bullets—and me from their shell, which fall every day. I cannot get the hang of this country, burning hot one minute and throwing it down the next, leaving everything under water. The wet brings thousands of flies into our tents, and some-times we have to sit on our saddles, such is the flow of water under the canvas. The people who have tunnelled themselves against the shelling are constantly being washed out, including the young lady from the hotel. I am afraid to say that she has not been paying me so much attention lately, but we are all tied up with siege work—which is to say, survival.

I had a bit of excitement today. While on picket duty I spotted a flashing in a clump of trees. We had been told to shoot on sight when seeing such, as there is a considerable problem with spies in the town. This I did, but as I was aiming at the flashing amongst the greenery I only hit the traitor's instrument: which I suppose pays tribute to my shooting, but did not please Lieutenant Norris, as I missed the culprit. On reaching the clump of trees, I caught a glimpse of a hefty figure disappearing down the slope. I did, however, discover the broken hand mirror with which he had been signalling, and a distinctive bootprint with a V in the middle. The authorities are on the point of arresting a man through the link of the mirror, but I doubt they have a case on which to convict him.

A farmer called Grimble died this morning, bombed while he was ploughing, which is not something you can say happens to us in Warwickshire. I had had a talk with him only last week. He said they can and do get two crops of everything here during the year, except tobacco; sad to relate that he will not be getting any more, thanks to Brother Boer. They are slovenly farmers here and very much behind the times as regards implements. Most of the ploughs are of the old-fashioned beam type and have one little wheel like a horse hoe. They just rout, not plough.

My worst news is that Norris has made me kill my horse Bashful, which is an awful thing to have to do. The blood went over my hands. He was becoming a rather pitiful creature through lack of forage, his ribs sticking out like corrugated iron. He could hardly trot any more, and the feeling of him sighing and giving up under me out of pure hunger was awful. But I could not bring myself to do it, and the Lieutenant threatened me with court martial when I argued. So I did it, and felt like a murderer as I cut him into joints—afterwards being put on a charge for my pains, for having argued with the officer. At least I will not have to eat Bashful myself. I swear that I will touch no horseflesh, all the same.

There have been many deaths from enteric since we have been here, now over fifty from the Green Horse alone during the last week. Pray for me on this front rather than any other, since I am in more peril from disease than the danger of shellfire. But I shall, I promise, keep myself hale and hearty, in spite of the tribulations Kruger and nature fling at us.

Your loving brother,

Tom.

33

Early in January, Bella determined that she would go up into town, despite Father having forbidden her to leave the protection of the tunnels. Anyway, it was her turn to go and queue for food at the Commissariat, which one of the women from her tunnel did each week. She was shocked by how dilapidated Ladysmith had become during her enforced absence: many more buildings had been damaged, and everywhere there were piles of rubble and rubbish, as well as the ubiquitous horse dung, invariably covered with fat blue flies. People, too, seemed more damaged: chalk-white, distracted, or plain bad-tempered. When a shell flew over during her journey, she saw a man shake his fist at the sky, as if remonstrating with the gods.

She made her way to the Commissariat, and joined the queue. The ration was pitiful: a bagful of slippery, slightly rotten carrots, two cans without labels, eleven brown bottles of the new horse drink, a jar of preserved pears from the late Mr. Grimble's half-destroyed orchard, and a small sack of maize meal. In addition, she received three tiny packets of coffee, tea and pepper, and a flask of vinegar. These last were "extras," the clerk informed her, as if she was lucky to get them. When she said she was from the tunnels and that there were babies there, he reluctantly reached beneath the desk and handed her two tins of condensed milk. Her requests for cheese, jam and bacon were turned down.

With her dismal load stowed in her suitcase—the same one in which she had brought her clothes to the tunnel (and it certainly felt no heavier than it had done on that occasion)—Bella set off for the hotel, hoping to find her father there. When she rounded the corner, and saw the now only half-familiar building, the sight almost brought tears to her eyes. The place was so derelict it looked as if it had been a ruin not for a fortnight, but for years. She climbed the steps of the veranda and went though into the bar.

Father didn't seem to have got much rebuilding done: the beams were still lying in the middle of the room, the flooring still sticking up. There continued to be glass everywhere, too, as well as pieces of collapsed wall and ceiling. She put her suitcase of food down in the middle of the devastation, and called up.

"Father? Are you there?"

No reply. And then a voice, which made her jump.

"He is out, mama."

She turned round to see the young Zulu boy, Wellington, leaning against a doorpost.

"Oh, it's you," she said, relieved. "Are you still here, then? I half thought you might have left. I am glad you are all right—my sister told me about your brave run to Intombi."

"Thank you, mama. The nkosi said we could stay here, even though there is little hotel work anymore. We have nowhere else to go."

"I understand. It's all right. It's not as if we have any other guests!"

The boy smiled.

"Look, do you know where he is?" asked Bella. "My father."

"I think he is at the Town Hall."

"I see. Is your mother here?"

"I will fetch her."

Wellington disappeared through the shattered doorway. He looked liked a skeleton, she thought; and all at once realized that if they, the whites, were getting so little food, the Africans must be getting even less. Her suspicion was confirmed when Wellington re-emerged with his mother, who also looked gaunt. The woman curtsied.

"Hallo, Nandi," said Bella, trying to sound as cheerful as she could amid the ruined scene. "How have you been managing to keep yourself?"

"I have been put onto cleaning by the soldiers, mama. It is very bad. I am very happy to see you. Although I am not happy in my soul. I am very hungry and the boy also, and our father is out there with the Mabunu, imprisoned by them."

"I did not know—you did not tell me that."

At this the Zulu woman started wailing, and got down on her knees in front of Bella, grasping at her skirts.

"Please, if you can help us . . . I gave the other mama my best pipe!"

Bella did not know what to do. She glanced at the boy, who looked embarrassed in return and then came over and began gently to pull his mother away from Bella.

"She is very upset," he said, nodding sagely, as if this were all part of normal life. Bella squatted down next to Nandi. There was something about this woman which moved her. She wiped away Nandi's tears with her handkerchief, and then opened the suitcase and gave her the sack of maize, a couple of bottles of Chevril, and one of the tins.

Nandi's thanks were as profuse as her tears. Embarrassed, Bella left them then and, carrying the now lighter suitcase, walked over to the Town Hall. On the way, she saw two things which brought home to her the effect upon Ladysmith of the siege. The first was the sight of a small group of children in tattered clothes scrambling over the ruins of the old dairy; one of them, a little girl in a red dress, was throwing empty bottles at a wall—just picking them out of a crate (by what miracle had it survived the bombardment?) and chucking them against the half-fallen wall, where the green glass exploded into tiny fragments and fell down among the rubble. It seemed so foolish and pointless—but if wise and just generals were doing much the same, it was little wonder that children began to act like this.

The other scene Bella observed was a flock of crows whirling and fighting over the carcass of a rat. Flapping and pecking at each other as they tumbled about over the body, they seemed to be one creature, a confused mass of black beaks and wings and feathers. It was horrible, but she could not draw her eyes away from it, as the beaks and claws tore into the furry flesh, lifting away portions of grey entrail.

Finally she walked on, trying to chase the images from her mind. As she did so, someone fell into step beside her.

"Hallo, my sweet."

She turned to see Tom Barnes. He had his cap on, a rifle slung over his shoulder, and looked very much the fierce soldier.

"Hallo," she replied, looking at the dusty street.

"Awful bad luck about the hotel. I'm sorry I haven't been able to come and see you, but—well, they've been keeping us hard at it."

"So I believe. Still, you might have come and found me. I saw you at the river."

"I know. Well, you saw me wave—but that Lieutenant Norris is a terror, and he would have hauled me over the coals if I'd stopped to chat."

He touched her back as they walked.

"Anyway, once things have quietened down, we'll get together, eh?"

"We'll see," she said, a little primly. "I am not certain it would be leading anywhere."

"It's just the war, Bella. I don't know . . . I don't know what to say. Maybe afterwards . . . Let me take that."

He relieved her of the suitcase and they walked on a few more paces in silence.

"Where you bound for?" Tom said then, pausing to tighten the rifle's sling on his shoulder, to keep it clear of the case.

"The Town Hall. I am hoping to find my father. I have seen little of him, too, since going into the tunnels."

"Well, I'm headed there, too. I got into an argument with Norris, so he put me on extra detail guarding prisoners."

"What did you argue about?"

"He put my horse on the butcher's list."

"Not Bashful?"

Tom nodded glumly, and they walked on in silence for a few paces.

"What does it involve, your extra duty?" Bella asked.

"Watching over the suspected spies and Boer sympathizers. There are more to be escorted to the Dopper Church today. I nearly potted a traitor myself the other day, saw him signalling while I was on picket. He got away, but the provosts have now arrested someone on suspicion. I have to be there as a witness too."

"Who was it?"

"Don't know. I didn't get a good look at him, but he left some bits and pieces behind when he ran off, and they reckon that's enough to get this chap on. I'm not so sure. I think they are being a bit over-zealous, since the last magazine was hit. They'll have the whole town in there before they are finished. Your pa sits on the council, doesn't he?"

Bella nodded. "I suppose that's why he must be there."

They had reached the steps of the Town Hall. It was a large build-ing, surmounted by a square tower with a clock in it, and a flagstaff bearing a red cross on a white ground, signifying that the place was being used as a hospital. But the fact that one part of it was also used for meetings was perhaps one of the reasons why, since Bella's short time in bed there, the Boers had felt justified in throwing four or five shells at the tower. The town clerk's room had been hit, and its stone wall carried out into the street, somewhat undermining the civic grandeur of the place.

"Better go in separately," said Tom.

Looking around furtively, he handed back the suitcase, gave her a quick peck on the cheek and went up the steps and through the big, woodworm-eaten doors. Bella waited at the foot of the stairs for a few seconds, wondering whether or not they had conducted themselves like lovers. Then she too went inside. The place smelt terrible, and looking across the entrance hall she could see the long lines of beds and stretchers with the nurses moving among them. She stopped and watched for a while, offering up a silent prayer of thanks that her own wound had been minor, and that she was no longer lying there among the injured. Then a man made a horrid noise of pain, and she shud-dered, and turned away.

With the suitcase in her hand, Bella went through the door into the chamber where the council met, to be confronted by a line of four or five despondent prisoners and a guard of soldiers, among whom Tom had taken his place. She did not really look at the prisoners at first, her eye being drawn by the sight of her father sitting in front of them at a table with a green baize cloth spread on it, together with Mayor Farquhar, Major Mott and two other officers. Then she looked back at the prisoners, and was horrified to see the tall, bearded figure of Antonio Torres among them.

She sat down at the back of the room, her heart beating hard. What had happened? Why was he being arraigned? The answer came soon enough, out of the mouth of Major Mott, who called Torres's name. The barber stepped forward between two armed soldiers with caps and belts, one of whom was Tom. As the Major read the charge, Bella saw her father frowning, having noticed her.

"Antonio Torres, in the opinion of the governing authorities of Ladysmith under military law, as represented here by the Legal Board of the Army and observing parties of Ladysmith Town Council, your loyalty to the Crown is called into question. As a Portuguese national, in view of the late activities of certain parties in ostensibly neutral Portuguese East Africa, you cannot in the opinion of the Legal Board be trusted with your liberty. Furthermore, you are called upon to explain the provenance of a looking-glass, of a brand known to be sold in your shop, which was discovered at a scene where signalling to the enemy is suspected to have taken place."

The Major held up a broken looking-glass. The roundel was only a quarter intact, and most of the remaining glass was missing, but Bella was shocked to recognize it as one of the very type that she herself had bought from Torres.

"Can you explain this?" demanded the Major. Torres, Bella saw, was trembling.

"Why are you doing this?" he said. "I have been a good citizen since I came to Ladysmith. I have no quarrel with the British. I just wanted to carry on with my business, and then the Boers hit it with a bomb. It is they who are my enemy. They have destroyed me!"

"What of this looking-glass?" barked Major Mott. "Is it yours?"

"It is certainly similar to ones in my stock," said Torres, in trembling tones. "But I have sold many of them, or did, when I still had a business from which to sell them. I cannot be held responsible for what happens to them after they leave my shop."

"You should be advised that the punishment for treason is death by firing squad. Can you tell the Board where you were on the afternoon of Friday last?"

"I don't know. I suppose I was in the caves at the Klip, as usual."

"Can you provide a witness to that effect?"

"I don't know!" said Torres, who was becoming even more agitated. "I suppose so. I can't remember. Go and ask some people there."

"We have made enquiries," the Major countered. "None of the people in your tunnel are willing to say for certain that you were there on that afternoon."

"Of course not," said Torres. "There are hundreds of people there. I may have been sleeping inside the tunnel, anyway, or giving someone a tattoo, or anything."

There was silence for a minute or so, as Major Mott made some notes on a pad, the ends of his sea-lion moustache drooping down before his bowed head.

Then he looked up.

"Is Trooper Barnes present?"

"Yes, sir," said Tom, smartly.

"Could you please verify the prisoner's bootprint? If you would oblige, Mr. Torres."

Tom went behind Torres and, bending down, grasped his ankle.

"This is lunacy," exclaimed Torres, as the trooper picked up his foot and inspected the sole of his boot.

The barber, made unsteady, was forced to put out an arm to keep his balance. If the situation had not been so tense, Bella would have found it comical. She could not think what the scene reminded her of, and then realized that it was reminiscent of someone checking a horse's hoof for stones or lesions—an extremely common sight in the horse-swelled town.

"It's not the same, sir," said Tom. "Not at all."

Major Mott addressed himself to Torres. "In the Board's opinion, you are suspected of treason, and will be remanded until such time as your guilt or innocence can be proved. If you are found guilty, you will be executed, as military law dictates. We will of course be searching among your belongings in the tunnels, taking care to verify your remaining footwear."

Bella watched as Torres rubbed his face with his hands, as though he had just seen rather than heard something he couldn't believe.

"Mister Mayor," he whispered. "Will you please stop this foolishness?"

"I'm sorry, Antonio," said Farquhar. "The order about Portuguese nationals has come down from General White, and is to be applied without exception. It has been issued to preserve the safety of the town. The matter of the looking-glass will have to be investigated further," he told Torres ominously. And then relented slightly. "But I am sure you will be released when it is all over."

"If you are innocent," added Major Mott, sternly.

"But I have no quarrel with any of you," said Torres. "Mr. Kiernan, tell them!"

Bella saw her father look down at the green baize.

"Take him away," said Major Mott. "Next!"

To her disbelief, Bella saw Tom and the other soldier move towards Torres, each taking one of his arms. She was so shocked by the picture—having come here simply expecting to have a talk with her father—that she was quite unable to move. Tom, giving her a wink, moved past with Torres, who on seeing her passed an accusing look in her direction. He must think I am a part of it, Bella realized, and the thought broke her inaction. She stood up and cried out, interrupting Major Mott, who was reading out the details of the charge against the next prisoner.

"Wait!"

The room fell silent.

"Bella!" said her father. "You should not be here. And you must not interfere."

"No," she said. "This is wrong. Father, Mayor Farquhar, I know Mr. Torres. He is a good man, you don't need to lock him up. This is pure cruelty. I myself have bought such a glass from him."

"Be silent!" bellowed her father.

Cowed, Bella sat down again. The Major looked at Kiernan, who shook his head, as if disowning her. Then Mott gestured at Tom and the other soldier that they should carry on. Torres began to struggle in their grip, and a chair was knocked over as they left the room. Bella sat for a second, shaking, and then got up and rushed out after them. She caught up with them at the bottom of the steps outside, where two other soldiers were tying a cord round Torres's hands, which had been pulled behind him. The barber's back was to her, and Tom stood nearby, leaning on his rifle.

"Tom! Wait, this isn't right."

"Army business, love. Best leave us to it." His voice seemed different, his whole manner altered—he was not like he was before. He turned to go.

"Stop," she said, tugging at his arm. "I'm telling you. You must help me."

His face softened a little. "I can't, Bella. It's orders."

"What the bloody hell?" said one of the other soldiers, disbelieving. "We better move on, Tom. You'll be put on report if anyone sees this."

"He's right," said Tom, embarrassed. "We've got to go."

Bella grabbed at his belt, and he took her by the wrist and removed her hand.

"Don't," she cried. "You're hurting me."

"Do not touch her," said an accented voice. Torres had turned round, and was watching the encounter. One of the other soldiers looked at him and, curling his lip, hefted his rifle and jabbed the butt into the barber's kidneys. Torres fell to the ground. Bella ran over, pushed past the soldiers and knelt by his side.

His dark eyes, filled with pain, looked up at her.

"It is all right. You must go. You will get into trouble."

She looked down at him as he lay there awkwardly with his hands bound behind his back, and discovered tears welling up in her own eyes. It was all so horrible, so cruel and unfair. Just plain wrong. Before she could say anything else, the two soldiers had lifted Torres up and began to drag him away.

"I'm sorry," Tom said, giving her an uncertain look, half crestfallen, half irritated.

Kneeling there on the ground, Bella looked back at him and loathed herself. She could not believe that she had let herself be touched by a man who could disregard her wishes so directly.

"I'm sorry," he said again. Then he hitched up his rifle onto his shoulder and followed his companions and their prisoner. Standing up, Bella walked back over to the Town Hall, sat down on the steps with her arms clasped around her knees, and began to cry. It was all too much—Jane, the hotel, and now this.

From above her came a harsh voice. "What the hell did you think you were playing at?"

With solemn, tear-filled eyes, she looked back over her shoulder and saw her father standing on one of the higher steps. He walked down and stood in front of her, breathing heavily.

"What on earth possessed you? I thought I told you to stay in the caves, in any case."

Bella said nothing, just looked at the dusty ground at his feet.

"Why did you do it? For what reason? I can't understand it. Surely you don't care about that hair-cutting buffoon?"

"Father, please don't talk like that," she mumbled.

"Have you fallen in love with him? With a damn barber? Is that it?"

"No," she said, sulkily. "It's wrong, that's all—what you did. You know that he is no threat to anybody. He might end up being executed."

"It's military law, Bella. We must accept it until things get back to normal."

"What is normal?" she answered angrily. "It's never going to be any good in this town. It never was going to be."

"Bella," he said, in a heavy voice. "Stop acting so wilful. Go back to the Klip and look to yourself. Forget about Torres."

"And you?" she said, with a note of sarcasm.

"Why are you defying me? I have been a good father to you. God knows it has not been easy. I don't understand. You've been a good girl up till now. Why are you behaving like this, at a time when your sister is in hospital and our home is destroyed? Do you not think I have enough to worry about?"

"I had to speak up for him."

"Look. Someone has been passing information about targets in the town to the Boers. I am not saying it is Torres, but as a Portuguese, he is bound to fall under suspicion as a traitor and a spy. There is nothing I can do about it."

"You could have spoken up for him."

"Why should I have done so? I don't like the man, and unless I had some particular reason, the army would have taken no notice of me. I don't understand why you are making such a fuss. Can you not settle for the fact that it has happened and go back to the caves and wait for the siege to end?"

"He was kind to me," Bella said, meekly.

"Don't be so stupid."

Scrawny, sallow, tense, a bundle of nerves crouched there on the steps, Bella Kiernan looked up at her father and found that even she was surprised by the force of feeling in her. All the dissatisfactions of her existence, the knowledge that her life—in that town, in that era— was set to be one of narrow, miserable renunciation, welled up in her. All her daughterly feelings—of respect, of love, and of fear too— evaporated in that moment. She felt a space—wide and empty as the veld, full of possibilities, but hollow also—open up inside her.

She spat the words out. "I hate you."

34

Back in the tunnels the night after her outburst, Bella was both wretched and resentful. On the one hand, she felt both sadness and fear on account of her hateful words; on the other, she was filled with righteous indignation at the treatment of Mr. Torres. Confusion, too, was compounded with her clearer thoughts and feelings: why did she feel this anger at—this contempt for, even—their subjugation to military law? Probably the generals, and Father, were right; if the town was to continue its defence, such measures had to be taken. Perhaps Torres was a spy, after all?—but even as she asked the question in her mind, she knew it could not be true. What they had done *was* wrong, and she felt an unaccountable urge to right it. The question was not so much one of morality as of her own self-determination, and this troubled her. When she had spoken those words to her father, she had for the first time in her life felt she was being her true self. It was a disturbing feeling, one that she was scarcely able to recognize for what it was . . .

The images of the day played through her mind. Father had actually raised his hand as if to strike her. Then, letting it fall, he had simply turned on his heel and walked away from her. She had gone back inside the Town Hall and collected the abandoned suitcase of food, then walked disconsolately back to the Klip.

Now, unable to sleep and trying to put these awful pictures away, she was sitting in the opening of the tunnel. Everyone else was in their cave, and the embers of the supper fire glowed in front of her. Other fires, Boer fires, shone on the hills here and there, indistinctly. It was a murky night. The moon was covered over, the hills shrouded. Now and then, clusters of stars showed through the cloud, as it moved its ragged chariots across the night sky. The stars made her think of her father; perhaps even now he was focusing his telescope upon them from the window of the Star Room, or walking out among the sentries with his haversack on his back. She shivered. He could be shot!

From time to time, as if to confirm her anxiety, came the boom of a gun or the sudden effulgence of a flare. Then the entire landscape was transformed, taking on a hellish cast. It made her think of sin, and as she looked up into the stars she thought of all the dead people who had gone heavenwards, and all the thousands more that this war was sending there.

It was Mrs. Frinton, whose devotion was of a dissenting stamp, who had put her in this frame of mind. Earlier in the evening, she had discovered Bella weeping in her cave.

"What is troubling you, my dear?" she had asked.

"I have a difficulty in finding the right course of action," Bella had replied, not wanting to reveal to the widow the details of her discomfort.

In the lamplight, Mrs. Frinton's creased, careworn face had been full of kindness, but also a sort of excitement. "Whatever the quality of your difficulty, the Lord will show you the way. You are of the Roman faith, I take it, being Irish?"

"Yes," Bella had said, although the family rarely went to church.

"Well, I suppose that as long as you believe, virtue will come to you—and then you will be happy, knowing that your path is the right one. I cannot describe that happiness. It is unspeakable. I have been with the Lord for over half a century and, as the Good Book says, my cup overflows."

The widow had brought a collection of devotional texts down to the riverside. Mention of the Psalms spurred her, and she insisted on fetching a tome for the troubled girl.

"It's by a Papist saint," she had said, on re-emerging. "But it's still one of my favourite books, and I think you might like it too."

Once the old woman had kissed her goodnight and retired to her own tiny chamber, Bella read a little of the book by candlelight. There was one passage which affected her powerfully, where the author described a vision that had come to her: "A most beautiful crystal globe, made in the shape of a castle, and containing seven mansions, in the seventh and innermost of which was the King of Glory, in the greatest splendour, illuminating and beautifying them all. The nearer one got to the centre, the stronger was the light; outside the palace limits everything was foul, dark and infested with toads, vipers and other venomous creatures."

The sentiments seemed very pertinent: a part of Bella identified strongly with the author's suggestion that solace was something to be found inside one's own heart. But another part of her, the more practical side, found the text quite unhelpful. What was she to do? She stared into the embers. Should she go and apologize to her father? Should she go and visit Torres in the Dopper Church? How did all this leave things between her and Tom Barnes? Unable to answer any of these questions, she retired to her pallet, and dreamed of a condition in which all of them could be resolved.

In the morning she decided that she would, at any rate, visit Torres, and in due course set out determinedly to do so. It was a relief to get out of the warren and even though several shells fell along the way, she felt better for the walk. This feeling disappeared when she reached the Dopper Church, however. The wire fence which the soldiers had erected around it gave it a most peculiar look—Bella didn't think there must be a church in the world like it—and if the wire alone made the picture peculiar, the faces behind it made it horrible. There were even children in there, no less spectral than their mothers, and all of them looked mournfully out between the strands of steel. She looked for Torres among those trapped, furtive faces, but could not see him. Eventually she approached the gate, where a little wooden shack had been built for the sentries.

She looked in at its open doorway, half expecting to find Tom there. He was not, but his friend with the whiskers—the one she had met at the camp—was inside, sitting on a chair, smoking his pipe and reading a *Ladysmith Lyre*. His rifle was propped against the wall next to him. There was something about its smooth brown lines, and the smoky metal of bolt and muzzle, that drew the young girl's eye.

"Hallo again," the man said, on looking up and seeing Bella. "If you are searching for Tom, I am afraid you have come at the wrong time. He only does nights here."

"I actually wanted to speak with one of the prisoners."

The trooper put down his *Lyre*. "Oh yes? I'll have to get permission from an officer if you want to come inside, and there isn't one here right now."

"Couldn't you just fetch the prisoner for me? It's Mr. Torres."

"That Portuguese fellow? Tom told me about the business outside the Town Hall."

"Please," Bella said. "I'd be so grateful if you could just fetch Mr. Torres for me."

"All right, love," the bewhiskered man said, with a grin. "I'll go and have a look for him. But you'll have to wait here." He picked up his rifle and, unlocking the gate with a key from a bunch on his belt, went through into the exercise area in front of the church. Bella watched him climb the steps and go in by the big wooden doors. A minute or so later he emerged with Torres. The barber looked strained, and coming up to the wire, gripped it with his hands. Bella looked through at him.

"I have come to apologize for my father's involvement in all this," she announced.

Torres took a deep breath, and gave a stoical smile.

"It's not your fault. You were just trying to help, I could see that."

"There must be something we can do," said Bella. She reached up and clasped his fingers, with the wire between them. Torres gave a dry laugh, but he did not remove his hand.

"I cannot see how. Unless you mean to bring guns and spring me out."

Bella looked into his dark eyes, scanning the aquiline face with its generous, full-lipped mouth and pointed beard. She felt a nervous fluttering in her breast, a mixture of frustration at his imprisonment and an almost maternal feeling of wanting to take him in her arms. She shook her head.

"I will try to help. I will do whatever I can."

He smiled again. "You are a good woman, too good to concern yourself with this. Go back to the tunnels. Keep your head down against the shells. I will be all right here. My scores I will settle myself, when this is over." With that, he squeezed her hand, turned about and walked back to the steps of the church, where a number of men and women had seated themselves. How many others, thought Bella, are waiting, inside and outside the town, for the walls and fences, the wire and earthworks, to come down?

She decided that she must confront Father again, and instead of heading straight back to the Klip, made her way to the hotel. The sight of it, of the torn-up floors and lumps of scattered masonry, was still distressing, even though she knew to expect it this time. She stepped carefully through the mess and climbed the staircase—the banister had quite gone, which made the climb a sobering experience. At one point the stairs creaked terribly and she thought the whole structure was going to come down. But it held, and when she reached the Star Room, she found the door open.

Her father was sitting at his desk with his back to her, and she stood for a second in the doorway and looked at him there under his toy universe: the thick neck and red hair, the broad, uncompromising shoulders.

"I've come to talk to you," she said.

He spoke in a low voice, without turning round.

"I am surprised you dare show your face here."

She walked up to him, her heart beating fast, and touched him on the arm. He almost jumped up, seeming to shake a little. Then he spun round in his chair, and she saw that his face had lost its usual florid tones and become unnaturally white. It was the face of someone under great strain. Gripping the edges of the chair, he spoke very slowly.

"Bella, I am sorry that we fell out in such a disagreeable manner. That is not important. What is, and I want you to listen to me very carefully, is that you keep away from here, and from me, until the siege is ended. There are too many things at stake here for a young girl to be around."

Not knowing what to say, she looked into his eyes, and saw that there were tears in them. In the distance, she heard the sound of a shell.

"Do you understand?"

Her gaze fell, unable to meet his any longer, and she noticed that his revolver was lying amid the clutter on his desk: a long-barrelled, heavy-looking thing that was usually kept locked in a drawer. Seeing her look, he stood up suddenly, his voice louder and more peremptory.

"You must go. Now."

"I want to talk to you," Bella said. "About Mr. Torres."

"Never mind that," he said, taking her arm and propelling her towards the door. "I want you to go back to the tunnels and keep away from here. You must do what I say."

"What about Torres?" she said, stubbornly.

He looked at the floor.

"Why won't you talk to me?" she pleaded, facing him in the doorway. But he said nothing, just folded his arms and stood there.

"Father," she said. "I'm sorry for what I said."

He reached out and touched her face. "Go now. I don't want you to come back here, or look for me, until the siege is finished. Promise me."

"I promise," she said, bewildered, and then he began to close the door, almost pushing her out onto the landing.

She descended the unsteady staircase in a daze, unable to make sense of the encounter. The breath piled up in her chest. She wished Jane were there, to talk to about it, and then felt a surge of guilt about her sister. If only she could get to Intombi . . . But mainly it was the vision of her father that possessed her, the vision of him standing there in front of her: silent, fortified, impregnable.

Emerging, blinking, into the daylight, she almost tripped over a dead horse lying in the street. It must have been hit by the shell she had heard. Strange how it had sounded further away. She walked back to the tunnels with a mind full of unresolved desires.

When she reached the Klip, she saw that the diggers had been busy again, sinking a shaft to make a new section of tunnel. Everywhere there were men smeared with clay and sweat. She made her way past them, nodded at Mrs. Frinton, and went straight through to her own cave.

Inside, exhausted, she lit a candle and began to take off her clothes. If she went to bed early, maybe all the confusion in her head would go away. Once in her nightgown, she sat on the edge of the pallet. The hammering-in of new support posts by the men outside was thumping through the whole network. She shivered. She felt the power of these fortifications arranged in and beyond Ladysmith as something vital and dangerous, pressing both upon her and from within her. As she sat there in the trembling candlelight, she tried to understand the notion. It was as if there were earthworks inside her very soul, stopping the impetuous flow of her natural feelings.

She looked at her feet. The mud of Ladysmith was between her toes. This—this earth—was what all the trouble was about, the shelling and the firing and the bayoneting, and yet she knew she would have given it all up for two pins if she could only be the person she wanted to be—a person whose character she could hardly place. General White had said that Ladysmith was co-existent with Britain, "one and the same," and yet she felt utterly apart from all that; surely somewhere, out there, was a place that was co-existent with *her*.

Perhaps, when sleep came, it was these thoughts, combined with the accumulated anxieties of three months of close beleaguerment, that cast the dream upon her. In the morning, the vividness of it was positively shocking. The bristling, perfect defences of the town had appeared to her as the red face and hair of her father. The face was that of a colossus, and she was riding over his hair on a horse, as if over grass. In spite of its vividness, the effort of collecting up all the broken pieces of the dream was draining. How to understand it all? There lingered in particular a secondary image of the horse as it galloped away from the town; she was still riding it, and yet she was also watching herself come towards her, the horse getting closer and closer. It had Torres's face.

Whatever this fantastical vision meant, she knew then that she had to try to help the barber, in spite of what Father had said. She got up and splashed some water on her face from a tin bucket. The water had not been boiled, but Mrs. Frinton had dripped a few drops of carbolic into it as a germicide. She supposed that the typhoid germs would not be able to sink through the pores in her skin—but in any case the disease was now so prevalent that one almost took a careless attitude to it. Wiping her face, she caught a glimpse of it reflected in the bucket: her eye sockets had become deeply sunken, her cheeks concave. She went through to the main gallery, feeling ugly—and hungry.

As she sipped a mug of Chevril, her warm breath made shapes in the cold morning air. They were having the musky, brown-bottled stuff for breakfast, lunch and supper now, as not keeping sweet for long it had to be drunk immediately. She looked out over the hills—vast and rolling, with thin tendrils of mist draped over the low summits. Her eye was caught first by some flaming red lilies on the opposite bank of the Klip, and then by the sight of the war balloon ascending over the range of hills.

She had hardly finished her Chevril when the firing started. There was a flash and a rasping, steel-throated bang. The Hindu sentinel on Wagon Hill cried out: "L-o-o-o-n-g T-o-o-o-o-m!" She didn't bother to move. Somewhere back in the town the shell exploded, and then there was a noise of shrapnel falling on tin roofs. She thought of poor Foster, and then of Jane.

Then another gun began. She could see its muzzle projecting from behind a large bank of earth. That was the one they called Lazy Susan, because it took longer than the others to load. There were so many guns around them now that people were running out of nicknames. They had all grown used to spotting the positions of the different guns from their reports. Lazy Susan was smaller than Long Tom: she made a *pip-pip* sound and her shells left little snowballs of white smoke suspended above the rocks and bushes. Bella watched them mix in with the remainder of the morning mist, and then the great orb of the observation balloon drifted into her field of vision again. It seemed to be altogether romantic and otherworldly—nothing to do with sieges and wars—and, in its slow, floating way, to offer passage to another time. She watched it move across the turbid sky.

Amours de Voyage

PART

THREE

35

Nevinson watched men of the Royal Engineers wind the balloon down to the copse behind which its winch had now been anchored. The previous tethering point, outside the hotel, had been deemed too dangerous after the riddling of that establishment. Now this scrub-entangled hole behind the Dopper Church—in the pre-siege era, the kind of place where a runaway prisoner might have hidden—was the most envied place in town.

As he watched the men hauling down the balloon, which pulled back at them like something alive, two of the Boers' big guns began to concentrate a crossfire upon the town. Nevinson heard a dog yelp, and, rounding a corner, saw the corpse of a brown-and-white pointer lying on the ground with a small shrapnel wound in its skull the size of a jigsaw piece. It almost brought tears to his eyes: there was something human concentrated in this animal tragedy, as if the whole use-lessness of the enterprise were summed up in a dead dog. He hurried homewards, as all around him the roofs of houses cowered under the bombardment and men and horses ran about madly. The shops of the main street had become ghostly shacks, and the Town Hall a model ruin.

He reached the supposed safe haven of the cottage to see one of their few remaining fowls killed by shrapnel—fluttered up in the air, leaving nothing but a cloud of feathers. He went inside and sat down at the kitchen table to catch his breath. He was sick of the siege, the way it raised hopes and then threw them back. He was sick of what had, since Christmas, passed for food: in front of him on the table were two brown-smeared plates, upon which he and MacDonald had eaten a stew of horseflesh, now the main source of fresh meat in the town. He himself had watched the slaughtering, seen poor Tom Barnes lift the knife to his colt's throat and, with tears in his eyes, cut the thick cord of the artery. The beast had collapsed, and its blood pumped out onto the soil of the parade ground; by the time the Green Horse had finished, the place was a shambles of rib cages and entrails and discarded hoofs and heads. As the flies began to gather, the poor men had collected up these pieces—these pieces of animals they had lately ridden—and taken them for cooking at the railway station.

Human casualties had also been mounting. The farmer, Mr. Grimble, had ploughed his last furrow, Mr. and Mrs. Star had been killed, and many others had also fallen victim to shellfire and disease. Five of the Devons had been hit by a shell while eating their breakfast, the body of one being split open, his head burnt and smashed to mummy. Others had lost legs, fingers or eyes to shrapnel. Nearly a thousand people had enteric, and the stench of infected human waste was everywhere. Sickness stalked the streets, the gutters after heavy storms becoming fever beds, stewing under the fierce sun.

Some, like MacDonald, were quick to blame the non-white races. "Drainage in its true, wholesome sense is unknown here," he had observed. "The reason why ninety per cent of the town is down with sickness is because what methods of sanitation there are, are entirely worthy of the people by whom they are carried out—coolies and kaffirs. It's no cause for wonder."

"Don't be a greater ass than you need to be," was Nevinson's response. "One type of ordure is much the same as another."

The condition of their colleague, Steevens, had worsened considerably, after a brief period in which he had seemed to be out of danger. Raving had now become his normal behaviour, so far had his constitution broken down. The effort of caring for him becoming overwhelming, they had sought out a nurse to take charge of him at night. To give him fresh air, he had also been moved to a tent, in a scooped-out hollow by the river. Around this Nevinson and MacDonald built a sandbag fort, with the help of Maud, the admirable artist of the Graphic.

A strange thing had happened on the night Nevinson engaged the nurse. He was walking with Maud along the main road, under a crescent moon, when he caught sight of something black moving swiftly across the dirt before them. About three feet long, it inched forward in quick little darts.

"It's a snake!" cried Maud—but Nevinson had already leapt forward to crack it across the back with his stick. It kept moving, stopping only when Nevinson crushed its head with his boot, Maud stamping on its tail for good measure.

They then continued on their journey. Nevinson returned on his own later that night, the nurse having been duly instructed. Passing the spot where the snake-killing had taken place, on a whim he picked up its remains on the end of his stick and brought them back to the cottage, throwing the corpse under a tree with the intention of inspecting it in the morning.

As it happened, that morning brought a huge bombardment, one of the heaviest the town had yet received. Coming out into the garden of the cottage to watch it—as he had recklessly taken to doing—Nevinson was nearly hit by a fragment of shell. The lump of iron passed by his head and winged into the eucalyptus tree under which he had tossed the body of the snake. Dazed from his narrow escape, he went over to look. He found that the piece of shell casing had struck the snake's body, cutting it in two.

As he later recorded it: "To my astonishment, I noticed that the snake's inside was pure white. I looked closer. It was white cotton wool. The skin was a silken umbrella case. The body was carefully wound round with black thread, and a long piece of cotton projected from the mouth—the place where the deadly fangs ought to have been."

Maud's china-blue eyes widened in amazement when Nevinson told him about it, and the affair of "the magic snake," as it came to be known, provided much material for discussion in later days and weeks.

So did the grievous condition of Steevens, who continually asked for them to fetch his wife. Whenever the nurse came into the tent, he would think it was her. At other times he believed himself in a ship journeying homewards, and would cry out "Five bells! Five bells!" in a most distressing manner.

Nevinson suspected this last fantasy was due to Steevens's memory of his final trip outside the cottage before his confinement, during which he had visited one of the naval gun emplacements. He had read

Steevens's notes on the subject, and could divine in them clear signs of delirium, for his colleague had written of being on deck among white-clad ladies in long chairs, of swishing through cool blue water with the hot iron hills of Natal swimming away in the background. It was poetic, but pitiful. *Amours de voyage?* Hardly.

They had been feeding Steevens with Chevril. The bottled horse extract issued by the Commissariat was sustaining but frightful stuff. Far stronger than the Bovril in imitation of which it was named, it went off quickly, often smelling high when the brown bottle was opened. The brew was made by stewing the bones and flesh of the horses, the strength being raised by successive bouts of boiling and evaporation. It was said to be the intestines and other internal organs of the animals that gave Chevril its flavour, and since many of the animals had simply withered away, dropping in the street and lying there unable to get up again, it did seem likely that there could not be much taste in the muscles that had once been their pride, and were now simply meat.

Many of the Indians and Africans were dropping in the street as well, being on still skimpier rations than the Europeans, in spite of the sterling service they were now doing in trench-digging, domestic work and scouting. The young lad Wellington was now employing himself sneaking supplies through the Boer lines into Intombi Camp, and had been commended for it by Major Mott. No one had really been counting the casualties among these races, but Nevinson suspected that they suffered more than their fair share, given the paucity of shelter that was left to them. The Hindus especially were brave in the face of shellfire, looking on Destiny with fateful resignation. Rashid, former carrier to Gunner Foster, had since the latter's death become famous in the town for falling reverently to his knees and uttering prayers at the approach of a shell from Long Tom.

At evening, with his stick under his arm, Nevinson took his customary constitutional. His route happened to take him up by the railway station. Unused for its true purposes since the beginning of the siege, the engine shed was now the soup manufactory where the corpses of the recently slaughtered horses were boiled up to make the Chevril and other new products which necessity had generated: jellies, lozenges and a rather ghoulish "sandwich spread" made of pounded bone. Every day, huge red sides of horseflesh were run through the town in trolleys up to this place.

The vapours resulting from the boiling—which went on every night now—could be smelt a good five hundred yards away. Yet despite feeling queasy, Nevinson couldn't resist having a look. He pushed open the large wooden door of the shed and went in. It was a veritable hell's kitchen, filled with smoke and greasy steam. The men from the Commissariat had lit wood fires in the long trenches where the engineers had hitherto worked beneath the engines, and left them to burn overnight under seventeen large steel tanks. These cauldrons—in fact, iron trucks with the wheels removed—had been plastered round with clay to keep in the heat. Inside them (as Nevinson peered in) could be seen bluish joints of horsemeat, tumbling about in the simmering water. There was something hypnotic about this sight, and he stood there for a good five minutes watching pieces of flesh detach themselves from bones and flick up in the grey foam: every now and then a recognizable fragment could be seen—a piece of rib cage, or a skull's empty eye socket.

On seeing this, Nevinson had to avert his own eyes, though he was not so sickened that he failed to take advantage of there being no one about to scrape up a bit of fibrous matter from the bottom of an empty tank with his stick. At the same time as making him feel nauseous, the smells had made him realize how hungry he was; or more specifically, how he craved protein. He chewed this meaty residue as he walked back to the cottage, reflecting that it was rather like bits of mashed-up rope, and probably didn't actually contain much nourishment. Still, it filled the belly, and he slept well that night.

The following morning was unremarkable except for the arrival by runner of a newspaper reporting the escape of Winston Churchill from the Boers. Apparently he had climbed over the wall of the place in which he had been imprisoned, and without maps or food had decided to head for the border with Portuguese East Africa, nearly three hundred miles away. This he had achieved by following the railway and using the stars to guide himself. After diverse excitements, including hiding down a mine, he had secreted himself in a goods train and finally reached Delagoa Bay, and was now bound for Durban by the steamer *Induna*. Knowing that Steevens would be interested in the adventures of his old friend (who now had a Boer price on his head), and thinking it might help him regain his senses, Nevinson took the paper down to the sick man's tent.

But before he even got to the tent, he knew that Steevens was in no condition to read the story. The poor man was singing, at the top of his voice and to the tune of "Three Blind Mice": "Yes please, sirs! Yes please, sirs! Yes please, sirs!"

"He was convalescent yesterday," said the nurse, who was sitting outside, "but he has been raving ever since he woke up this morning. I am afraid that he hangs by a thread."

Nevinson pulled aside the tent flap and went in. The air was filled with a typhoid stench, and Steevens was thrashing about on the camp bed. On seeing his friend, he froze, looked him in the eye and said peremptorily, "On deck! Get me up on deck!"

At a loss as to what to do, Nevinson sat down and read him the article about Churchill. Every now and then, as he read, Steevens moaned, or shouted a scrap of verse:

There was an Old Person of Troy
Whose drink was brandy and soy . . .

36

MR. WINSTON CHURCHILL'S ESCAPE
Details of His Journey
From our special correspondent
By Eastern Telegraph Company Cable

Chieveley Camp, Monday, 5:35 p.m.

Mr. Winston Churchill has arrived here. He tells us that the Boers treated him with kindness and even unselfishness. When he refused to answer questions, they admitted that it was not fair to put them, and they were scrupulous not even to contradict a prisoner in argument. He returns with very high opinions of the Boer military genius. Before leaving Pretoria he left letters for the officials regretting that the circumstances did not permit him to take a formal farewell.

In a special edition published yesterday, the *Morning Post* prints the following telegram from Mr. Churchill:

Lourenço Marques, December 21, 10 p.m.

I was concealed in a railway truck, under great sacks. I had a small store of good water with me. I remained hidden, chancing discovery. The Boers searched the train at Komati Poort, but did not search deep enough, so after sixty hours of misery I came safely here.
I am very weak, but I am free. I have lost many pounds weight, but I am lighter in heart.
I shall also avail myself of every opportunity from this moment to urge

with earnestness an unflinching and uncompromising prosecution of the war.

On the afternoon of the 12th, the Transvaal Government Secretary for War informed me that there was little chance of my release. I therefore resolved to escape the same night, and left the State schools prison in Pretoria by climbing the wall when the sentries' backs were turned momentarily. I walked through the streets of the town without any disguise, meeting many burghers, but I was not challenged in the crowd.

I got through the pickets of the town guard and struck the Delagoa Bay railroad. I walked along it, evading the watchers at the bridges and culverts. I waited for a train beyond the first station. The 11:10 goods train from Pretoria arrived, and before it had reached full speed I boarded it, with great difficulty, and hid myself under coal sacks. I jumped from the train before dawn and sheltered during the day in a small wood, in company with a huge vulture who displayed a lively interest in me. I walked on at dusk. There were no more trains that night.

The danger of meeting the guards of the railway line continued, but I was obliged to follow it, as I had no compass or map. I had to make detours to avoid the bridges, stations, and huts.

My progress was very slow, and chocolate is not a satisfying food. The outlook was gloomy, but I persevered, with God's help, for five days. The food I had to have was very precarious. I was laying up at daylight and walking on at night time, and meanwhile my escape had been discovered and my description telegraphed everywhere.

All the trains were searched. Everyone was on the watch for me. Four wrong people were arrested. But on the sixth day I managed to board a train beyond Middleburg, whence there is a direct service to Delagoa.

News in brief

THE PLAGUE
Oporto, Wednesday

There was one fresh case of plague here today, and one death from the disease.

Election Intelligence

SOUTH MAYO

Mr. John O'Donnell and Major John MacBride of Westport, County Mayo, who is at present leading the Irish Brigade of the Transvaal Boers, were yesterday (says the *Globe*) nominated at Claremorris to contest the vacancy in the representation of South Mayo caused by the resignation of Mr. M. Davitt as a protest against the war. Several papers were handed in on behalf of each candidate, and afterwards a large public meeting was held. The polling takes place on Monday.

The Theatres

THE YEOMAN OF THE GUARD AT SADLER'S WELLS

The leading members of the D'Oyly Carte Opera Company who are this week playing Gilbertian opera are all well known to audiences. Miss Lina Carr, who is once more prima donna, was effective as usual, and she was very well supported by Mr. Leon Graham as Fairfax. The humours of Miss Billington's gaoler were enjoyed as on many previous occasions. Sergeant Meryll was represented by Mr. Kavanagh and Dame Carruthers by Miss Kate Forster, and another performance none the less successful for being familiar was Miss Gaston Murray's as Phoebe. Mr. Workman was to have played Jack Point the jester, but owing to indisposition he was replaced by Mr. Alfred Beers. *The Gondoliers* will be given this evening and *The Mikado* at the matinee on Wednesday. The rest of the week's programme includes *Trial by Jury* and *Utopia Limited.*

Letters to the Editor

TAM O' SHANTERS

Sir—I am given to understand that wool Tam-o'-Shanters are very beneficial as sleeping caps for soldiers. I shall be pleased to provide sufficient wool for at least 200 caps, if a number of ladies volunteer to make them. I sincerely hope that a few of the ladies of Manchester who have the time and can do this class of work will communicate

with me at once, so as to get the task in hand as early as possible.—
Yours, &c.,

(Mrs.) T. M'Cormick, Director, Crosby & Walker Limited, Oldham
Street, Manchester, November 18, 1899.

Advertisements

MONUMENTS in Granite, Marble and Stone:—Memorial Tablets,
Fonts, Busts and Medallions. Ackroyd's Funeral Works, 36–38
Commercial Road, London. Opposite front entrance cemetery.

OLD FALSE TEETH BOUGHT:—Many ladies and gentlemen have by
them old or disused false teeth, which might easily be turned into
money. Messrs. R., D. and J. R. Fraser of Ship Street, Ipswich (established since 1853), buy old false teeth. If you send your teeth to them,
they will remit you by return of post the sum at value, or, if you prefer,
they will make the best offer and hold your teeth over for your reply. If
reference necessary, apply to Messrs. Bacon and Co., bankers, Ipswich.

MOST TYPEWRITERS:—Most typewriter brands for sale, second-hand
but in good condition. Write to Cape & Pilcher, 14 Lancashire Road,
Stockport.

> *. . . which he took with a spoon,*
> *By the light of the moon,*
> *In sight of the city of Troy.*

37

Nevinson stayed with Steevens late into the night, dozing in the nurse's chair outside the tent. At about 3 a.m., he was awoken by rifle fire. Nothing new in that—except that it seemed very near. On getting up to investigate, he discovered that the Boers were making a concerted effort to storm the town from several directions, concentrating their attack on the crucial point of Caesar's Camp, which along with Wagon Hill next to it was the strategic key to the town's defence.

He rushed up to General White's headquarters to see what was happening. The place was chaos, with staff officers, signallers and messengers running in and out, bringing news of a battle of increasing intensity. The new field telephones came into their own that night—it was the first time they had been used in combat. As each line rang, and the message came down the gleaming wires that streamed across the town and its surroundings, a signaller would take advice from a post commander and pass it to a staff officer, who would then shout to General White the latest developments. Above the hubbub could be heard the squeal of the dynamos as the telephone operators wound them up, and then spoke in a gabble before the charge ran out.

"Heavy firing on southeast and west!"

"NMR in fight, five killed, twelve wounded."

"A hot action at Wagon Hill. Pickets are retiring. Being shot against skyline. Reinforcements requested."

"Boers have captured southeast of Caesar's. Artillery support requested."

Although the General had a scale model of the town and its fortifications on a table in front of him, and was moving garishly painted blocks of wood (representing contingents of troops) around it, he seemed somewhat bemused by the scale of the attack. In places the Boers had broken through the lines and were shooting into the tents, killing and wounding men through the canvas.

Unable to determine much in the confusion of White's HQ, Nevinson decided to go and see for himself. On riding up to Caesar's Camp as dawn began to break, he saw that the Boers were indeed in possession of a part of it. If they take it outright, he reflected, we might not hold Ladysmith for very much longer. He wondered how near to go, and then the matter was settled when a volley of bullets flew by close enough for him to hear the whine of their flight. None hit him, luckily, but he took the precaution of dismounting and taking shelter in a nearby sangar. And there he remained for most of the day, in the company of some men of the Irish Fusiliers, under a Major Churcher. Shells and bullets came whistling from every direction for the next twelve hours, as seemingly endless waves of Boers came on and were repulsed by the troops General White was sending into the breach. Nevinson watched the panoramic show of the actions and, as the new men moved in over the dead, imagined the General where he had left him in the telephone room—the controlling Immanent Will, spinning out his electric messages across a brain-like web of resonating, twitching wires. Then he saw a real brain smashed open as a man next to him went down to a bullet, lumps of pink jelly and chipped bone spilling out with the blood.

The sun grew fierce above the sangar. Through a loophole in the stone breastwork, Nevinson could see the ambulance wagons and the stretcher-bearers going to and fro. There were no more casualties in his fort, although splinters of rock from bullet strikes were continually falling on him. Partly this was because the Fusiliers had put up a line of straw dummies, as though peering over the parapet, to draw the Boer fire and enable some of them to get out and move forward. These dummies, which even had sun helmets, uniforms and rifles strapped to their vestigial hands, must—through the smoke of the battle—have seemed quite lifelike to the Boers, for they certainly kept shooting at them.

The dummies' camouflage received a boost later in the day, when a heavy storm came on and rain and hail obscured the opposing sides. The downpour also added to the discomfort of the living bodies. No one manning the defences had any food, nor any water except what was in the canteens on their belts, and after having burned up earlier, all were now shivering with cold.

Nevinson managed to get out at about five in the afternoon, but returned after half an hour with a tin of milk and some arrowroot for Major Churcher, who was exhausted. By this time, the British were gaining the upper hand, and at about six the Devons carried out a successful bayonet charge over on Wagon Hill. By seven, control over the two hills had been re-established. The mopping-up lasted till dark. On getting back to the cottage and taking off his soaking clothes, Nevinson went straight to bed feeling ill. He'd be damned if he'd catch a chill.

The morrow brought a dull, damp day, as if to thwart him in his determination to ward off a cold. He sat down to write up the battle, after getting an idea of the casualties from Colonel Hamilton at White's HQ. Altogether, about five hundred men had been killed or wounded on the British side, to some eight hundred on the Boer side. He was about to set this down when, struck by a thought, he stopped and laid aside his pen in disgust. He did not seem to be able to get beyond the background of glory, the military shorthand with its "algebraic signs and formulae of slaughter" (he had picked up his pen again, and was writing this instead), its "conventional language that conceals reality as well as any legal convention can": the bayonets sliding into flesh as though it were butter, the overpowering smell of horses, the gashes in a stomach raked by shrapnel. Journalism was not up to the task. Nor was literature: only Mr. Hardy came close. No wonder that the armies of the past vanish, their ancient dead only rising from the furrows of buried time to laugh, invisibly, at the very pageants of memory by which we seek to summon them.

38

By January 15, Steevens had lost consciousness. He looked so much worse that Nevinson, who saw him that morning, decided to send off a warning message to Mrs. Steevens by heliograph. After despatching the nurse to fetch Major Donegan of the Royal Army Medical Corps, said to be the best doctor in the town, Nevinson climbed up to each of the signal stations in turn. But to his irritation he found them busy with military traffic. He left instructions with a signaller, and rushed back down to Steevens's tent. Major Donegan was already inside. He decided to inject strychnine, and about noon things began to look a bit more hopeful. Nevinson went outside and sent a galloper to prevent the heliograph message. There was no point in causing unnecessary distress to Mrs. Steevens.

The strychnine stimulant proved relatively effective, and Steevens regained consciousness. MacDonald and Maud were fetched, and Steevens lay there blinking at his three fellow correspondents—Donegan having left to see to other patients.

"He's sweating heavily," observed MacDonald.

"You don't say sweating, Mac," said Steevens. "You say perspiring." Then he lifted his hands to his face and groaned.

"Come on, George," said Maud. "You've got to fight it. It's gripped you, and you've got to strengthen yourself—will it away."

Steevens took his hands away, and gave Maud a cynical look. "All right then," he said, "let's have a drink."

The war artist went and fetched some champagne, part of a cache that had been hidden against the event of relief, and poured it into a beaker, which he held against Steevens's lips. Nevinson was pained to see how swollen and split they had become. The sick man winced when the fizzy liquor went into the cracks, although he managed to finish the beaker. It seemed to have a good effect, and he began talking—about another colleague, Churchill.

"I remember once, when he came to dinner at my house, he said we were all worms, but he was a glow-worm. It made me laugh, but even then you could see how ambitious he was. It came off him like light off a lamp. Astonishing. I'm so glad he has escaped. Nevinson, if I don't make it, tell him that I love him."

"That you love him?" The signs of raving were coming back, and along with it a high-pitched, tumbling tone of voice, so different from his usual restrained yet casual tones.

"Yes, he is a nice boy. You will tell him, won't you? But don't tell him what a worm you feel when the enemy is plugging shells into you and you can't plug back."

He tried to struggle up out of the camp bed, but then fell back exhausted.

"Don't be thinking like that," said Maud, laying a hand on his shoulder. "You are going to be all right."

"And if Lynch ever comes back, tell him I will let him off the bet."

"What's that?" queried Nevinson.

"I had a bet with him of a dinner. I backed our cottage to be hit against another that he selected; and I won. He was to pay the dinner at the Savoy when we returned. He said, too, that the shells were like angels' visits, more or less. Well, soon I will be in a place where I can verify his conjecture. Tell him that, too."

"Stop talking now, old chap, you'll tire yourself," said MacDonald.

"Well, you are in command. I'll do what you like. We are going to pull through."

Then he rolled over and went to sleep, and between four and five o'clock that afternoon, passed quietly from sleep into death. The funeral was set for that very night. It was the rule of the town: so many were dying now that they could not be left unburied for more than a few hours, for fear that the corpses, rapidly decaying in the heat, would spread the disease.

On their way back to the cottage, Nevinson and MacDonald walked in silence at first, falling into step so that they matched each other pace for pace.

Then MacDonald spoke. "I shall miss the cocksure, logic-chopping blighter."

"I too," said Nevinson.

"I am surprised he went. I thought he really was going to pull through. You don't think that champagne was an indiscretion?"

"Of course not. It was a dying man's comfort. The fever had him by the throat. The doctor reckoned he had a weak heart, and that that was what got to him."

"God, this is a wretched, man-eating place. It is taking the best of us. He was good, wasn't he? Next to Bennet Burleigh, the ablest in the field."

"The best, I think. Look how Burleigh ran out on us here. George had a touch of genius, beyond question. I can't think of any other journalist who was able to give such a kick to his reports. Everything was dramatized. What Kipling does for fiction, he did for fact."

"Yes . . . I suppose so," said MacDonald, with some hesitation.

They buried Steevens that night. It took until half-past eleven for the coffin to be built—the wood for the job having been ransacked from a ruined building—and the ceremony took place at midnight. Most of the correspondents turned out for it, together with a good many officers and a few civilians. About twenty-five people in all, mounted on horseback, followed a small, glass-covered hearse up the hill to the graveyard. A soft rain was falling and, every now and then the donkey pulling the hearse let out its ghastly bray, which echoed between the silent rocks. On the way, Nevinson saw Tom Barnes and his friend, who stopped and saluted in the moonlight. This silvery pall, falling down through ragged edges of cloud, reflected on the hearse, the glass of which was covered in black and white embellishments; reflected too on the lines of white crosses marking the graves of earlier fatalities. As the thin ropes lowered the coffin, the Boer searchlight on Umbulwana began to play inquisitively on the scene, sweeping from side to side, and then settling its full glare on the grave. White and open, with its fringe of grass and waiting lid of earth, the hole looked, thought Nevinson, like an eye. Then the light went off, and all was dulled, and the rattle of soil began to sound on the wood.

39

Snare drums and trumpets sounded him down the gangplank. On his arrival in Durban from Delagoa Bay, Churchill was met by a large crowd, cheering him in praise of his escapade. He also received a large number of telegrams from all over the world.

To wit: "My heartiest congratulations on your wonderful and glorious deeds, which will send such a thrill of pride and enthusiasm through Great Britain and the United States of America, that the Anglo-Saxon race will be irresistible."

He took them with a pinch of salt, and after visiting the hospitals in the city—the sight of British wounded, the amputees in particular, had a profound effect on him—he hastened back to the British lines. He learned the news about Ladysmith, and how White's force was still stuck there, in spite of considerable advances by Buller. He rejected the suggestions he heard in Buller's camp that Ladysmith should be abandoned to its fate, and threw himself into the efforts to relieve the beleaguered town. Yet even he had doubts, and he watched the bombardments of the Boer positions with circumspection. Then he sat down to eat his luncheon.

The Biographer was one of the first to pass his congratulations to Churchill on the hero's rejoining the relief column. In fact he did so during that very luncheon, after which he made a tour of the camp looking for images with which to fill his machine. The troops were hungry. In one part of the camp tales of a wagonload of hams that had got through to some other contingent seemed to thicken the air with the odour of the frying pan. The chap who told the tale larded it with pictures of the slices sputtering in the pan, and by the time he had finished it was almost too much for one soldier.

"Oh," he cried. "Say them greasy words again!"

The Biographer wished again for some device that could record a voice, as an adjunct to the lens. He had, furthermore, come to recognize the limitations of the technology that he did possess: during Colenso and subsequent actions, he had become aware of how, in spite of his best efforts to get a full picture of the conflict, even the Biograph's panoramic view ended up being partial and confused. It was a matter of some concern to him that the officers in charge—Generals Buller and Coke, Warren and Woodgate, Colonels Crofton and Thorneycroft and Hill—really had no better a perspective on things than he did with his lens. The whole business seemed to be turning into a shambles. Every day, it was mooted that they would ford the Tugela, and—as it was said—"uncork the bottle" in which Ladysmith was stowed. But at every attempt the Boers threw them back. Christmas passed. There were muted celebrations. Then the firing resumed. So it went on. Only by the New Year came good news: the campaign in Cape Colony was going well, and the Boers were gradually being "sidled and coaxed," as Churchill put it, out of there. "Perhaps," he remarked to the Biographer, "1900 will mark the beginning of a century of good luck and good sense . . ."

And yet the guns still thundered. On January 6 there was so terrible a cannonade over Ladysmith that even Churchill and the Biographer could hear it at the relief column's camp. How much longer could that heroic garrison survive? That day, at any rate, they did so, a message coming over on the heliograph to the effect that "General attack on all sides by Boers—everywhere repulsed—but fight still going on."

The decision was taken to try to draw some of the Boer fire from the besieged town by creating a diversion nearby. Perry Barnes was in the action; indeed, Churchill—taking notes for his next letter back to the *Morning Post*—heard him speculating on the effect of a Maxim machine gun the Boers possessed. "You watch it . . . we'll have that fucking laughing hyena let off at us in a minute."

In his notebook, the correspondent marked the expletive down as a double dash.

That night, dashes were to the point, and points also: the searchlights at Buller's camp and in the invested town again communicated by flashing Morse on the clouds. This time a Boer searchlight joined the party, its beam flickering over the signals, trying to confuse them. The news got through, however—how the Boers had tried to rush the pickets on the outskirts of the town, but had been pushed back. Unsurprisingly, however, the details—who had died, who had survived—were missing from the account. Nonetheless, the news heartened the relief column, and as he sat in his tent watching Long Tom puff his pipe on Bulwan Hill, spitting down sheaves of orange flame on Ladysmith for the seventy-second day of siege, Churchill reckoned that the curtain was about to rise. The relief of Ladysmith was imminent.

The signs were everywhere, as each hour brought new reinforcements and supplies into camp, including more volunteer stretcher-bearers to join Gandhi's corps.

"They are sons of Empire, after all," muttered Churchill, watching them line up for their lentils at lunchtime.

A few days later, at dawn, General Buller gave the order to march. The column was to force the Tugela at Potgieter's Drift. Kit and correspondent, Biograph and stretcher-bearer, mule and machine, amid line upon line of khaki-clad soldiers—infantry, cavalry, gunners, sapper and service corps, all manner of uniforms. At least ten miles long, the column wound its way west through the hills. The place where the proposed crossing was to be made lay in an arabesque of river; over on the other side, the slopes and plains bristled with the ant-like figures of Boer gunners and horsemen. Among them, were he to be spied by some greater magnifying machine than Winston Churchill's spyglass, was the Boer doctor, Felix Sterkx.

The impending collision was inevitable, the tragedy set to unwind like clockwork. Still it did not happen. Battle tomorrow, thought Churchill, but never battle today. And then the day did come. Sappers began fixing pontoons in the river at various points. Slowly, with halts and hindrances, various contingents tried to cross. It was raining heavily, and mules and oxen bogged down in the quagmire. The Boers held their ground in any case, and back and forth the bullets whistled. This was not the place, after all; this was not the time. Except to die, for each attempt added to an ever-increasing casualty list. So far, Buller's efforts to relieve Ladysmith had cost the lives of some two thousand men. Was the bargain worth its price?

Buller climbed Mount Alice, a thousand feet above the river, and considered the Boer defences on the other side. Another plan was needed. He decided to send General Warren westward with twelve battalions and thirty-six guns, to cross the Tugela five miles upstream, while another commander was directed to make a diversionary attack there at Potgieter's Drift, thus splitting the Boer defences. The plan worked. From his new camp at Three Tree Hill, Warren was to throw his battalions forward, attempting to secure the small mountain known as Spion Kop. Forced to meet this turning movement in the British attack, the Boers had had to extend their line. Churchill reported it so: "Their whole position was, therefore, shaped like a note of interrogation laid on its side."

Soon enough, that question would be answered. Positively, it was believed. The Biographer had moved his cart forward to take a snapshot of Warren's men as they crossed, up to their breasts in the silvery water; the sun was setting, the Cape doves were cooing, and the omens seemed good. Now he was back near Buller's HQ on Mount Alice, on the south side of the river. He set up the camera between two big 4.7-inch guns, retired to his cart, and laid his head down to sleep. In the morning, he was woken by Biograph, his pet kitten, climbing over his face. As he was dressing, he heard the shout of one of the gunners outside one of the tents.

"Get up, for we shall be firing soon."

And fire they did. The earth shook beneath the camera, such were the vibrations from the guns, and the Biographer suspected the image would prove unsatisfactory. Once again, its panorama offered just one slice of the action, cut out of time; unable to record, for instance, how for seven hours of the previous night a column of Warren's men under Woodgate, Crofton and Thorneycroft had climbed their way up the gullies, ridges and boulder-strewn flanks of Spion Kop. On reaching the top they had successfully driven the Boers off with musketry and the bayonet. The force then tried to dig themselves in as reinforcements moved up. But their entrenching tools proved next to useless in the stony ground and, fumbling about in the darkness, they had to resort to piling up into low breastworks such boulders and rubble as they found on the summit. Still, it was a victory of sorts, and cheerful signals were sent by starshell to Warren over at Three Tree Hill, and Buller at Mount Alice. And from there in code to Ladysmith.

The cheer did not last long. When the morning mist lifted,

Warren's men—Perry Barnes among them—found themselves on something like a *tafelkop,* as the Dutch would have it: a semi-circular tabletop, on which had been scored the miserly, boomerang-shaped trench into which they were now packed.

"Like stockfish in a barrel," Barnes said, to no one in particular.

And then the killing began. From positions in front and high above on either side, Boer rifles began to rake them. Crossfire. The cracking of whips in the air. Underneath, the burden of the guns: six field pieces and two pom-poms. A formula for slaughter. Behind the low walls of that pitiful trench the casualties piled up. General Woodgate was mortally wounded, Colonel Thorneycroft rallied the men, Colonel Crofton—well, some were to say he dilly-dallied.

By mid-morning, the heads of Boer sharpshooters appeared over the edge of the tabletop opposite Perry Barnes and his companions. Far beyond, showing between the burghers' broad-brimmed hats and the muzzles of their rifles, a green smudge on the plain, supposed oasis: Ladysmith. Crofton sent a message down to Warren: "Help us, Woodgate dead." The Boers came on; soon they were only thirty feet away. The message came back: "Hold on to the last, no surrender." Confusion. Now it was hand to hand, and bloody as a butcher's slab . . . Among the soldiers there was a move to surrender, but this idea Thorneycroft firmly quashed, his large, red-faced figure standing oblivious to the Boers' fire.

He made his point to them too, shouting loudly enough for his words to be heard across the lines: "You may go to hell. I command this hill and allow no surrender. Go on with your firing!"

They did, and faced with the onslaught Perry Barnes and anyone else who survived the terrible riposte to Thorneycroft's challenge jumped out of the trench and fell back two hundred yards, scattering. Again the Colonel rallied them. Still the fire came. But spurred on by Thorneycroft, the British inched forward, recovered their lost ground at bayonet point. Sitting down in their trenches again, they made a long spiny hedgehog of bloodied blades and waited.

So it went on. Noon came, and with it more death. All day long the noise of battle rolled. Men like Perry Barnes, men who were there, saw what they saw, did what they did. Farther away, others saw nothing, or saw something obscured. For all of it, every human thrust and counter-thrust, was shut off to the likes of the Biographer, back there on Mount Alice with Buller. His hand on the shutter switch, in the lens some milky panorama of hills, drifts and more hills; but not the truth. Vague impressionist puff of battle; the men in the trenches rising and falling, but they were too far away. Only a telescope (Buller had one, Churchill had one) could catch them, and even then the images were questionable. In this context, thought the Biographer, gauziness and dubiety were utterly inappropriate: truth only was excellent, and a far-off dream it seemed, too.

For Churchill, watching the picture show or otherwise simply sitting around in Buller's camp was a good deal less than satisfactory. It was against his nature and his character. He had, in any case, had himself recommissioned, so he could be soldier again as well as journalist. At around four, he rode up the hill to see what was going on. It shocked even him, veteran of the Sudan and the Frontier, to see the stream of mutilated men coming down the slope in front of him. He got as near as he dared to the top, and watched the Boer Maxims lay waste to the British ranks.

Buller, too, through his muddy little disc of glass watched men cut to pieces. A shambles, in the old sense of the word: even the mushrooms of dust could not hide it. The Boers were winning. The messages had come in from the summit, forwarded from Warren: "Reinforce at once or all is lost. General dead." If he had received this message, why hadn't Warren committed more troops already? He was a sapper, that was the reason; a defensive man with a yen for trenches and fortifications, when what was needed up there was a fighter, not a hole-digger. If only Warren had been in Ladysmith . . . So Woodgate was gone. Through the glass, Buller saw Thorneycroft's large figure as he strove to rally the men. He sent an order to Warren to the effect that Thorneycroft was to take over command on Spion Kop from Crofton, with immediate local promotion to brigadier-general. Then he applied himself to the eyepiece again, sweeping his glass over the Boer positions . . .

In the early hours of that terrible day, Doctor Sterkx had been woken by the rattle of small arms. At daybreak he had heard that the British had taken the crest of Spion Kop. The bastion was theirs. This morning the counter-attack would begin. Sterkx had been ordered to go with it as medical officer. In the midst of a body of men, three or four hundred, he had climbed the grassy hill, struggling with his heavy surgical bag in one hand, grasping at the slippery tussocks with the other. Fire had been poured into them from the British trench; all around him men fell, and fell, and fell. Shot through the lungs, shot through the chest, shot through the forehead. There was mist everywhere, morning mist and blood mist.

Now it was afternoon. As Buller watched, Sterkx found a little hollow in which to do his work of cutting and binding. All around him the ground was blood-spattered. Still the fire came. From either side, the big guns pounded an acre of grass. A tremendous din. The mist dispersed, and the sun came out, and still the fire came. Point-blank fire. The crash of Lee-Metfords, incessant, and the British hidden by mounds of tumbled earth and the rough *schanses* of boulder and rubble they had scrabbled around them. Perhaps only a hundred Boers were left now, facing the narrow belt of rocks that comprised the British trenches on the crest. Surely this was a British victory. Sterkx watched men slip away beside him, dispirited, thirsty, burned by hot sun and hot bullets.

Others went over the rim, and fought hand to hand with the *rooineks*. Few of those came back to his dressing station: shot, disembowelled, torn by shells, they lay on the grass. This was the end. He spotted Janssen there, and van Zyl, one shot in the throat, the other bayoneted. He saw Spijkers with an eye put out by a shell splinter, holding his hand to the gushing socket. This was the end.

Another thought so too. Sickened, Churchill had watched it, had watched it all until dusk fell. He resolved that Warren, waiting for the outcome down at the bottom, had to be told how bad it was. Heavy guns would have to be brought up, or better cover found for the poor men on the summit. But Warren, like Crofton, was in dilatory mood. Churchill was sent up the stony track once more, this time in darkness, to find out what Thorneycroft thought. On the way up, his path obstructed by a stream of wounded men and stretcher-bearers, he nearly collided with two Indians carrying the body of General Woodgate.

"I have seen some service," he said to them, looking down at the dead man's pallid, moonlit face. It seemed as if it were made from wax. "But nothing like this."

"We are in the grip of elemental forces," intoned one of the Indians, much to Churchill's surprise. "Only when we look into our hearts and prevent the violence surging in them will you no longer see sights like this."

"Buck up, man," said Churchill. "We've got a battle to win."

On the other side of the plateau, among the burghers, everyone thought that the British were indeed winning. The hours had gone by. Six, seven, eight o'clock . . . The bodies had piled up. Surely before morning the British would sweep through, roll up the Boer line; they could be in Ladysmith by daybreak. It was clear the position would have to be abandoned. Sterkx felt his nerve go; he gathered up his instruments and bag and slithered down the hill. At the bottom, he found more wounded, and spent the rest of the night tending to them by lamplight.

Nine, ten, eleven . . . Perry Barnes thought of his brother, shut up in Ladysmith. Before night had fallen, it had been possible, just, to see the town beyond the ridge of the last hill. Now it was nearly midnight and they had been here—what? sixteen hours?—on this Spion Kop, pinned down by rifle fire, and swept by Long Toms. Oh Tom, what a beast of a weapon you have given your name to. Carnage here: men blown to pieces, heads torn off, holes in the middle of torsos. Just limbs left. He had watched a headless man get up and stagger three paces before falling. They say they are getting some heavy guns to us; but when? The CO, Thorneycroft, was beside himself, sitting on the ground and shaking uncontrollably. At least Perry thought he was the CO: he had been arguing with Lieutenant-Colonel Hill and General Coke, who disputed his promotion. What a load of idiots: around Perry, the bodies were three deep. He tried to make himself as small a target as possible.

Great confusion. Lieutenant Churchill, the one who made that famous escape, was up here with a message from Warren. Reinforcements were finally coming, he said, and guns. At last. But Thorneycroft says they are to go down, what's left of them. So that's what they did, Perry and his comrades, dragging wounded men under the very moon by whose light, the night before, they had climbed the blasted hill. On the way down, they met the party sent to rescue them. God, what a mess.

It was past two in the morning. All night long, the Biographer had listened to the guns; watched Gandhi and his Indians come and go under flare and torchlight; watched the barrels smoking and spurting orange flame as the gunners continued to rain death on the Boer positions beyond Spion Kop; watched the men smoking as they lay on the stretchers, pulling furiously on pipes to ease their pain. It was as if, he thought, the shells were going off inside them. Terrible slaughter. He tried to sleep, but it brought no respite: the distorted faces of those smokers haunted him like ghosts, and in his dreams the ambulance wagons became wagonloads of human hams.

Sterkx woke with a start, realizing that he had fallen asleep on the chest of a dead man. Where was he? At the foot of Spion Kop. He looked up at the grim, mist-shrouded slope, expecting to see a phalanx of British troops in front of him. The sky paled, and a figure emerged from the mist, his hat dripping with dew. It was a broad-brimmed hat, a Boer one.

"It is ours," the man said, in the Taal. "Look."

He pointed up at the summit, where rays of sun were beginning to penetrate the mist shroud. There at the top were two more figures, waving their rifles. They had broad-brimmed hats as well.

"My commando," said the man, grinning. His beard, Sterkx noticed, was stiff with dried blood. "We have won, meneer."

Once more, Sterkx climbed the hill. Breasting the ridge, he saw the remains of the British trench in the clearing mist. Between them lay an expanse of grass, dotted here and there with Boer corpses. He checked each one to see if any were living. No. Of course not. Then he walked further over towards the silent British trench, still slightly nervous. Peering over the parapet, he suddenly came face to face with a British trooper; the man was squatting in the trench, his feet gathered on the body of another, with his rifle grasped between his thighs and hands. It looked as if he had coiled himself up in a ball, like a porcupine. Sterkx looked around: everywhere there were bodies, parts of bodies, and parts of parts: feet, heads, arms, all torn asunder . . . Here was humanity blown to atoms.

Later that morning, the Biographer tried to take his cart closer to the site of battle, was dissuaded by an officer, and so waited by the banks of the river. Another armistice had been agreed to gather the dead. Once again, he saw Gandhi toiling down the narrow track from the summit, rallying his volunteers. He learned that the Indian had had the honour of carrying General Woodgate's stretcher. Others were now being carried on the backs of the Indians. There was a want of stretchers, and those wounded who had not been tended to staggered alone, or leant on the arm of a comrade. All by the sides of the track lay those whose strength had failed: ripped by shell and bullet, they bled to death. Slowly, as flies clustered in black heaps on bloodstained uniforms, the picture became clearer, and it was ghastly. Over thirteen hundred men lost. The ridge abandoned, and no ground gained. A pointless sacrifice.

40

57109 Trooper Barnes, P.,
Military Camp No. 3,
Spion Kop,
Natal.
January 27th, 1900

Dear Lizzie,

The first month of the new century sees me in the clear-up stage of a bloody slaughter, which cannot bode well for the next hundred years. I have seen such sights. Dead and wounded men lying all in heaps in a long trench or on open grass, killed or maimed. They look like bits and pieces of clothing, thrown down when you are going to bed. But they are people, and are covered with black stains of blood. The man with the camera has been photographing their faces, which are dreadful, since the eyes and mouths tend to have fallen open and all the muscles frozen.

It should never have happened, and I can only say I don't want another lot like it. They are saying it is the heaviest cannon fire ever. No reprisals could be too severe for the monsters of iniquity who did this to our men, and I mean our own Generals as well as the Boers.

On the battlefield afterwards, Boers were picking bits of kit off our dead men. They are as keen for curios as we are, but to my mind it is a disrespectful thing for either side to do after such a fight.

I am going to write another letter to Deacon, a chap who was invalided home after this do. I shall tell him to call and see you as he lives in Cubbington. Lucky dog. I never want to see a battlefield again as long as I live.

It is hard for me to think about how things are with you at this time, but rest assured that I desperately want to be back with you. I think much on the business of life on the farm, missing my forge in particular; my own furnace and tools, not the shoddy portable stuff they give me here. I didn't hear what sort of man Father got in response to the advertisement I saw in the Mail. I hope he is good with the beasts.

Thank-you for the pipe and the 1/4 lb of Tobacco. I have also been sent a woollen Tam-o'-Shanter by a lady from Manchester, as a charitable donation, so that will serve as a smoking cap. The Tobacco here is awfully strong stuff. The white clay pipes the Africans use are not bad but not like the one you sent me, which is a little gem. I have degenerated into quite a big smoker, I am afraid. But so would you have done if you had seen what I have seen.

Hoping you are all in the best of health and temper, I will now close with love to all.

I am as ever

Yours etc,

Perry

p.s. You might send me some tea tabloids and saccharine, which we carry in our wallets and are handy when we go on these flying expeditions with nothing but what we carry on our horses. Be certain that when we "fly" into Ladysmith I will give some to Tom.

41

Keeping flies off was the worst of it. But under Doctor Sterkx's attentions, over the course of two months, the entry wound in his thigh had slowly begun to close up. He saw it whenever the doctor changed the bandages: a ragged hole, with the purple skin around it puckered and stained with cordite. The exit wound was still causing him a great deal of trouble: messier and more ragged, it continued to be painful. Both wounds were difficult to keep clean, and the doctor had warned him that if it began to show signs of infection he might lose the leg. Sometimes the Zulu wondered if he would ever get out of the camp. He had talked no more of his escape, but as the days crawled by, he began to get up and limp around the camp, trying to strengthen his withered muscles. With or without Sterkx's help, he was determined to go.

Then, unexpectedly—after a particularly fierce bombardment of Ladysmith by the Boer guns—Sterkx came into the hut one evening, carrying a bundle wrapped in grey cloth. He sat down next to Muhle.

"I have got the things you asked for. A knife, too. I still think you have little chance of getting into the town, but I cannot stand the thought of my Frannie being hit by one of our own shells."

Muhle looked at the anxious white face of the doctor, then reached out and grasped his hand.

"I will do everything I can to help her. Have you put a letter in?"

Sterkx shook his head. "It is too dangerous. Joubert would have me shot if he knew I was letting you go into the town with your knowledge of our camp. I would come under suspicion of being a spy. No, I want you to find her, if you get inside, and tell her that I am all right. And also that when it is over she is to try to get to her mother's house in Lichtenburg. I will leave instructions for her there."

Muhle sat up. "What about you? Why don't you come with me?"

Sterkx shook his head again. "I must stay here and do my duty. I still believe in the cause of this war: if we don't drive the British out, we will never have freedom in our land."

Muhle bit his lip. "You are good doctor," he said, in even tones. "And a brave man. Well you deserve the Zulu name of Nkombose, surrounder of hills. When this is over, you will come to my kraal at Inanda, on the Mngeni river, and the women shall do a dance in honour of that name."

Before Muhle had finished speaking, Sterkx stood up. "Good luck, kaffir. If you are caught, I will deny all knowledge of this."

Brooding, Bella kept the siege, looking out over the yellow Klip with hooded eyes. The guns were briefly silent. Only the rats could be heard, and the sighs of the wind as it rippled over the water. The winder of a hand-line sat in her lap, the line's free end attached to a hook baited with a worm. Besides eels, what they mostly caught was a kind of barbel, a frightful thing that sat in the mud at the bottom. It tasted powerfully stale, and she doubted whether the flesh was not poisonous. From where she sat, she could see the lumps of horse dung slowly breaking up in the slow-moving, stagnant water. A week or so ago, the Boers had tried to dam the river upstream, in the hope of diverting its flow into the middle of the town, to flood people out: the plan had not worked, but the attempt at damming did seem to have made all the waste come to the surface.

Every now and then, a rat would pop up its head by the bank, and chatter its teeth. She wished it was those horrible creatures which were damaged by the shells, not the birds and flowers. Only the other day, she had seen a mockingbird knocked out of the air by a fragment of shell. It was still alive when she got to it, one leg smashed and its wings fluttering hopelessly. She had picked it up and broken its neck. Mrs. Frinton, she knew, was in the habit of bringing such casualties to the cooking pot, but unable to do so herself, she had buried the poor little thing. There was, in any case, something a bit ghostly about the whole episode, insofar as the mockingbirds had taken to imitating the whine and buzz of shells, and of the whistles that the wardens blew to warn of them.

As she looked out over the lilies and swamp grass on the riverbank—as she had looked out over them for so many weeks now—the whole view, with its wind-swayed palette of reds and greens, became soft and hazy in a way that could not simply be accounted for by the breeze. It was as if, without hard concentration, particular objects and colours would slip away from her. Sometimes she seemed to feel herself sliding into the scene, becoming a part of it . . . just another shape among all the others ranged along the river. Other times, she was distinct, alive and alert inside herself. All the while, she hoped for something to emerge from the picture in front of her. But she did not know what it was: the departure she had wished for, the longed-for scenes—they had all been shipwrecked in a living sea of waking dreams.

It was no wonder she was so shaken and confused. The relentless pounding of iron and explosive, hurled four miles through the air, reduced all to a terrible sameness. For while the sights and smells and sounds of the town had become shocking and extraordinary—the horses with their skeleton ribs and drooping eyes, the soldiers with bare, bleeding feet, the oxen bellowing as they tried to tear themselves from the yokes out of pure hunger—the constant noise and brightness of explosion dulled the power of the senses to register these things. Some days, she felt she might never see or hear straight again.

And yet another part of her felt that she had never really done so anyway. Only when she had spoken back at her father had she felt clear of all the things that were jammed up inside her. That was why she had to do it, that was why she had to do what she had been planning and pondering all these long weeks. When she was ready, and had amassed a store of food, a pair of pliers and other requisites, she would go and talk to Nandi and Wellington about it.

On February 5, Nevinson fell sick. He took to his bed in the cottage, mindful of the parallel with Steevens, but telling himself this was just one of his usual spells of ill health. But on the ninth, MacDonald called for the Hindu doolies to carry him away to one of the hospitals, in a high fever.

Knowledge of his innocence, and frustration at his imprisonment, bred a kind of despair in the barber. The dreary tempo of life in the

Dopper Church weighed down on Torres's spirits. He sank very low, and began wishing that he had never left Lourenço Marques. At least, there, he had had his freedom. Each week it became harder not to rage at the doltish English guards, or run full-pelt at the wire and try to climb it, regardless of the consequences. During the day, he would pace round the dusty ground inside the fence. At night—sour, depressed and hungry—he would lie on one of the mats the army had provided and try to ignore the crying children. There was no division of prisoners by gender nor (and this annoyed the Boers greatly) by race, and they all dressed, washed and ate together. The children's wails, echoing under the roof of the big church, had an eerie, unearthly quality that was very disturbing in the blackness. They were mostly Boers, and some had lost their mothers in the confusion of the early days of the war.

The orphaned children were being looked after by a blonde, plumpish Dutchwoman. One of the most curious sights of the prison yard was the pet goose which she took around with her on a lead, thereby providing much amusement for the children. She was a brisk, businesslike person who paid little attention to anyone or anything except the children and the goose.

At six o'clock one evening, however, while making his final tour of the yard, Torres found her crouched in a corner, sitting in a little alcove between an outhouse and the main building.

She was weeping, holding the goose between her knees. He got down next to her. "What is the matter?" he said, reaching out to touch the stained white linen of her sleeve.

She looked up at him with tear-stained eyes, and said something in Dutch.

"I don't understand," said Torres. "Do you speak English?"

She smiled thinly, and shook her head. Then, pointing at her chest, she said the word *"Vrouw."*

Wife, he knew that.

Then she pointed at the hills where the Boer guns were massed, and said another word which Torres could not catch. At that moment there came a distant puff of smoke and, as if by command of her speech, the guns began to thunder. The Boer woman curled herself into a ball next to Torres. As the shells screamed over, making the air throb, the two of them found themselves holding each other in the dank little corner of masonry, with the goose squirming between them. Torres found his lips were softly pressed against the Boer woman's hair, and his arms grasping her trembling body. The yellow beak of the goose flapped from side to side, hissing with anxiety. All around was noise and explosion. Sparks flew off the roof of the church. Torres couldn't believe that the Boers would take such risks in landing shells so close to the church; surely they knew that some of their own people were inside. A red flash blazed; there was a cracking sound; the British were firing back.

All told, the encounter must have lasted half an hour or so. Once the Boer shelling had slackened slightly, they released each other. Torres stood up, sweating heavily. He nodded at the woman, and she got to her feet. They walked back round to the front of the church, where the sentry at the gate regarded them closely. Torres realized it was one of the soldiers who had brought him in when he was first detained, the one who had talked with Miss Kiernan outside the Town Hall. Their eyes held each other's for a second, and then the soldier waved his rifle in the direction of the doors. It was getting dark; it was time to go in.

42

It was time to get out; it was getting dark—and the British shells were falling. Tying the bundle to his belt, Muhle poked his head out of the hut. All around were the tents and abandoned campfires of the Boers, the whole lot encircled by the laager of wagons; several of these had been tipped over by shells, and the canvas covering of one was burning. That was where to head for, the smoke would mask him . . . though there was not enough, not yet. He waited for another shell to fall, watching the shadowy figures of Boers running about between the tents, heading for the rock-walled schanses in front of the laager. They were swearing and shouting; then, as he watched, the force of another explosion swept across the encampment. It picked up the white glow of a tent as if it were nothing but a handkerchief—picked it up, crumpled it, and tossed it aside.

We moya! Hail, wind. Crouching, and moving along the ground quickly in the pall of green lyddite smoke with every muscle tensed, Muhle reached the edge of the laager, slipped underneath a wagon, and rolled down a slope. At the bottom of the incline, the bundle banging uncomfortably into his hip, he threw himself into a thicket of low underbrush. Time to gauge the situation, time to catch his breath. The green smoke had begun to fill his lungs and sting his eyes, and he was coughing loudly; but it was better to do that now, while the noise of the engagement still covered him. Behind him he could see the tips of Boer guns, and here and there the brimmed hat of a sentry ducking beneath the wall of his schanse. In front of him, lit by moonlight and the afterglow of shellfire, was another, taller hill, split up the middle by a donga, a gully filled with rocks and boulders. He ran towards it.

Before he could gain it, he heard the snap of a Mauser bullet, plucking at the earth next to his feet. One of the sentries must have seen him. *Nayaphi?* Where should he go now? Think. Follow the way of the *isidawana,* the weasel. Cunning his only salvation. They would expect him to go up the donga. Instead, he waited for another shroud of smoke to drift across the escarpment, then veered sideways, away from the gully, heading for some more undergrowth. The physical effort of it almost broke him: his wound felt as though someone was turning a knife inside it. Worse still were his eyes, which were streaming from the effect of the lyddite fumes. He crashed into a patch of brush and, lurching and gasping and tripping over branches, made his way through to the other side. The edge of the thicketed piece of ground fell away towards a long, open area of country affording no cover whatsoever, and then rose to another crest. He knew that as soon as the bombardment had ceased, the Boer sentries would come down looking for the strange dark figure they had glimpsed in the moonlit smoke.

There was nothing for it but to try to work the flank of the hill on the other side of the open country, where—through his burning eyes   he could see the night outline of some thorn trees poking up at the top of the ridge. He began to move swiftly towards them, expecting at every moment to feel the burn of a bullet in his back or shoulder. He had a vague idea where he was, that if only he could get over the ridge, the British lines would be within sight. He had almost reached it when another shot rang out. Realizing they must have started following him already, he dropped down and started to wriggle forward on his stomach. Just a few hundred yards to go. He squirmed like a reptile, all the time the coarse grass rubbing against his trousers and the wound beneath.

Behind him he heard faint voices, and then the bark of a dog. He tried to speed up. The bombardment had stopped now, and the clouds of smoke were thinning out. By the hoe of Shaka, his eyes hurt. Surely the moonlight would show him full now. He had only a few minutes left. Forward a bit more in his snake track. The trees were above him; he reached out and scrabbled with his hand, pulling himself up. Now he could grasp a root. He pulled again. Then he turned on his side and looked round. Appearing and disappearing in the blackness were the flames of torches, a straggly line of fire-spots. But they were not coming in his direction. He had made the right choice. They were going up the donga. He released a sigh from his lungs and stood up. Stumbling, he made his way through the mimosa thicket. The thorns tore at his sides, and every now and then he stopped and raised his hands to his eyes. They felt thick, gummy. When he got to the other side of the trees, he looked out over a series of undulating ridges and saw, through his swollen lids, the lights of Ladysmith, two or three miles away. Between lay various smaller Boer outposts and batteries, blocking his way.

Around him, another light—the generous, dangerous moon of Natal—illuminated patches of ground. He picked out the stripe of a path coming up from the town, passing between the circular shapes of the British defences, and suitably obscured from the Boer outposts by hills. He crawled down towards it, collecting up stones as he went, pulling out his shirt and using it as a pouch in which to carry them. When he got to the edge of the path, he crouched down and started making a pile of stones. Not enough. He went back and picked up more, until the pile was knee-high. To the innocent eye, it looked like nothing, indistinguishable from any of the other cairns that dotted the slopes above the town. To his eye, though—and, he hoped, that of another—it was a clear sign written on the ground. A letter.

He retreated to the trees and, finding a small area free from roots, opened the bundle. He laid the cloth on the ground and spread out the contents upon it: water canteen, knife, and a small packet. He took the knife and began to scrape a hole in the ground. It seemed to take an age, but after a while he had made enough of a depression to hide most of his body. He broke off some branches and, using strips of bark to bind them together, made a cover for the hole, stuffing leaves into the bindings to complete the camouflage. Then, exhausted, he crawled inside his burrow, pulling the lid down on top of him. His wound was throbbing—it felt warm, as if a coal had been placed in a cavity beneath the soft, fresh-healed skin—and he was hungry. He took the packet out of the bundle, undid it, and felt something rough, like tree bark. Biltong, dried meat. Mabunu food. Boer food. He lifted it to his mouth and tore off a piece. It was extremely tough, taking a long time to soften.

43

Time passed. Time grew, the roots of trees sending out bright green suckers into people's bomb-proof shelters. And time, like the ever-decreasing bundles of forage the Green Horse spread out each day on the parade ground, rotted. Tom felt he was rotting too, the lack of purpose fermenting inside him. He hated being on guard duty at the prison; it was a lowly activity for a soldier. He wished he wasn't there. More than anything, he wished he hadn't got caught up in the business with Bella and the Portuguese prisoner. When he was off-duty, he had gone down to the tunnels to see her, but on being fetched out by an old woman she had simply given him a hard look and marched back inside her cave without a word.

Without: that was the word which pressed down on his mind. Without meat (how fondly he remembered those days at home, pulling ribs of tender yearling from the pickle tub), without the physical comfort of a woman (the memory of his encounter with Bella in the orchard, too, played through his mind, at once arousing and depressing him), without drink, without tobacco. Without, also, in another sense, the Boers. By Christ, how would it end, when would it end? If someone had said to him in November that he would still be shut up here in February, he would have laughed. The mutter of Buller's guns on the Tugela, now clearly audible, merely emphasized the deadlock in which they were fixed: news of the British defeat at Spion Kop had made everybody very miserable, and they were all as likely to imagine the distant thunder as being the fire of a retreating army as that of an advancing one. The messages coming through from Buller's heliograph had—from the point of view of a hungry, dispirited garrison—descended to a quite unbelievable level of banality and uselessness, one reading "Sir Stafford Northcote, Governor of Bombay, has been made a peer."

Apart from dreaming about Bella's soft white hands, Tom concerned himself, as he sat on a milking stool outside the Dopper Church guardhouse, with the identity of the spy out of whose hands he had shot the looking-glass. In spite of his arrest, he was pretty certain it wasn't the Portugee: all the boots at his ruined shop and living quarters had been checked, and none of them printed the tell-tale V-sign. Whenever he was on his way from Green Horse Valley to the church, he looked out for it in the dust of the street; but he never saw it. It was just the same as everything else in the town. Nothing happened, nothing except shells, sunstroke and dysentery—and the constant craving for tobacco, which seemed to take on great, almost philosophical proportions in that place. There was a shortage, but there were also secret stocks. A black market had grown up—especially in the pungent Dutch shag, which could be sweetened with peach blossom. There were also those among the Indian and other merchants who made a small fortune by rerolling the fragments from cigar butts picked up around the town, and then selling the second-hand article in their shops.

It was while buying an ounce of plug tobacco at such a shop, one evening before going on duty at the church, that Tom saw her: not Bella (although she had continued to occupy his thoughts) but a coffee-coloured woman with beads round her neck and long coils of dark hair. She was a Cape Malay, a descendant of one of the indentured labourers brought to South Africa by the Dutch. Her father, seeing Tom look at her in the murky room beyond the counter, grinned toothlessly from under his red fez and made a sign with his head, jerking it back towards her with a suggestive look. Tom glanced at the woman again. She was wearing a light shift, printed with swirling patterns of blue and orange. In the semi-darkness, her eyes—larger and more oval than those of Europeans—looked back at him impassively.

The shopkeeper lifted up the flap in the counter and Tom—forced to heft his rifle awkwardly in order to fit through the gap—went through into the dimly lit room. The place smelt of patchouli, and the low flame of an oil lamp guttered in a corner, giving off a smoky light. The woman smiled at him, and then went over to the bed and lay down. She had a large number of bangles on her arm, made of horn and metal.

Tom cleared his throat. "How much?"

The woman shook her head—which he took to mean that she did not understand English—and, sitting up on the bed, held up the fingers of both hands. Ten shillings. He had enough: it was cheaper than the tobacco, at any rate, which had cost him twenty-five shillings. He calculated that at the usurious rate of exchange that obtained in Ladysmith, this woman's body would cost him no more than he could expect to pay for three-quarters of a pound of sugar.

He stood there for a second, not knowing what to do. Finally he unhitched his rifle, took off his helmet, and started to undo the buttons of his tunic. As he was doing so, the woman pulled her shift over her head, the bangles sliding down her arm with a clanking sound. Tom looked at her bared, pointed breasts, and then clumsily lifted up his right foot to undo the laces of his boot; as he did so, he nearly lost his balance, and the woman made a noise something like a laugh and got up out of the bed. Coming over to him, she knelt down on the floor and began to unlace his boots, holding the leg with one hand as she pulled at the heel with the other. Tom looked down at her bent back beneath him, the bones of her spine pressing out through the caramel flesh like the keys of a musical instrument.

She put her hands flat against his thighs, rubbing her palms against them in slow, circular movements. He felt himself grow hard, and looked down through the gloom at the woman's hair streaming down her back, at the smooth groove between her buttocks and the sharply defined muscles of her calves, which tapered out towards feet folded flat against the floor. Her soles were face up, skin reflecting the lamplight in feathery creases.

She began to undo his breeches. As she tugged them down, his eye was caught by his boots lying on the floor to either side of her— tipped over, their tongues and laces falling out around them. There was something fascinating about those boots of his, or so it seemed, and as the Malay woman released him from his underclothes, he stared at them dumbly. Still kneeling, the woman reached an arm between his thighs and started caressing his buttocks. Her cheek, the whole side of her face, was laid against his hip, and as she moved her hair brushed against him, making him shudder with pleasure. His hands felt trembly and useless, so he put them on her shoulders; but then she made a slight disapproving sound and stood up, dragging her breasts against his stomach, until she was face to face with him. She moved closer until, almost imperceptibly at first, a soft warm hood of flesh began to press itself over the tip of him. He gasped.

At this she laughed softly, and immediately uncoupled herself. She turned around and—holding his prick as if it were the bridle of a horse—led him over to the bed. They lay down next to each other, he flat on his back and she up on one arm, stroking his chest and stomach with her free hand. Her hair and breasts hung down near his face, the dark nipple of the nearest breast touching his cheek. After a while, she pushed back her hair over her ear, leant down over him, and took his crown between her lips. For a while she was motionless, except for fluttering her tongue upon him a little. Then she took the root of him in her hand and began to move her head slowly up and down. When she pulled his shaft tight with her hand, he had to stop a groan in his throat, conscious that the shopkeeper was not far away. Looking up at the ceiling of the room, which was spotted with dark marks and blotches, he was just beginning to feel a warm, rising sensation in his balls when she stopped, climbed on top of him, and drew him into her.

She started to move, and he groaned again and gripped her hipbones. In response, she stopped and waited, immobile except for the slightest pulse. As she did this, she looked down into his face with mocking eyes. He had to look away, concentrating on the dark shape of his rifle, propped up against the wall. Soon, when he was calmer, she put her hands on his chest and started to move again. She used her hands as levers to get the rhythm; and then the rhythm got him, the tempo increasing until, helpless, he closed his eyes and unloaded himself deep inside her.

44

"Come on," shouted the Biographer, "come on in."

Naked, Perry Barnes hovered on a pale sandbank at the edge of the Tugela, and then jumped.

The Biographer approached him like a greedy crocodile. "Now I can touch your fudge-box," he murmured lasciviously.

Once, unobserved under the cover of the river's silvery surface, they had finished (for they had been lovers for weeks) and the Biographer had frigged him off under the water—Perry's white string, seed of his forefathers, floating off downstream to God knew where—they got out and towelled themselves down.

The two men walked back to camp in silence, glowing with shame and the after-warmth of pleasure. The Biographer smoked a cigar.

Then Perry said, "If I get potted . . . when you get into Ladysmith, tell Tom he was a good brother."

"Don't be silly," said the Biographer. "You'll be able to tell him that yourself, when you see him."

45

Each eye had its own vision, thought Nandi, but some eyes saw nothing at all. To be specific, white eyes. They did not see that all this digging and cleaning of latrines to which she had been put by the military might be beneath her. It was simply *kafferwerk,* her natural lot, this carrying of shit and earth, sometimes with her bare hands. It amazed her, the extent to which the whites failed to see her as human. It was not even that they thought her nearer to the beasts, the oxen and mules; it was that they failed even to see her at all. To them, all blacks were invisible, and silent too. The truth, of course, was that the voices of all her people were as noisy as the shells which, even now, screamed in the air above her; it was just that the whites did not understand the language. Not Zulu or Xhosa—she meant something deeper than that: the blackness which shut like prison bars.

Another shell went over. It had grown dark, and she could see the orange mark the shell made in the sky. She just shrugged now when the bombs came; whereas earlier, like everyone else, she had crouched and cringed. Now it was all simply part of the routine. No shelling—that would have been extraordinary, that would have broken the pattern of events. But in Ladysmith now, with the siege in its one hundred and tenth day, the routine was as set and fixed as the passage of the earth round the sun.

And yet, that day, a strange thing had happened. The young mama, Miss Bella, had come up from the tunnels to the small shack she and Wellington had built in the ruined garden behind the Royal (the original servants' quarters having been hit) and asked for their help. She had never known anything like it before. Wellington had not been there, and it had been to him in particular that the young mama had wanted to talk. He had been out beyond the lines, checking for heaps of stones, for *isivivane*. According to her son, Muhle had made some pledge about meeting him by one—but to her own mind, in spite of missing her husband terribly, it would be better if Wellington did not go outside the perimeter, as he put his life in danger each time he did. He had now stopped going on missions for the white men, and spent all the time scouring the hills and the plain for his father.

A kind of mania about this had come over him, and it was all she could do to prevent him from spending all day and night out there. At least the young mama's suggestion (for which she had already made a payment) kept Wellington in the town, even if it did seem dangerous enough in itself. She would tell him about it when he came back, and send him down to see Miss Bella at the tunnels. Nandi, who had once taken some food down there on Mr. Kiernan's instructions, was glad she didn't have to go herself. The holes by the Klip made her think of the *umgodi,* the mine shafts on the Rand—and those she associated with death, only death. Whatever happened, after all this, she would rather cut her wrists than go back there.

She heard a noise, and looking out of the shack, saw Wellington appear in black silhouette, standing out against a vague red glow of shellfire. When he came in, she told him what the young mama had said. He went immediately down to the tunnels to meet with Miss Bella. All that night Nandi Maseku lay awake, smoking her second-best pipe.

Across town, in the hospital, Nevinson too lay awake, waiting for his dose of morphia. That, and douching his head with boiling hot water, were the only ways of easing the pain in his skull, which seemed to have swelled to the size of a football. He craved the needle like a lover. Aping Chatterton, he dangled his arm from the bed. Chatterton the poet-forger, whose supposititious verses were attacked by another, eighteenth-century George Steevens. Was the scholar an ancestor of his departed friend? He'd never had time to ask.

A gowned figure glided over. The nurse's cool fingers plucked up the flesh of his arm; the prick was over before he felt it; and he waited for the vial's brown liquid to do its magic. Afterwards, once the warm feeling had flooded through him, he felt unassailable. Nothing in the world was evil, everything was possible, and all lived happily in joyous anarchistic communities. He heard a voice, and seemed to see a white light above him.

46

Above him, Torres saw the dark roof of the church. He could feel something worrying at his shoulder, pulling at his shirtsleeve. He looked down and saw a thin black face.

"Get dressed, nkosi," the face said. "We go."

Torres looked around; everyone was asleep.

"What's happening?" he whispered back.

"Do it quick please, nkosi, mama waits outside. She says you are to escape."

The barber dragged on his clothes quickly and followed the boy to the vestry. Its door creaked awfully, and in front of him Torres heard the boy catch his breath. Once they were inside, the boy lifted away the iron grille that covered the window. It was clear that he had undone the screws from the outside, and then replaced the grille loosely after he himself had climbed in. Now he motioned that the barber should climb up out of the window. Torres looked at him askance: the gap was narrow, and to go through it presented a hazard of the sharpest character. But then he thought of all the long days he had spent locked up in the place, and the ever-present threat of being shot by the British on a cooked-up charge. With these thoughts in mind, he lifted himself up and poked his head out of the window. The moon shone brightly over the yard, but the eastern fence was in shadow. That must have been where the boy came in. Holding on to the window frame, he put first one leg out and then the other. Then, with some difficulty, he manoeuvred himself through the gap, the iron frame scraping his back. Falling awkwardly to the ground, he looked over to the sentry's hut, just twenty yards away, and saw that he would be plainly visible if the man sitting outside happened to look.

His rescuer dropped down beside him.

"Wait," said the boy, and pointed over towards the sentry hut.

In the moonlight, Torres saw the slim figure of Bella Kiernan approaching the soldier where he sat on the stool outside the hut. The soldier sprung up immediately on seeing her and, as Torres watched, the two of them were soon locked in an embrace.

"Now," the boy said, and began to run across the yard towards the eastern fence. Mystified, and not at all sure of the good sense of embarking upon this adventure, Torres followed. There was no point in hesitating now. On reaching the fence, the boy knelt down and crawled through a neat square hole, evidently cut by pliers. Again Torres followed. Suddenly they were outside. He wanted to stop, wanted to catch his breath, but the boy was running on, with light, quick steps. As they passed from an area of ruined, deserted buildings to scrubland covered with bush and trees, the details of the plan which had, for reasons deep in the heart of Bella Kiernan, been hatched on his behalf, suddenly became apparent to the barber.

"You must get inside," said the African. "Miss Bella, she said wait for her."

Wellington pushed aside the branches of the trees, into the clear space they fringed. Torres came behind, nearly tripping over one of the straining mooring ropes. The brazier which heated the air had been lit earlier in the night, and the great linen-clad shape was now full and warm. Torres stood motionless for a second, and then climbed into the basket. He understood now, this was what it had all been leading up to, this was where fate had been pointing.

His guide handed him a knife. "For the ropes. I must go now, nkosi. If the soldiers find me here, they will kill me."

"Me also, I should think," said Torres. "How can I thank you for this?"

The Zulu boy stood there in his ragged clothes, the whites of his eyes picked out by the glow of the brazier.

"You do not need to thank me. I was paid."

"All the same," said Torres, "you have been very brave."

Wellington said nothing, just turned his head, and then was gone, into the shadows.

Alone, Torres waited. He warmed his hands over the coals, and looked out into the foliage, hoping to spot the white of a petticoat or bonnet. Above him, the quilted membrane fluttered and flapped. The only other noise was the hiss of the brazier and, now and then, the faint sound of a falling coal knocking against the iron, near by and visible, but so faint that it sounded like something heard over a long distance. He looked into the fire and, as his thoughts drifted, seemed to see into the depths of life. How had this happened to him? He shook his head, as if to shake off an illusion.

When Bella came, panting from having run, Torres was like a man in a trance, and it was almost as if he did not know what he was doing as he cut the ropes. The balloon, shrugging itself free of the copse like someone trying to evade grasping hands, lifted from the earth into the night air above Ladysmith.

By imperceptible gradations, the moon-flushed grey linen sphere rose into the sky. Tom, himself flushed from Bella's kisses, bemused by her inexplicable change of heart and her sudden departure, saw it in the sky, and thought it odd that the observers should take it out so late at night. Gleaming, an exclamation mark of reflected light, the balloon slid above the town, passing over the journalists' cottage, over the battered roof of the Royal Hotel, where Bella's father slept the uneasy sleep of the guilty, over Mr. Grimble's untended fields, where starved, released horses roamed loose, over Mrs. Frinton, as her gentle snores drew in the damp air of the tunnels, over the oxbow of the Klip, over the V where the railway branched, over the thorn-tree-dotted scrub of a hill—in the lee of which lay Muhle Maseku, curled up in his burrow, under its lid of leaves and branches.

47

At Intombi, one evening towards the end of February, Jane Kiernan found Tom Barnes shading his eyes against the setting sun and looking in the direction of the hills above town. She asked him what he was looking at.

"Men," he said.

"Boers?" she queried.

"I think," he said, quietly, "that they might be our own."

Although exhausted from the heavy work there at the hospital camp, Jane found herself flinging her arms round the battered soldier, who winced when she did so. She said she was sorry, and then shouted out. Others came to look, straining their eyes at the specks on the red horizon. But soon it grew too dark. Everyone was so excited they could hardly speak, still less sleep . . .

That night, by candlelight, Jane applied more Condy's fluid to the lacerations on Tom's back. He had arrived at Intombi in a bad way, having been ordered flogged by Lieutenant Norris for allowing Torres to escape. They talked about Bella again. Neither could believe what had happened.

Among the others who had gathered at the hospital camp to watch the silhouettes of the distant soldiers that evening was Wellington Maseku. He was quite well known there now, but his arrival there this last time, on the same day as Tom, had caused quite a stir. With a tramp-like, leaf-covered, leg-dragging figure leaning upon him, he had burst into the wounds tent demanding attention for his companion. It was his father, whose burrow he had finally discovered, having stumbled across the *isivivane*.

Under normal circumstances, the doctors and nurses would not have countenanced treating a stray African, but they were grateful for the supply runs Wellington had made in the past, and considered that the least they could do was clean and dress Muhle's wound. Full of dirt and badly infected, it had deteriorated considerably, on account of the long, dangerous walk from his hiding place to the camp. One doctor said he thought the leg was turning gangrenous, and might have to be amputated.

So as Wellington watched the figures on the horizon with the others, his mind was elsewhere. The relief of Ladysmith did not seem, to the young Zulu boy, the most important thing at all. He decided that in the early morning he would make his way back to the town to bear the bittersweet news to his mother. Once again, he would brave the Boer lines—the lines in which Dr. Sterkx, trying to keep his mind occupied with his work, thought constantly about his wife, and whether the kaffir had got through. It was the last time Wellington Maseku would pass through those lines, and it was the worst of all his journeys, as the battle round Ladysmith began in earnest that day.

In the town itself, about a week later, Nevinson—recovered from his illness, and just about free from the lure of morphine—noted through his glass a great disturbance in the Boer camps. Lines of men and wagons had started moving towards the railway junction, and the roads that led to the Free State. A derrick or tripod of wooden posts, like a huge letter "A," had been erected above the remaining Long Tom, to lift it from its pit. It gave the correspondent great pleasure to see the whole machinery brought down by a shot from one of the naval guns. Later in the day, he rode up to one of the outposts with MacDonald to get a better view of the long silver snake of Boer wagons disappearing into the green background of the hills. The silvery aspect came, he realized, from the sun reflecting off the white covers on the Boer wagons.

"What do you make of it?" asked MacDonald, who was standing next to him.

"It's a trek," said Nevinson. "A great trek."

On either side of the line of wagons were black- and brown-coated horsemen moving forward in dense groups, sweeping across the landscape in ever extending curves.

"They are pulling back their columns," observed Nevinson.

"That's not a column in retreat," said MacDonald. "That's an army."

"It's a shame our cavalry and galloper guns cannot pursue them."

"Not a chance," said MacDonald. "We've eaten our horses into immobility. Anyway, our kit is too heavy. He must fly light who goes in pursuit of the flying Boer."

As they watched, they heard a loud boom and saw a great cloud of debris appear on the plain.

"Blowing up the bridges behind them," said Nevinson.

On their return, the correspondents sat down to what would prove to be their last dinner of horseflesh. They were just about to tuck in when a shout came from outside.

"Buller's cavalry are in sight! They are coming across the flats!"

Going into the centre of town, the two correspondents found a great crowd of people running through the streets, shouting and cheering—a confused throng of military and civilians, white and black and all the races, mixed together in an ecstasy of joy. All were headed for a drift in the Klip, the place where any incoming column would have to cross, and together they presented a skeletal, hollow-cheeked, spindle-shanked collection.

Tumbled along in this bony crowd, MacDonald and Nevinson could hardly see when they got to the river. Then, craning their necks above the battered, mud-stained helmets of soldiers, the bonnets and straw hats of white womenfolk, above the red fezzes of the Malays and the turbans of the Sikhs and the heads of the leaping, chanting Zulus, they caught a glimpse of a column of khaki-uniformed horsemen splashing through the water.

Two squadrons of Light Horse and mixed irregulars. Nevinson knew they must be from outside, as their mounts were far too plump and sleek to be Ladysmith horses. The crowd opened to let them trot past, and then followed as they swung into the main street, the van-guard of an exultant avenue of humanity, each crying or laughing as the moment took them, letting go their emotions as if siege walls had tumbled in their very breasts. There was no sense, anymore, of the mark of the superior race or caste.

The procession came to a climax when General White came out on horseback to meet the rescuers. Straightening up in the saddle, he began to speak.

"Citizens . . ."

The old man's voice trembled. The tumult of the crowd died down. He tried again.

"Citizens and soldiers, this . . . is a great day. It is the time for you to rejoice and not, any longer, for me to give you orders . . ." He faltered, and then continued. "I thank you for your loyalty, and your cooperation in the defence of the town . . . Thank God we kept the flag flying!"

Laughs and cheers drowned him out.

"It cut me to the heart," he continued, "to reduce your rations as I did."

Then he broke down again, and had visibly to steel himself to control his feelings. He was helped along by the encouraging shouts of the crowd—among whom, it must be said, were many who had cursed him in earlier days. Finally, a smile passed across his face.

"I promise you, though, that I'll never do it again."

There were more laughs and cheers from among the mass of straining voices and shrunken faces. Jostled by the crowd, Nevinson was separated from MacDonald. He glimpsed Bobby Greenacre running round and round in a circle, and Mrs. Frinton kneeling on the ground in the middle of it, her hands held up in an attitude of prayer.

Others saw the raising of the siege from different aspects. Looking down on Ladysmith from the back of a wagon, Dr. Sterkx fretted about the fate of his wife, cursing in the same breath the stubbornness of the English and the treachery "of kaffirs who don't deliver messages as they promise."

Up in the Star Room of the wrecked Royal Hotel, other eyes, those of Bella's father, also watched the performance. Under simulacra of Orion and Cassiopeia, he cradled his heavy revolver in his hand, and wondered what to do.

Below the Irishman, too close to the broken frontage of the Royal for Kiernan to see them, MacDonald encountered a Zulu woman, sitting on the wooden stoep. She was weeping. There was a young boy by her side, whom he recognized as Nevinson's runner.

Looking up at him, with tears streaming down her face, the woman said something in Zulu to the Australian.

"What's that she's saying?" MacDonald asked the boy.

"She said—the English can conquer everything but death; why can't they conquer death?"

"Why's she saying that then?"

"We have just heard that my father has died."

It was true. Wellington had made several trips between Intombi and Ladysmith as the siege was being raised, in the course of which Muhle's leg had been operated on by surgeons of the Army Medical Corps, who had already reached the hospital camp, and were engaged in helping ease the strain among the weary doctors there. A young Indian auxiliary, Mohandas Gandhi, had been among the attendants at the operation, holding Muhle's hand, and looking into the Zulu's eyes as they enquired the surgeon's preparation of his knives and saw. Once morphia had been injected, and its creeping numbness had taken effect, the operator cut the flesh swiftly, and then set to work on the bone with the saw. Within a couple of minutes, the leg was being wrapped in a blanket on the floor; within an hour, Muhle had departed into the world of the spirits. Efficient as he had been, the surgeon had cut too close to an artery in the groin, and had been unable to staunch the flow of blood.

There were many other casualties in the last days of the siege. In the final battle to secure the town, the toll was heaviest among regiments of the Irish Brigade. The Connaught Rangers, Dublin Fusiliers and Inniskilling Fusiliers together lost nearly five hundred men in under twenty-four hours. "My brave Irish," as Queen Victoria said on receiving the news.

Another who died was Perry Barnes—riding along when a shell struck off his head. The horse carried on down the line with its headless rider still in the saddle. After about a hundred yards, he had fallen off, to be dragged along, like Hector at Troy, with one foot in the stirrup.

The Biographer, who had been filming his chum as he rode, had turned his head away from the eyepiece and promptly fainted. He was hysterical for several days afterwards, and when, together with Churchill, he entered the town, it was with a broken heart, and a heavy message to deliver to Perry's brother.

Churchill would always maintain that he was with the first column to reach Ladysmith, but in fact he did not arrive until that night, after the initial celebrations were over. He was not the only one to present a "colour piece" as one of the correspondents might have called it. On March 1, Buller came into the town in secret, and departed incognito after a meal with General White. Two days afterwards, a triumphant entry into the town was staged, with the garrison lining the route as Buller's army marched in. Unable to stand through weakness, they sat down on the kerbs and pavements. In the vanguard of the triumphant procession was Buller, large and powerful-looking on his horse, as he rode up towards where General White and his staff waited to salute them on the steps of the shell-damaged Town Hall. Everyone expected Buller to come over and shake hands, or even embrace his counterpart; but he just rode on.

As Nevinson would write, looking back in later years: "In various antiquated inns and lodging houses, one still may admire a picture representing Buller and White meeting with enthusiastic grip of hands, while lusty crowds applaud the patriotic triumph. Nothing of the kind happened."

People did celebrate, but the cheers they gave this time were thin and wavering. For by now many in the emaciated garrison were in fact giving vent to frustration that the relief column had taken so long to arrive. So much for the "intense enthusiasm" recorded by Churchill—though we may be fairly sure that the sadness he recorded on learning of the death of his friend and mentor, Steevens, is genuine.

However it was thought to have ended, the siege was over, having lasted one hundred and eighteen days. The facts, under their particular descriptions (some people said it was a hundred and nineteen), were transmitted by cable, newspaper article and letter to Britain, and her rejoicing was mighty. Journals were written up and published, even a couple of novels. The siege was indeed over.

The Monologues
of the Dead

PART

FOUR

Tom

We have been uprooting the Boers, burning their farms and driving them off their lands. We strip the houses bare and the sheep we just kill and leave there, stopping only to cut out their hearts and livers. These choice pieces are put in gunny sacks and later cooked over our campfires.

In this way, it is said, we hope to prosecute the real end of the war, by preventing the guerrillas getting supplies from their wives and from the few farmers who have stayed put. It is General Kitchener's plan, and to my mind it is a beastly business. It is like driving pheasant for a shoot. The latest thing is that the dispossessed people are being put into camps.

We have also been building things called blockhouses, made of tin and concrete, right across the land. The Boers snipe at us as we build; they are using expanding bullets, which make a horrible mess of our fellows. But in spite of these attentions there is now a line from here to Klerksdorp. The grim little buildings we make are connected by barbed wire, which we unroll from large wooden drums, dividing up the country across hundreds of miles in an endless web. The idea is that our columns will chase the Boers into the grids made by this arrangement, going from blockhouse line to blockhouse line.

The Boers have recently been trying to get through by driving herds of bullocks against the fences, to crash them down. But there is always another square beyond in which we can catch them. They are all so short on stores now that they dress in the strangest costumes— some with sacks with holes in for trousers, others with women's bonnets and skirts. All in all, it is an odd way to wage a war, in my opinion more blockhead than blockhouse. I cannot say when or how it will end.

We are now using native troops, which raises the enemy to a pitch of anger. Whenever they capture any, they kill them outright. General Smuts's troops did this at a village outside Modderfontein lately. When we came there, the bodies of the blacks were still unburied, lying there rotting in the sun. They were all put in one grave, yours truly wielding one of the shovels.

For myself, all I know is that I am quite done in now. Once I heard of Perry's death, the fighting spirit went out of me. I no longer look after myself either, eating my food with one hand and delousing myself with the other, taking dozens of the vermin out of my shirt simply by running my finger down a seam.

This is, it seems to me, the worse-run campaign ever. We have to replace our horses every two or three weeks now. Many of the mares are in foal, and the other day one foaled while we were actually on the move. The poor thing was half out before someone shouted, "Look out, she's foaling down," and the column halted.

When I came out here, I was full of Queen and Country. I am no longer. Partly it is the conditions and the time it is taking to wrap things up, but also it is Kitchener. He is very unjust and arrogant, and untouchable to ordinary soldiers—of an altogether different kidney to White or Buller.

As for the rest, the business with Bella Kiernan, flying off like that with the Portugee, I was outraged and shamed by it, especially when her gulling of me came to light. Her sister gave me some calming comfort at Intombi, that is true, but I doubt I shall go back to Ladysmith when I am discharged, even though I have promised her that I will try. I must confess a certain amount of self-distrust about my motives towards Jane in this respect.

In truth, maybe it would be better if I just went home. This is a cruel land that has been too much overrun by war. At one farm, there was a woman who was about to give birth in a few days. She was weeping her eyes out, since her man had been killed. We were marching on and there was nothing much we could do. I did help arrange a cart to get her to a rail junction, so as she could be taken to a camp, but whether she or the baby survived I do not know.

December, 1901

Mrs. Sterkx

Epidemic has struck in this place I am being held in, adding to the burden of starvation. My goose, I am sad to say, has long been eaten. I have no idea where my husband is, and can only pray that he is still alive. When the train brought us in, like animals in open trucks, many of the children were already lying on the floor, sick with fever. At least fifty of those in my train are now dead. A girl from a place outside Lichtenburg gave birth on the train, but the baby was lifeless when it came out. She too has gone now.

On arrival the soldiers pushed us into dirty bell tents: often fifteen or more of us in a space meant for eight. The stink is beyond belief. No soap, not enough water, and hardly any beds or mattresses at all. I myself sleep on bare earth. We do our toilet in steel pails and throw the doings into pits behind the tents, where great clouds of flies swarm over them.

We are given only a little food, nor much fuel to cook with. More and more people are being sent in. Thousands at a time. If it wasn't for the numbers dying—nearly a hundred each day now—there would be no room for them, and as it is we get packed closer and closer. It is said there are nearly two hundred thousand people in camps such as this now. Many of those interned are kaffirs, and it does us great dishonour to live cheek by jowl with them. They too are dying by the score.

Sometimes we have to wash our clothes in water thick with human foulness. Most of us have no clothes apart from those we stand in. All our linen is filled with lice. I know one woman who has taken to wearing male kaffir clothes, giving up her last bit of money to a black who is in authority here. It is typical of the English that they should use the kaffirs in this way.

Apart from the soldiers guarding the wire, the only English person I have seen here is a woman who has come to write a report on the conditions, which she says she will send to their parliament. She says they are pursuing a policy of extermination against us. I can believe it, which is more than can be said for the British newspapers. Someone who can read English says their *Times* has reported that "the enemy's wives are being fed and looked after." It is a lie.

March, 1902

Nevinson

The landing of troops here, mainly Anzacs in this area, was surely a dangerous and almost unachievable task from the start. Now we are withdrawing, and the Gallipoli expedition comes to an end after more than eight months. Far longer than the siege of Ladysmith, of which it greatly reminds me for some reason, though it dwarfs that episode in its human cost. Here the sound of the big guns blazing, and the sight of Tommies squeezed together in trenches as the shells fall upon them, makes the South African war seem like firecrackers at a party.

The sand is crimson with Australian and New Zealand blood. And that of Indians and other races from the farthest corners of the Empire. Mule carts ply to and fro picking up the corpses amid the barbed-wire entanglements on the beach. The Indians manage the mules like well-trained dogs, with the Turks taking pot-shots at them all the while.

Many are hit. I do not think I have ever seen so many bodies in one place. I will not discuss policy, but people are furious at Mr. Churchill for setting this fiasco in motion, some saying he ought to be publicly hanged. One of the Australian press corps, Keith Murdoch, is planning to blow the whistle on the whole shambles. He says he knows MacDonald. Another ghost of Ladysmith days: Lieutenant-General Hamilton has been here too, and Major Mott, my old censor, now Inspector-General of Communications.

It is strange how that place comes back to haunt me. Or perhaps it is not. It may be that every moment in the history of humankind is a crucible like that. In any case, one could not account for even the tiniest fraction of the sparks that fly out—unless every single thing that moved our ancestors, that spurred their appetites and emotions, came down to us as a message with the colour of our hair and the shapes of our noses. But still it would not be enough, as the role of chance and of the incalculable dooms us to a continuous functioning. The mightiest moments pass uncalendered. No tables could compute them. Like the white-hot particles that we now know to whirl round sun and stars, like the myriad points of this bloodstained sand in front of me, the sum of events outstrips our understanding.

December, 1915

Bobby Greenacre

I would prefer to be fighting than convalescing. I have just been down to Estcourt to sign up, and would by now be on my way to Europe, if I hadn't done something stupid on the way. I went for a swim in the famous "Map of Africa" pool at Dalton Bridge, it being very hot. Just my luck to get bitten by a puff adder as I was dressing. If I hadn't already got my trousers half on, the damn thing's fangs would have gone a lot deeper into me. Half an inch long, and yellow, they were.

It pleases Mother though, who wants to save me from the trenches to be a lawyer. They are thinking of moving to Australia. God knows why. As I lie here in my bed, one thing about the adder episode has cheered me up: remembering how those two correspondents fell for that magic snake trick I used to play when I was a boy. I could hardly contain myself as I sat, hidden behind my wall, pulling on the cotton thread and they danced up and down on it. And when I heard one of them saying he'd picked it up and taken it home on his stick, still without realizing, well that was the end.

January, 1916

Nevinson

Back on the dope again. On my sickbed, where I have so often found myself since returning from Gallipoli, I have been reading Yeats's autobiographical *Reveries,* which he gave to me. I think I prefer his previous title for it, *Memory Harbour.* But that's as may be; he is a greater man than I. It will be a relief to get off my back and resume the literary life, not least my visits to his chambers at Woburn Place. Last time I was there, he was entertainingly full of his psychical researches, harking on Leo Africanus, his sixteenth-century attendant spirit, who converses with him in Italian; and also on Freud and Jung and the Sub-Conscious Self.

He did apply his own self to present matters too, however. He is worried about the fate of Maud Gonne, his erstwhile love. I believe she is in Northern France, nursing wounded soldiers. My own admiration for that beautiful woman has worn off somewhat. Well, whatever the danger, she is better off there than with that drunken bounder MacBride, who brought nothing but evil back with him from South Africa. I always knew that marriage would end in disaster: as was the case with that family in Ladysmith (Leo Kiernan was also a Nationalist, I have learned), it shows that domestic and political virtue don't necessarily go hand in hand.

In spite of my support for the Irish cause, I can shed no tears for MacBride; indeed, my harsher part thinks it is a good thing that they executed him in Dublin—not for the charge, his supposed role in the Easter Rising, but for the unnatural molestations he visited upon Maud's daughter.

As for Kiernan and his poor girls, I heard a story about the one who escaped in the balloon with the barber. What was her name?

Bella? Yes, Bella the barmaid . . . My informant told me that when the balloon came down, they disposed of the empty linen and basket by giving it to the nearest black tribe, who between them carved it up and distributed it in roughly the same manner in which they deal with the corpses of elephants—and that even now, in the region, pieces of the fabric are highly prized, having an almost cult-like status. I don't know whether this is true or not.

November, 1916

The Biographer

(voice-over)
British Movie-tone News
It Speaks for Itself!

Only recently released from prison, Mr. Gandhi arrives to attend negotiations with the Viceroy of India at his new palace, designed by Sir Edwin Lutyens. The scantily-clad Mahatma said afterwards that he is aware he must have given the Viceroy cause for irritation, and also have tried his patience, but that right is on his side. Mr. Gandhi, shown here with his famous spinning wheel, said that the agreement reached with the Viceroy represented a truce, and that his goal remained complete independence for India.

February, 1931

Churchill

"It is alarming and also nauseating to see Mr. Gandhi, a seditious Middle Temple lawyer, now posing as a fakir of a type well known in the East, striding half-naked up the steps of the Viceregal palace, while he is still organizing and conducting a defiant campaign of civil disobedience, to parley on equal terms with the representative of the King-Emperor."

Speech to the West Essex Conservatives,
February, 1931

Jane

Two months ago I buried Tom. Last month I sold the farm. Now I am in an hotel by the port, at Lourenço Marques. It hurt me to see all our ploughs and other implements up for auction, but I knew I had to do it. Every day, I have had to steel myself, and only the thought that a long-overdue meeting is shortly to take place has kept me going.

There is a pretty piece of Portuguese embroidery in a frame on the wall of this room, showing a flower with red petals. I have closed my eyes now, but the image is still there in front of them. It is strange how that happens.

Tom died peacefully, in his sleep, although he had been ill for some time. I have not cried so much since hearing of Bella's disappearance and then finding Father on the floor of the Star Room as the siege ended at Ladysmith, all those years ago. He was lying on his back in a puddle of blood, with the revolver in his hand. The hole, which was in his throat, was only small. I couldn't believe that there could be so much blood from it. Father had left a note, saying that he was sorry and that he had "betrayed his family for his country," and that he loved us both very much.

At first I did not know what this talk of betrayal meant, but in later years heard from Boers how he had been working with Major MacBride's Irishmen on their side. That MacBride was a bad man, he fathered a bastard child in the Cape later, and got up to God knows what when he returned to Ireland. It shocks me that Father was associated with him, though both are still seen as heroes by the Boers round Ladysmith.

Tom was with me when we discovered the body. It was then that he promised to come back once the war was over. We had grown close at Intombi; it was almost by mistake, but I suppose we were both healing each other's wounds over Bella. When, at the end of the war in May 1902, he never came, I had given up hope of him. Those were my worst months, running the hotel on my own, with only Nandi and Wellington to help me. Father was dead and I had no idea at all where Bella was. Then, one day in early 1903, Tom just turned up.

At first it was difficult, as I did not trust him. But as the months went by, we rekindled the feelings we had discovered at Intombi and eventually were married. It was natural. We sold the hotel later, and bought a farm in Bechuanaland. We have had thirty years of happy life together. My only regret is that we were never able to have children.

By the time Tom and I were together, I had long given Bella and her Portuguese man up for dead. When the news got out about the balloon, the army had sent out patrols looking for it. There were rumours that it had been shot down by the Boers and that Bella and Torres had been killed in the descent. But not a trace of it was found. After the war, I put advertisements in the papers seeking information, but received no replies, except crank ones.

It was some years later that Nandi told me, during a visit back to Ladysmith, where she had a little stall. She was ill then, her limbs swollen and her voice faint from shortness of breath. I almost fainted myself when she revealed the truth: how, shortly after we had left for Bechuanaland, Bella and Torres had turned up at the hotel. The new owners had sent them to Nandi. When Nandi told her what had happened between me and Tom, she said that Bella was very distraught. That Bella told her not to tell me that she had come; that it was better that way, lest she destroy my happiness. I railed at the old woman then, and would have struck her had she not been so ill. But later I knew that, in her terms, she had done right. As she pointed out, she was keeping a promise.

Nandi died of heart failure not long after. Keeping it all secret from Tom, I set myself the task of tracking Bella down. I wrote to Portuguese East Africa, where they had gone, and after long correspondence with the British Embassy and others learned that they had left there for Portugal itself. Lisbon. I discovered that Torres had made a deal of money from a bauxite claim he bought with an inheritance, and they had decided to go to the mother country—or his mother country, rather—to live in luxury. So then I started writing to the embassy there too, and newspapers and any other places I could think of.

At long last, in the final months of Tom's illness, I received a letter from Bella—and a photograph. It shows her with Torres, standing next to a fancy white motor car. Bella is wearing a cocktail dress, with a feather boa, Torres a linen suit and spotted tie. He has his foot up on the running board and looks very tanned and handsome, although his hair and beard have gone white.

Bella said in the letter that she is "sorry that she has been so selfish, that her adventures have taken precedence over family duty." It was eerily like father's note, so long ago. Lord, how it all comes back: the sight of him there on the floor, his complexion drained to a terrible paleness, and his hair soaked with blood. I wonder whether I will ever be able to forgive Bella for leaving me to face that on my own; but we shall have to see. And will, as my present journey takes me to Portugal to meet with her.

As for her so-called adventures, she says she will tell me all when I see her. The long and short of it is that when the balloon came down, they sank the empty linen and basket in a lake, weighting them with stones. Then walked for miles across the bush, going through great difficulties until, like Mr. Churchill before them, they hit the Delagoa Bay railway and boarded a train covertly.

Tomorrow, when my ship leaves, I will sail out in the shiny blue water of that bay myself. The barman downstairs says you can see porpoise swimming by the side of the ship; only the way he said it, with a strong Portuguese accent, it sounded like "purpose," and at first I didn't know what he meant. It is only just now that I have realized. I am looking forward to it.

May, 1933

MacDonald

Today I ran into—of all people—Bobby Greenacre, who in his prime has become a top-notch barrister (Robert Greenacre KC!) at the Australian Bar. I was giving evidence in a patent action brought against another paper. Greenacre was our adversary's lawyer. The action had reference to the printing of "stop press," or late news, in newspapers. My own company, as the plaintiffs, were owners of a special "fudge box," a technical device by which late news can be inserted while the rest of the paper is being printed. We were alleging that the other lot had infringed our patent with a so-called new invention. Greenacre spoke well, but the judge, Mr. Justice Kelly, upheld our case, on the grounds that their device had been anticipated by prior patents.

The case relates to the form of newspaper printing machine known as the endless-web letterpress. These machines were the outcome of the discovery of how to make up and print quickly with small cylindrical stereotypes. They are especially important to evening newspapers, which have to publish rapidly the latest news arriving: the speed in the insertion of late news is the essence of our patent. The point is, our gadget gave us the chance to revise or review our record of events in the very act of putting them on record.

December, 1938

Gandhi

I was never given the chance to explain that my supporters would not actually help the Japanese if they invade India, only resist them passively. The Viceroy sent police to pull me from my bed in the early morning. They have taken me to this prison: one of the Aga Khan's palaces near Poona, a ludicrous and desolate place to be incarcerated.

As soon as they had locked me up, the people began rioting—setting fire to police stations and government buildings, breaking up railways and killing a number of British officials. The Viceroy presents it all as my fault, printing some grossly inaccurate statements in the newspapers. I used to feel able to see myself as others see me—but now I am not so sure. None of them make themselves sure of their facts; everything is distorted and misrepresented.

I suspect that I will soon have to fast—crucify the flesh by taking only water, with a little salt. If the Viceroy calls it political blackmail, then so be it. I believe a Higher Tribunal will say otherwise; and if I perish, I will face the Judgement Seat with innocence in my heart.

August, 1942

Churchill

MOST SECRET CIPHER TELEGRAM
FROM PRIME MINISTER TO VICEROY OF INDIA

"BEGINS. Thank you so much for your most interesting letter of April 29. I was sure you would find the problems set you of absorbing interest, and everyone here thinks you are addressing yourself to them with extraordinary energy and tact. I am fully aware of the weakness of the machine which you have at your disposal, but this is largely due to the great diminution in white officials which has marked the last twenty-five unhappy years. I assented to your letting Gandhi out on the grounds of his grievous state of health. He seems to have recovered a good deal of political vitality since then.

He is a thoroughly evil force, hostile to us in every fibre, largely in the hands of the native vested interests and frozen to his idea of the hand spinning wheel and inefficient cultivation methods for the overcrowded population of India. I look forward to a day when it may be possible to come to an understanding with the real forces that control India and which, at any political settlement, will be allied with a marked improvement in the wellbeing of the masses, whom the reformers often forget, but who constitute for us a sacred duty. ENDS."

Sent: 27.5.44
Copyright: Public Record Office

The Biographer

It is twilight, and the summer air above the bay is stirred only by the gulls. Peace: I think I will have myself a gin on the terrace before the boy comes. The eve of the election, and with Germany defeated and the Allied leaders gathered in Potsdam, it seems sad that the British people will repay Winston's heroism with ingratitude by voting in the Socialists.

Still, maybe it is time for a change, and a well-deserved rest for him. The sad thing is how he does not seem to be able to let go of the romance of Empire, the whole nineteenth-century edifice, however modern and practical he is in other respects. There is no chance of us staying in India, of course; we will be out of there pretty sharpish once the Japanese war has ended, in my opinion.

I recently saw a newsreel—they've got a bit fancier since my retirement—of Winston giving his V for Victory sign as he disembarked from an American plane, a Fortress or Liberator or some such name. He was still wearing an aviator's oxygen mask as he came down the steps—and smoking his cigar! He had the mask specially adapted.

History's impresario. I remember him on the long trek to Ladysmith all those years ago: even then, as time was fashioning him for the struggles ahead, he was the consummate showman. But he saw the action right enough too, and transmuted his experiences of personal danger into a philosophy of Imperial greatness, at the heart of which was the vital importance of Britain's survival.

Courageous, indefatigable, bloody-minded: sometimes it seemed as if nothing but his lion's roar stood between us and the Nazi threat. That was the illusion, anyway, and like all the best ones, it worked. I do not mean to denigrate his statesmanship. Forged on the steel of instinct, tempered in the waters of experience, it struck a blow for freedom that will reverberate through the history of mankind. Yes, this Vulcan let you know he was hammering. Yes, he was a self-dramatist. But no one else could have done what he did.

July, 1945

Wellington

Kaffir, waar's jou pas? Nigger, where's your pass? I heard that as a young boy in the mine shanty. I heard it—albeit spoken in English—at Ladysmith. I have heard it ever since. If there is one thing that has characterized the oppression of native people in South Africa, from before the Union between Cape Colony and the Boer Republics and afterwards, it is the iniquity of the pass system. On March 21 of this year, 1960, that history fulfilled its bloody legacy, with the cold-blooded gunning down of sixty-nine people outside the police station at Sharpeville, gathered there only because of the Pass Laws.

I was not there. A few days after those tragic events (as I sit in my cell, some two hundred people are being treated for bullet wounds), I joined Chief Luthuli, who like me had been giving evidence as one of the accused at the so-called Treason Trials, and followed him in publicly burning my passbook before the press cameras. Now I am in gaol, along with many others of my brothers in the ANC. Why they should see an old man like me as a threat, I cannot say.

We are still organizing, concerning ourselves greatly with the planned boycott of South African goods by the rest of the world. Not everyone is supporting us, of course. The other day a strange tale came into the prison about Viscount Montgomery, of Alamein fame, who has been visiting the country. We had hoped he would come and talk to us, but he did not, consorting only with members of Dr. Verwoerd's government and the representatives of big business. Apparently he has now asked the world "to give Dr. Verwoerd a chance," as Chief Luthuli put it. I cannot understand how such a valiant enemy of Nazism can take such a position.

Every now and then they drag us from the cells to attend further sessions of the Treason Trials. Our defence is now being conducted by two young leaders of the Congress, themselves also accused, Duma Nokwe and Nelson Mandela. They are young but resourceful, although the legal proceedings are so farcical (even in court the seating arrangements follow the apartheid rules) that I do not believe they will be able to help us very much. Privately, Nelson has confided to me that if he is released he will call for the use of violent tactics. Luthuli holds to his line of passive resistance, sharing Gandhi's old view that moral weight will prevail.

I am not so sure. This morning I was slapped about by a white policeman, and I cannot say that the gentle approach did me much good. I am fearful as to what will happen. Outside, the government is sending our people to the so-called Bantustans. Tourists are being taken to selected villages to see the plump noble savage in his element, but it is all faked. The truth is bony animals, parched fields full of stones, and sub-human conditions in the huts. There are reports of barbed-wire enclosures in Pondoland.

I find myself thinking much of Ladysmith and its siege, just over sixty years ago. Perhaps it is the feeling of being in prison. I often wonder how life treated that man and woman I helped to escape. I remember watching—from that bowl of trees—their balloon rise up into the pure depth of the night and thinking, it cannot be as easy as that. I was right. For one like myself, at least, the siege has never really ended. I suppose that is just politics, which I have made my life; which is why what I see, right now, is bars across a little square of blue.

A few months after my father was buried, I walked from Ladysmith to Groutville, where I joined the mission school. Mother remained in Ladysmith, at first working for the sister of the balloon woman, and then running a little shop of her own. Before she passed away, I used to visit as often as I was able. Whenever I went back, I would return to the site of the old hospital camp at Intombi where my father died. There is just grass there now, acres of it, studded with clumps of mopani trees. Underneath one lies his body, and also the new *isivivane* I built in his memory. It does not state who he was or how he died; but I know, and my children know.

Last time we were in Ladysmith—which is a big modern town these days—we made a discovery of a Bushman cave in one of the hills outside the town. We were having a picnic; it was the nearest place we were allowed to do so, without the police chasing us away.

The edges of the cave's entrance were obscured by tall grass and saplings, and I do not think anyone had been in there for many years. It smelled very musty. On striking a match inside, we found it to be full of paintings. Drawn on the walls in ochre paint, they depicted the First People in little groups, hunting eland and gazelle with bows and spears. They were like ghosts, those pictures, the wind in the cave seeming to mimic the voices of the dead men and women as we stood looking at them, striking matches until our thumbs blistered. We were glad to make our way outside, my children and I, following the oval gap at the mouth of the cave, as it drew the sky towards us.

Acknowledgements

This novel was inspired by my great-grandfather, a British trooper at Ladysmith. Looking some years ago for fishing tackle in the family attic, I found a keep-net and a tatty black book—into the latter of which an unknown hand had made copies of my ancestor's letters. The letters themselves were never found.

I have employed many other sources in this book, but owe a particular debt to H. W. Nevinson's three volumes of memoirs: *Changes and Chances* (1923), *More Changes, More Chances* (1925) and *Last Changes, Last Chances* (1928). Although the material account is largely different, acknowledgement is also naturally due to Nevinson's *Ladysmith: The Diary of a Siege* (1900), Donald MacDonald's *How We Kept the Flag Flying* (1900) and G. W. Steevens's posthumously published *From London to Ladysmith* (1900). These accounts are often contradictory: none contains "The Magic Snake, or Things Are Not What They Seem," which can be found in Nevinson's *Essays in Freedom* (1909).

Other helpful works were *From London to Ladysmith via Pretoria* (1900) by Winston S. Churchill, *The Biograph in Battle* (1901) by William Dickson, and Thomas Pakenham's magisterial overview *The Boer War* (1979). Thanks are also due to the Churchill Archive Centre in Cambridge, to the Ladysmith Museum and Information Centre in Natal, and to the Ladysmith Historical Society. Tim Padfield at the Public Record Office kindly granted permission for the use of a Crown Copyright document, while Toby Buchan, Alex Clark, J. M. Coetzee, Lindsay Duguid, Bridget Frost and Randolph Vigne helped to save the manuscript from itself; any errors remain entirely my own.

A NOTE ABOUT THE AUTHOR

Giles Foden was for three years an assistant editor of the *Times Literary Supplement*, and is now on the staff of the *Guardian*. His first novel, *The Last King of Scotland*, won the 1998 Whitbread First Novel Award and the Somerset Maugham Prize. He lives in London.

A NOTE ON THE TYPE

This book was set in Adobe Garamond. Designed for the Adobe Corporation by Robert Slimbach, the fonts are based on types first cut by Claude Garamond (c. 1480–1561). Garamond was a pupil of Geoffroy Tory and is believed to have followed the Venetian models, although he introduced a number of important differences, and it is to him that we owe the letter we now know as old style. He gave to his letters a certain elegance and feeling of movement that won their creator an immediate reputation and the patronage of Francis I of France.

Composed by Stratford Publishing Services,
Brattleboro, Vermont
Printed and bound by R. R. Donnelley & Sons,
Harrisonburg, Virginia